THE BEET QUEEN

BOOKS BY LOUISE ERDRICH

NOVELS

Love Medicine
The Beet Queen
Tracks
The Bingo Palace
Tales of Burning Love
The Antelope Wife
The Last Report on the Miracles at Little No Horse
The Master Butchers Singing Club
Four Souls
The Painted Drum

WITH MICHAEL DORRIS

The Crown of Columbus

POETRY

Jacklight
Baptism of Desire
Original Fire

FOR CHILDREN

Grandmother's Pigeon
The Birchbark House
The Range Eternal
The Game of Silence

NONFICTION

The Blue Jay's Dance
Books and Islands in Ojibwe Country

THE BEET QUEEN

A NOVEL BY

LOUISE ERDRICH

HARPER PERENNIAL

NEW YORK • LONDON • TORONTO • SYDNEY

HARPER ● PERENNIAL

Grateful acknowledgment is made to the editors of the following publications in which parts of this book appeared, in slightly altered form: "The Branch" and "Chapter One: 1932," *The Paris Review* as "The Beet Queen." "Chapter Two: 1932, Sita Kozka, Mary Adare, Celestine James," *New Native America*, a book by University of New Mexico Press, as "The Manifestation at Argus." "Chapter Two: 1932, Sita Kozka," *Ms.* magazine, August 1986. Part of "Chapter Three: 1932, Karl Adare," *The American Voice*, Fall 1986. "Chapter Six: 1952," *Antaeus* as "The Air Seeder." "Chapter Seven: 1953, Celestine James," *Minneapolis-St. Paul* magazine, August 1986, as "Chez Sita." Part of "Chapter Seven: 1953," *Chicago Magazine* as "Knives." "Chapter Eight: 1953," *Formations* as "The Little Book." Parts of Chapters Nine and Fifteen, *The Georgia Review* as "Mister Argus." Part of Chapter Ten, *New England Review*, Fall 1986. "Chapter Eleven: 1964," *Atlantic Monthly* as "Destiny." "Chapter Thirteen: 1972, Celestine James," *The Kenyon Review* as "Pounding the Dog."

The author would like to thank the National Endowment for the Arts and the Guggenheim Foundation for their support during the years this book was written.

A hardcover edition of this book was originally published in 1986 by Henry Holt and Company, Inc. It is here reprinted by arrangement with Henry Holt and Company, Inc.

A previous paperback edition was published in 1987 by Bantam Books.

P.S.™ is a trademark of HarperCollins Publishers.

HarperCollins books may be purchased for educational, business, or sales promotional use. For information please write: Special Markets Department, HarperCollins Publishers, 10 East 53rd Street, New York, NY 10022.

First HarperFlamingo edition published 1998.
First Harper Perennial edition published 1999.
Reissued in Perennial 2001.
Reissued in Harper Perennial 2006.

Family tree hand-lettered by Martie Holmer

The Library of Congress has catalogued the HarperFlamingo edition as follows:
Erdrich, Louise.
    The beet queen : a novel / Louise Erdrich.— 1st HarperFlamingo ed.
      p. cm.
    ISBN 0-06-097750-7
    1. Orphans—North Dakota—Fiction. I. Title.
PS3555.R42 B4
813'.54—dc21   97-51170

ISBN-10: 0-06-083527-3 (pbk.)
ISBN-13: 978-0-06-083527-9 (pbk.)

06 07 08 09 10 RRD 10 9 8 7 6 5 4 3 2 1

To Michael

Complice in every
word, essential
as air.

ACKNOWLEDGMENTS

Grateful acknowledgments are made, first, to my father Ralph Erdrich, and also to my grandmother Mary Erdrich Korll, to our editor and publisher Richard Seaver, to our Aunt Virginia Burkhardt for her generous enthusiasm and advice, to Charles Rembar, and to Barbara Bonner, friend and passionate reader.

CONTENTS

THE BEET QUEEN

Pete = · = · = Fritzie   Mr. · · · (1) Adelaide (2) · · · Omar
Kozka   Adare   Ober   Adare

Jimmy = · = · = (1) Sita (2) = · = · = Louis
Bohl   Kozka   Tappe

Dutch = · = · = (2) Regina (1) = = = "Montana" Eli
James   Puyat   Kashpaw   Kashpaw

Isabel   Russell
Kashpaw   Kashpaw

Celestine = · = · = Karl   Mary   Jude
James   Adare   Adare   Miller
{adopted by
Martin &
Wallacette   Catherine
Dot }   Miller}
Adare

LEGEND
= = = = Traditional Ojibwe marriage
· · · · Sexual affair or liaison
= · = · = Catholic or civil marriage

The Branch

Long before they planted beets in Argus and built the highways, there was a railroad. Along the track, which crossed the Dakota–Minnesota border and stretched on to Minneapolis, everything that made the town arrived. All that diminished the town departed by that route, too. On a cold spring morning in 1932 the train brought both an addition and a subtraction. They came by freight. By the time they reached Argus their lips were violet and their feet were so numb that, when they jumped out of the boxcar, they stumbled and scraped their palms and knees through the cinders.

The boy was a tall fourteen, hunched with his sudden growth and very pale. His mouth was sweetly curved, his skin fine and girlish. His sister was only eleven years old, but already she was so short and ordinary that it was obvious she would be this way all her life. Her name was square and practical as the rest of her. Mary. She brushed her coat off and stood in the watery wind. Between the buildings there was only more bare horizon for her to see, and from time to time men crossing it. Wheat was the big crop then, and the topsoil was so newly tilled that it hadn't all blown off yet, the way it had in Kansas. In fact, times were generally much better in eastern North Dakota than in most places, which is why Karl and Mary Adare had come there on the train. Their mother's sister, Fritzie, lived on the eastern edge of town. She ran a butcher shop with her husband.

The two Adares put their hands up their sleeves and started walking. Once they began to move they felt warmer, although they'd been traveling all night and the chill had reached deep. They walked east, down the dirt and planking of the broad main street, reading the signs on each false-front clapboard store they passed, even reading the gilt letters in the window of the brick bank. None of these places was a butcher shop. Abruptly, the stores stopped, and a string of houses, weathered gray or peeling gray paint, with dogs tied to their porch railings, began.

Small trees were planted in the yards of a few of these houses, and one tree, weak, a scratch of light against the gray of everything else, tossed in a film of blossoms. Mary trudged solidly forward, hardly glancing at it, but Karl stopped. The tree drew him with its delicate perfume. His cheeks went pink, he stretched his arms out like a sleepwalker, and in one long transfixed motion he floated to the tree and buried his face in the white petals.

Turning to look for Karl, Mary was frightened by how far back he had fallen and how still he was, his face pressed in the flowers. She shouted, but he did not seem to hear her and only stood, strange and stock-still among the branches. He did not move even when the dog in the yard lunged against its rope and bawled. He did not notice when the door to the house opened and a woman scrambled out. She shouted at Karl too, but he paid her no mind and so she untied her dog. Large and anxious, it flew forward in great bounds. And then, either to protect himself or to seize the blooms, Karl reached out and tore a branch from the tree.

It was such a large branch, from such a small tree, that blight would attack the scar where it was pulled off. The leaves would fall away later on that summer and the sap would sink into the roots. The next spring, when Mary passed it on some errand, she saw that it bore no blossoms and remembered how, when the dog jumped for Karl, he struck out with the branch and the petals dropped around the dog's fierce outstretched body in a sudden snow. Then he yelled, "Run!" and Mary ran east, toward Aunt Fritzie. But Karl ran back to the boxcar and the train.

PART ONE

PART ONE

MARY ADARE

So that's how I came to Argus. I was the girl in the stiff coat.

After I ran blind and came to a halt, shocked not to find Karl behind me, I looked up to watch for him and heard the train whistle long and shrill. That was when I realized Karl had probably jumped back on the same boxcar and was now hunched in straw, watching out the opened door. The only difference would be the fragrant stick blooming in his hand. I saw the train pulled like a string of black beads over the horizon, as I have seen it so many times since. When it was out of sight, I stared down at my feet. I was afraid. It was not that with Karl gone I had no one to protect me, but just the opposite. With no one to protect and look out for, I was weak. Karl was taller than me but spindly, older of course, but fearful. He suffered from fevers that kept him in a stuporous dream state and was sensitive to loud sounds, harsh lights. My mother called him delicate, but I was the opposite. I was the one who begged spotted apples from the grocery store and stole whey from the back stoop of the creamery in Minneapolis, where we were living the winter after my father died.

This story starts then, because before that and without the year 1929, our family would probably have gone on living comfortably in a lonely and isolated white house on the edge of Prairie Lake.

We rarely saw anyone else. There were just us three: Karl and me and our mother, Adelaide. There was something different about us even then. Our only visitor was Mr. Ober, a tall man with a carefully trimmed black beard. He owned a whole county of Minnesota wheatland. Two or three times a week he appeared, in the late evenings, and parked his automobile in the barn.

Karl hated Mr. Ober's visits, but I looked forward to each one because my mother always brightened. It was like a change of weather in our house. I remember that on the last night Mr. Ober came to visit, she put on the blue silk dress and the necklace of sparkling stones that we knew had come from him. She wound and pinned her dark red braid into a crown, and then brushed my hair one hundred light, even strokes. I closed my eyes and listened to the numbers. "You didn't get this from me," she said at last, letting the hair fall limp and black about my shoulders.

When Mr. Ober arrived, we sat with him in the parlor. Karl posed on the horsehair sofa and pretended a fascination with the red diamonds woven into the carpet. As usual, I was the one whom Mr. Ober singled out for petting. He put me on his lap, called me Schatze. "For your hair, Little Miss," he said, pulling a green satin ribbon from his vest pocket. His voice was deep pitched, but I liked the sound of it in counterpoint to or covering my mother's. Later, after Karl and I were sent to bed, I stayed awake and listened to the grown-up's voices rise and tangle, then fall, first in the downstairs parlor and then, muffled, in the dining room. I heard both of them walk up the stairs. The big door closed at the end of the hall. I kept my eyes open. There was darkness, the creaks and thumps that a house makes at night, wind in the branches, tapping. By morning he was gone.

The next day Karl sulked until our mother hugged and kissed him back into good humor. I was sad, too, but with me she was short of temper.

Karl always read the comics in the Sunday paper first, and so he was the one who found the picture of Mr. Ober and his wife on the front page. There had been a grain-loading accident, and

Mr. Ober had smothered. There was a question, too, of suicide. He'd borrowed heavily against his land. Mother and I were cleaning out drawers in the kitchen, cutting white paper out to fit them, when Karl brought the piece in to show us. I remember that Adelaide's hair was plaited in two red crooked braids and that she fell full length across the floor when she read the news. Karl and I huddled close to her, and when she opened her eyes I helped her into a chair.

She threw her head back and forth, would not speak, shuddered like a broken doll. Then she looked at Karl.

"You're glad!" she cried.

Karl turned his head away, sullen.

"He was your father," she blurted.

So it was out.

My mother knew she'd lose everything now. His wife was smiling in the photograph. Our big white house was in Mr. Ober's name, along with everything else except an automobile, which Adelaide sold the next morning. On the day of the funeral, we took the noon train to the Cities with only what we could carry in suitcases. My mother thought that there, with her figure and good looks, she could find work in a fashionable store.

But she didn't know that she was pregnant. She didn't know how much things really cost, or the hard facts of Depression. After six months the money ran out. We were desperate.

I didn't know how badly off we were until my mother stole a dozen heavy silver spoons from our landlady, who was kind, or at least harbored no grudge against us, and whom my mother counted as a friend. Adelaide gave no explanation for the spoons when I discovered them in her pocket. Days later they were gone and Karl and I owned thick overcoats. Also, our shelf was loaded with green bananas. For several weeks we drank quarts of buttermilk and ate buttered toast with thick jam. It was not long after that, I believe, that the baby was ready to be born.

One afternoon my mother sent us downstairs to the landlady.

This woman was stout and so dull that I've forgotten her name, although I recall vivid details of all else that happened at that time. It was a cold late-winter afternoon. We stared into the glass-faced cabinet where the silver stirrup cups and painted plates were locked after the theft. The outlines of our faces stared back at us like ghosts. From time to time Karl and I heard someone cry out. Once something heavy hit the floor directly above our heads. Both of us looked up at the ceiling and threw out our arms, as if to catch it. I don't know what went through Karl's mind, but I thought it was the baby, born heavy as lead, dropping straight through the clouds and my mother's body. I had a confused idea about the process of birth. At any rate, no explanation I could dream up accounted for the long scream that tore through the air, turned Karl's face white, and caused him to slump forward in the chair.

I had given up on reviving Karl each time he fainted. By now I trusted that he'd come to by himself, and he always did, looking soft and dazed and somehow refreshed. The most I ever did was hold his head until his eyes blinked open.

"It's born," he said when he came around.

As if I knew already that our disaster had been accomplished in that cry, I would not budge. Karl argued and made a case for at least going up the stairs, if not through the actual door, but I sat firm until the landlady came down and told us, first, that we now had a baby brother, and second, that she had found one of her grandmother's silver spoons under the mattress and that she wasn't going to ask how it got there, but we had four weeks to move out.

That night I fell asleep sitting in a chair beside Mama's bed, in lamplight, holding the baby in a light wool blanket. Karl was curled in a spidery ball at Mama's feet, and she was sleeping hard, her hair spread wild and bright across the pillows. Her face was white, sunken, but after she spoke I had no pity.

"I should let it die," she mumbled. Her lips were pale, frozen in a dream. I would have shaken her awake, but the baby was curved hard against me.

"I could bury it out back in the lot," she whispered, "that weedy place."

"Mama, wake up," I said, but she kept speaking.

"I won't have any milk. I'm too thin."

I looked down at the baby. His face was round, bruised blue, and his eyelids were swollen almost shut. He looked frail, but when he stirred I put my little finger in his mouth, as I had seen women do to quiet their babies, and his suck was eager.

"He's hungry," I told her.

But Adelaide rolled over and turned her face to the wall.

Milk came flooding into Adelaide's breasts, more than the baby could drink at first. She had to feed him. Milk leaked out in dark patches on her light-green plaid shirtwaists. She moved despairingly, burdened by the ache. She did not completely ignore the baby, although she refused to name him. She cut her petticoats up for diapers, sewed a layette from her nightgown, but often left him to howl. Sometimes he cried such a long time that the landlady came puffing upstairs to see what was wrong. She was troubled to see us so desperate and brought up food left by the paying boarders. Still, she did not change her decision. When the month was up, we still had to go.

The spring clouds were high and the air was warm on the day we went out looking for a new place. All of the ordinary clothes Mama owned had been cut up for the baby, so she had nothing but her fine things, lace and silk, good cashmere. She wore a black coat, a black dress trimmed in cream lace, and delicate string gloves. Her hair was in a strict and shining knot. We walked down the brick sidewalks looking for signs in windows, for rooming houses of the cheapest kind, barracks, or hotels. We found nothing and finally sat down to rest on a bench bolted to the side of a store. In those times, the streets of towns were much kindlier. No one minded the destitute gathering strength, taking a load off, discussing their downfall in the world.

"We could go back to Fritzie," Mama said. "She's my sister. She'd have to take us in."

I could tell from her voice that it was the last thing she wanted to do.

"You could sell your jewelry," I told her.

Mama gave me a warning look and put her hand to the brooch at her throat. She was attached to the things that Mr. Ober had given her over the years. When we begged, she showed them off: the complicated garnet necklace, the onyx mourning brooch and drop pearl earrings, the Spanish comb, and the ring with the good yellow diamond. I supposed that she wouldn't sell them even to save us. Our hardship had beaten her and she was weak, but in her weakness she was also stubborn. We sat on the store's bench for perhaps half an hour, then Karl noticed music in the air.

"Mama," he begged, "it's a fair!"

As always with Karl, she began by saying no, but that was just a formality and both of them knew it. In no time, he had wheedled and charmed her into going.

The Orphans' Picnic, a bazaar held to benefit the homeless children of Saint Jerome's, was taking place at the city fairground just a few streets away. We saw the banner blazing cheerful red, stretched across the entrance, bearing bright yellow handmade letters. Plank booths were set up in the long brown grass leftover from winter. Nuns swished between the scapular and holy-medal counters or stood poised behind racks of rosaries, shoe boxes full of holy cards, tiny carved statues of saints, and common toys. We swept into the excitement, looked over the grab bags, games of chance, displays of candy and religious wares. At a booth that

10

sold jingling hardware, Mama stopped and pulled a dollar bill from her purse.

"I'll take that," she said to the vendor, pointing. He lifted a pearl-handled jackknife from his case and gave it to Karl. Then she pointed at a bead necklace, silver and gold.

"I don't want it," I said.

Her face reddened, but after a slight hesitation she bought the necklace anyway. Then she had Karl fasten it around her throat. She put the baby in my arms.

"Here, Miss Damp Blanket," she said.

Karl laughed and took her hand. Wandering from booth to booth, we finally came to the grandstand, and at once Karl began to pull her toward the seats. I had to stumble along behind them. Bills littered the ground. Posters were pasted up the sides of trees and the splintery walls. Mama picked up one of the smaller papers.

THE GREAT OMAR, it said, AERONAUGHT EXTRAORDINAIRE. APPEARING AT NOON. Below the words there was a picture of a man, sleek, moustachioed, his orange scarf whipping in a breeze.

"Please!" Karl said.

And so we joined the gaping crowd.

The plane dipped, rolled, buzzed, glided above us like some kind of insect. I did not crane my neck or gasp, thrilled, like the rest of them. I looked down at the baby and watched his face. He was just emerging from the newborn's endless sleep, and from time to time now he stared at me in deep concentration. I stared back. In his face I found a different arrangement of myself— bolder, quick as light, ill-tempered. He frowned at me, unaware that he was helpless, troubled only at the loud drone of the biplane as it landed and taxied toward the crowd.

Thinking back now, I can't believe that I had no premonition. I hardly glanced when The Great Omar jumped from the plane, and I did not applaud his sweeping bows and pronouncements. I hardly listened when he offered rides to those who dared. I

11

believe he charged a dollar or two for the privilege. I did not notice. I was not prepared for what came next.

"Here!" my mother called, holding her purse up in the sun.

Without a backward look, without a word, with no warning and no hesitation, she elbowed through the people collected at the base of the grandstand and stepped into the cleared space around the pilot. I looked at The Great Omar for the first time. The impression he gave was dashing, like his posters. The orange scarf was knotted at his neck and certainly he had some sort of moustache. I believe he wore a grease-stained white sweater. He was slender and dark, much smaller in relation to his plane than the poster showed, and older. After he helped my mother into the passenger's cockpit and jumped in behind the controls, he pulled a pair of green goggles down over his face. And then there was a startling, endless moment, as they prepared for the takeoff. The aeronaught exchanged signals with two men who had helped him turn the plane.

"Switch on! Switch off! Contact!"

"Clear prop!" Omar shouted, and the men leaped away.

The propeller made a wind. The plane lurched forward, lifted over the low trees, gained height. The Great Omar circled the field in a low swoop, and I saw my mother's long red crinkly hair spring from its tight knot and float free in an arc that seemed to reach out and tangle around his shoulders.

Karl stared in stricken fascination at the sky, and said nothing as The Great Omar began his stunts and droning passes. I could not watch. I studied the face of my little brother and held myself tense, waiting for the plane to smash.

The crowd thinned. People drifted away. The sounds of the engine were harder to hear. By the time I dared look into the sky, The Great Omar was flying steadily away from the fairgrounds with my mother. Soon the plane was only a white dot, then it blended into the pale sky and vanished.

12

I shook Karl's arm, but he pulled away from me and vaulted to the edge of the grandstand. "Take me!" he screamed, leaning over the rail. He stared at the sky, poised as if he'd throw himself into it.

Satisfaction. It surprised me, but that was the first thing I felt after Adelaide flew off. For once she had played no favorites between Karl and me, but left us both. Karl dropped his head in his hands and began to sob into his thick wool sleeves. I looked away.

Below the grandstand, the crowd moved in patternless waves. Over us the clouds spread into a thin sheet that covered the sky like muslin. We watched the dusk collect in the corners of the field. Nuns began to pack away their rosaries and prayer books. Colored lights went on in the little carnival booths. Karl slapped his arms, stamped his feet, blew on his fingers, but I wasn't cold. The baby kept me warm.

The baby woke, very hungry, and I was helpless to comfort him. He sucked so hard that my finger was white and puckered, and then he screamed. People gathered. Women reached out their arms, but I held my brother tighter. I did not trust them. I did not trust the man who sat down beside me, either, and spoke softly. He was a young man with a hard-boned, sad, unshaven face. What I remember most about him was the sadness. He wanted to take the baby back to his wife so she could feed him. She had a newborn of her own, he said, and enough milk for two.

I wouldn't answer.

"When is your mother coming back?" the young man asked.

He waited. Karl sat mute staring into the dark sky. All around, the large interfering people told me what to do.

"Give him the baby, dear."

"Don't be stubborn."

"Let him take the baby home."

13

"No," I said to every order and suggestion. I even kicked hard when a bold woman tried to take my brother from my arms. One by one they grew discouraged and went off. Only the young man remained.

It was the baby himself who finally convinced me. He did not let up screaming. The longer he cried, the longer the sad man sat beside me, the weaker my resistance was, until I could barely hold my own tears in.

"I'm coming with you then," I told the young man. "I'll bring the baby back here when he's fed."

"No," cried Karl, coming out of his stupor suddenly. "You can't leave me alone!"

He grabbed my arm so fervently that the baby slipped, and then the young man caught me, as if to help, but instead he scooped the baby to himself.

"I'll take good care of him," he said, and turned away.

I tried to wrench from Karl's grip, but like my mother he was more stubborn when he was frightened, and I could not break free. The man walked into the shadows. I heard the baby's wail fade. I finally sat down beside Karl and let the cold sink into me.

One hour passed. Another hour. When the colored lights went out and the moon came up, blurred behind the sheets of clouds, I knew for certain the young man lied. He wasn't coming back. And yet, because he looked too sad to do any harm to anyone, I was more afraid for Karl and myself. We were the ones who were thoroughly lost. I stood up. Karl stood with me. Without a word we walked down the empty streets to the rooming house. We had no key, but Karl displayed one unexpected talent. He took the thin-bladed knife Adelaide had given him, and picked the lock.

The cold room was filled with the faint perfume of the dried flowers that our mother scattered in her trunk, the rich scent of the clove-studded orange she hung in the closet, and the lavender

14

oil she rubbed into her skin at night. The sweetness of her breath seemed to linger, the rustle of her silk underskirt, the quick sound of her heels. Our longing buried us. We sank down on her bed and cried, wrapped in her quilt, clutching each other. When that was done, however, I acquired a brain of ice.

I washed my face in the basin, then I woke Karl and told him we were going to Aunt Fritzie's. He nodded without hope. We ate all there was to eat in the room, two cold pancakes, and packed a small cardboard suitcase. Karl carried that. I carried the quilt. The last thing I did was reach far back into my mother's drawer and pull out her small round keepsake box. It was covered in blue velvet and tightly locked.

"We'll have to sell these things," I told Karl. He hesitated but then, with a hard look, he took the box.

We slipped out before sunrise and walked to the train station. In the weedy yards there were men who knew each boxcar's destination. We found the car we wanted and climbed in. We spread the quilt and rolled up together, curled tight, with our heads on the suitcase and Mama's blue velvet box between us in Karl's breast pocket. I clung to the thought of the treasures inside of it, but I had no way of knowing that the comforting rattle I heard once the train started moving that afternoon was not the rich clatter of heirlooms that could save us—the garnet necklace and the good yellow diamond—but pins, buttons, and one silent ticket of retrieval from a Minneapolis pawnshop.

We spent all night on that train while it switched and braked and rumbled toward Argus. We did not dare jump off for a drink of water or to scavenge food. The one time we did try this the train started up so quickly that we were hardly able to catch the side rungs again. We lost our suitcase and the quilt because we took the wrong car, farther back, and for the rest of that night we did not sleep at all because of the cold. Karl was too miserable even to argue with me when I told him it was my turn to hold Mama's box. I put it in the bodice of my jumper. It did not keep me warm, but even so, when I shut my eyes, the sparkle of the diamond, the patterns of garnets that whirled in the dark air, gave me something. My mind hardened, faceted and gleaming like a magic stone, and I saw my mother clearly.

She was still in the plane, flying close to the pulsing stars, when suddenly Omar noticed that the fuel was getting low. He did not love Adelaide at first sight or even care what happened to her. He had to save himself. Somehow he had to lighten his load. So he set his controls. He stood up in his cockpit. Then in one sudden motion he plucked my mother out of her seat and dropped her overboard.

All night she fell through the awful cold. Her coat flapped open and her black dress wrapped tightly around her legs. Her red hair flowed straight upward like a flame. She was a candle that gave no warmth. My heart froze. I had no love for her. That is why, by morning, I allowed her to hit the earth.

When the train stopped at Argus I was a block of sullen cold. It hurt when I jumped, scraping my cold knees and the heels of my hands. The pain sharpened me enough to read signs in windows and to wrack my mind for just where Aunt Fritzie's shop was. It had been years since we visited.

Karl was older, and I probably should not hold myself accountable for losing him too. But I didn't help him. I ran to the end of town. I couldn't stand how his face glowed in the blossoms' reflected light, pink and radiant, so like the way he sat beneath our mother's stroking hand.

When I stopped, hot tears came up suddenly behind my eyes and my ears burned. I ached to cry but I knew that was useless. I turned back, looking carefully at everything around me, and it was lucky I did this, because I'd run past the butcher shop and, suddenly, there it was, set in from the road down a short dirt drive. A white pig was painted on the side, and inside the pig, the lettering KOZKA'S MEATS. I walked toward it between rows of tiny fir trees. The place looked unfinished but prosperous, as though Fritzie and Pete were too busy with customers to care for appearances. I stood on the broad front stoop and noticed everything I could, the way a beggar does. A rack of elk horns was nailed overhead. I passed beneath them.

The entryway was dark, my heart was pounding. I had lost so much and suffered so badly from the grief and cold that I'm sure what I saw was quite natural, understandable, although it was not real.

Again, the dog leapt toward Karl and blossoms fell from his stick. Except that they fell around me in the entrance to the store. I smelled the petals melting on my coat, tasted their thin sweetness in my mouth. I had no time to wonder how this could be happening because they disappeared as suddenly as they'd come when I told my name to the man behind the glass counter.

Uncle Pete was tall and blond and wore an old blue denim cap the same color as his eyes. His smile was slow, sweet for a butcher, and hopeful. "Yes?" he asked. He did not recognize me even after I told him who I was. Finally his eyes rounded and he called out for Fritzie.

"Your sister's girl! She's here!" he shouted down the hall.

I told him I was alone, that I had come in on a boxcar, and he lifted me up in his arms. He carried me back to the kitchen where Aunt Fritzie had been frying a sausage for my cousin, the beautiful Sita, who sat at the table and stared while I tried to tell Fritzie and Pete just how I'd come to walk in their front door out of nowhere.

They watched me with friendly suspicion, thinking that I'd run away. But when I told about The Great Omar, and how Mama held up her purse, and how Omar helped her into the plane, their faces turned grim.

17

"Sita, go polish the glass out front," said Aunt Fritzie. Sita slid unwillingly out of her chair. "Now," Fritzie said. Uncle Pete sat down heavily and pressed his fists together under his chin. "Go on, tell the rest," he said, and so I told all of the rest, and when I had finished I had also drunk a glass of milk and eaten a sausage. By then I was so tired I could hardly sit upright. Uncle Pete lifted me. I remember sagging against him, then nothing. I slept that day and all night and did not wake until the next morning.

I lay still for what seemed like a long while, trying to place the objects in the room, until I remembered they all belonged to Sita.

This was where I would sleep every night for the rest of my life. The paneling was warm stained pine. The curtains were patterned with dancers and musical notes. Most of one wall was taken up by a tall oak dresser with fancy curlicues and many drawers. On it there was a wooden lamp in the shape of a wishing well. A full-length mirror hung on the back of the door. Through that door, as I was taking in my surroundings, walked Sita herself, tall and perfect with a blond braid that reached to her waist.

She sat down on the edge of my trundle bed and folded her arms over her small new breasts. She was a year older than me and one year younger than Karl. Since I'd seen her last, she had grown suddenly, but her growth had not thinned her into an awkward bony creature. Sita grinned. She looked down at me, her strong white teeth shining, and she stroked the blond braid that hung down over one shoulder.

"Where's Auntie Adelaide?" she asked.

I did not answer.

"Where's Auntie Adelaide?" she said, again, in a singsong furious voice. "How come you're here? Where'd she go? Where's Karl?"

"I don't know."

18

I suppose I thought the misery of my answer would quiet Sita, but that was before I knew her.

"How come she left you? Where's Karl? What's this?"

She took the blue velvet box from my pile of clothes and shook it next to her ear.

"What's in it?"

I snatched the box with an angry swiftness she did not expect. Then I rolled from the bed, bundled my clothes into my arms, and walked out of the room. The one door open in the hallway was the bathroom, a large smoky room of many uses that soon became my haven since it was the only door I could bolt against my cousin.

Every day for weeks after I arrived in Argus, I woke slowly, thinking I was back in Prairie Lake and that none of this had happened. Then I saw the dark swirls in the pine and Sita's arm hanging off the bed above me. The day started. I smelled the air, peppery and warm from the sausage makers. I heard the rhythmical whine of meat saws, slicers, the rippling beat of fans. Aunt Fritzie was smoking her sharp Viceroys in the bathroom. Uncle Pete was outside feeding the big white German shepherd that was kept in the shop at night to guard the canvas bags of money.

I got up, put on one of Sita's hand-me-down pink dresses, and went out to the kitchen to wait for Uncle Pete. I cooked breakfast. That I made a good cup of coffee at age eleven and fried eggs was a source of wonder to my aunt and uncle, and an outrage to Sita. That's why I did it every morning until it became a habit to have me there.

I planned to be essential to them all, so depended upon that they could never send me off. I did this on purpose, because I soon found out that I had nothing else to offer. The day after I arrived in Argus and woke up to Sita's accusing questions, I had tried to give them what I thought was my treasure—the blue velvet box that held Mama's jewels.

I did it in as grand a manner as I could, with Sita for a witness and with Pete and Fritzie sitting at the kitchen table. That morning, I walked in with my hair combed wet and laid the box between my uncle and aunt. I looked from Sita to Fritzie as I spoke.

"This should pay my way."

Fritzie had my mother's features sharpened one notch past beauty. Her skin was rough and her short curled hair bleached platinum. Her eyes were a swimming, crazy shade of turquoise that startled customers. She ate heartily, but her constant smoking kept her string-bean thin and sallow.

"You don't have to pay us," said Fritzie. "Pete tell her. She doesn't have to pay us. Sit down, shut up, and eat."

Fritzie spoke like that, joking and blunt. Pete was slower.

"Come. Sit down and forget about the money," he said. "You never know about your mother. . . ." he added in an earnest voice that trailed away. Things had a way of evaporating under Fritzie's eyes, vanishing, getting sucked up into the blue heat of her stare. Even Sita had nothing to say.

"I want to give you this," I said. "I insist."

"She insists," exclaimed Aunt Fritzie. Her smile had a rakish flourish because one tooth was chipped in front. "Don't insist," she said.

But I would not sit down. I picked up a knife from the butter plate and started to pry the lock.

"Here now," said Fritzie. "Pete, help her."

So Pete got up, fetched a screwdriver from the top of the icebox, sat down and jammed the end underneath the lock.

"Let her open it," said Fritzie, when the lock popped up. Pete pushed the little round box across the table.

"I bet it's empty," Sita said. She took a big chance saying that, but it paid off in spades and aces between us growing up because I lifted the lid a moment later and what she said was true. There was nothing of value in the box.

Stickpins. A few thick metal buttons off a coat. And a ticket describing a ring and the necklace set with garnets, pawned for practically nothing in Minneapolis.

There was silence. Even Fritzie was at a loss. Sita nearly buzzed off her chair in triumph but held her tongue until later, when she would crow. Pete put his hand on his head. I stood quietly, my mind working in a circle. If Sita had not been there I might have broken down and let the tears out again, like in the rooming house, but she kept me sharp.

I sat down to eat out of range of Sita's jabbing elbow. Already my mind was working on what revenge I would exact from her, and already I was way ahead where getting even was concerned, because Sita never saw me clearly until it was much too late. And so, as the years went on, I became more essential than any ring or necklace, while Sita flowered into the same frail kind of beauty that could be broken off a tree by any passing boy and discarded, cast away when the fragrance died.

I put the jewel box on the dresser I now shared with Sita, and never looked inside again. I didn't let myself think or remember, but got on with living. Still, I couldn't stop the dreams. At night they appeared, Karl, Mama, my baby brother, and Mr. Ober with his mouth full of grain. They tried to reach through air and earth. They tried to tell me there was rhyme and reason. But I put my hands over my ears.

I'd lost trust in the past. They were part of a fading pattern that was beyond understanding, and brought me no comfort.

Karl's Night

When Karl lay down in the freight again that morning, he decided not to move until he died. But then the train didn't travel on as it was supposed to. Not ten miles out of Argus, Karl's boxcar separated from the rest of the train and stopped. All that day he dozed and woke and saw the same two tall silver grain elevators just down the line. By late afternoon he was so thirsty, cold and hungry, so tired of waiting to die, that when a man swung through the door he was glad for the excuse to put it off.

Karl had buried himself in hay from the broken bales, and the man sat down not more than two feet away without seeing him. Karl watched the man closely. He seemed old to Karl at first. His face was burned a leathery hard brown. His eyes were almost lost in squinting folds; his lips were thin. He looked flint hard under his clothes, the remains of an old army uniform, and when he lit a cigarette stub the match reflected two thin flames in his eyes. He blew the smoke out in a ring. His hair was longish, the color of sand, and his beard was half grown.

Karl watched the man smoke his cigarette carefully down to the paper end, and then he spoke.

"Hello?"

"Huahh!" The man jumped up and floundered backward, then caught himself. "What the . . ."

"My name is Karl."

"Gave me a hell of a scare." The man glared into the shadows around Karl and then laughed abruptly. "You're a kid," he said, "and God don't you look the fool. Come here."

Karl stepped out and stood in the wide shaft of light from the door. The hay he'd slept in had matted to his overcoat and stuck out of his hair. He stared at the man from beneath a headful of

22

grasses, and his look was so mournful that the man softened.

"You're a girl, aren't you?" he said. "S'cuse my language."

"I'm not a girl."

But Karl's voice hadn't finished changing yet and the man was unconvinced.

"I'm not a girl," Karl repeated.

"What'd you say your name was?"

"Karl Adare."

"Karla," the man said.

"I'm a boy."

"Yeah." The man rolled a new cigarette. "I'm Saint Ambrose." Karl nodded cautiously.

"It's no joke," said the man. "My last name's Saint Ambrose. First name's Giles."

Karl sat down on the bale next to Giles Saint Ambrose. Hunger was making his head swim. He had to blink to keep his vision clear. Still, he noticed that the man was not as old as he had thought at first. In fact, once he was sitting close, Karl saw that his face was marked by sun and wind, not age.

"I'm from Prairie Lake," Karl managed to say. "We had a house."

"And you lost it," said Giles, looking at Karl through plumes of smoke. "When'd you eat last?"

The word *eat* made Karl's jaws lock, his mouth water. He stared speechlessly at Giles.

"Here." Giles took a newspaper-wrapped square from his jacket pocket. He unwrapped the package. "It's good, it's ham," he said.

Karl took it in both hands and ate with such swift ferocity that Giles forgot to draw on his cigarette.

"It was worth it just to watch," he said when Karl had finished. "I was going to ask you to save me a hunk, but I didn't have the heart."

Karl folded the newspaper and gave it back to Giles.

23

"That's all right." Giles waved the paper away. He reached down and picked up the stick Karl had brought into the boxcar. A few wilted gray blossoms still clung to the nodes. "This would make a good mosquito whip," said Giles.

"It's mine," said Karl.

"Oh?" said Giles, thrashing the air. "Not anymore it isn't. Call it a trade."

What happened to Karl next would shame him later on, but he couldn't help it. The branch made him think of the leaping dog, its snarling muzzle, of Mary standing rooted in the street and himself tearing at the tree with all his strength, managing to twist off the branch and strike. Karl's eyes filled with tears and spilled over.

"It was only a joke," said Giles. He jiggled Karl's arm. "You can have it back." Giles wrapped Karl's fingers around the branch and Karl held tight to it but could not stop crying. He melted inside, overflowed. Sobs burst from his chest.

"Quiet down," said Giles. He put his arm around Karl's shoulders and the boy fell against him, weeping now in long tearing jagged moans. "You're going to have to practice. Boys don't do this," said Giles. But Karl kept crying until the fury of his grief was exhausted.

When Karl woke later it was dusk. He could hardly see, and the air was full of a dull confusing roar that sounded like torrents of rain or hail. Karl reached for Giles, afraid he'd vanished, but the man was there.

"What's that?" Karl asked, running his hands over Giles's rough army jacket. He fell back, reassured, when Giles mumbled, "It's just the grain loading. Go to sleep."

Karl stared up into the dark exciting sound of the avalanche. He planned how he and Giles would travel in the boxcar, occasionally jumping off at a town they liked the look of, stealing

24

food, maybe finding an abandoned house to live in. He pictured them together, in danger from dogs or police, outrunning farmers and store clerks. He saw them roasting chickens and sleeping together, curled tight in a jolting boxcar, like they were now.

"Giles," he whispered.

"What?"

Karl waited. He'd touched other boys before but just in fun, down the alleys behind the boardinghouse. This was different, and he was not sure he'd dare, but then his body filled with the rushing noise. He took the chance, put his hands out, touched Giles's back.

"What do you want?"

Karl put his hand underneath Giles's jacket, and the man turned to him.

"Do you know what you're doing?" Giles whispered.

Karl felt the breath from Giles's lips and tipped his mouth up to kiss him. He put his hands under Giles's clothes again and edged close. Giles rolled on top of him and pinned him deep in the hay. Karl shivered then flushed warm when Giles began.

"You're no girl," Giles mumbled into Karl's hair, then he kissed Karl on the throat and began to touch him in a new way, all over, roughly but also carefully, until Karl's body tightened unbearably and then let loose, abruptly, in a long dark pulse. When Karl came back to himself he wrapped his arms very tightly around Giles, but the moment had passed. Giles loosened his arms gently and rolled over next to him. They lay together, side by side, both looking up into the sound of the grain, and Karl was certain of what he felt.

"I love you," Karl said.

Giles did not answer.

"I love you," Karl said again.

"Oh, Jesus, it wasn't anything," said Giles, not unkindly. "It happens. Don't get all worked up over it, okay?"

25

Then he turned away from Karl. After a long moment Karl got up on his knees. "Giles, you asleep?" he asked. There was no answer. Karl felt Giles's breathing slow, his body slacken, his legs jump as he fell into a deeper level of sleep.

"Bastard . . ." Karl whispered. Giles didn't waken. Karl said it, a little louder, again. Giles slept. Then Karl went into a black turmoil, a revery where things got mixed up in time and Adelaide's hair flew out of its knot, once again, to snarl around the shoulders of the slender pilot. He saw her fly off into the sky and then remembered the knife she had given him. He took it out, for the first time since Minneapolis, and tested its point with his finger.

"This is sharp," he warned. He stabbed it once or twice through the dark, even brought it down close enough to prick the torn wool of Giles's jacket. But Giles did not wake, and after a while Karl folded the knife and put it back in his pocket.

The roar stopped abruptly. Giles stirred but didn't wake. Through the cracks between the boards, Karl saw lanterns arc and swing and move away. And then there was a sudden jolt, another and another all down the line of cars, until theirs moved too, pounding, slowly gathering speed.

"It happens," Karl said then, repeating Giles's words. "It happens."

When he said that, it felt like his heart ripped open. Even in his storm of weeping he had not touched the depth of his loss. Now it swallowed him. There was the branch, still faintly good to smell. He picked it up and then stood in the blackness. He didn't want to vomit or scream. He didn't want to cry on the lap of anyone again. So he stood frowning keenly at nothing as the train rolled on, and then, light and quick as a deer, he leaped forward and ran straight out the door of the moving boxcar.

SITA KOZKA

My cousin Mary came in on the early freight train one morning, with nothing but an old blue keepsake box full of worthless pins and buttons. My father picked her up in his arms and carried her down the hallway into the kitchen. I was too old to be carried. He sat her down, then my mother said, "Go clean the counters, Sita." So I don't know what lies she told them after that.

Later on that morning, my parents put her to sleep in my bed. When I objected to this, saying that she could sleep on the trundle, my mother said, "Cry sakes, you can sleep there too, you know." And that is how I ended up that night, crammed in the trundle, which is too short for me. I slept with my legs dangling out in the cold air. I didn't feel welcoming toward Mary the next morning, and who can blame me?

Besides, on her first waking day in Argus, there were the clothes.

It is a good thing she opened the blue keepsake box at breakfast and found little bits of trash, like I said, because if I had not felt sorry for my cousin that day, I would not have stood for Mary and my mother ripping through my closet and bureau. "This fits perfectly," my mother said, holding up one of my favorite blouses, "try it on!" And Mary did. Then she put it in her drawer, which was another thing. I had to clear out two of my bureau drawers for her.

"Mother," I said, after this had gone on for some time and I was beginning to think I would have to wear the same three outfits all the next school year, "Mother, this has really gone far enough."

"Crap," said my mother, who talks that way. "Your cousin hasn't got a stitch."

Yet she had half of mine by then, quite a wardrobe, and all the time it was increasing as my mother got more excited about dressing the poor orphan. But Mary wasn't really an orphan, although she played on that for sympathy. Her mother was still alive, even if she had left my cousin, which I doubted. I really thought that Mary just ran away from her mother because she could not appreciate Adelaide's style. It's not everyone who understands how to use their good looks to the best advantage. My Aunt Adelaide did. She was always my favorite, and I just died for her to visit. But she didn't come often because my mother couldn't understand style either.

"Who are you trying to impress?" she'd hoot when Adelaide came out to dinner in a dress with a fur collar. My father would blush red and cut his meat. He didn't say much, but I knew he did not approve of Adelaide any more than her older sister did. My mother said she'd always spoiled Adelaide because she was the baby of the family. She said the same of me. But I don't think that I was ever spoiled, not one iota, because I had to work the same as anyone cleaning gizzards.

I hated Wednesdays because that was the day we killed chickens. The farmer brought them stacked in cages made of thin wooden slats. One by one, Canute, who did most of the slaughtering, killed them by sticking their necks with the blade of his long knife. After the chickens were killed, plucked, and cut open, I got the gizzards. Coffee can after coffee can full of gizzards. I still have dreams. I had to turn each gizzard inside out and wash it in a pan of water. All the gravel and hard seed fell out into the bottom. Sometimes I found bits of metal and broken glass. Once I found a brilliant. "Mother!" I yelled, holding it out in

28

my palm. "I found a diamond!" Everyone was so excited that they clustered around me. And then my mother took the little sparkling stone to the window. It didn't scratch the glass at all, of course, and I had to clean the rest of the gizzards. But for one brief moment I was sure the diamond had made us rich, which brings me to another diamond. A cow's diamond, my inheritance.

It was a joke, really, about the inheritance, at least it was a joke to my papa. A cow's diamond is the hard rounded lens inside a cow's eye that shines when you look through it at the light, almost like an opal. You could never make a ring of it or use it for any kind of jewelry, since it might shatter, and of course it had no worth. My father mainly carried it as a lucky piece. He'd flip it in the air between customers, and sometimes in a game of cribbage I'd see him rub it. I wanted it. One day I asked if he would give it to me.

"I can't," he said. "It's my butcher's luck. It can be your inheritance, how about that?"

I suppose my mouth dropped open in surprise because my father always gave me anything I asked for. For instance, we had a small glass candy case out front, over the sausages, and I could eat candy anytime I wanted. I used to bring root-beer barrels into class for the girls I liked. I never chewed gum balls though, because I heard Auntie Adelaide tell mother once, in anger, that only tramps chewed gum. This was when my mother was trying to quit smoking and she kept a sack of gum balls in the pocket of her apron. I was in the kitchen with them when they had this argument. "Tramps!" my mother said, "That's the pot calling the kettle black!" Then she took the gum from her mouth and rubbed it into Adelaide's long wavy hair. "I'll kill you!" my Auntie raged. It was something to see grown-ups behaving this way, but I don't blame Auntie Adelaide. I'd feel the same if I had to cut out a big knot of gum like she did and have a shorter patch of hair. I

29

never chewed gum. But anything else in the store I wanted, I just took. Or I asked and it was handed right over. So you can see why my father's refusal was a surprise.

I had my pride even as a child, and I never mentioned it again. But here is what happened two days after Mary Adare came.

We were waiting to be tucked in that night. I was in my own bed, and she was in the trundle. She was short enough to fit there without hanging off the edge. The last thing she did before going to sleep was to put Adelaide's old keepsake box up on my bureau. I didn't say anything, but really it was sad. I guess my papa thought so, too. I guess he took pity on her. That night he came in the room, tucked the blankets around me, kissed me on the forehead, and said, "Sleep tight." Then he bent over Mary and kissed her too. But to Mary he said, "Here is a jewel."

It was the cow's diamond that I wanted, the butcher's luck. When I looked over the edge of my bed and saw the pale lens glowing in her hand, I could have spit. I pretended to be asleep when she asked me what it was. Find out for yourself, I thought, and said nothing. A few weeks later, when she knew her way around town, she got some jeweler to drill a hole through one end of the lucky piece. Then she hung the cow's diamond around her neck on a piece of string, as if it were something valuable. Later on she got a gold link chain.

First my room, then my clothing, then the cow's diamond. But the worst was yet to come when she stole Celestine.

My best friend, Celestine, lived three miles out of town with her half brother and much older half sister, who were Chippewas. There weren't all that many who came down from the reservation, but Celestine's mother had been one. Her name was Regina I-don't-know-what, and she worked for Dutch James, keeping his house when he was a bachelor and after, once they married. I overheard how Celestine came just a month past the wedding, and how Regina brought down the three other children

30

Dutch James hadn't known about. Somehow it worked out. They all lived together up until the time of Dutch James's peculiar death. He froze solid in our very meat locker. But that is an event no one in this house will discuss.

Anyway, those others were never court adopted and went by the last name Kashpaw. Celestine was a James. Because her parents died when Celestine was young, it was the influence of her big sister that was more important to Celestine. She knew the French language, and sometimes Celestine spoke French to lord it over us in school, but more often she got teased for her size and the odd flimsy clothes that her sister Isabel picked out of the dime store in Argus.

Celestine was tall, but not clumsy. More what my mother called statuesque. No one told Celestine what to do. We came and went and played anywhere we felt like. My mother would never have let me play in a graveyard, for example, but when visiting Celestine, that's what we did. There was a cemetery right on the land of Dutch James's homestead, a place filled with the graves of children who died in some plague of cough or influenza. They'd been forgotten, except by us. Their little crosses of wood or bent iron were tilted. We straightened them, even recarved the names on the wooden ones with a kitchen knife. We dug up violets from the oxbow and planted them. The graveyard was our place, because of what we did. We liked to sit there on hot afternoons. It was so pleasant. Wind ruffled the long grass, worms sifted the earth below us, swallows from the mudbanks dove through the sky in pairs. It was a nice place, really, not even very sad. But of course Mary had to ruin it.

I underestimated Mary Adare. Or perhaps I was too trusting, since it was I who suggested we go visit Celestine one day in early summer. I started out by giving Mary a ride on the handlebars of my bicycle, but she was so heavy I could hardly steer.

"You pedal," I said, stopping in the road. She fell off, then jumped up and stood the bicycle upright. I suppose I was heavy, too. But her legs were tireless. Celestine's Indian half brother, Russell Kashpaw, approached us on the way to Celestine's. "Who's your slave today?" he said. "She's cuter than you'll ever be!" I knew he said things like that because he meant the opposite, but Mary didn't. I felt her swell proudly in my old sundress. She made it all the way to Celestine's, and when we got there I jumped off and ran straight in the door.

Celestine was baking, just like a grown-up. Her big sister let her make anything she wanted, no matter how sweet. Celestine and Mary mixed up a batch of cookie dough. Mary liked cooking too. I didn't. So they measured and stirred, timed the stove and put out the cooling racks while I sat at the table with a piece of waxed paper, rolled out the dough, and cut it into fancy shapes.

"Where did you come from?" Celestine asked Mary as we worked.

"She came from Hollywood," I said. Celestine laughed at that, but then she saw it wasn't funny to Mary, and she stopped.

"Truly," said Celestine.

"Minnesota," said Mary.

"Are your mother and father still there?" asked Celestine. "Are they still alive?"

"They're dead," said Mary promptly. My mouth fell open, but before I could get a word of the real truth in, Celestine said.

"Mine are dead too."

And then I knew why Celestine had been asking these questions, when she already knew the whole story and its details from me. Mary and Celestine smiled into each other's eyes. I could see that it was like two people meeting in a crowd, who knew each other from a long time before. And what was also odd, they looked suddenly alike. It was only when they were together. You'd never notice it when they weren't. Celestine's hair was a tarnished red brown. Her skin was olive, her eyes burning black. Mary's eyes were light brown and her hair was dark and lank. Together, like I said, they looked similar. It wasn't even their build. Mary was short and stocky, while Celestine was tall. It was something else, either in the way they acted or the way they talked. Maybe it was a common sort of fierceness.

After they went back to their mixing and measuring, I could see that they were friendlier too. They stood close together, touched shoulders, laughed and admired everything the other one did until it made me sick.

"Mary's going to Saint Catherine's next fall," I interrupted. "She'll be downstairs with the little girls."

Celestine and I were in the seventh grade, which meant our room was on the top floor now, and also that we would wear special blue wool berets in choir. I was trying to remind Celestine that Mary was too young for our serious attention, but I made the mistake of not knowing what had happened last week, when Mary went into the school to take tests from Sister Leopolda.

"I'll be in your class," said Mary.

"What do you mean?" I said. "You're only eleven!"

"Sister put me ahead one grade," said Mary, "into yours."

The shock of it made me bend to my cookie cutting, speechless. She was smart. I already knew she was good at getting her way through pity. But smartness I did not expect, or going ahead a grade. I pressed the little tin cutters of hearts, stars, boys, and girls into the cookie dough. The girl shape reminded me of Mary, square and thick.

"Mary," I said, "aren't you going to tell Celestine what was in the little blue box you stole out of your mother's closet?"

Mary looked right at me. "Not a thing," she said.

Celestine stared at me like I was crazy.

"The jewels," I said to Mary, "the rubies and the diamonds."

We looked each other in the eye, and then Mary seemed to

33

decide something. She blinked at me and reached into the front of the dress. She pulled out the cow's diamond on a string.

"What's that?" Celestine showed her interest at once.

Mary displayed the wonder of how the light glanced through her treasure and fell, fractured and glowing, on the skin of her palm. The two of them stood by the window taking turns with the cow's lens, ignoring me. I sat at the table eating cookies. I ate the feet. I nibbled up the legs. I took the arms off in two snaps and then bit off the head. What was left was a shapeless body. I ate that up too. All the while I was watching Celestine. She wasn't pretty, but her hair was thick and full of red lights. Her dress hung too long behind her knees, but her legs were strong. I liked her tough hands. I liked the way she could stand up to boys. But more than anything else, I liked Celestine because she was mine. She belonged to me, not Mary, who had taken so much already.

"We're going out now," I told Celestine. She always did what I said. She came, although reluctantly, leaving Mary at the window.

"Let's go to our graveyard," I whispered, "I have to show you something."

I was afraid she wouldn't go with me, that she would choose right there to be with Mary. But the habit of following me was too strong to break. She came out the door, leaving Mary to take the last batch of cookies from the oven.

We left the back way and walked out to the graveyard.

"What do you want?" said Celestine when we stepped into the long secret grass. Wild plum shaded us from the house. We were alone.

We stood in the hot silence, breathing air thick with dust and the odor of white violets. She pulled a strand of grass and put the tender end between her lips, then stared at me from under her eyebrows.

Maybe if Celestine had quit staring, I wouldn't have done what I did. But she stood there in her too-long dress, chewing a stem of grass, and let the sun beat down on us until I thought of what to show her. My breasts were tender. They always hurt. But they were something that Mary didn't have.

One by one, I undid the buttons of my blouse. I took it off. My shoulders felt pale and fragile, stiff as wings. I took off my undervest and cupped my breasts in my hands.

My lips were dry. Everything went still.

Celestine broke the stillness by chewing grass, loud, like a rabbit. She hesitated just a moment and then turned on her heel. She left me there, breasts out, never even looking back. I watched her vanish through the bushes, and then a breeze flowed down on me, passing like a light hand. What the breeze made me do next was almost frightening. Something happened, I turned in a slow circle. I tossed my hands out and waved them. I swayed as if I heard music from below. Quicker, and then wilder, I lifted my feet. I began to tap them down, and then I was dancing on their graves.

MARY ADARE

HOW LONG WAS Sita going to shimmy there, I wondered, with her shirt off and thunderclouds lowering? I heard Celestine walk into the kitchen below and bang the oven door open, so I came down. I stood in the kitchen door watching her lift each cookie off the sheet with a spatula. She never broke one. She never looked up. But she knew I was there, and she knew that I'd been up on the second floor, watching Sita. I know that she knew because she hardly glanced up when I spoke.

"It's dark all of a sudden," I said; "there's a storm."

"Sita's mother'll be mad," said Celestine, dusting flour off her hands.

We went out to get Sita, but before we were halfway across the yard Sita came, walked right past us, jumped on her bicycle, and rode away. That is how I got caught in the rain that afternoon. It swept down in sheets while I still had a mile left to walk. I slogged in the back door of the house and stood dripping on the hemp mat.

Fritzie rushed at me with a thick towel and practically took my head off rubbing it dry.

"Sita! Get out here and apologize to your cousin," she hollered. She had to call Sita twice before she came.

On the first day of school that next fall, we walked out of the door together, both carrying fat creamy tablets and new pencils in identical wooden pencil boxes, both wearing blue. Sita's dress was new with sizing, mine was soft from many washings. It didn't bother me to wear Sita's hand-me-downs because I knew it bothered her so much to see those outgrown dresses, faded and unevenly hemmed by Fritzie, diminished by me and worn to tatters, not enshrined as Sita probably wished.

We walked down the dirt road together and then, hidden from Fritzie's view by the short pines, we separated. Or rather, Sita ran long legged, brightly calling, toward a group of girls also dressed in stiff new material, white stockings, unscuffed shoes. Colored ribbons, plumped in bows, hung down their backs. I lagged far behind. It didn't bother me to walk alone.

And yet, once we stood in the gravel school yard, milling about in clumps, and once we were herded into rows, and once Celestine began to talk to me and once Sita meanly said I'd come in on the freight train, I suddenly became an object of fascination.

36

Popular. I was new in Argus. Everybody wanted to be my friend. But I had eyes only for Celestine. I found her and took her hand. Her flat black eyes were shaded by thick lashes, soft as paintbrushes. Her hair had grown out into a tail. She was strong. Her arms were thick from wrestling with her brother Russell, and she seemed to have grown even taller than a month ago. She was bigger than the eighth-grade boys, almost as tall as Sister Leopolda, the tallest of all the nuns.

We walked up the pressed-rock stairs following our teacher, a round-faced young Dominican named Sister Hugo. And then, assigned our seats in alphabetical order, I was satisfied to find myself in the first desk, ahead of Sita.

Sita's position soon changed, of course. Sita always got moved up front because she volunteered to smack erasers together, wash blackboards, and copy out poems in colored chalk with her perfect handwriting. Much to her relief, I soon became old hat. The girls no longer clustered around me at recess but sat by her on the merry-go-round and listened while she gossiped, stroked her long braid and rolled her blue eyes to attract the attention of the boys in the upper grade.

Halfway through the school year, however, I recaptured my classmates awe. I didn't plan it or even try to cause the miracle, it simply happened, on a cold frozen day late in winter.

Overnight that March, the rain had gone solid as it fell. Frozen runnels paved the ground and thick cakes of ice formed beneath the eaves where the dripping water solidified midair. We slid down the glossy streets on the way to school, but later that morning, before we got our boots and coats from the closet for the recess hour, Sister Hugo cautioned us that sliding was forbidden. It was dangerous. But once we stood beneath the tall steel slide outdoors, this seemed unfair, for the slide was more a slide than ever, frozen black in one clear sheet. The railings and steps were coated with invisible glare. At the bottom of the slide a pure glass fan opened, inviting the slider to hit it feet first and swoop down the center of the school yard, which was iced to the curbs.

I was the first and only slider.

I climbed the stairs with Celestine behind me, several boys behind her, and Sita hanging toward the rear with her girl friends, who all wore dainty black gum boots and gloves, which were supposed to be more adult, instead of mittens. The railings made a graceful loop on top, and the boys and bolder girls used it to gain extra momentum or even somersault before they slid down. But that day it was treacherous, so slick that I did not dare hoist myself up. Instead, I grabbed the edges of the slide. And then I realized that if I went down at all, it would have to be head first.

From where I crouched the ride looked steeper, slicker, more dangerous than I'd imagined. But I did have on the product of my mother's stolen spoons, the winter coat of such heavy material I imagined I would slide across the school yard on it as if it were a piece of cardboard.

I let go. I went down with terrifying speed. But instead of landing on my padded stomach I hit the ice full force, with my face.

I blacked out for a moment, then sat up, stunned. I saw forms run toward me through a haze of red and glittering spots. Sister Hugo got to me first, grabbed my shoulders, removed my wool scarf, probed the bones of my face with her strong, short fingers. She lifted my eyelids, wacked my knee to see if I was paralyzed, waggled my wrists.

"Can you hear me?" she cried, mopping at my face with her big manly handkerchief, which turned bright red. "If you hear me, blink your eyes!"

I only stared. My own blood was on the cloth. The whole playground was frighteningly silent. Then I understood my head was whole and that no one was even looking at me. They were all crowded at the end of the slide. Even Sister Hugo was standing there now, her back turned. When several of the more pious students sank to their knees, I could not contain myself. I lurched to my feet and tottered over. Somehow I managed to squeeze through their cluster, and then I saw.

The pure gray fan of ice below the slide had splintered, on impact with my face, into a shadowy white likeness of my brother Karl.

He stared straight at me. His cheeks were hollowed out, his eyes dark pits. His mouth was held in a firm line of pain and the hair on his forehead had formed wet spikes, the way it always did when he slept or had a fever.

Gradually, the bodies around me parted and then, very gently, Sister Hugo led me away. She took me up the stairs and helped me onto a cot in the school infirmary.

She looked down at me. Her cheeks were red from the cold, like polished apples, and her brown eyes were sharp with passion.

"Father is coming," she said, then popped quickly out.

As soon as she was gone, I jumped off the cot and went straight to the window. An even larger crowd had collected at the base of the slide, and now Sister Leopolda was setting up a tripod and other photographic equipment. It seemed incredible that Karl's picture should warrant such a stir. But he was always like that. People noticed him. Strangers gave him money while I was ignored, just like now, abandoned with my wounds. I heard the priest's measured creak on the stairs, then Sister Hugo's quick skip, and I jumped back.

Father opened the back door and allowed his magnificence to be framed in it for a moment while he fixed me with his most penetrating stare. Priests were only called in on special cases of discipline or death, and I didn't know which one this was.

He motioned to Sister Hugo, and she ducked from the room.

He drew a chair up beneath his bulk and sat down. I lay flat, as if for his inspection, and there was a long and uncomfortable silence.

"Do you pray to see God?" he asked finally.

"Yes!" I said.

"Your prayers were answered," Father stated. He folded his fingers into the shape of a church and bit harshly on the steeple, increasing the power of his stare.

"Christ's Dying Passion," he said. "Christ's face formed in the ice as surely as on Veronica's veil."

I knew what he meant at last, and so kept silent about Karl. The others at Saint Catherine's did not know about my brother, of course. To them the image on the ice was that of the Son of God.

As long as the ice on the playground lasted, I was special in the class again, sought out by Sita's friends, teachers, even boys who were drawn to the glory of my black eyes and bruises. But I stuck with Celestine. After the sliding, we were even better friends than before. One day the newspaper photographer came to school and I made a great commotion about not having my picture taken unless it was with her. We stood together in the cold wind, at the foot of the slide.

GIRL'S MISHAP SHAPES MIRACLE was the headline in the *Argus Sentinel*.

For two weeks the face was cordoned off and farmers drove for miles to kneel by the cyclone fence outside of Saint Catherine's school. Rosaries were draped on the red slats, paper flowers, little ribbons and even a dollar or two.

And then one day, the sun came out and suddenly warmed the earth. The face of Karl, or Christ, dispersed into little rivulets that ran all through the town. Echoing in gutters, disappearing, swelling through culverts and collecting in basements, he made himself impossibly everywhere and nowhere all at once so that all spring before the town baked hard, before the drought began, I felt his presence in the whispering and sighing of the streams.

CELESTINE JAMES

I HAVE A BACK view of Mary when she shoots down the slide to earth. Her heavy gray wool coat stands out like a bell around the white clapper of her drawers, but the wind never ruffles her blue scarf. She is motionless in her speed, until she hits. Then suddenly things move fast, everywhere, all at once. Mary rolls over twice. Blood drenches her face. Sister Hugo runs toward her and then there are screams. Sita draws attention to herself by staggering to the merry-go-round, dizzy at the sight of her cousin's blood. A tortured saint, maybe even Catherine herself, she drapes her body among the iron spokes at the center of the wheel, and calls out, in a feeble but piercing tone, for help.

Sita is five times as strong as she looks, and can beat me in a fight, so I do not go to her. Sister Hugo is now leading Mary up the stairs with her handkerchief and the blue scarf pressed on Mary's forehead. I have backed down the iced-over slide steps like magic, and now I run after the two of them. But Sister Hugo bars me from the door once they reach the infirmary.

"Go back down," she says in a shaking voice. Her eyes blaze strangely underneath her starched linen brow. "It may not last," she says. "Run to the convent! Tell Leopolda to haul herself right over with the camera!"

I am confused.

41

"The ice, the face," said Sister Hugo frantically. "Now, *get!*"

And so I run, so amazed and excited at how she has expressed herself, not like a teacher but just like a farmer, that I do not ring the convent bell but leap straight into the entryway and scream up the echoing stairs. By then I know, because it is in the air of the school yard, that some kind of miracle had resulted from Mary's fall.

So I shout, "A MIRACLE" at the top of my lungs. To do that in a convent is like shouting fire in a crowded movie. They all rush down suddenly, an avalanche of black wool. Leopolda springs down last of all, with a fearsome eagerness. A tripod is strapped on one shoulder. Drapes, lights, and a box camera are crammed in her arms. It is like she has been right behind her door, armed with equipment, praying year in and year out for this moment to arrive.

Back on the school ground, all is chaos. A crowd has formed around the end of the slide. Later on, the face they stare at is included in the catechism textbooks throughout the Midwest as The Manifestation At Argus, with one of Sister Leopolda's photographs to illustrate. In the article, Mary is described as "a local foundling," and the iced slide becomes "an innocent trajectory of divine glory." The one thing they never write about is how Sister Leopolda is found several nights after Mary's accident. She is kneeling at the foot of the slide with her arms bare, scourging herself past the elbows with dried thistles, drawing blood. After that she is sent somewhere to recuperate.

But that day, in all of the confusion, I sneak back into the school building. As I walk down the hall Father comes out of the infirmary door. He is lost in a serious thought and never lifts his head, so he does not see me. As soon as he is down the hall I slip straight in, alarmed because a priest near a sick person spells doom.

But Mary is recovered from the blow, I think at first, because she's sitting up.

42

"Did you see him!" she says immediately, clutching my arm. She looks deranged, either with her sudden importance or with the wound. Her head is taped in gauze now, which would give her a nun-like air except that the pits of her eyes are beginning to show disreputable black and purple bruises.

"They say it's a miracle," I tell her. I expect her to laugh but she grips my hand hard. Her eyes take on a glitter that I start to suspect.

"It was a sign," she says, "but not what they think."

"How do you mean?"

"It was Karl."

She has never mentioned Karl before, but from Sita I know he is her brother who has run off on a boxcar heading west.

"Lay back," I tell Mary. "Your head got knocked."

"He's got to bother me," she says loudly. "He can't leave me alone."

Her face screws up. She is thinking deeply like the priest and has lost all track of me or even of herself. Her eyes glare into the distance, light and still, and I see that she is very annoyed.

After Sister Hugo sends me out of the infirmary, I walk down the stairs, out into the cold overcast weather, and join the throng clustered around the miraculous face. Only to me, it is not so miraculous. I stare hard at the patterns of frozen mud, the cracked ice, the gravel that shows through the ice, the gray snow. Other people looking from the same angle see it. I do not, although I kneel until my knees grow numb.

That night the face is all that Russell and my big sister Isabel can talk about.

"Your girl friend's going to put us on the map," declares Isabel. She's all we have, and she takes care of us by holding down jobs with farmers, cooking, and sometimes even threshing right along with the men. "Girls have been canonized for less," she now says. Isabel carries the banner in Saint Catherine's Procession every year, looking huge and sorrowful, but pure. My mother was big too. It seems like I got all of my father's coloring, but am growing very quickly into my mother's size.

"I bet Sita's about ready to kill that little Mary," Russell says with a sharp laugh. Sita has made fun of him for being an Indian, and he is always glad to see her taken down a notch.

"They are taking a picture of Mary for the papers," I tell him. Isabel is impressed, but not Russell, because he plays football and has been in the papers many times for making touchdowns. People say he is one Indian who won't go downhill in life but have success, and he does, later, depending on how you look at it.

The next morning, before school starts, he comes with me to inspect the ice. During the night, someone has put up a low slat and wire fence around the sacred patch. Russell kneels by the fence and blesses himself. He says some sort of prayer, and then walks his bicycle down the icy road to the high school. He has seen it too. I am left at the bottom of the slide again, kneeling and squinting, even crossing my eyes to try and make the face appear. All the while the nuns are setting up the altar, right there in the school yard, for a special mass. I begin to wish that I had asked Russell to point out the features for me exactly, so that I can see Christ, too. Even now, I consider questioning the nuns, but in the end I don't have the courage, and all through the mass, standing with the seventh grade, watching Mary, Sita, Fritzie and Pete take communion first, I pretend that I am moved by the smashed spot, which is all I can see.

Rescue

In a small frame house in Minneapolis, a young woman sat reading the newspaper, her fingers rustling in and out of the pages. Her husband sat across the room watching her read. Their son was in his arms.

"Here's another ad," said Catherine Miller.

"Why do you look for them anyway?" said her husband, Martin.

She lowered the paper and stared calmly at him. Her brows were plucked into slender bows that made her eyes seem intelligent. Her light brown hair was poked into a swirling topknot.

"You know why," she said, flipping the paper back and forth. "The police, Martin. Kidnapping's a criminal offense."

Having no answer, Martin looked down at the baby. The child's eyes lost focus, his mouth drooped, and Martin held him closer, taking such pleasure in the sleeping baby's trust that he did not notice when his wife tensed, held her breath, scanned an article quickly, and then lowered the paper.

She sat with the paper in her lap, watching Jude, her son, the tiny baby she had named for the patron saint of lost causes, lost hopes, and last-ditch resorts. She remembered that first night after their other son, the one who had only lived three days, was buried.

That night was a small quiet place in her she rarely visited. But now she thought back. How still the world had been, and the sky, such a dark spring blue. Her bound breasts ached unbearably. Her mind was frozen blank with loss, yet every nerve throbbed. She could not sleep.

From time to time such blind agony had swept over her that she thought she would drown, or lose her mind. She had even refused anodynes. She wanted nothing to dull the pain, no laudanum, not even a glass of whiskey. But with Martin gone that night, she decided suddenly she needed something. So she stumbled to the cabinet where the bottle was hidden and poured a quick, large toothglass full of bootleg. Standing alone in the cold dark house, a tall frowzy figure in a nightgown printed with flannel roses, she drank. The liquor burned with a clear fire. She poured another glass and downed it more slowly, allowing the heat to envelop her. To her surprise, the whiskey helped. At least it was a distraction, and as she floated back to bed and straight into sleep, the pain, duller now and heavier, was held at arm's length and not cradled inside of her.

Relaxed in dead exhaustion, she had not heard Martin come through the front door. Once he entered the bedroom and put the baby in the crib, she heard it howl, but she retreated mentally from the sound. Even in her stupor she was certain that it was some sort of terrible hallucination. She felt Martin's hands at her breasts, untying the strips of cloth now soaked with her faintly sweet milk, and she tried to fight him away. Martin calmed her with words and low croons, as if she were a frightened animal, and once she lay still again he put the baby to her breast.

Instantly, although she knew it could not be happening, she let go and fed the child, as if from her own heart. Even in her confusion she realized that the child was different, as small as her first, but older, more adept.

Now, waiting for Martin to look up and see her expression, a tide of feeling that she'd held back without knowing it rolled out. Even looking at the baby warmed her. What a marvel—those dark red curls!

"You look like the cat that ate the bird," said Martin, smiling at her.

"I'm happy."

"I'm happy too," said Martin cautiously. "He's ours."

"I know it."

And then she read the article aloud, the one accompanying the usual ad with the reward offered for information leading to the recovery of a month-old baby boy. The article described the mother, her incredible behavior, and said that she was also sought by the Kozka family of Argus.

After she finished reading the article, Catherine Miller saved the paper away carefully in a drawer, along with the tiny cap of pale blue, the thick blanket pieced from scraps of coat fabric, and the strange little green plaid gown the baby had been wearing on the night he came to her rescue.

CHAPTER THREE *1932*

KARL ADARE

I HAD LANDED in tall dead grass. It was daylight. The pain in my legs was horrible and the ground under me was cold. As the day wore on the light warmed, grew hotter, and beat through my clothes. The pain spun me long and shrank me into a knot. Any slight movement made it worse, and so I lay still.

I thought Giles would come back when he found out what I had done. I saw him waking up alone in the jerking boxcar. He would wait until the train slowed, then hike back and take me in his arms. I trusted that since I hadn't died I certainly would be saved.

My salvation dragged a cart of scavenged boards down the tracks. Its wheels were shrieking iron. The sound stopped just above me. She was massive. Her shadow fell from above. I opened my cracked throat, but no word came out of it, then a woman stumbled down the low embankment. Her head was bound in a white scarf that blazed against her dark skin. Twin silver mirrors dangled from her earlobes, flashed, dizzied me. She crouched over me, lifted my eyelids with fingers tough and flexible as pliers. Then she opened my jaw and poured raw whiskey down my throat. It went through me like a rope of fire, tangling my guts, lighting a pinpoint of sense in my brain.

"Feet," I said.

She bent closer.

But I couldn't stand to have them touched, and twisted away from her probing fingers.

Blue in the dusk, a formation of scarves and blankets, she

disappeared. There was a clattering and banging beyond my sight, and I slept until she came back and carried me over to the fire. Water was steaming in a pot on a hook. I saw a knife, a few packets of flour, some dried beans and dirty roots. She put me on a mound of reeds.

"What are you going to do!" I struggled in her arms.

Days would pass before I realized that Fleur Pillager almost never spoke, though she had the ability. She told me only her name, but I heard her sing and talk to herself.

She covered me with a horse blanket then dribbled more whiskey between my lips until my coughing stopped her. She cut off my shoes, slicing carefully into the leather, then my socks too. I begged her to use that same knife to cut my feet off, but when she put my feet firmly in her lap I arched into blackness. At the first squeeze of her hand, she told me later, I passed out.

While I was dead to the world, Fleur Pillager proceeded to knead, mold, and tap the floating splinters of my bones back into the shape of ankles, feeling her own from time to time to get the shape right. The packets I thought were flour were really plaster of Paris. Out of it she made my casts and shaped them with carved splinters from the only branch within a mile of the railroad track, the apple branch, torn from an Argus tree, that she found lying next to me.

She bundled me into oilskins and more blankets and got me drunk, but I could not sleep that night. The sky changed gradually, black to gray, red to pink, and then the sun broke out. Fleur had drawn her cart down the railroad embankment onto the margin of a reedy slough almost deep enough to be a lake. The cattails were the tallest things in sight. The world was bare as far as the eye could see. We were the only detail in it. Fleur poked up the fire, mixed bread in a pan, and heated the sloughwater coffee. I sipped a rank, sweet cup of it and studied her as best I could.

Her face was young, broad and dark, but fine around the edges, even delicate. Her heavy mouth curved at the corners, her nose arched like the nose of a royal princess. She was an Indian, a Pillager, one of a wandering bunch that never did take hold. She made her living by peddling whatever came her way to sell. Pans hung from her cart, and bundles that held packets of needles, colored string. Calico dress lengths were piled on top. She dealt in mismatched plates, mended cups, and secondhand forks. She bought handmade white lace from the mission school and traded it for berries pounded into jerky, birch-bark picture frames.

I wanted to tell her who I was, to tell her everything. But then, just as I started to speak, the sky rushed down. The earth pressed close, so close I couldn't breath.

"There's something wrong with me," I choked.

Fleur pounded my chest, put her ear on my heart, then got up and started throwing things off her cart. I had pneumonia, a common hazard of sleeping in cold boxcars. Most every longtime hobo walked around with it, died of it or survived. Fleur put rocks in the fire to heat, but the reeds smoked too much. So she split some railroad ties and stoked the blaze until the rocks were red hot.

The sun lowered. The grass rustled in the slight breeze and the noise seemed unnaturally loud, and the ducks too, mumbling in their soft nests, and the muskrats. I seemed to hear them slapping through the water after insects. Even the massing clouds seemed to make a light *whooshing* sound as they puckered and folded and gained color.

Fleur rolled the hot stones, sizzling, onto the mud by the slough, and then she put the wagon box over them. On it she put a chair that had been tied on top of everything. She stripped me naked in a few short jerks and rolled me back up in a dry blanket. She sat me on the chair on top of the box, as on a throne, and then wound a length of rope around me. Over it all, down to the ground, surrounding me like a cape and tied firmly around my shoulders, she draped her blankets.

Then I was sealed into a sweltering cone.

I was the highest point in the world. I was out of my mind. I faced west as the sun settled in a fierce glow that lit my face. I shone back like a beacon through my transparent skin and imagined I could be seen as the dark came on, red like a lantern, glowing like a heart in crackling papers. The outlines of my bones were etched black. I was a signal. All through the night I pulsed on and off, calling any of them back to me—Giles or Mary, my mother, even the baby who'd ruined my life by driving her away.

Animals surrounded the edges of my heat. I saw the eyes of skunks, red marbles, heard the chatter of coons, watched the bitterns land, blacker than the black sky, and drowsy hawks. A bear rose between the fire and the reeds. In the deepest part of the night, the biggest animal of all came through in a crash of sparks and wheels.

It was not quite dawn when Fleur took me down. I was limp and sodden but breathing more easily. My fever had broken sometime during the night. She rolled me in the outermost dry blankets and put me on the reeds again. She piled more reeds on top of me. And over all that, she lay herself, a crushing weight, and at first I was cold again and felt my lungs tightening, but then, from above, her warmth pressed down.

When I was better we moved on. Fleur's cart ran on specially grooved wheels, and she pulled it, her head through a horse collar. We traveled slowly, our ears stopped with cattail down to muffle the wheels' shocks and groans. I was lashed on top, in my chair, legs sticking out and an umbrella tied to shade me. Because both of our ears were stopped up, I worried about hearing trains. But Fleur wore hobnail boots with flattened cans nailed upon the toes. Those slats of metal vibrated to signal a train's approach, and Fleur had time to lift the cart off and trundle it to one side.

I didn't know where we were going, didn't care. We passed

farms, some near the tracks, some far, and each time Fleur took the cart off and dragged it overland or down a road until we reached the yard. You would have thought dogs would worry her, farmers would lock their doors. But outside each yard the dogs met us eagerly. Next came the children, clutching nickels, to get the first look. Then the women appeared, hesitating, faces flushed with steam, hands raw from the laundry, feet aching. Fleur showed them buffalo-horn buttons, twinned geese in an agate, a brooch made of claws. At last, the men arrived for ax heads and lengths of twine. Fleur's customers were wary and approached her with a hint of fear, as if she were a witch or maybe a saint cast off to wander.

And they looked at me, Fleur's captive in every way, shamefully dependent on her. I don't know what they saw. A stick boy. A poor fool.

Sometimes we stayed in a tool shed or barn, and once a man with lumps on his neck big as goose eggs invited us to sleep in his dead wife's parlor. We never stayed more than one night anywhere. At dawn Fleur packed the wagon piece by piece, with me on top. She put her head in the collar, and pulled me along the track.

Between farms, I had plenty of time to think, and sometimes the first few days I took out my knife with the mother-of-pearl handle. Holding it tight, I could see my mother sweeping the floor with short, bored strokes or pinning her hair up. When she did that she hardly looked in the mirror. I saw the milky white underside of her arms, the little frown by which she clenched pins in her mouth, her fingers precisely stabbing. I longed for her then and I let myself cry, beneath Fleur's umbrella. It wasn't long, though, before I tired of weeping and began inventing scenes of my mother that gave me more pleasure. For instance, her suffering when we finally met again and I ignored her, turning a marble cheek. Or the shock with which she tried to comprehend my cruelty.

"I shall never forgive you," I murmured, out loud sometimes to increase the thrill.

But as my fantasies grew harsher, she began to sob in my pictures, to pound her fists into her mattress, scratch her smooth skin, and even to tear out her hair by the handful, until at length I was frightened by the violence of her shame and sorrow. I began to believe, then, that she hadn't really abandoned me. It came to me quite naturally that the man in the white sweater, leather helmet, orange gold scarf had stolen her off against her will.

I realized this one day when we had stopped to let a train pass by. I thought of the way my mother's lips had grazed mine before she thrust her arm up, to offer her money for a plane ride with the skinny barnstormer. Her lips were cold, in spite of the full sun. Her jaw was clenched. She had never gone up in a plane before and she must have been afraid. Although her gesture was bold, her smile, as she tendered the bill from her purse, was too bright, too hollow. An adventure to break the tedium was all she'd wanted. Her fear and the cool kiss proved it. Naturally, Omar had been taken with her, had fallen in love with her when she offered the bill, had then secretly planned not to bring her back but to keep on flying no matter how she pleaded, how loud her cries rang above the engine.

Even now, as I sat with Fleur in the wind of approaching trains, my mother was captive to that man.

I would save her. Once I could walk I'd hunt him down. One morning I would stand at his door. He'd appear, wiping soap from his chest, and with no warning I'd strike. I killed the pilot many times and in many ways as we traveled. Always, at the end of each episode, my mother rushed to me over his dead body. She held me close, and when she kissed me her lips were lingering and warm.

I suppose it was a week or two before we got to the reservation where Fleur lived. We traveled not more than a mile or two each day, because the farms were spread evenly along the route and required detours. During that time, the wind seared my face. The rain hardened my skin. If it was cold at night or drizzly, Fleur rolled me in a mound of blankets and oilcloths. Sometimes, by morning, I was rolled up tight and warm next to her, close but never quite touching her skin. I think I could have gone on living endlessly under her protection, but then, suddenly, we got where we were going.

One day Fleur left the track and we began down two ox-trail ruts, passing out of farm country and into open prairie. It was a long time before there were any houses. We began to visit low cabins of mud-mortared logs, inhabited by Chippewa or fiercer-looking French-Indians with stringy black beards and long moustaches. There were board houses, too, with wells, barns, and neat screen doors that whined open when we approached. The women who came out of these doors wore housedresses and had their hair cut, curled, and bound in flimsy nets. They were not like Fleur, but all the same they were Indians and spoke a flowing language to each other.

After a few days of walking the paths deeper into the small hills, we came to a settlement. It wasn't much. A few board houses and two larger buildings that looked like schools or offices. We headed up a winding road to a church. Fleur left her cart at the bottom of the hill and carried me in her arms straight up to the back door of a whitewashed house.

"What's this!" cried a nun who opened the door. She was fat and mild and very clean looking. I smelled so bad that she covered her mouth with her hand.

Fleur continued to hold me like an offering. No explanation. And after a while the nun opened the door wider and gestured us in. She rang a small bell near the entryway, and several of her sisters gathered.

"She picked me up," I said. "I fell off the westbound train."

They peered at me with round eyes, then turned and held a conference as to whether I would stay or not, whether they should tetch their Superior or the priests, whether or not I was an Indian, or dangerous. As it happened, their talk was useless, for even while they hissed and murmured Fleur bent over, laid me in a heap on their polished linoleum, and walked back out the door.

I'd been cast off so many times that by then it didn't matter. It occurred to me while I was sitting on the floor that the three things I'd done on my own had caused my life to go from bad to worse. These were, first, hopping the train back out of Argus, then Giles Saint Ambrose and finally jumping off the boxcar. I'd ended up completely helpless. So this time I simply sat still until the next person took charge of me. I did not resist sleeping on a pallet in the broom closet of the priest's house and then drudging in the churchyard when I was finally healed. I went along when the nuns found the money to send me back to Minneapolis, where other members of their order met the train and then walked me back full circle, beneath the red banner of Saint Jerome's, past the trees that had been strung with colored lights for the Orphans' Picnic, around the grandstand, and still farther, to the large brick orphanage with many doors and windows where I spent the next year before I entered the seminary.

I had a great talent for obedience. I was in love with the picture of myself in a slim black cassock, and felt that the green lawns of the seminary and white brick of the chapels set me off to good advantage. While I walked the grounds, reading my daily lessons, I was exposed to many eyes. Between the lines of sacred texts, I rendezvoused with thin hard hoboes who had slept in the bushes. Ghostly, rank in their own sweat and travel dust, they saw me as a pure black flame. They could not resist me. I always knew that if I kept my eyes moving strictly down the page of print, if I paused in the darkest corners of the landscape, if I closed my eyes as if in communion with someone greater, they would come. They would force me to worship them like an animal. I would fall. I would burn and burn until by grace I was consumed.

Aerial View of Argus

One day Aunt Fritzie invited Mary into her office, where the black and gold safe was kept, where ledgers filled six shelves and white tape from the adding machine curled like spindrift across the floor. The long strips tangled around Mary's ankles when she sat down next to the gray steel desk. Fritzie rummaged in the drawers and pulled out clips, paper, more adding tape. A stand-up ashtray was handy at one elbow; a radio hummed in the oak cabinet above her head. The plants that grew in Aunt Fritzie's office had leaves flat as dollar bills and never needed water. The fluorescent lights she turned on at night buzzed and snapped and attracted soft brown moths.

This office was Mary's favorite place. Already she had decided that when she was in high school, she would learn how to keep books like Aunt Fritzie. She wanted to sit among the dry plants on cold nights and work with numbers. On one night at the end of every month, when Fritzie sent the bills out, Mary fell asleep to the soothing *tick, tick, whirr* of Aunt Fritzie's fingers on the adding machine keys.

"I guesss you're old enough to figure this out for yourself," said Aunt Fritzie now. She had found what she was looking for and handed the card to Mary. It was a postcard. Mary observed the picture carefully before turning it over. On the front, a man in a formal suit was photographed standing in the branches of a tree. *The largest Live-oak in So. Jacksonville, Fla.* was written in ornate green script below him. On the back of the card there was a short message.

I am living down here. I think about the children every day. How are they? Adelaide.

Mary glanced up in time to catch the way Aunt Fritzie blew the smoke out, in two thin streams of contempt. Then she looked down at the card again. Fritzie was waiting for a reaction, but Mary didn't feel anything in particular.

"Well," said Aunt Fritzie, "what are you going to do?"

In Aunt Fritzie's loud voice, Mary heard a conspirator. Fritzie was Adelaide's only sister, after all. Adelaide had abandoned her too.

"I don't know yet," said Mary.

"Of course not," said Fritzie. She put out her cigarette with one harsh stab. "I'd like to horsewhip her."

Mary pulled a dead leaf off the plant that crowded the window.

"Write her back if you want, she's your mother. But I washed my hands of Adelaide when you walked in the door."

Mary stole a look at Aunt Fritzie's expression. But Aunt Fritzie caught her eyes and Mary couldn't break free.

"Don't go back to her, is all I ask," said Fritzie.

Something like a tight band in Mary's chest snapped and she laughed, a sudden awkward bray of intense relief that embarrassed her.

"Fat chance," she said. "you're more a mother to me."

Fritzie fumbled another cigarette from her pack. Her yellow skin flushed golden and she squinted at her automatic lighter. "Why don't I quit? These things are killing me."

"They stink too," said Mary.

"That's according to Sita."

Mary laughed.

"After this pack," Aunt Fritzie promised.

"After this pack," Mary agreed.

Aunt Fritzie picked up a green pen labeled KOZKA'S FOR THE FINEST IN MEAT PRODUCTS and started paging through her bound ledger. Mary shook the curls of paper away from her ankles.

"I'll take this," Mary said, holding up the postcard, and then she left.

Mary didn't think specifically about the postcard, but it was there in the back of her mind all the next few weeks, and sometimes she would find herself addressing long imaginary letters, full of hatred and grief, to Adelaide. Then one day she answered her mother's postcard with one that she chose almost unthinkingly from the rack at the corner drugstore. *Aerial View of Argus, North Dakota* it said on the front. Argus's brown dots of buildings, bare streets, and puffs of green trees were surrounded by a patchwork of dull brown fields. What she wrote on the back of the card surprised Mary as much as it would have surprised and gratified Aunt Fritzie, whose name and style of handwriting she carefully copied.

All three of your children starved dead, Mary wrote.

She addressed the card and walked down to the post office with it in her hands. She bought a stamp, licked it, and placed it in the upper right-hand corner. When her fingers released the card into the mail slot she thought that she felt nothing. But that night, the last night of the month, as she was falling asleep to Aunt Fritzie's adding machine, she imagined that she saw the postcard alight in her mother's hands. Adelaide stared down and examined each detail of the picture, but although she searched the fine marks, she could not see her daughter, who was too small to tell of, looking directly through her, not dead but securely hidden in the aerial view.

Mary's postcard, forwarded through two addresses and held for several weeks at the booking agency that handled The Great Omar, came into Omar's hands just after the accident. He put

58

it in his pocket and would have forgotten about it except that, in the hospital watching Adelaide, he had nothing to distract himself. And so he painfully extracted the card with his burnt hands, looked at it several times, and put it back.

Omar tried not to move much and took shallow breaths, his face white from the pain of his bound ribs, his shattered leg splinted from the hip. Only his eyes moved, from the peak of Adelaide's feet under the hospital sheet, to the curve of her wrist, to the stern plane of her left cheekbone and back again. There was a small window over her head, a patch of Florida indigo. The day was sweltering. Just behind the rubbery curtain someone groaned, and farther down the ward water gushed on and on until he wondered if any could be left. He opened his mouth, tried to speak, but he rarely knew what to say to Adelaide when she was alive, and now that she was so near death he felt even less sure of himself.

He couldn't even touch her. His hands were puffy soft clubs, bound in lengths of gauze. During the accident, sparks had jumped from the controls but he had not taken his hands away. He'd screamed while everything was happening, but Adelaide had not, that he could remember, and now he could imagine that she'd sat beside him, ice cold as he tried to arrest their plunge.

He had, remarkably, brought them to earth and avoided a total crack-up, although what happened was bad enough. They had been flying a county fair, so there were plenty of people to run for doctors, ice, splints, bandages, stretchers, and salts. He remembered the commotion and, above it, the roaring of the alligator wrestlers, the tinny twinkling of some Ferris wheel tune. He'd called Adelaide's name, but the eyes of the strangers who held him were wide with excitement and told him nothing.

He still didn't know how badly she was hurt, or whether she'd wake up sound in the mind or whether she'd wake up at all. He didn't know it would turn out that her injuries were far less serious

59

than they seemed, or that she would carry one scar only, at the nape of her neck, while he would live on with pains in his knees and a rolling limp. He thought that any moment could easily be her last and he would never know it.

A nurse strode in, clanged a few pans, and withdrew. On the other side of the curtain the groans changed to a low and monotonous curse. Adelaide's hand trembled. Omar almost called the nurse back, then stopped himself, afraid the shaking might signal some turn for the worse. He kept watch. It was a shock to him when she spoke.

"I've got to send Mary a sewing machine," said Adelaide.

Her voice came from the unseen area beyond her cheekbone, drifted down over Omar, and drew him. He leaned over to her.

"If Mary learns how to sew, she'll always have a skill to fall back on."

Her lips were pursed in the practical frown Omar knew from the evenings when she counted money, the day's take, and decided how much for the room, whether they'd eat high or low, and what they'd put aside for repairs and gas. Adelaide was good at this. Since she had joined him they not only managed to have enough but some left over, which she kept in her winter account and would not let him withdraw.

Omar reached toward Adelaide. He gasped at the stab in his ribs, but she didn't seem to notice him anyway.

"Look at me," he said.

Her gray-blue eyes focused on the wall, her lovely eyebrows drew imperiously together.

"There's enough money saved for a Singer," she said.

Then she shut her eyes. It was real sleep this time. She frowned as if daring anyone to wake her up. Omar moved away, disturbed and jealous. Adelaide almost never talked about her children or her life before him.

Flies threw themselves busily against the screened blue. The

60

air was close. Omar didn't like to think that while Adelaide was sleeping now it might be Mary, or that other one, a boy, that she dreamed of and not him. He'd never had the slightest doubt about her before. He was proud that she'd left her children and her whole life, which he gathered had been comfortable from her fine clothes and jewelry, for a bootlegger with nothing to his name but a yellow scarf and an airplane held together with baling wire.

Now the airplane was painted, in the repair shop even now, and his name was known on the circuit. He didn't drink, either.

Thanks to her, he thought. Her hand was still. He watched it for a sign of weakness that did not come. Her knuckles pinked, as if she had been knocking on a door. She made a fist and began to tighten it over and over. Omar felt his throat shut, even though she was just squeezing air.

He sat with Adelaide until he fully understood that she was out of danger. Then he got to his feet, took the card from Argus out of his pocket, and propped it on the wood nightstand where she would see it.

PART TWO

MARY ADARE

AFTER THE MIRACULOUS sheets of black ice came the floods, stranding boards and snaky knots of debris high in the branches, leaving brown leeches to dry like raisins on the sidewalks when the water receded, and leaving the smell of river mud, a rotten sweetness, in the backyards and gutters. Long into the drought there would be evidence of how far up the river had come: oddities like snails in the wet straw of the stock pens, and the moldy ring halfway up the wall of Pete's garage. The pipes clogged with sewage and backed up all that summer, letting off a sharp ammonia that gave Sita terrible headaches. She spent days lying perfectly still in our darkened bedroom, with her head packed in ice.

For a while I was still the girl who had caused the miracle, an attraction to customers and neighbors who stopped to touch me, holding their fingers out as if my body was filled with divine electricity. I wished it was. I wished something else unusual would happen. But nothing special came of their touching, no luck at cards or last-ditch cures, no sudden grace. There were no spectacular side effects to anything I did. And so the touching stopped. I became an ordinary girl again, and maybe something worse than that, in the town's eye, as years went by.

I was never much for looks, and I saw that right off. My face was broad and pale, not homely, but simply unremarkable, except for the color of my eyes. That was the feature I liked best about myself. My eyes turned a light brown almost yellow, and I had no eyebrows to detract from the effect. They never grew back after the accident with the slide. My hair stayed thin, black as tar. Although I washed it, like Sita, in beer and eggs, it could only be worn lank or tied in two pencil braids. For years I used Sita's hand-me-downs, let out at the seams and shortened. Then I dressed to suit myself. But by that time I couldn't have cared less. So what if I smelled like white pepper from the sausage table? So what if I was plain? At least I had the shop, Pete and Fritzie, and Celestine, although sometimes even she wearied of my blunt ways.

I said things too suddenly. I was pigheaded, bitter, moody, and had fits of unreasonable anger. Things I said came out wrong, even if I thought first. All through school it bothered me when other children turned away, or just looked shocked when I spoke. I don't apologize, and there's really no excuse, but what happened in the Minneapolis grandstand, the boxcar, and on the playground in Argus had affected me, set me above the rest in my differentness. I had perspective. Sometimes before sleep I looked down from my bed and saw Argus as in the postcard view I sent to my mother. It was small, a simple crosshatch of lines on the earth, nothing that an ice age or perhaps even another harsh flood could not erase.

As the town around me ceased to matter, though, Celestine mattered more. And Pete and Fritzie too, even Sita, although I was less important to her. We never actually liked one another, only grew in tolerance and became accustomed to each other's presence in the way only people who sleep in the same room can. Night after night we blended and fought in dreams. Vibrations left our minds and hung trembling about us. By morning, our ghostly selves had made peace.

So maybe I was closer to Sita than I ever was to Celestine, even though by daylight I couldn't stand Sita's careful slenderness and practiced voice, her way of turning with an eyebrow raised and trying to shut me up, her thin mouth that she painted and blotted a dozen times while waiting for customers. I couldn't stand her. I felt relieved when Celestine came by the shop. She had quit school before she was half finished and taken a job with the telephone company. This job made her seem older, but there was still an ease between us.

Celestine looked good in those days, big and lean. She wore tailored suits instead of dresses and carried a leather shoulderbag. Striding into the kitchen, she was handsome like a man. Her voice was low and penetrating and she smoked Viceroys like Fritzie. We sat and complained about her boss and read V-mail. Leaving, she would light a last cigarette and smoke it halfway down before she got into Russell's car. The cigarette dangled from her lips as she pulled out.

I kept hoping I would get some of Celestine's height. But I stopped growing at eighteen, still short. For a while I was depressed to realize that as long as I ran the shop I would have to look through, not over, the lighted case at customers.

The shop was my perfect home. The house was built on one level. The floors were cast of concrete with hot-water pipes running through them for warmth. The thick walls were finished off with stucco, painted a smooth glossy white. Because so many of the doorways were rounded, the place seemed like a cave carved out of a hillside. The light fell green and watery through thick glass window-blocks except in the kitchen where the screen door let through a blast of sun. Customers came back there to talk. Across Fritzie's garden and the wide yard, they could watch cows and sheep moving in the darkness of the stockpens, half visible between the heavy rail ties.

Pete brought links of his sausages in for them to taste, and they ate them with soda crackers or soft white bread, comparing the summer sausage and the beerwurst and the Swedish. They

67

were heavy people, Germans and Poles or Scandinavians, rough handed and full of opinions, delicate biters, because their teeth hurt or plates did not fit well. Grizzled hairs sprouted from surprising places upon them. Their hands were misshapen and calloused. Their light eyes did not shift nor their conversation falter when they happened to look up, on a slaughtering day perhaps, to see a pig penned in the killing chute, having its throat cut.

Sometimes I waited on customers. But more often, Fritzie and I cut meat or ground it or spiced it in the big room. Sita refused to do much more than help out when back orders pressed. On the day everything changed, when I was still eighteen, I was at the steel-plate table cubing stew meat and Fritzie was standing at the big electric saw. I might have heard some sound she made under the saw's shrill whine, or perhaps I just felt it. Anyway I turned as she was falling to her knees. Beet red and choking, she pounded the floor for air while I pounded her, but not enough air came and she slumped, unconscious, dragging only an occasional shuddering breath to let us know she was still alive.

What struck me then, suddenly, as Pete carried her out the door to the ambulance that saved her life, was the frailty of her body once she wasn't there to move it. She was a stick figure, cartoon thin and broken in Pete's arms. Later that night, at the hospital, when she was sealed in a tent of oxygen, and alert, I sat beside her and watched her fingers trace the hem on the sheet. In that gesture I saw everything. Her wonder, her awareness of the texture of the thin material, her surprise that she wasn't dead after all.

When Fritzie came home she stopped smoking for good. She sat at the kitchen table, in the light from the screen door, chewing gum, sucking sourballs, nibbling buttered toast. After a few tobaccoless, idle months, her face bloomed from acid yellow, to peach, to rose. She gained weight and let her hair grow from the peroxide bleach to brown. She had been hard, one track, always someone to reckon with, but now she softened. Overnight she became a stout woman of no particular menace. She began to feel that she'd neglected her girls, and took up crocheting some afghans she had started when she was young. The old blocks were faded, the tint in the yarn was dull, but she surrounded them with blazing colors and then branched off in ever more complicated efforts. Piles of patterned wools collected at her feet.

"You keep these in your hope chest," she told me one afternoon.

"I don't have one," I said.

So Sita got the afghans, but I didn't care. I was going to need a lot more than afghans. Even then I knew that the shape of my life was to be no tunnel of love in darkness, no open field.

I did not choose solitude. Who would? It came on me like a kind of vocation, demanding an effort that married women can't picture. Sometimes, even now, I look on the married girls the way a wild dog might look through the window at tame ones, envying the regularity of their lives but also despising the low pleasure they get from the master's touch. I was only tempted once, but that was to romance. Marriage would not have been a comfort with Russell Kashpaw, or likely even possible. He was not the type to marry, even in the years he was able.

It began the second time he came home from a war, from Korea, on the night Celestine got the news that her brother was wounded in action. She came by the house late, tapping at my window until I woke up. Although Sita didn't make a sound, I sensed her building up an insomniac fury in the dark. So I signaled Celestine to the kitchen door. I let her in, and when she showed me the news about Russell I went straight to the cupboard. I chose the thickest of Pete's little shot glasses and poured us a whiskey. We drank the first one quick, the next slow, and then we went outside to smoke underneath the cold white stars. The shock wore off after some time, and she came back down to earth.

He would recuperate. We got the news of it soon after. I sent a get-well card to his hospital address in Virginia. *We'll see you soon in Argus,* my note said. Nothing personal. Still I expected an answer, even a message through Celestine. But the thing about Russell was he had no manners or consideration. Having gone through high school as a football star, then having hit the big time with the war, he was even more socially backward than I was. Before I knew this, though, I thought he would come by the shop when he first got home. But nothing, not a word, not a hello or kiss my foot, only rumor that he'd taken a good bank-clerk job Argus National had offered him as a returning home-town hero, even though he was an Indian.

The first time I saw Russell after he returned was on the muggy summer day I went over to deposit the week's total. I knew I might run into him but hadn't yet pictured him as changed. I still imagined the same bull-chested boy with the soft voice, teasing eyes, the shaggy hair.

The air was humid, the sky hung low, but the lobby of the bank was cool. A procession of veined green marble, brass, and velvet ropes led to his cage. I paused before I walked it, and let the fans beat down.

He recognized me when I finally stood before him. "I got your card," he said.

"It's about time," I answered.

That was all. He took my canvas money bag, and then I looked straight at him and stood rooted in surprise. The scars stretched up his cheeks like claw marks, angry and long, even running past his temples and parting his hair crooked. I could see that they went downward, too, mapping him below. He counted my money. The sight of him embarrassed me, not because he was ugly, but just the opposite. Scarred, his face took on an unsettling dark grandeur. He was richly carved and compelling in those terrible wounds. I looked down. But even there I was not safe. Russell's hands were thin and muscular, softening from mechanic's into banker's, and on one finger he wore a pink rubber cap.

He used that capped finger to press the bills up so that he could count them swiftly. I couldn't tear my gaze away.

"Here's your receipt," he said, breaking the spell.

I left in a daze at myself. I didn't even say good-bye.

All right, I thought, I am in love with the half brother of my best friend, Celestine. Or at least I am in love with his scars and the rubber cap on his finger.

So I decided to get to know Russell.

One day I told Celestine to bring him by for dinner.

"How come?" she asked.

"He's your brother," I said.

"Well, he won't," she told me.

"He can suit himself." I wouldn't show it meant something. But Celestine caught on.

"I'll try and convince him," she promised.

When Russell came to dinner, he was hardly even civil. He spent the whole time staring out the door, straight past me, at the stockpens and the heavy barred gates. The pens were empty, but he watched them anyway. Several times I turned in spite of myself and glanced across the yard. He seemed to make Pete uncomfortable, too. A heavy silence fell at the table and Pete finally left. He went back to the utility room, where we soon heard him tinkering with and cursing his broken motors.

The rest of us, Celestine, Sita, Fritzie, Russell, and myself went out back to sit in the wood-slat and cedar chairs Pete had built so that Fritzie could lounge in the open with visitors. I made a pitcher of cold whiskey sour. The four of us women talked easily, our glasses cooling our fingers, but our talk was like waves that washed in to break on Russell's silence. He sat there, like a stiff, as the last of the sun burned the weeds beyond the smokehouse.

71

"You're a real ball of fire," I said to him, annoyed.

He looked at me for the first time that night. I'd drawn my eyebrows on for the evening in brown pencil. I'd carefully pinned my braids up and worn a black chiffon scarf to set off my one remarkable feature, yellow cat eyes, which did their best to coax him. But I don't know coaxing from a box lunch.

Russell turned, unaffected by any of my charms, and looked at Sita in a way that I was meant to see. I understood that if he was going to think that way of anyone, it was her. She had been talking more than usual and had a rare color in her cheeks. Her hair washed down her neck in a clean shining sweep. But when she saw that Russell Kashpaw was looking at her, she tipped her head away and her red lips tightened. She pulled a white hankie from her sleeve, turned a cold cheek, and let him know that Sita Kozka was off limits to his type.

I suppose most girls who had set their cap for a man would have despised him for looking at another, but I was different. It was Sita whom I wanted to kill.

"I'm going to tell your fortune," I said, leaning toward her, brushing her pale arm. "I'll get the deck."

Fortune-telling was a pastime that Sita hated herself for loving. It never failed. She always always tried to look disgusted, as if telling the future was the most low-class idea in the world, but then she bent, spellbound, to the cards as they were laid out. She bit her lips but could not refuse a small glimpse into the beyond. So I walked inside and got a deck from the kitchen drawer. Then I laid the cards out one by one on the broad arm of her chair.

"There's the jack of hearts," I said, "and here's a deuce. What's this?" I paused. She had drawn the queen of spades.

"What's it mean?" Sita flushed in helpless shame at her curiosity. I sat straight up in my chair and took a long drink of whiskey sour.

"Well?" asked Sita.

"Well," I said flatly.

"*Come on,*" she said.

I hesitated, took another drink, shook my head until she fidgeted.

"I hope you like Buicks," was my only comment.

"For Godsakes!" Now Sita was ready to explode. Celestine hated arguments, so she got up and walked into the shop to get more ice. Russell craned to see the cards. Sita stood and ordered me to tell her. "What's the matter, run out of miracles?"

"Sit back down," I said. "You should be sitting when you hear this." She sat. I told her. "I hope you like Buicks, because I see that you'll be riding in a Buick on the day you croak."

Her mouth opened. She made a hoarse little furious sound and struck all the cards off the end of her chair. "Dry up like a prune," she shouted.

"You girls give each other such a hard time," observed Fritzie. Her face was mildly bored. She was used to us pecking at one another, but Russell wasn't.

"So," he said. "Sita will be riding in a Buick. What about me?"

He picked the cards up off the grass and put them in my hands. He couldn't help but smile when, all business now, I slapped the cards down on the arm of his chair. When they were all laid out he studied them in silence, along with me. Celestine came through the door with a big red plastic bowl of ice in her hands.

"What did I miss?" she asked.

"Tales of doom," Fritzie said.

"You're always telling someone they're going to die or get mangled or divorced." Celestine settled next to Fritzie, lit a Viceroy, and breathed thick blue smoke. "Why don't you ever predict something good? For instance, here's Russell, home safe. Why don't you predict something good like that?"

73

"What's there?" Russell said.

"A woman," I answered, looking straight into his eyes.

"Only one?" Celestine said, then caught herself, remembering how I'd wanted Russell to come out to dinner, I suppose. She moved abruptly, dropping ice in everybody's glass to shut herself up.

"Whoever she is," said Russell, "I know one thing."

"What's that?" I said.

"I'm not going to marry her," he answered.

The bottom fell out for a moment, but then I recovered. I got my wits back.

"That's right," I said, "you're not. But you're going to owe her a lot of money."

"I am?" He looked distressed.

"See what I mean?" Celestine settled back. "Why can't you ever predict something good?"

"This is good," I insisted, raking the cards up. "He'll pay through the shorts."

Russell started to laugh. He was getting loose on the whiskey sours. All of us, even Sita, were beginning to feel disconnected and bumbling. We laughed easily now over nothing and hardly even noticed the mosquitoes that swarmed us as the sun went down.

"Light the citronella candle," Fritzie said at one point. But no one paid any attention until she said it louder. That was why there must have been some light, enough to see by. Maybe it was me who lit the yellow candles in their buckets; I don't remember. But I haven't forgotten what came after, when Russell pulled his shirt up high, on a dare from Sita, and showed us his hidden scars.

I got up and went over to see them closer. I bent until I felt his warmth. The wounds had been so deep that he was ridged like a gullied field. His chest had been plowed like a tractor gone

74

haywire. I reached out. He said nothing, and so I touched him. And then everyone was silent with drunk surprise.

"God she's fresh!" said Sita, upsetting the quiet in a shrill and disapproving voice.

Russell shifted beneath my hands, and when I still didn't move them he took them off gently and folded them together.

"Bless you, my child," he said, so that we all laughed. I shook my head to clear it, but the shaking only set my teeth on edge. I went to bed soon afterward, and fell into a deadening sleep.

I was exhausted when I woke, thick and swollen with unknown dreams, but I was cured, as though a fever had burned off. One thought was clear. I would never go out of my way for romance again. Romance would have to go out of its way for me.

Pete and Fritzie sent away for brochures from the chamber-of-commerce departments of cities like Phoenix and El Paso. The doctor said that Fritzie's lungs needed dry warmth, a desert climate, and she shouldn't undergo even one more Dakota winter. So all of a sudden Pete was making plans to send her south, but then, once she put her foot down and refused to go alone, he included himself. This all happened without the benefit of any discussion over what would become of the shop, or of Sita, or me.

So I sat down with Fritzie one day. She was making something out of plum-colored bits of yarn. Because of her, I had taken up crocheting now and then myself. But I didn't find it relaxing. I pulled the yarn so hard it broke, and the things I made ended up as tight useless lumps.

"I've got to ask you something," I said, "about the shop. Are you selling it when you go down south?"

She was surprised, enough to pull a stitch. "We thought you'd run it," she told me.

"I will then," I answered. And that was settled, although the complicated part of it was not. "But Sita," I wondered. "What will she do?"

Fritzie frowned into the purple network she was slowly enlarging. "Sita could run the grocery section," she said. "She could help if she wanted to." Both of us knew Sita wasn't interested in the shop. I knew more. She hated it, in fact, and wanted only to move down to Fargo and live by herself in a modern apartment, and model clothes for DeLendrecies. She imagined that she would also work behind the men's hat counter. There she would meet a young rising professional. They would marry. He would buy her a house near the county courthouse, on the street of railroad mansions not far from Island Park. Every winter she would walk down the hill to skate. She would wear powder blue tights and a short dress with puffs of rabbit fur at the sleeves, collar, and all around a flared hem that would lift as she twirled. I knew all of this because, on an evening of friendliness, Sita had told me it was her dream.

"Sita wants to go to Fargo," I told Fritzie, "and work in a department store."

Fritzie nodded and said, "She might as well."

So that was how it happened that fall. Sita made plans to move to Fargo. Fritzie and Pete packed all of the suitcases and trunks that they owned for the trip. I did nothing special. In fact, the only way I can account for Sita's last night is that I did the most customary thing that day. I washed down steel tables in the preparations room with the same strong milky cleaning solvent that we always used. But maybe it was an odd batch that affected my hands.

Whatever it was, Sita was upset by the incident to the point that she never speaks of it. Perhaps she pretends it never happened. I don't know anything about Sita's mental habits anymore, not since she moved to Blue Mound and stopped communicating with us all. But that night we went to sleep in our twin beds as

76

usual. Sita liked the curtains shut tightly. I wanted them open for moonlight. But as always, since it was her room, she got her way. The old furnace at the end of the hall woke me in the middle of the night. It came to life with a wild and throbbing complaint that no one ever noticed in the day. It often woke Sita too. I kept my eyes shut because I knew what the noise was, and tried to let myself drift off again. That wasn't Sita's habit. She awakened and lay with teeth clenched, arms rigid, praying for sleep to take her but at the same time too maddened to let it happen. I usually slept all the better, sensing her alert watch in the dark. But that night I did not drift off again, because she spoke.

"My dear God, my dear God," she said in a pinched little voice. "Mary, I know you're awake."

I heard the tense undertone, but I sighed as if falling to a deeper level in my dreams. She'd probably heard a mouse behind the walls, or thought of some drastic mix-up she'd made in managing her boyfriends during this important move. Or maybe it was her hair. She'd suddenly realized the tight new wave she'd got to impress the manager of DeLendrecies, the curly bangs, the slight yet bold tint job, was wrong for her shape of face.

But it was none of these.

"Mary," she shrilled, "WAKE UP."

So I opened my eyes. The room was half lit. I thought at first that she had left the curtains open, but the light in the room was coming from me, or from my hands, to be entirely exact. They glowed with a dead blue radiance.

I lifted them in wonder. The light began to weaken and fade. I shook them, and for a moment they pulsed brightly, as if there had been a loose connection. Then they dimmed no matter what I did until the room was pitch dark again. Only when their light was put out did Sita dare jump from bed, hop to the end of the room, and throw the switch. Her teeth clicked together in fear.

"I'm so goddamn glad I'm getting out of here," she whispered.

She stepped back into the room just long enough to pull the blankets off her bed, and she slept the rest of the night on the living room couch. As for me, for once I caught Sita's insomnia and lay awake.

After a long while, the thickly curtained windows went light gray and I heard Pete get up to switch off the yard light and let the dogs out. Soon, when they'd left for Arizona, I'd be up at Pete's hours, doing just as he did, making the rounds to assure myself that the temperatures were proper in the freezers and the smoke rooms, that the safe was still locked, that the back door was open for Canute, who started work at seven, and that coffee was boiling for the men who came in later.

I imagined myself doing all that Pete did, alone in the early stillness, and again at night when the stillness was blue-black. I'd go around to rattle each door lock, pull down the front blinds, check the thermostat and gauges. When it came to running the shop in the daylight, I'd do a few things differently too, like change the front sign, put an add in the *Sentinel* now and then, plus more pepper in the blood sausage. I'd change this very room, sleep with the curtains open if I wanted, or throw the damn curtains out. To hell with the full-length mirror and the wishing-well lamp. Sita could take them, the way she'd already taken Adelaide's blue velvet box. I'd seen her hide it in her suitcase.

After she left I missed Sita more than I thought I would. For weeks I slept fitfully and woke, disturbed by the absence of her level breathing, often overwhelmed by my own dreams. They became too real now that there was no one to distract my sleeping mind. I passed some nights caught in blizzards, or startling orchards, or cramped in the cages of small animals.

One dream in particular I had for months running. I walked into a rickety wooden house, no place I had ever lived in, but

78

one I knew. Inside, there were many small empty rooms, some hidden deep in the interior. I wandered through the whole place, never lost but never quite certain of where I was until I came to the room I recognized, the room where I would wait for him. It was always the same. I entered this last room carefully. The floor creaked as I stepped over the threshold and edged along the whitewashed and peeling wall. This room was stark and windowless, but full of flimsy doors that opened out in each direction.

Always, when he entered, I was certain that the floor would break beneath him. It gave as he walked toward me, but even when he reached for me, stepping down heavily, nothing snapped. His lips were deep and curved. His eyes were the same burnt-butter brown as his hair, and his horns branched like a young buck's.

I grew impatient for him, for the way he bent toward me, breathing eagerly, for his long smooth thighs and for the sound of the doors that never fitted their frames, tapping back and forth as we moved.

The Orphans' Picnic

Karl walked quickly through the wrought-iron gate onto the fair-grounds, and then stopped at the edge of the crowd. He was waiting to be seen. They were all here. Fathers Mullen and Bonaventure. Sisters Ivalo, Mary Thomas, Ursula, and George. As always, each presided over a game, cakewalk, a table for knitting or white elephants. Each was busy taking tickets or making change from a cigar box. When they failed to recognize him immediately, Karl bought a lemonade and sat down in their plain view.

He lounged for a good half an hour, shifting his feet in the dry spring grass, smoking one heavy cigarette after another and crushing them out on the metal frame of his chair. His black hair gleamed like shoe leather, and his teeth were very white. He made a lot of easy sales to women and had come up in the world. The new clothes, he thought, and the thick wad of dollar bills would throw the priests off. The truth was he'd turned out worse than their wildest dreams.

"Step up! Step up! You there in the gangster suit!"

Someone laughed. Karl turned. It was a chubby redheaded seminarian running the nearest booth, a fishing booth. With one quick glance Karl dismissed him as unattractive. He knew the type: cheerfully pious and self-important, a raffler of door prizes, a shiner of the priests' shoes.

"Help out the orphans," the boy grinned. His creamy white neck bulged in the tight collar of his cassock. He was about sixteen. His eyes were long lashed, like Karl's, but they were a deep, sweet hazel color. His hair, dark red and springy, curled back from his forehead in a way that struck Karl, suddenly, as familiar. It was just like Adelaide's. Karl frowned at the coincidence. There was more too, once he looked. The marble skin. The pointed cheekbones. The arch of the boy's black eyebrows was picture perfect. He was a ringer except for the baby fat. He was almost too much like her.

Karl's face went numb. The memories of this place jolted him. He sat not twenty feet from the spot where Adelaide had flown away, and again he saw the luminous sky into which Omar's plane vanished. He heard his tiny brother's loud relentless cries.

The young man who stole the baby must have lived in the neighborhood. He must have come to the Picnic because he was a Catholic. He would have raised his son a Catholic too, and the boy would probably have been a day student at Saint Jerome's.

Karl took a dollar from his roll and stood up.

The boy's smile sharpened when Karl approached with money in his hand.

"Fish today, sir? Three chances for a quarter."

Karl put the bill down.

"What's your name?" he said.

"Jude Miller," said the boy. "How many chances?"

"How many have you got?"

Jude attached a basket to a hook and dropped it over a wall painted with blue waves.

"Fishy fishy in the brook," he began in a practiced drone, "come and nibble on my hook."

"Cut that," said Karl.

Jude was flustered. "I have to tell Sister what prize to give you, sir, boy's or girl's. It's in the rhyme." He jumped to tug the basket back over the wall. It already held the prize, a small picture of a juicy-looking sacred heart.

"Throw it back, it's too small," said Karl.

The boy gripped the basket stupidly. "But it's a holy card."

"It's a piece of crap," Karl said. "I expect something better for my money."

81

At the mention of money, Jude closed the lid of his cigar box. "Aren't you a Catholic?" he asked.

Karl looked down. A creamy white owl guarded the bills and small change. Jude's long-fingered, quick, fat hands rested protectively on either side. Karl decided that he disliked his brother as intensely now as he had long ago.

"You're a piece of crap too," said Karl.

Jude Miller looked wildly around for help. He was penned in the booth. "Step right up!" he called to a woman and child who passed near. He craned around Karl to attract them, but they continued toward the midway with only a smiling glance. The priests and nuns paid him no attention either. He turned and knocked on the waves.

"Sister? Could you come out here?"

"No doubt about it," said Karl.

"About what?"

"You," said Karl.

"What is it, Jude?" said a woman's voice through the wall.

Karl leaned right into the boy's face and said, "Do you know who you are?"

Jude's face was red and straining. He bit his lip, almost in tears. His hands had locked in panic around the cigar box full of money.

"I'm crap," he whispered.

"Jude?" said the voice again.

Karl laughed. "Just like your mother. Now who am I?" He let the light flood his face, and looked expectantly at Jude. The boy didn't hesitate.

"You're the devil," he said.

Karl touched his moustache, and laughed again.

"That's what Father Mullen said. Tell him Karl Adare came back to say hello."

SITA KOZKA

EVEN THOUGH IT was winter and snow blew through the fine black screens of my apartment porch, I liked to sit there and look out on the street. Broadway in Fargo, just above the downtown area, was always full of nurses walking to the hospital, nuns gliding back from the cathedral, and long-term patients tottering between their relatives.

I was doing well enough in spite of a married doctor who strung me on for three years before I knew he would never leave his wife, the old story. I got away from him, then came Jimmy, who stepped in to help me recover from the experience. I was grateful to Jimmy at the time, but then I could not get rid of him. It seemed like he was outside my door, waiting in his plush car, every other night. He drove down from Argus whenever I modeled in a DeLendrecies style show. He clipped out and saved the fuzzy newsprints of me posing in a ballgown, a coat with platter-sized buttons, even matching swimwear. Jimmy was persistent, and always showed me a good time, but he belonged in Argus where he owned a steakhouse. The right man hadn't come along.

I kept my looks up with more care than ever. I was ten years older than some of the girls I modeled with and I was no longer the one most sought after. I had to wonder how much time I had left. The years were showing, the wear and tear. I kept slim, kept my waist the 22 ½ of Vivien Leigh's, kept attending refresher courses at The Dorothy Ludlow Evening School of Charm. The most important thing Dorothy taught me was to sit up straight and never, under any circumstance, to frown. One trick I learned was that dining in the evening alone, or playing cards with girl friends, I should wear a Band-Aid tightly taped across my forehead to keep it smooth. Frown lines aged a woman more quickly than her hands. I bought a little metal grinder to pulverize apricot kernals, which I mixed with cold cream and rubbed on my skin. After bathing I freshened my face with a bit of cotton dipped in white vinegar. I wore kidskin glove liners when I walked outdoors in winter.

Determination, that's what it was. I made good money and bought a television. But I was thirty years old. Something more should have happened. People told me I should have gone to Hollywood, and now I had to agree. Hollywood had been a missed chance I should have taken when I could. The only thing that would save me, now, was to find the ideal husband. So I was looking. I kept an eye out, but Mr. Right refused to show his face and the months ticked by. Maybe if I'd found him, or gone to Hollywood, or even gotten a big promotion at DeLendrecies, the letter would not have mattered when it came and I would have sent it back to Mary instead of using it as an excuse to put off Jimmy.

I was sitting on the little porch I mentioned. It was a sunny winter Saturday and I was waiting for Jimmy to come and pick me up in his coupe. We were going ice skating and I worried that he would make some romantic gesture. Perhaps that evening as we sat around the oil-drum fire, drinking cocoa, he'd pop the question or draw the jewelry store box from his thick plaid jacket. I imagined ways I could discourage him, not completely, but just enough to give me time. As it happened, though, the postman arrived before Jimmy.

I went downstairs when I heard the letter slide into the box. I didn't get much mail. This letter had been forwarded, readdressed in black grease marker and in Mary's peaked script. I always told Mary that her handwriting looked like the writing of a witch. Mine is close to perfect, at least so the nuns said. The letter itself was written in an unfamiliar hand and addressed to the Kozka family. Since Mama and Papa had still not settled in a permanent residence, Mary had sent the letter on to me.

Dear Mrs. Kozka,

I saved the newspaper ads ever since he was a baby. And now I had to come clean about him in confessional, as I asked Father Flo about it. Father Flo says to write you, telling you the circumstance. Well it happened I lost my own and couldn't have any after that. So I kept Jude when my husband brought him over from the fairgrounds. I always might have given him back except I heard about the mother flying off. So I raised him. My husband's heart gave out six years ago. But now that baby's going to have his ordination in one week. He's going to be a deacon, on his way to a priest. February 18, at the Cathedral in Saint Paul is where he'll be ordained. Jude doesn't know he's adopted. Now is the time to tell the whole thing if you want. Father Flo says this letter is the right thing to do, so I wrote. You may reply to me.

His mother,
Mrs. Catherine Miller

I read the letter over like it was gibberish, and then I read it again. I was about to read it a third time when Jimmy pulled up outside and sat on his horn. Try as I might I couldn't get him to ring the bell, or to develop any manners whatsoever when it came to dating. He always said there were no parking spaces big enough to fit his car on my side street, but the avenue was wide and, in places, completely curbless. There was always room. Jimmy was just too lazy to get out, lock his car, walk the half block, and ring my doorbell. He could dance, play cards all night, ice skate in toe loops and waltz steps and figure eights. But he couldn't get out of his car and ring my bell. It was irritating. And so, even more on that day than most, we started off on the wrong foot.

I put down the letter and ran outside to stop his racket. I'd tied my skates over my shoulder and they knocked. The blades could have hurt me if I'd fallen. Jimmy reached across the car seat and flipped the handle. That was another thing. He had no courtesy for opening a girl's door. In restaurants he barged through and let me fend for myself behind him. But I suppose he was better than my married doctor, even so.

"How many times have I told you to park, then ring?" I said this first, then slid into the passenger's side of the car.

"Sita Cakes!" He shouted, then revved the engine above my voice.

"Don't say anything about the parking spaces, Jimmy!" I screamed. "And don't call me Cakes."

Another thing. He called me by his favorite desserts. Sweetpie. Muffin. Sugardonut. No wonder he was getting fat. Being called these names made me feel puffed up too, unpleasantly sweet, and too soft, like risen dough.

"Come on over here," he said, patting the upholstery beside him.

And at once, although I had been so annoyed I wanted to slap his cheek, I slid over and wedged myself against Jimmy's side. This was how he always won me—at the last minute and against my better judgment. Once there, however, I relaxed and got comfortable. I could just be myself with Jimmy, that was for sure. Since he didn't appreciate anything I really stood for, or even acknowledge the improvements as to culture and charm I had made in myself, I went back to being Sita Kozka, daughter of Pete, the butcher. Or just about. I never let Jimmy forget that I was a model and had paid my own way in life.

We drove over to the Moorhead side, to try out their rink. Someone had put up a little warming shack there, and inside, after the brilliance of the snow, the air seemed steamy as a lagoon. The benches were scored and gouged by children's blade tips, carved with initials and arrow-pierced hearts. We laced up and stowed our boots in a corner, then clattered down the splintery ramp onto the ice. The rink was frozen a clear deep gray. I could see the cracks running down several feet and the brown oak leaves floating, suspended where they'd fallen. We crossed our arms and held hands, started gliding back and forth. We went around and around the rough oval rink.

"Sita," said Jimmy after some time. He hesitated. Then at last he blurted out, "Let's get married."

I panicked. I didn't want to have to say yes or no. Maybe it was instinct, a flair for self-preservation, that caused me to suddenly realize the sense of the letter that came in the mail that morning. It was strange how the meaning of it popped into my mind just then. But it did, hitting me so unexpectedly that I gasped.

Jimmy stopped and looked at me in amazement.

"That's yes?" he asked.

"I don't know. Wait," I said, "I've figured something out."

Jimmy balanced, holding tight to my shoulders, very still.

"You know that baby brother Mary had? The one they lost? No . . . you don't know." I shrugged off his hands and skated forward. "Don't say anything. I have to think." The snow along the edge of the pond was piled in crisp boulders. It had fallen deep and packed hard. The shadows were a flimsy blue.

"It's that baby," I said out loud. I knew all about it, not from Mary, who never spoke about her life before she came to Argus, but from overhearing Mama's conversations in the kitchen. Her friends came by to sit with her and drink watery coffee. They smoked each other's cigarettes and chewed on tough molasses

87

cake. As they talked I used to stand just outside and listen in. They went on and on about Aunt Adelaide, how the children's father had not married her, and why she had left her children. They speculated on what might have happened to the baby. When the young man took him out of Mary's arms, and walked away, had it been a curse or a blessing? Had he really had a wife?

And now, at last, there were answers to these incompletes. I had the letter that could solve the mystery.

"So, enough thinking?" said Jimmy, behind me. He touched my arm.

"I know what I'll do," I said, turning to face him.

"What?"

"I'll go to Minneapolis. He's getting ordained this week."

Jimmy's face was a study.

"Look," I said, "something real important has come up. I'll have to think about . . ." I waved my hand in the direction of the place we had been skating when he proposed. ". . . all of that. But right now I've got to pack."

Jimmy didn't sulk. He was too upset and too confused. Perhaps I worried him with my sudden conviction and the firm plans about my travel. Perhaps it seemed unusual. At any rate, he dropped me off with only a peck on the cheek. I was impatient to read the letter once more and to make the arrangements necessary in my work schedule. I'd take the train, a small overnight bag, stay at a hotel. I wouldn't call this Catherine Miller long distance or let her know that I'd appear. I'd simply slip into the crowd at the baby's ordination, incognito, and after I had seen Mary's lost brother I'd decide what to do, select the right moment to reveal who I was. I'd make a drama of it.

I packed. I made my arrangements and booked the ticket. The night before I was to leave I lay awake in excitement. What was happening was so interesting, like a plot in the mystery books I read to soothe myself. Of everything that happened, of all the circumstances that had caused my cousin Mary to arrive by freight one early spring, the letter was now the only other clue besides Adelaide's blue velvet box. I'd packed that, for no reason except that it seemed appropriate. I put a photograph of Adelaide inside the box among the old pawn tickets and popped-off buttons. If the boy wanted to know what his mother looked like, I'd have her picture. I shivered, knowing the letter had been in Mary's own hands, the hands that glowed blue in the dark and yet picked up no unusual vibrations as to the envelope's contents.

Minneapolis was a nice town then, built up by Minnesota grain and railroad fortunes. Spanking new sidewalks ran along the wide streets and trees were everywhere, not like in Fargo, which would always have a bare old cowtown look about it even when the big money came in from sugar, beans, and wheat. This was a real metropolis, with a landmark skyscraper called Foshay Tower amid miles of fine residential areas. My hotel room had good thick furniture in it, drapes with big ferns on them, and a smart dresser with a long rectangular mirror.

I hadn't slept the night before, so that night I was out. I woke up at the late-winter dawn, just as the first light filtered through the pattern on the curtains. I knew exactly where I was, knew just what I would do. I'd have black coffee in the hotel café. I would take an elevator to the top of Foshay Tower, then I would visit a department store. After that I'd just have time to get a taxi to the cathedral.

The black coffee came in an elegant cup with a paper doily underneath it, but I never got past the doors of the Foshay elevators. The operator said, "Coming up, ma'am?" But I just shook my head, suddenly dizzy. The latticed metal gates unfolded shut in front of me. The doors were inscribed with shining plaques of the tower. To focus my vision I stared at the replica, rising mighty from crests of gilded brass, radiating beams of light from its heavy peak. The department store visit was even worse. I should have known how it would affect me just from looking in the windows at the pinch-waisted mannequins. Their eyes were deep and black, painted on with a fringed brush. Their mouths shone wetly as if they'd just drunk something from a glass. They wore hats with little poked stitchwork designs and carried purses in shapes I'd never seen. Worse then that, they wore dresses with off-center buttons and a hemline that was lower, strictly lower, than the style our store had ordered.

"How could this have happened?" I said out loud. "Who decreed?"

I marched in the store to check the racks and it was true. Even the shopgirls were wearing this new look. My legs felt long, revealed, clumsy, and outdated. I took off my gloves and touched the dresses. I wanted the black one with inset stripes.

"May I help you?"

It was as if one of the mannequins had come to life, she was so perfect. Her hair was set in the kind of finger wave it was impossible to get in Fargo. And her ensemble! I could have thrown myself down on the carpet.

"I'm just looking."

Her eyes were flat, gorgeously indifferent. She didn't work on commission, I was sure of it. Either that or she was independently rich and only sold clothing for amusement. I held the dress up without a word. She took it and whirled off, expecting me to follow. I did. I tried on the dress. When I stepped out and looked into the three-way mirror, I was thrilled. But then she appeared behind me and I was just an imitation of her.

"Are you visiting here in Minneapolis?"

"No," I said.

Before she could say anything else, I twirled the skirt and said, "I'll take it."

She didn't smile. She didn't offer the slightest compliment. Then, back in the dressing room, I took the dress off and carefully hung it. The tag was beneath the sleeve and I didn't have enough money along with me to meet the price. I could have written a draft on my bank account, but the amount was simply too high. It was way out of line. I stood there in my slip, so unnerved I could hardly think straight. I read the numbers over and over, as if I could change them by force of will. But they stayed the same, written out in a thin black flourish. I dressed slowly and walked out, hoping that the shopgirl had gone off on coffee break. But she was waiting at the counter.

"Shall I wrap that for you, miss?" she asked in a bored, flat voice.

"I've changed my mind," I told her.

"Ah."

"I was looking for something more formal."

"Of course."

She turned to wait on another customer, and I escaped.

The cathedral was lovely in the snow, and already cars had pulled up to the curbs for blocks in advance. I walked up the stone steps with others, family and friends of those who were about to take the Holy Orders. The door closed behind us with a great crash that echoed, and the ceiling sprang upward, higher than high, enormous. Wheels of blue, green, golden light fell through the round stained-glass windows. The church was already filled downstairs, so I climbed the back steps to the organ loft. There were a few seats left, extra folding chairs beside the pews. I genuflected and sat in a wedge of gold light that seemed to warm me although the church itself was not well heated. Soon I heard the whine of bellows as an aged nun flipped switches and set the pipe organ breathing close by.

She began to play. Her small arched feet fled up and down

the low register. The music swelled. I took a missal and opened it, just as those young men to be ordained filed in, dressed in white robes, each carrying a long, lit candle and a stole. I tried to see them but they were too far away. I hadn't pictured this. I'd given no thought to how I'd recognize this Jude Miller. The young men made a half circle around the bishop's faldstool. Then the bishop himself entered and knelt down and prayed. The church was full of white chrysanthemums, white gladiolas, white carnations. The people smelled of mothballs and hair oil and perfume. Fat white satin bows were draped at the saints' feet, and the colored candles in the racks were lit in faltering rows.

The bishop went to his seat and put on his vestments with slow and studied gestures. I observed each young man in turn. The boy would be about eighteen, short perhaps, like Mary, perhaps red haired, perhaps a handsome version of Adelaide. But then again he might be like his father. I'd never seen a picture of the man or even heard him described, except as married.

And then, once the service began and the bishop spoke, I realized that my visit could be more than dramatic anyway. It could be dangerous. I realized that I could spoil Jude Miller's future.

Large and splendid in his robes and mitre, the bishop addressed the whole assembled crowd in Latin. We followed in our dark green missals.

Reverendissimus in Christo Pater, et Dominus, Dominus, Dei.

I read along with him on the opposite side of the page.

THE MOST REVEREND FATHER IN CHRIST, BY THE GRACE OF GOD AND THE FAVOR OF THE APOSTOLIC SEE, ORDERS AND COMMANDS, UNDER PENALTY OF EXCOMMUNICA- TION, ALL AND EACH HERE PRESENT FOR RECEIVING ORDERS, THAT NONE OF THOSE WHO MAY PERCHANCE BE IRREGULAR OR EXCOMMUNICATED BY THE CANONS OR BY HIS SUPERIOR, OR UNDER INTERDICT, OR SUS-

He went on listing those who shouldn't dare come forward to
receive the Orders. But I kept seeing *illegitimate*. The candidates
stretched out prone on the floor as the Litany of Saints began. I
followed the text out of habit and asked to be delivered from the
spirit of fornication, from lightning and tempest, from the scourge
of earthquakes, plague, famine, war, and everlasting death.

Now those who were to be deacons stood, stepped forward,
and made a kneeling semicircle close to the bishop. Although I
looked closely I still couldn't see them well enough to decide
which was Mary's brother. The bishop laid his hands on their
heads, one by one. But he didn't say their names. He let them
touch the Book of Gospels, then prayed, and it was over. They
filed back to their places. Having come all this way I wished I
could at least solve the mystery for myself, but they all looked
perfectly normal, not special in any detail, and not familiar. So
I edged through the crowd and walked out of the cathedral onto
the wide sunny steps.

The air was fresh, cold, and full of ordinary sounds. Behind
me, the music was muffled and grand. I took the blue box from
my purse and opened it. Perhaps I needed to refresh my memory.
Perhaps I'd see some feature that would point to one of the young
men. But Adelaide looked like no one else. She stared boldly
from her locket-sized photograph, hair coiled, eyebrows arched
like wings. I poked the buttons about. I unfolded the pawn ticket.

It was a crumpled yellow scrap with a simple address, numbers,
and a description carefully written out in tiny script.

Flawed yellow diamond ring in gold setting. Fair condition.
Victorian garnet filigree necklace with individual settings.

I imagined the old necklace, the ring, first on Adelaide and then on me. I hadn't much good jewelry to my name beyond a string of cultured pearls.

I walked to the curb and held my hand up when a cab appeared. I wasn't sure of my destination until I got in. As if I'd always meant to, I read the driver the address off the pawn ticket. Then I settled back into the cracked leather.

We drove for miles. The streets turned shabby, and gray snow was piled off to either side in icy walls. I began to wonder if I wasn't crazy to come all this way. But the shop was still there. It was a hole filled with junk up to the windows. I got out without paying the full fare and asked the driver to wait, then I walked into the shop. JOHN'S, the sign said.

I stood beyond the door, in the overflowing gloom, and waited for my eyes to adjust. The place was cold and full of sour smells, littered with camera parts and broken musical instruments. An enormous young man in several topcoats walked through a pair of curtains and put his hands on the counter.

"Buying or selling?"

"I'm here for this ring and necklace," I said, handing him the ticket.

He pursed his lips, "Nineteen thirty-two." He laughed, looking at the handwriting. "John Senior took this," he said. "John Senior's dead."

He held the ticket out but I didn't take it.

"Oh please," I said. "I'm sure you could find it if you looked. It would mean so much."

He rubbed his beard. He couldn't say no. "Wait a minute," he sighed. "I still got a boxful of stuff I never sorted through."

He tugged a flat metal case from underneath a pile of newspapers and put it down on the counter. Inside, it was divided into tiny compartments, each holding some scrap. Jewelry, war medals, broken watches, tie clasps.

He sorted the rings from the rest of the stuff. Not one of them was a diamond by any stretch. But then, pawing through the rest of the heap, he nudged aside a blackened tangle of delicate links and spread it on the counter with his fingers.

"This could be it, I guess," he said, scratching at a setting with a dirty fingernail.

"That?" I was disappointed.

"We had this fire and things got covered with oil and soot. It's red stones all right. Maybe you could tell if you shined it up."

It was almost too filthy to touch, so I opened the blue box and let him drop it in. I wrote a bank draft, thanking heaven I hadn't bought the new black dress. I put the box in the bottom of my purse and walked out.

Back in Fargo I brought the necklace to a jeweler. He cleaned it, repaired a few of the settings, and gave it back. When I saw it laid out on a sheet of white cotton, I couldn't believe my eyes. The stones glowed like rubies. It was fit for royalty. I put it on, turned back and forth in front of the bathroom mirror. The jewels distinguished me. A low-cut dress of cream lace would set them off perfectly. I wore the necklace all that night while I made my dinner and watched my television programs. But when I unclasped it to go to bed, and put it in my drawer, there was the letter from Mrs. Miller, still unanswered. I sat down at my table with a sheet of my best stationary, and wrote.

February 19, 1950

Dear Mrs. Miller,

In answer to your letter, which was forwarded to me from Argus, as far as I am concerned what you tell your boy is up to you. He would be my cousin, and there is a sister too. He also had one brother, but no one knows what became of him. I, on the other hand, have become a leading fashion model and clerk for

DeLendrecies here in Fargo. My parents own a successful meat marketing concern on the east side of Argus, North Dakota. There is nothing else to say, so I will sign myself.

Yours truly,
Sita Kozka

I addressed the envelope, sealed the letter inside, even used a stamp. Perhaps I should have marched out there and then, however, even though it was midnight, and mailed it away, because even by the next morning I was starting to hesitate. I had enough to think about already.

For days that letter sat on the dresser. And then one night, as Jimmy was on his way to my apartment for dinner, I was straightening the tops of things, fussing with shades and lamps. I came across the letter and slipped it beneath a crocheted piece of linen. I needed everything just so.

Sita's Wedding

Beneath the loud polka music of The Six Fat Dutchmen, the brother and cousins of Jimmy Bohl huddled close in the Legion Pavilion booth and discussed how they would kidnap the bride from the wedding dance and where they would deposit Sita for Jimmy to find. Because they were loaded on sloe gin and schnapps, they agreed on everything and nothing. All they could do was laugh, their faces dark red, exploding, eyes popping, when they thought of Jimmy yelling, "WHERE'S SITA?" They nearly choked imagining his rage when he jumped into his toilet-paper-and-shaving-cream-decorated Lincoln, revved the motor, raced into the cold March night to find her, and suddenly smelled the terrible odor released from within the heater.

"Limburger cheese," was all one cousin had to say to make the other double up and fall sideways against the wooden panels of the truck.

"There he is now," said Jimmy's brother, nodding at the dance floor.

Jimmy whirled by, a tall, pudgy man barely saved from complete blandness by his short wavy pompadour and precise goatee. He was light on his feet, a practiced ballroom dancer. Sita wore a glazed look of surrender as she was flung back and forth across the floor.

"What about the Kozkas? Think they'll be pissed?" asked Jimmy's brother. The cousins took stock of Pete and Fritzie, but the two looked so placid in their new suntans and added girth, sipping beer and nodding at the dancers, that the possibility of their anger seemed remote. The bride and groom were waltzing now. Red stones glittered at her throat. Rhinestones sparkled in the tiara that held up Sita's veil. Her dress was special, the skirt enormous and layered, the bodice stitched with pearly beads. It seemed to the huddled men that a soft light glowed around Sita's face, a mist of loveliness, but that was only the effect of her wispy veil, and their drunkenness, for in reality Sita's smile was bleak and her stare, over Jimmy's shoulder, was razor sharp with nervous exhaustion.

Watching her, one of the cousins snorted.

"She's a looker, though," he said. His voice was malicious. Jimmy's brother hunched and pursed his lips.

"She used to think she was too good," he said. "Kept Jimmy on a string until she figured nothing better would show up." He winked blearily, at no one. "Tonight, even steven."

When the number was over, Sita fled down a corridor to the ladies' room, her veil wrapped over one arm. Seeing this, the cousins rose together in a common, unconscious agreement. Jimmy's eager brother led them, as one by one they slipped drunkenly through the dancers toward that same corridor where Sita had disappeared and which led, beyond the ladies' room, out into the beaten-dirt parking lot.

And so it happened. No one witnessed Sita's abduction when she stepped from the ladies' room door. By the time Jimmy finished dancing with all of his waitresses and looked for her, his new bride was well on her way up north on Highway 30, wedged in the backseat of Jimmy's brother's car between two of Jimmy's cousins, whose sex jokes and sweated-through rental suit coats threw Sita into a state of such repulsion that she lost her voice.

They did not speak to her anyway. The road was straight, slick looking under the cold stars, and the pint they passed around evaporated quickly. The sweetness of their schnapps breath was more than Sita could bear and she tried, once, to say she was sick and that they had to let her out. But her words came out a hoarse croak and when she lunged over a cousin's hard paunch for the back door handle they all, suddenly, noticed her.

"Oopsy daisy!"

"Catch her!"

"Soon enough!" Their voices knocked her back against the seat cushions, and their clumsy hands pinioned her. She sank into herself, hating them so thoroughly it sent a raw current down the middle of her. She glared at each of them in turn, wishing that her eyes could melt the flesh from their bones.

"Where we taking her?" Jimmy's brother finally wondered. He was driving.

"I don't know!" said a cousin, at which the others let loose in hoots of laughter that left them weak. After that they quieted, momentarily pensive.

"Let's go ice fishing this winter," said one of them. For half an hour they discussed which lake to visit, whose house they'd haul there. Sita drowsed, certain they'd turn and bring her back. But just when it seemed that they'd satisfied their urge to drive in the dark and perhaps even forgotten about her crushed among them, they came onto reservation land, unfenced, fallow, deserted except for one small yard light.

Jimmy's brother drove into the circle of light and stopped in front of a sagging wooden structure, unnamed but recognizable to all of the men.

"Hoo boy!" whooped a cousin, acknowledging Jimmy's brother's genius.

"Let her out now," Jimmy's brother instructed the backseat cousins. "And give her your jacket; goddamn it's cold out there!"

The cousin jumped out, deposited Sita, and fell back into the car. Frightened suddenly, she huddled in the shell of the suit jacket. But the cousin's warmth left it before Jimmy's brother had honked, blinked, and driven off. The wind tore at her veil like teeth. The cold flowed up her skirt, down her arms.

Sita tried to scream.

"Jackass!" she whispered.

The taillights vanished. The wind was harsh, a storm almost, and Sita had to fight it as she stumbled between the cars in the lot and tapped on the plain wood door. No one answered. She stood a moment and then the wind opened her dress suddenly from behind, turned it inside out and over her head like an umbrella, and tumbled her in the door.

What she entered was a small Indian bar, patronized on that cold night by seven quietly drinking old men, two loud women, and Russell Kashpaw, who was with both of the women for the evening. What the ten people and the bartender experienced coming at them through the door was a sudden explosion of white net, a rolling ball of it tossed among them by freezing winds. Two bare spike-heeled legs scissored within the ball, slashing lethal arcs, tearing one old man's jacket before he reared away in fright. And the white ball *was* frightening, for while the wind tumbled it about and the patrons of the bar dodged to avoid danger, it kept up a muffled and inhuman croaking. But then, when the door was finally slammed shut, the gown came to a slow rest, arms emerged and madly smoothed the dress down layer by layer until a face finally stood out within the torn foam.

"It's a fucking queen," said one of the women in the hush of amazement.

"Shut your mouth," said the other woman, clutching Russell's arm. "It's a bride."

And it was a bride, everyone could see that now. She rose to her feet, disheveled but normal in all respects except that her face was loose and raging, distorted, working horribly in silence.

KARL ADARE

GENTLEMEN AND LADIES *of the Crop and Livestock Convention,
I have come to unveil a miracle.*

That's how I begin my spiel.

*Each one of us survived the dust bowl, those clouds of blowing
grit. Precious topsoil on the whim of the wind! Well gentlemen
and ladies, plowing caused that, tilling made it happen, and one
way to stop that infernal process is not to till.*

But. . . .

I pause dramatically.

*I have to till to plant, you tell me. Well no more! Beneath this
tarp I've got the answer to nature's prayers. Gentlemen . . .*

I pull the string and drop the canvas.

THE AIR SEEDER!

And then I proceed to explain the mechanism. I point to the
thin tubes that conduct the seeds from the box down to the
surface. I explain how, assisted by a puff of the motorized bellows,
each seed is blown gently into the earth. The Air Seeder does
not disturb the soil, I tell them, thereby conserving moisture,
reducing your surface loss.

There are the usual questions, then, the usual scepticism. I
caught the man's eye, a yearning guarded glance, while I was
answering those questions, handing out leaflets, and demonstrat-
ing the process as best I could.

We were both at the convention in Minneapolis. He was a
slim man with a lot of thick blond hair, wide gray eyes, and an

easy manner about him. He asked questions relating to process and durability. He liked the concept, he told me. Innovation was his game.

"I'm Wallace Pfef. I speculate over in Argus," he said. "I'd like to do more promotional work, put the town on the map, boost agriculture. That's why I'm interested in your seeder," he went on.

I said this machine was the coming thing, showed him charts and farm news write-ups, but all the while I was thinking Why Argus? It seemed like that two-bit town popped up every time I turned around. Argus citizens were always shaking my hand. Or the newspapers were full of freak accidents, catastrophes, multiple births at Saint Adalbert's Hospital in Argus. I wondered if someday I'd read my sister's name in these accounts, and I knew that it wouldn't matter if I did. I'd never call, visit, even write a letter. It had simply been too long. Yet I had a fascination, a curiosity that drew coincidence, and it was probably this that led me to ask the man, Pfef, to join me for a drink.

And, too, a salesman makes friends where he can. He wasn't my type, but he wasn't as bad as some.

We walked out of the convention room, crossed the lobby, and entered the dim hotel bar.

"I'll stand you one," I said, putting down a five-dollar bill when our drinks arrived. The waitress took the right amount from the five and left the change on the table. I did not touch the change.

He thanked me, took a slow drink, and said nothing else, which at first I found unsettling, but then, when I purposely waited also and didn't fill in the space he'd opened up, it was clear we had allowed our drink to shift the ground between us.

"Are you from Minneapolis?" he asked. Somehow the subject seemed more personal now than when we'd spoken of his being from Argus.

"Here . . . different places," I told him.

102

"Which places?"

I paused, feeling the old discomfort over questions about my past, yet wanting to reveal just enough to keep him interested.

"Saint Jerome's," I said. "It's a Catholic home for bastards."

He clearly hadn't expected this. "I'm sorry," he said. "That's too bad."

I waved it off.

He didn't have much to say about anything now, but he kept that waiting look on his face, and although I don't usually talk about myself, try to keep my distance, I added what I never told anyone.

"I've got a sister," I said. "She lives in your town."

He looked expectant. Clearly, he knew everyone in Argus, and I realized I'd gone too far. He would tell Mary that he'd met me if I told him her name, which he clearly anticipated. I'd considered giving him a business card, but now I'd have to be more cautious.

"But I don't know who she is," I backpedaled. "It could be just a rumor. That kind of thing always happens in a home. Other kids pretend they've seen your files, or the nuns make up stories. . . ."

"You believe it though," he said, looking straight at me with conviction. At that moment, the ground dwindled considerably between us as it always does when one person admits to observing another that closely and meets your eyes. It was now my turn to say something that would penetrate still farther. I took my chance.

"Let's have dinner in my hotel room," I said.

His stare changed to surprise. We'd downed three quick drinks by then, and the five he'd insisted on putting down also lay broken between us. Three drinks was where I started feeling loose, and as I watched him stand up I knew the same was true of him.

"Oh no," he said, rummaging below his seat. "I dropped my pamphlets."

His hips were fine and thin, I noticed, but he wasn't strong

103

or muscular. There was more to admire about my appearance. I lifted weights, swam laps, or ran an occasional mile even when I was on the road. I took care of myself mentally too. I'd had enough setbacks with other people, and perhaps because of them I never let anything go far enough to cause me trouble.

"Coming?" I asked.

He had recovered his pamphlets. He stood up with a quick nervous smile, and together we walked down the carpeted corridor, up two flights of stairs, and entered my room. It was a single, dominated by a bed with a bright orange bedspread. Pfef managed to avoid looking at the bed by making a beeline for the window and admiring my view. Which was of the parking lot.

There really were menus in the desk-table drawer, and I was honestly hungry. I found that once we were alone in the room I didn't even care much what happened, one way or the other. It wasn't that Pfef was unattractive, it was his sudden nervousness that bored me, the awkward pretense when it was he who put his hand out once, stopping mine, when I'd tried to lay down another bill for drinks.

I sat on the bed and opened the menu. I knew what I was hungry for but it wasn't available.

"Game hens," I compromised, "even though they'll send them dry and tough."

He relaxed, sat down in the little chair beside the bed, and picked up a menu.

"The prime rib. That's my choice."

"We're settled then." I phoned the desk. While we waited for the trolley I poured him a shot from the bottle I kept in my suitcase.

"Is this your only water glass?" he wondered, politely, before raising it to his lips.

"I'm not particular," I said, taking a pull from the bottle; "not like you."

He had been the one with the bold observant statements downstairs, but once I tagged him he flushed and fell silent, swirled the whiskey in his glass, and then got that waiting look on his face again.

So I didn't say anything, just took the glass from his hand.

"The dinner," he said in a faint voice.

But he bent forward anyway, and I held his shoulders, drew him to me. Then we lay back on the startling spread.

By the time the bellhop knocked on the door we were back where we'd started, dressed, the only difference being now we shared the water glass. The truth is I liked drinking from a glass.

The boy just shoved the cart in, put his hand out for the tip, and left us. Maybe he thought we were plotting gangsters, or knew the truth. Pfef ate quickly, avidly, with obvious relief. He cut his meat into small squares and popped them into his mouth. It had not been as bad as he thought, I guessed, or now that it was over he could put it behind him, pretend it never happened, go quietly back to Argus and tell his wife how well the convention had gone and ply her with some Minneapolis souvenir to oil the creaky little hinge of his guilt.

"I've never done this before," he said.

I just turned away and carved the tiny birds, remembering the guarded yearning, his waiting eye. He was married for sure, at least I assumed it. He wore a wedding-type ring and had a cared-for look—pressed, shined, and starched.

"So how's the little woman?" I could not help myself. I said this with a sneer.

He looked up, uncomprehending, wiped his chin. I tapped his hand.

"Oh," he said. "I was engaged once, long ago."

"I bet you were."

Then he turned the tables, or tried to.

"What about you?" he asked.

"What about me?"

"You know."

"You mean women?" He nodded. I told him I'd known plenty and very closely, although the truth is I had always found their touch unbearable, a source of nameless panic.

"But no love and marriage for me," I told him.

He was fascinated.

"Why don't you let me try and find your sister?" he asked. This came out of the blue, unexpected, and when he looked at me with his clear sad eyes, I suddenly had the feeling that had always frightened me, the blackness, the ground I'd stood on giving way, the falling no place. Maybe it was true about him, the awkwardness, no experience, the awful possibility that he wanted to get to know me.

"I'm done," I said, shoving away my plate and, just to do something, just to stop the feeling, wheeling the cart madly out the door too. I came back in the room and leapt onto the bed. I had to stop myself from falling, so I jumped. I felt silly and light, bouncing in the air. I felt like a child who would ruin the bedsprings.

"You'd better stop," Pfef said, shocked, dropping meat from his fork. "The management."

"Screw the management!" I laughed at his maidenly face. "I've got a trick I'm going to show you." I didn't actually have anything in mind, but as I bounced, hitting the ceiling almost, I was suddenly inspired. I'd watched hard-muscled boys so closely on the diving boards downtown. They sprang up, whirled over, threw themselves precisely through the air in a somersault and split the water harshly with their toes. I would do the same. I took a great bounce. Then I tucked, spun, whirled, and I still believe that if it hadn't been for Pfef's sudden yell I would have landed perfectly on my feet. But the cry of alarm threw me off. I kept my body

106

tucked too long and hit the floor at the foot of the bed, in an area so small it seemed impossible I could have landed perfectly within it, but I did, and wrenched my back too.

I knew it was bad the instant I hit. I stayed conscious.

"Pfef," I said, the moment he bent down, "don't touch me."

He had the sense not to, the sense to call the hospital, the sense to sit beside me without talking and keep the orderlies from moving me until the doctor ordered up a plank. The stupid thing I kept thinking all this time, too, was not about my neck or how I could be paralyzed for life. For some reason I had no fear of it. No fear of anything. I looked at Pfef, and by the way he stared back, purely stricken, eyes naked, I knew if I wanted I could have him for life. But I didn't even think about that. It was my sister I remembered.

"Her name's Mary," I said out loud. "Mary Adare."

And then the injection took hold, the black warmth. I realized the place I'd landed on was only a flimsy ledge, and there was nothing else to stop me if I fell.

Wallace's Night

Nighthawks dived through his headlamps, small triangular shadows, their fringed mouths spread for insects. The air off the ditches smelled wet, and sometimes he caught the gleam of water standing mirrorlike between the endless black furrows. Far off the highway between Minneapolis and Argus, lone lights signaled like boats anchored far at sea. The first glimpse that Wallace actually had of Argus was the little tame red beacon that shone on top of the water tower.

He turned his car off the highway onto a small dirt road famous for harboring high school sweethearts. His friend, Officer Ronald Lovchik, was under pressure from certain parents to patrol this stretch on weekend nights. This Saturday night the road was deserted. He caught no reflections; no lovers blinked their headlights farther down the crooked, potholed rut. He let his car bounce softly to a halt and then cut the engine.

All around him a night music opened. Crickets sawed. The new wheat rustled. Dreaming birds that nested in the culverts and low windbreaks let out small sharp cries. Wallace slid low in the seat and breathed the mild sweet wind. The steering wheel curved like a smooth bone where he rested his fingers. Over him, the whole moonless sky was spread with planets and stars.

He didn't want to go back to his half-built empty house yet, but he didn't want to think too closely about what had happened to him in Minneapolis either. He shut his eyes but couldn't doze. He was too alert, too conscious. He tried to occupy his mind with anything but Karl.

There was the problem of the swimming pool that Wallace managed along with his other jobs. The pool had been a WPA project, an elaborate one, much too large and fancy for Argus.

Now the plumbing was rotten and cracks had appeared in the deep end. The filtering system was worthless and the valuable hand-painted friezes that adorned the dressing-room walls were chipping. Vandals had sliced the fence.

The pool was too big a headache. He thought about First National. He sat on the board that put the okay on its investments. He tried to keep his mind on the last stock portfolio he'd seen, but the smell of standing rain was in the breeze. He drifted. He saw Karl's hands, his dark hair, the drawn face in the crisp and disinfected hospital sheets. When the lights went on suddenly behind him, Wallace was dazzled.

A car door slammed. His front seat was full of the glare. Someone bent into his window.

"Wally Pfef!"

"Ron!"

"What are you doing here?"

"I'm . . ." what *was* he doing here anyway? ". . . thinking."

Lovchik straightened. Wallace groped along the front seat and grabbed a pile of pamphlets he'd taken back from the convention. He pressed them to his chest and sprang from the car.

"Look at this," he said, handing one out. Ron Lovchik looked put upon. He unhooked a flashlight from his belt and focused it on the pamphlet.

"It says here 'the Sugarbeet.' "

"That's it!" said Wallace, and swung an arm out toward the empty night, the vast and silent fields.

"These fields, everything you see, well it's beet country Ron."

Wallace grabbed Lovchik's arm, tapped his finger on the glossy paper booklet. "Listen. Table sugar is a staple of the worldwide menu. You like sugar. I like it. Sugar's got to come from somewhere, and it might as well be here. It could mean a face-lift for Argus! Money in the coffers. It could mean a new squad car. A two-way radio!"

109

Officer Lovchik shifted his weight and peered down at the small writing, at the picture of beets.

"Isn't it a lovely sight?" said Wallace. His voice soared. "A big white fat root just waiting to be made into $C_{12}H_{22}O_{11}$. That's sugar. Imagine it, Ron. All the fields around here planted. A beet refinery. The money flowing in. Your jail gets new windows. Argus builds two new swimming pools. When the wind blows off the piled beets the people hold their noses, but they smile, Ron. They know which side their bread is buttered on."

The ideas began to pour into Wallace's brain.

Officer Lovchik shook his head, looked down at the pamphlet again, flipped it in his hands. He gave Wallace a light whack on the shoulder.

"You never quit, Wally. You've even got plans for Lover's Lane.

Wallace jumped into his car, started the engine, and roared the gas enthusiastically.

"What a twist!" he shouted, driving off into the night. "This road will become a major bypass!" Before him, like Oz, the imaginary floodlit stacks of the beet refinery poured a stinking smoke straight upward in twin white columns.

CELESTINE JAMES

"ALL NIGHT LONG I've been grappling with killer robots," says Mary to herself, although I am working right next to her.

It is one whole decade before the president is shot and the world goes haywire, but Mary is ahead of her time. The idea of robots, which is current in magazines, has taken root in her mind along with other things. Atomic weapons. Space travel. Ginseng. She thinks that the beet sugar this town has gone crazy for is unhealthful. She has started to talk about raising bees. But her favorite is still the subject of mechanical people.

"Robots would have no feelings," she says now, darkly. "You could not appeal to their mercy."

"Since when," I say to her, "could you appeal to the common soldier? They sweat the mercy out of them in boot camp."

That's according to Russell, who should know. He has been discharged from the VA hospital, where he's been ever since he got back from his latest war, Korea. He is home now at last, never again to be a soldier. But he is riddled with even more wounds than before, so that now there is talk of making him North Dakota's most-decorated hero. I think it's stupid, that this getting shot apart is what he's lived for all his life. Now he must wait until some statehouse official scores the other veterans, counting up their wounds on a paper tablet, and figures out who gave away the most flesh.

He has been in the service so long that he's used to waiting. And then we hear the bad news about our sister Isabel, who married into a Sioux family and moved down to South Dakota. We hear she has died of beating, or in a car wreck, some way that's violent. But nothing else. We hear nothing from her husband, and if she had any children we never hear from them. Russell goes down there that weekend, but the funeral is long past. He comes home, telling me it's like she fell off the earth. There is no trace of her, no word.

Russell stays in the bars all night, or mopes around the house with his toolbox, until Mary gets wind of this and hires him to work on the shop's delivery van and motorized cooling system. Now he's in and out all day, limping, creased head to foot with new scars and stripes that almost look like the markings of an animal. He works for such long hours on the freezers that his hands are frostbit and raw, but he seems to improve a bit, mentally, to take an interest in life.

As Russell is getting better, the bottom is falling out of Sita's situation. Not that we hear it directly from her, more from rumors that customers bring through the door, and from things we observe ourselves. She has been heard out back in the kitchen of The Poopdeck Restaurant, criticizing her husband Jimmy for his method of frying food. Everything The Poopdeck makes is first dipped in batter then fried in deep fat. His food is fixed the way people around here like it. But Sita wants to make The Poopdeck into a first-class restaurant, a *four star*, our customers have heard her yell. They have seen Jimmy storm out stamping his small, sharp-toed feet, popping red in the face. He sits down at the edge of the counter, to a whole plate of glazed cinnamon rolls, and snaps them up daintily without losing his pout. He has gained so much weight from sweets eaten in anger that he hardly fits into a booth anymore.

Sita, however, remains toothpick thin and sour. To stay beautiful, she has to work harder than ever on herself. She spends hours at the hairdressers, money on skin treatments, and she ends up looking stuffed and preserved.

So Russell has war depression. Sita's pickled in her own juice. And Mary has a million ideas bouncing off the wall. The killer robot army that I have mentioned was in her dreams the night before.

"They came at me," she says with vigor, "shooting death rays from their fingers." We are sitting in plastic chairs out back of her kitchen on the cement slab floor of her glass porch. It is a rich and tangled garden of steamy vines. I think her whole idea's out of the ball park, and I tell her so.

"Of course," she returns, "it takes a mind that's unusual."

"You are unusual," I tell her. "I'm sure that nothing could make you happier."

Whether she hears this or ignores it, I don't know. She seems to have grown heavier in the past few years, not stouter, just more unshakable in deed and word. What she doesn't like, she doesn't hear. Now she walks among the teeming pots and cold-frames where she practices her ideas on growing plants.

In these flats, the soil is mixed fine with coffee grounds and broken eggshells. Her roses grow dark red and electric on crushed bones. The tiny heads of lettuce tighten in garters. The tomato plants droop on thick stems mulched with dried blood and oak leaves. Asparagus fern and chives blow everyplace like hair. Mary uses anything around her that's available. She bends over, tying her tomatoes up on thin steel rods that I think she has lifted from a construction site.

We have stopped for lunch, but now the boy, Adrian, who helps out anywhere he's needed and is supposed to be a cousin of mine, shouts that there's customers.

"Don't get too caught up," I warn Mary as I walk through the door, "we've got the liver sausage waiting." It is mixed up in a huge steel vat, but now one of us has to wash the beef casings, send the mixture spurting through the nozzle of the sausage machine, then tie the long tube into rings.

"I know, I know," she says, but whether she's answering me

113

or merely soothing her tomatoes I can't tell. I walk down the hall, out to the counter, and the customer I see standing there is our old classmate, Wallace Pfef, now the head of the chamber of commerce and still a bachelor. He is watching our steaks intently through the thick glass, as if they might suddenly shake off their green paper frills. The lights from the case glow up into his face, making purple shadows beneath his eyes and nose.

"What can I get you today?" I ask. Wallace is usually a regular, but has not been in for weeks.

"Good afternoon, Celestine," he says. "I was hoping to see Mary." He looks around me, but she is not visible down the hall or through the window that leads to her office.

"She's out back," I tell him, "tying up her tomato vines."

He looks both relieved and disappointed. "Never mind, I'll talk to her next time," he says. I ask if it's important, but he only smiles his little businessman smile and taps the glass with a fingernail.

"Could I see that one?" he asks.

Pfef must be shown his meat up close, as if it were jewelry from a case. I display the red steak on a piece of waxed paper and he examines it before nodding his acceptance.

"Wrap it up," he says, "and one-quarter pound of the longhorn cheddar."

I cut this, wrap both of his purchases in white paper. And then, because his interest in Mary has made me curious, I ask him if he's sure I shouldn't get her.

"No," he waves away my offer, "no, please don't. It was only this."

He shows me *The Sentinel*. It is an ad. One full page. GRANDE OPENING, it says, CHEZ SITA, HOME OF THE FLAMBÉED SHRIMP. The ad goes on to talk about "your dining pleasure," "subtle ambiance," "food exquisitely displayed." A menu is listed.

114

"Doesn't it look delicious," says Wallace. "You know, Sita's restaurant is a prestigious addition to our town." His voice is raised in such enthusiasm that Mary hears him as she walks down the hallway with the ball of string.

"What's this?" she says.

"Mary!" says Wallace. He smiles at her and offers a small whitish envelope from the inner pocket of his suit jacket. He explains. "All the businesses in town are getting these, but your cousin Sita asked me to make especially sure that you received it."

"I'll bet she did," says Mary. She has opened the envelope and I see that it's an invitation. Engraved. Mary hands it to me. I read how we are cordially invited to the grand opening of Chez Sita, one week from this evening. There is a note on the bottom, in Sita's tight little handwriting, that tells us ties and suitcoats are required wearing for men, and also that ladies must dress in an appropriate fashion. This is Sita's way of telling us she doesn't really want us to come, her low-class former friends and relatives. She is sending us the invitation just to rub our faces in the subtle ambiance of her new and very prosperous life.

While I'm musing on the creamy little card, Mary is reading the newspaper ad.

"Chez Sita." She says *Chez* to rhyme with *Pez*. She does not seem impressed by the menu or the ad. And I find, as soon as Wallace has left us, that a customer has already told Mary the story behind Sita's restaurant. As we stand at the counter, Mary relates it to me. Sita and Jimmy have finally divorced, she says. It was all a secret and now it's final. They are living apart. Jimmy took the real estate agency, the scrapyard, the storage and rental warehouse, even The Trampoline, which is a bar he thought up to attract the younger set; and also his miniature golf course. Sita took the house and the restaurant. She closed The Poopdeck, remodeled the interior and hired all new staff including a chef,

Mary says, *all the way from Minneapolis*. This last fact clearly angers Mary, and her face clouds in the telling.

"It is expensive," I say, looking at the menu. "Who do you think will eat at Chez Sita?"

Mary cannot say, cannot imagine. But the customer's story explains to us what I've noticed over the past few weeks about the outer transformation of The Poopdeck.

I've watched workers tear the colorful plastic banners from The Poopdeck's mast, lower the lifeboat, and finally cover all the blue and white nautical trim with a dark wine-red paint. Still, there is no disguising the shape of the building's hull, the portholes, the mast that probably cannot be severed without structural damage to the building below. Now, approaching the restaurant from the edge of town, it is not a boat that you see, beached cheerfully like before, but a ship so dark it's almost frightful. It is Sita's black ship, unmoored in tossing yew shrubs, ready to sail as if gathering souls.

It is an odd thought, but I was traveling with Mary when we first saw the changes and she maintained that the place looked like the ship of the dead.

Now Mary tosses the invitation into the trash and walks out to the liver sausage table. She does not intend to go to Sita's grand opening, that is evident, but I follow behind her and pick the card from the bin.

"Don't you want to know what it's like on the inside?" I ask.

"What what's like." Mary is sorting out the dishpan of casings now, untangling the long opaque strings, preparing them to be filled.

"Sita's place."

"Why waste money?"

I don't answer, to see if she will go on from there.

"That place gives me the creeps," she says.

"Some people feel like that about butcher shops," I say, and

116

I turn from her, annoyed at how she won't understand what she doesn't want to think about. I take the cover off the sausage machine and start packing the liver mixture into its bin with a flat trowel. Mary fits the end of the casing onto the nozzle, and then wipes her hands off on her apron.

"I'm going anyway," I tell her. "With or without you."

One week or so later, on the very day of the grande opening, Mary changes her mind and asks what time I'm leaving.

"Suppertime," I answer.

"Then let's take the shop truck."

I'd rather not show up in Sita's parking lot in the low maroon van lettered boldly on each panel HOUSE OF MEATS, but it's not worth the price of arguing. So we gather that night, dressed in our finest summer clothing. Russell slides into the driver's seat. Mary settles into the passenger's side. I must crawl into the back and crouch behind them, taking care not to ruin the knees of my stockings.

Russell is dressed in the new gray suit, which I bought him because his two dress uniforms were asked for by the county museum. They now hang off a tailor's dummy in a display case along with a list of Russell's medals and a photograph. That picture shows him as he was when he came back from Germany, before Korea, when his scars were more attractive than now. Mary has twisted her salt-and-pepper hair into a French knot, and she is dressed in electric sea-blue. Her dress is made of a shiny taffeta, and fastened on the shoulder with rhinestone bows. The dress is not Mary's color, or her style either with its tight bodice and enormous gathered skirt. It is the kind of mistake that ladies shops sell cheap at their year-end clearance, and that is very likely where Mary acquired it. For my part, I have always been advised, with my height and big bones, to dress in a soft yet tailored style. I wear a ruffled pink shirt, a brown suit jacket

117

and pleated skirt out of summer-weight wool. Except for Mary, I think, we look presentable. She is hunched over, polishing the tops of her shoes with a piece of newsprint, and then she is muttering into the glove compartment. She doesn't like Russell driving, but I've convinced her to let him, I'm not sure why, except that I'm anxious about appearances and it's customary for the man to take the wheel. I still wish we didn't have to use the van. I don't want to stick out in the elegant surroundings.

"Where in the hell are my yarrow sticks!" says Mary, peering up at us, one hand still groping through the maps and sunglasses and delivery orders.

These sticks are supposed to tell what is going to happen in the short run. But I doubt they could have predicted much about that night. Lately, Mary has been sending off for special offers and reading books on mental projection. She claims she had psychic ability when she was young and caused the face of Christ to appear where she hit the ground beneath the school slide. That event is so old no one here remembers it anymore. And for myself, I never saw it no matter how hard I looked so I don't buy it. I tell Mary that she has started to believe her old newspaper clippings, but nothing seems to shake her deep faith.

"Here we are," I say. My eyes are full of the glaring fabric of Mary's dress. Russell gets out of the van. I am used to the way his face looks, all sewn together, but he often startles others. And I do not even feel so sure about myself. I tower. My face is too broad. My teeth look fierce when I grin, a trait from my mother's side. But I know that any concern for how we look to others is absolutely useless on my part, so I resign myself.

Walking into the restaurant I do not shrink or sidle. I take my usual long step and tell the puffy little hostess in her prom gown that I've got reservations.

"James?" she says, simpering into her leather-covered guest book. "I'm afraid not."

"Adare," says Mary, and starts to spell it.

"Oh yes," the hostess says. "We have your table waiting, madam. Right this way."

She leads us through doors that have been padded like the walls of a lunatic's cell, and on into the high-class gloom.

"What did I tell you," says Mary. "This is eerie."

I throw my arm out to stop her comment, but hit thin air. I think I see a ghostly flare of light off her dress, but the room is so deceptive, so large and full of shadows. As we walk, we grip each other's sleeves. Russell, up front, has taken the arm of our hostess, who is surefooted in this atmosphere as a guide in a cave. At each table we pass, a candle flickers in a bowl and I see that many of these tables are occupied. People have come, drawn by the novelty like us, or perhaps even the legitimate wish to experience dining pleasure. I think at first they are squinting at huge photograph albums, but once we sit down and are handed our own I see that of course they are menus.

"Our proprietor, Mrs. Sita Bohl, will be by to greet you personally," says the hostess.

"Tell her not to bother," says Mary before I kick her.

The hostess lifts her eyebrows then vanishes into the shade between the tables. A waiter comes. We all order highballs. But it is really too dark in here, and I believe that Sita has covered the portholes, which is too bad, because even a gleam of starlight would help us read our menus. Our candle is especially dim, too, in its bowl. It does not shed enough light to read by. But luckily Russell smokes, or not so luckily, because as chance would have it, while he is holding his lighter close to the pages to see the words, he sets his menu on fire. He doesn't notice it at first. None of us notice, except that the glow at our table gets brighter. I take advantage of the flare to quickly make my selection. Then Russell is slapping the fire out with his napkin, a heavy starched linen that was folded into a crown. The napkin absorbs the fire, puts it out.

"Excitement's over," Russell assures the waiter who stands

behind us, poised with a pitcher of iced water. A small cloud of smoke now drifts in the dark air above our table. We have created a stir that I know will inevitably draw Sita. And sure enough, she soon materializes, with us suddenly, dressed in a black sheath and pearls. She bends over the table, trying not to make a scene, and hisses something indistinguishable. The light from below distorts her face into a Halloween mask, witchlike and gruesome. It is a moment before I register the fact that she is whispering not about the charred paper, the cloud of smoke, the disturbance we have created, but about some dilemma of her own.

"Come out back," she says. "Follow me."

But Mary asks in a loud voice, "What for?"

Sita tries to hush her but Mary is adamant.

"We're not going to budge," she says from deep in her chair.

Sita is forced to plead with her, but nothing she whispers convinces Mary, who fairly shouts, "You in some kind of trouble, or what?"

"Come on." I finally cannot bear the suspense. "Let's go with Sita." I pull Russell to his feet, so then Mary is forced to follow or sit alone. Sita leads us. But she blends into the darkness in her black dress, and we fumble, banging into other people's tables, before we finally locate some door that leads us into the bright kitchen area. There we see, blinking, that Sita has transformed herself. She wears an apron, stands before an open grill, and behind her two long tables are covered with a welter of open cookbooks and empty pots.

A waiter leaps through the door.

"Anything!" he cries out. "They're chewing on their forks!"

"My God," says Sita, stirring a pot of soup with one hand, checking a piece of meat with the other, "hold them off! Give them each a free drink!"

"They're already drunk!"

"My chef," gasps Sita, explaining over her shoulder to us,

"came down with food poisoning. All the helpers too. It was the shrimp stuffed with crab."

I had been going to order that.

"Too bad," Mary says. In her voice there is victory, and I feel somewhat ashamed of her because Sita is driven to her limit. Her face is strained with shock. Her hair is fairly on end. Her movements are jerky and stunned, like the robots in Mary's dream. Even after all that Sita has done to make us feel beneath her, I can't enjoy watching this. But Mary has the most to complain about in Sita's case, and I pause in the feeling that she should decide what to do next.

"All right," she says. "Let's get to work."

Sita sags as if the wire that held her up was severed, and then unties her apron. She hangs it on a hook, smoothes her hair, and moves out the door.

"Put these on," Mary orders, handing white coats and wide aprons down from a shelf to Russell and me. "Now you," she tells the next waiter who pokes his head in through the door, "go out there and tell the customers that their side dishes are on the house and their whole total meal is twenty percent off. That'll shut them up."

The waiter darts out. On the counter there is a tall stack of orders. I start to read them. The renovators, luckily, have left behind one of The Poopdeck's large deep fryers. I turn the controls up to high. Mary finds plastic bags of jumbo breaded shrimp in the freezer. Once the grease bubbles, Mary fries up a batch, then another, and Russell sends a plateload, twelve or fifteen, to every table. "Home of the Flambéed Shrimp," Sita's ad declared. Almost every order included shrimp.

I am trying to read cookbooks, meanwhile, and figure out how to poach frog's legs, ball *Foie Gras*, prepare a *Velouté de Volaille Froid*, not to mention the main courses: *Poulet Sauté d'Artois*, *Filet de Boeuf Saint-Florentin*, *Huîtres à la Mornay*, and of course the nearly fatal shrimp-and-crab dish. But that is temporarily not available.

"I can't do this," I say to Russell in despair.

He has grated potatoes next, having finished the shrimp. He is frying an enormous load of golden hashbrowns.

"Relax," he says, grinning beneath his chef's hat. He seems to be enjoying this. "No one out there understood the menu," he explains. "In case you hadn't noticed, the damn thing was in French."

I don't get his drift.

"They won't know what their food is supposed to be," he says; "just cook it up the way you would at home."

He's right, so that's what I do.

We make fried chicken, roast beef, oysters in a pie. Mary tosses together Pete's famous Polish noodle soup. Russell finds several boxes of delicate French wafers and coats them with chocolate, berry glaze, sherbets, and ice cream. We make something out of everything we uncover in the kitchen. Sita pops in occasionally. Her look, as the waiters carry plates of fried chicken past her, is both beaten and full of relief.

It is well past eleven o'clock before we get a breath. The regular employees, sons and daughters of our customers, have been sworn to secrecy concerning the state of the chef's health and our contribution. But of course, I can see it from their eyes, there is no way they will be silent about what has taken place.

The food was good, too. The customers left satisfied, full, ready to come back, and declaring that the French deep-fry method was expensive but delicious, and the quantity was worth it for the price. Almost every one of them goes out with a white, foil-lined bag that says *"pour le chien."* We three sit down at last, in the wreckage of the kitchen.

The hostess has rolled down her stockings and dropped the straps of her gown. She sits with us, feet up on a chair. Slowly, the waiters and waitresses straggle in, exhausted and hungry. The dishwashers are still going. Everyone begins to eat scraps of this, tastes of that, bits of Russell's confections and leftover hashbrowns.

"You saved the night," says the same waiter who stood behind us with the pitcher of iced water. "She's still out there totaling up."

She, of course, is Sita, who finally comes through the door.

"Well," she says, massaging her temples, "I suppose I should thank you."

"Don't mention it," says Russell.

"Wait," Mary holds Sita's gaze, "if you want to thank something, go ahead and thank your father's noodle soup."

Sita nods briefly, but that's all she can bring herself to do. After a while she turns around and walks out the door.

After Sita departs, things loosen up. "Have a drink?" the hostess asks us in a friendly voice. We agree. There is plenty of open wine, which we polish off, and even champagne. The hostess slumps lower in her chair, makeup blurred, and lets Russell rub her back.

It is almost dawn before Mary, Russell, and myself are finally let out the door beneath the dark ship's prow. The air is cool and gray. The sky sparkles and the dew makes everything smell fresh, even the gravel in the parking lot. Russell lounges on the side of the truck for a moment, lighting a cigarette between his palms. The cupped glow reflects onto his face. Mary glows too. Her dress is spectral, floating across the flat ground. She is rummaging in her purse for the keys, forgetting Russell has them. Before he can give them back to her, Mary's hand lights on something.

"My sticks," she exclaims, drawing out a thin bundle that looks like broomstraws.

"Throw them here, on the car hood," says Russell. "Let's see the future."

So Mary chants beneath her breath, and tosses her yarrow sticks according to some mail-order instruction. They land every which way, in a jumble, but she looks at them with keen eyes as though their exciting design is plain. No matter how we pester Mary she will say nothing of what she sees, and just leaves them scrambled on the hood when Russell gives her the keys to the truck. We get in and Mary starts driving. As we move along, the sticks slide off the hood one by one and we laugh every time this happens, as though we're throwing caution to the winds.

Not long after the night in which we rescue Sita from the grande opening's certain disaster, more rumors start to fly about her. A customer comes into the shop and says that the state health inspector, who was sent over from Bismarck to investigate Chez Sita after word leaked out on the food poisoning, has been back and forth many times. He does not always wear his badge or carry his briefcase, and no one knows whether he is paying social calls or if there is yet more to fear from the unfamiliar food. The hostess and most of the waiters are laid off, we hear. Chez Sita is usually empty. But this fact does not seem to bother Sita.

One day, picking up some barrels of salt down at the warehouse in Fargo, I see her snapping a green bean, then sniffing the end to determine its freshness. A man is standing with her. He is tall and sober, with gray steel glasses and gray hair. Sita holds the end of the green bean to his nose and he frowns. She smiles and looks almost girlish again. Her hair is tousled. I turn away before she sees me there, watching. The man with Sita looks like the kind of expert you see on television commercials, the type whose low calm voice advises us on pain relief. I feel he must be the state health inspector, and from Sita's smile I think that his visits are probably not so official anymore. This man seems a way out of the restaurant business, a chance for Sita to make a new start in life. I am relieved for her, glad of her good spirits.

But as I am driving back from the big market with the barrels of preserving salt, I think of Sita's face again, and see the crisp bean in her fingers. It makes me wonder about myself. Will I ever smile, flush, offer a tidbit of food? Are these things that Sita feels, these pleasures I have read about in books, the sort of feelings I might experience? It has never happened yet, although I've known men. Perhaps, I think, I'm too much like them, too strong or imposing when I square my shoulders, too eager to take control.

I drive for a distance among the quiet, flat fields, but the long views of crops do not calm me, nor the clouds, just scratches high in the atmosphere, nor the strung poles that endlessly pass and revolve. I'm not calm even when I reach the shop. I find Mary's note saying that she left and I should lock up for the night. Perhaps because I'm in this mood—strange, disturbed, lonely at the core—perhaps because Mary is unexpectedly not there, I'm not at my best when the man comes through the door.

He is fine boned, slick, agreeable, and dressed to kill in his sharp black suit, winy vest, knotted brown tie. His hair is oiled. His lips are fevered and red as two buds. For a long while he stands there, eyeing me, before he opens his mouth.

"You're not pretty," are the first words he speaks.

And I, who have never bit off my words even to a customer, am surprised into a wounded silence although I don't look in the mirror for pleasure, but only to take stock of the night's damage.

I am standing on a stool, changing the prices I chalk above the counter each week on a piece of slate. Blutwurst. Swedish sausage. Center-cut chops. Steak. I keep writing and do not give him the satisfaction of an answer. He stands below me, waiting. He has the patience of a cat with women. When I finish, there is nothing left for me to do but climb down.

"But pretty's not the only thing," the man continues smoothly, as though all my silence has not come between.

I cut him off. "Tell me what you want," I say. "I'm closing shop."

"I bet you never thought I'd come back," he says. He steps close to the glass counter full of meats. I can see, through the false, bright glare inside the case, his dumbbell-lifting chest. His sharp, thick hands. Even above the white pepper and sawdust of the shop, I can smell the wildroot, tobacco, penetrating breath mint.

"I never saw you the first time," I tell him. "I'm closing."

"Look here," he says, "Mary . . ."

"I'm not Mary."

"Oh, my God, *Sita*?"

"Sita's gone," I say. "She lives in the biggest house in Blue Mound. That's the next town over."

He goes rigid, puts his hand to the back of his skull, pats the hair in place thoughtfully.

"Who are you then?"

"Celestine," I say, "as if it's any of your business."

I have to ring out the register, secure the doors, set the alarm on the safe before I can walk home. Around that time of early evening the light floods through the thick block-glass windows, a golden light that softens the shelves and barrels. Dusk is always my time, that special air of shifting shapes, and it occurs to me that, even though he says I am not pretty, perhaps in the dusk I am impossible to resist. Perhaps there is something about me, like he says.

"Adare. Karl Adare."

He introduces himself without my asking. He crosses his arms on the counter, leans over, and deliberately smiles at my reaction. His teeth are small, shiny, mother-of-pearl.

"This is something," I say. "Mary's brother."

"She ever talk about me?"

"No," I have to answer, "and she's out on a delivery right now. She won't be back for a couple of hours."

"But you're here."

I guess my mouth drops a little. Me knowing who he is has only slightly diverted what seem like his firm intentions, which are what? I can't read him. I turn away from him and make myself busy with the till, but I am fumbling. I think of Sita testing vegetables. Now it seems as though something is happening to me. I turn around to look at Karl. His eyes are burning holes and he tries to look right through me if he can. This is, indeed, the way men behave in the world of romance. Except that he is slightly smaller than me, and also Mary's brother. And then there is his irritating refrain.

"Pretty's not everything," he says to me again. "You're built . . ." He stops, trying to hide his confusion. But his neck reddens and I think maybe he is no more experienced at this than I.

"If you curled the ends at least," he says, attempting to recover, "if you cut your hair. Or maybe it's the apron."

I always wear a long white butcher's apron, starched and swaddled around my middle with thick straps. Right now I take it off, whip it around me, and toss it on the radiator. I decide I will best him at his game, as I have studied it in private, have thought it out.

"All right," I say, walking around the counter. "Here I am." Because of the market visit I am wearing a navy blue dress edged in white. I have a bow at my waist, black shoes, and a silver necklace. I have always thought I looked impressive in this outfit, not to be taken lightly. Sure enough, his eyes widen. He looks stricken and suddenly uncertain of the next move, which I see is mine to make.

"Follow me," I say. "I'll put a pot of coffee on the stove."

It is Mary's stove, of course, but she will not be back for several hours. He does not follow me directly, but lights a cigarette. He smokes the heavy kind, not my brand anymore. The smoke curls from his lips.

"You married?" he asks.

127

"No," I say. He drops the cigarette on the floor, crushes it out with his foot, and then picks it up and says, "Where shall I put this?"

I point at an ashtray in the hall, and he drops the butt in. Then, as we walk back to Mary's kitchen, I see that he is carrying a black case I have not noticed before. We are at the door of the kitchen. It is dark. I have my hand on the light switch and am going to turn on the fluorescent ring, when he comes up behind me, puts his hands on my shoulders, and kisses the back of my neck.

"Get away from me," I say, not expecting this so soon. First the glances, the adoration, the many conversations must happen.

"How come?" he asks. "This is what you want."

His voice shakes. Neither one of us is in control. I shrug his hands off.

"What I want." I repeat this stupidly. Love stories always end here. I never had a mother to tell me what came next. He steps in front of me and hugs me to himself, draws my face down to his face. I am supposed to taste a burning sweetness on his lips, but his mouth is hard as metal.

I lunge from his grip, but he comes right with me. I lose my balance. He is fighting me for the upper hand, straining down with all his might, but I am more than equal to his weight-lifting arms and thrashing legs. I could throw him to the side, I know, but I grow curious. There is the smell of corn mash, something Mary has dropped that morning. That's what I notice even when it happens and we are together, rolling over, clasped, bumping into the legs of the table. I move by instinct, lurching under him, my mind held up like a glass in which I see my own face, amused, embarrassed, and relieved. It is not so complicated, not even as painful, as I feared and it doesn't last long either. He sighs when it is over, his breath hot and hollow in my ear.

"I don't believe this happened," he says to himself.

128

That is, oddly, when I lash out against his presence. He is so heavy that I think I might scream in his face. I push his chest, a dead weight, and then I heave him over so he sprawls in the dark, away from me so I can breathe. Then we smooth our clothing and hair back so carefully in the dark, that when we finally turn the light on and blink at the place where we find ourselves, it is as though nothing has happened.

We are standing up, looking anyplace but at each other.

"How about that coffee?" he says.

I turn to the stove.

And then, when I turn around again with the coffeepot, I see that he is unlatching a complicated series of brass fittings that unfold his suitcase into a large stand-up display. He is absorbed, one-minded, not too different from the way he was down on the floor. The case is lined in scarlet velvet. Knives gleam in the plush. Each rests in a fitted compartment, the tips capped so as not to pierce the cloth, the bone handles tied with small strips of pigskin leather.

I sit down. I ask what he is doing but he does not answer, only turns and eyes me significantly. He holds out a knife and a small rectangle of dark wood.

"You can slice," he begins, "through wood, even plaster with our serrated edge. Or . . ." he produces a pale dinner roll from his pocket, "the softest bread." He proceeds to demonstrate, sawing the end of the block of balsa wood with little difficulty, then delicately wiggling the knife through the roll so it falls apart in transparent, perfect ovals.

"You could never butter those," I hear myself say. "They'd fall apart."

"It's just as good with soft-skinned vegetables," he says to the air. "Fruits. Fish fillets."

He is testing the edge of the knife. "Feel," he says, holding the blade toward me. I ignore him. One thing I know is knives and his are cheap-john, not worth half the price of the fancy case. He keeps on with his demonstration, slicing bits of cloth, a very ripe tomato, and a box of ice cream from Mary's freezer. He shows each knife, one after the other, explaining its usefulness. He shows me the knife sharpener and sharpens all Mary's knives on its wheels. The last thing he does is take out a pair of utility shears. He snips the air with them as he speaks.

"Got a penny?" he asks.

Mary keeps her small change in a glass jar on the windowsill. I take out a penny and lay it on the table. And then, in the kitchen glare, Karl takes his scissors and cuts the penny into a spiral.

So, I think, this is what happens after the burning kiss, when the music roars. Imagine. The lovers are trapped together in a deserted mansion. His lips descend. She touches his magnificent thews.

"Cut anything," he says, putting the spiral beside my hand. He begins another. I watch the tension in his fingers, the slow frown of enjoyment. He puts another perfect spiral beside the first. And then, since he looks as though he might keep on going, cutting all the pennies in the jar, I decide that I now have seen what love is about.

"Pack up and go," I tell him.

But he only smiles and bites his lip, concentrating on the penny that uncoils in his hands. He will not budge. I can sit here watching the man and his knives, or call the police. But neither of these seem like a suitable ending.

"I'll take it," I say, pointing at the smallest knife.

In one motion he unlatches a vegetable parer from its velvet niche and sets it between us on the table. I dump a dollar in change from the penny-ante jar. He snaps the case shut. I handle my knife. It is razor sharp, good for cutting the eyes from potatoes. But he is gone by the time I have formed the next thought.

In my stories, they return as a matter of course. So does Karl.
There is something about me he has to follow. He doesn't know
what it is and I can't tell him either, but not two weeks go by
before he breezes back into town, still without ever having seen
his sister. Russell looks outside one morning and sees him strad-
dling the chubstone walk to our house.

"It's a noodle," says Russell. I glance out the window over his
shoulder and see Karl.

"I've got business with him," I say.

"Answer the door then," Russell says. "I'll get lost."

He walks out the back door with his tools.

The bell rings twice. I open the front door and lean out.

"I can't use any," I say.

The smile falls off his face. He is confused a moment, then
shocked. I see that he has come to my house by accident. Maybe
he thought that he would never see me again. His face is what
decides me that he has another thing coming. I am standing there
in layers of flimsy clothing with a hammer in my hand. I can
tell it makes him nervous when I ask him in, but he thinks so
much of himself that he can't back down. I pull a chair out, still
dangling the hammer, and he sits. I go into the kitchen and fetch
him a glass of the lemonade I have been smashing the ice for. I
half expect him to sneak out, but when I return he is still sitting
there, the suitcase humbly at his feet, an oily black fedora on his
knees.

"So, so," I say, taking a chair beside him.

He has no answer to my comment. As he sips on the lemonade,
however, he glances around and seems slowly to recover his
salesman's confidence.

"How's the paring knife holding out?" he asks.

I just laugh. "The blade snapped off the handle," I say. "Your
knives are duck-bait."

He keeps his composure somehow, and slowly takes in the

living room with his stare. When my ceramics, books, typewriter, pillows and ashtrays are all added up, he turns to the suitcase with a squint.

"You live here by yourself?" he asks.

"With my brother."

"Oh."

I fill his lemonade glass again from my pitcher. It is time, now, for Karl to break down with his confession that I am a slow-burning fuse in his loins. A hair trigger. I am a name he cannot silence. A dream that never burst.

"Oh well . . ." he says.

"What's that supposed to mean?" I ask.

"Nothing."

We sit there for a while collecting dust until the silence and absence of Russell from the house grows very evident. And then, putting down our glasses, we walk up the stairs. At the door to my room, I take the hat from his hand. I hang it on my doorknob and beckon him in. And this time, I have been there before. I've had two weeks to figure out the missing areas of books. He is shocked by what I've learned. It is like his mind darkens. Where before there was shuffling and silence, now there are cries. Where before we were hidden, now the shocking glare. I pull the blinds up. What we do is well worth a second look, even if there are only the squirrels in the box elders. He falls right off the bed once, shaking the whole house. And when he gets up he is spent, in pain because of an aching back. He just lies there.

"You could stay on for supper," I finally offer, because he doesn't seem likely to go.

"I will." And then he is looking at me with his eyes in a different way, as if he cannot figure the sum of me. As if I am too much for him to compass. I get nervous.

"I'll fix the soup now," I say.

"Don't go." His hand is on my arm, the polished fingernails

clutching. I cannot help but look down and compare it with my own. I have the hands of a woman who has handled too many knives, deep-nicked and marked with lines, toughened from spice and brine, gouged, even missing a tip and nail.

"I'll go if I want," I say. "Don't I live here?"

And I get up, throwing a housecoat and sweater over myself. I go downstairs and start a dinner on the stove. Presently, I hear him come down, feel him behind me in the doorway, those black eyes in a skin white as veal.

"Pull up a chair," I say. He settles himself heavily and drinks down the highball I give him. When I cook, what goes into my soup is what's there. Expect the unexpected, Russell always says. Butter beans and barley. A bowl of fried rice. Frozen oxtails. All this goes into my pot.

"God almighty," says Russell, stepping through the door. "You still here?" There is never any doubt Russell is my brother. We have the same slanting eyes and wide mouth, the same long head and glaring white teeth. We could be twins, but for his scars and except that I am a paler version of him.

"Adare," says the salesman, holding out his perfect hand. "Karl Adare. Representative at Large."

"What's that?" Russell ignores the hand and rummages beneath the sink for a beer. He makes it himself from a recipe that he learned in the army. Whenever he opens that cupboard I stand back, because sometimes the brew explodes on contact with air. Our cellar is also full of beer. In the deepest of summer, on close, hot nights, we sometimes hear the bottles go smashing into the dirt.

"So," says Russell, "you're the one who sold Celestine here the bum knife."

"That's right," Karl says, taking a fast drink.

"You unload many?"

"No."

133

"I'm not surprised," Russell says.

Karl looks at me, trying to gauge what I've told. But because he doesn't understand the first thing about me, he draws blank. There is nothing to read on my face. I ladle the soup on his plate and sit down across the table. I say to Russell, "He's got a suitcase full."

"Let's see it then."

Russell always likes to look at tools. So again the case comes out, folding into a display. While we eat, Russell keeps up a running examination of every detail a knife could own. He tries them out on bits of paper, on his own pants and fingers. And all the while, whenever Karl can manage to catch my eye, he gives a mournful look of pleading as if I am forcing this performance with the knives. As if the apple in Russell's fingers is his own heart getting peeled. It is uncomfortable. In the love magazines, when passion holds sway, men don't fall down and roll on the floor and lay there like dead. But Karl does that. Right that very evening, in fact, not long after the dinner, when I tell him he must go, he suddenly hits the floor like a toppled statue.

"What's that!" I jump up, clutching Russell's arm. We are still in the kitchen. Having drunk several bottles in the mellow dusk, Russell isn't clear in the head. Karl has drunk more. We look down. He is slumped beneath the table where he's fallen, passed out, so pale and still I fetch a mirror to his pencil-moustache and am not satisfied until his breath leaves a faint silver cloud.

The next morning, the next morning after that, and still the next morning Karl is here in the house. He pretends to take ill at first, creeping close to me that first night in order to avoid deadly chills. The same the night after, and the night after that, until things began to get too predictable for my taste.

Sitting at the table in his underwear is something Karl starts doing once he feels at home. He never makes himself useful.

He never sells any knives. Every day when I leave for work the last thing I see is him killing time, talking to himself like the leaves in the trees. Every night when I come home there he is, taking space up like one more piece of furniture. Only now, he's got himself clothed. Right away, when I enter the door, he rises like a sleepwalker and comes forward to embrace me and lead me upstairs.

"I don't like what's going on here," says Russell after two weeks of hanging around on the outskirts of this affair. "I'll take off until you get tired of the Noodle."

So Russell goes. Whenever things heat up at home he stays up on the reservation with Eli, his half brother, in an old house papered with calendars of naked women. They fish for crappies or trap muskrats and spend their Saturday nights half drunk, paging through the long years on their wall. I don't like to have him go up there, but I'm not ready to say good-bye to Karl.

I get into a habit with Karl and don't look up for two months. Mary tells me what I do with her brother is my business, but I catch her eyeing me, her gaze a sharp yellow. I do not blame her. Karl has gone to her only once for dinner. It was supposed to be their grand reunion, but it fell flat. They blamed each other. They argued. Mary hit him with a can of oysters. She threw it from behind and left a goose egg, or so Karl says. Mary never tells me her side, but after that night things change at work. She talks around me, delivers messages through others. I even hear through one of the men that she says I've turned against her.

Meanwhile, love wears on me. Mary or no Mary, I am tired of coming home to Karl's heavy breathing and even his touch has begun to oppress me.

"Maybe we ought to end this while we're still in love," I say to him one morning.

He just looks at me.

135

"You want me to pop the question."

"No."

"Yes you do," he says, edging around the table.

I leave the house. The next morning, when I tell him to leave again, he proposes marriage. But this time I have a threat to make.

"I'm calling the state asylum," I say. "You're berserk."

He leans over and spins his finger around his ear.

"Commit me then," he says. "I'm crazy with love."

Something in this all has made me realize that Karl has read as many books as I, and that his fantasies have always stopped before the woman came home worn out from cutting beef into steaks with an electric saw.

"It's not just you," I tell him. "I don't want to get married. With you around I get no sleep. I'm tired all the time. All day I'm giving wrong change and I don't have any dreams. I'm the kind of person that likes having dreams. Now I have to see you every morning when I wake up and I forget if I dreamed anything or even slept at all, because right away you're on me with your hot breath."

He stands up and pushes his chest, hard, against mine, and runs his hands down my back and puts his mouth on my mouth. I don't have a damn thing to defend myself with. I push him down hard on the chair and sit, eager, in his lap. But all the while, I am aware that I am living on Karl's borrowed terms.

They might as well cart me off in a wet sheet too, I think.

"I'm like some kind of animal," I say, when it is over.

"What kind?" he asks, lazy. We are laying on the kitchen floor.

"A big stupid heifer."

He doesn't hear what I say though. I get up. I smooth my clothes down and drive off to the shop. But all day, as I wait on customers and tend fire in the smoke room, as I order from

136

suppliers and slice the head cheese and peg up and down the cribbage board, I am setting my mind hard against the situation.

"I'm going home," I say to Mary, when work is done, "and getting rid of him."

We are standing in the back entry alone; all the men are gone. I know she is going to say something strange.

"I had an insight," she says. "If you do, he'll take his life."

I look at the furnace in the corner, not at her, and I think that I hear a false note in her voice.

"He's not going to kill himself," I tell her. "He's not the type. And you . . ."—I am angry now—"you don't know what you want. At the same time you're jealous of Karl and me, you don't want us apart. You're confused."

She takes her apron off and hangs it on a hook. If she wasn't so proud, so good at hardening her heart, she might have said what kind of time this had been for her alone. She might have said how all this hurt because she once made a play for Russell, and he resisted.

But she turns and sets her teeth.

"Call me up when it's over," she says, "and we'll drive out to The Brunch Bar."

This is a restaurant where we like to go on busy nights when there is no time for cooking. I know her saying this has taken effort, so I feel sorry.

"Give me one hour, then I'll call you," I say.

As usual, when I get home, Karl is sitting at the kitchen table. The first thing I do is fetch his sample case from the couch where he parks it, handy for when the customers start pouring in. I carry it into the kitchen, put it down, and kick it across the linoleum. The leather screeches but the knives make no sound inside their velvet.

"What do you think I'm trying to tell you?" I ask.

He is sitting before the day's dirty dishes, half-full ashtrays,

137

and crumbs of bread. He wears his suit pants, the dark red vest, and a shirt that belongs to Russell. If I have any hesitations, the shirt erases them.

"Get out," I say.

But he only shrugs and smiles.

"I can't go yet," he says. "It's time for the matinee."

I step closer, not close enough so he can grab me, just to where there is no chance he can escape my gaze. He bends down. He lights a match off the sole of his shoe and starts blowing harsh smoke into the air. My mind is shaking from the strain, but my expression is still firm. It isn't until he smokes his Lucky to the nub, and speaks, that I falter.

"Don't chuck me. I'm the father," he says.

I hold my eyes trained on his forehead, not having really heard or understood what he said. He laughs. He puts his hands up like a bank clerk in a holdup and then I give him the once over, take him in as if he was a stranger. He is better looking than I am, with the dark eyes, red lips and pale complexion of a movie actor. His drinking has not told on him, not his smoking either. His teeth have stayed pearly and white, although his fingers are stained rubbery orange from the curling smoke.

"I give up! You're the stupidest woman I ever met." He puts his arms down, lights another cigarette from the first. "Here you're knocked up," he says suddenly, "and you don't even know it."

I suppose I do look stupid, knowing at that instant what he says is true.

"You're going to have my baby," he says in a calmer voice, before I can recover my sense.

"You don't know."

I grab his suitcase and heave it past him through the screen door. It tears right through the rotten mesh and thumps hard on the porch. He is silent for a long time, letting this act sink in.

"You don't love me," he says.

"I don't love you," I answer.

"What about my baby?"

"There's not a baby."

And now he starts moving. He backs away from me toward the door, but he cannot go through it.

"Get going," I say.

"Not yet." His voice is desperate.

"What now?"

"A souvenir. I don't have anything to remember you." If he cries, I know I'll break down, so I grab the object closest to my hand, a book I've had sitting on the top of the refrigerator. I won it somewhere and never opened the cover. I hold it out to him.

"Here," I say.

He takes the book, and then there is no other excuse. He edges down the steps and finally off at a slow walk through the grass, down the road. I stand there a long time, watching him from the door, before he shrinks into the distance and is gone. And then, once I feel certain he has walked all the way to Argus, maybe hopped a bus or hitched down Highway 30 south, I lay my head down on the table and let my mind go.

The first thing I do once I am better is to dial Mary's number.

"I got rid of him," I say into the phone.

"Give me ten minutes," she says, "I'll come and get you."

"Just wait," I say. "I have to have some time off."

"What for?"

"I went and got myself into the family way."

She says nothing. I listen to the silence on her end before I finally hear her take the phone from her ear, and put it down.

In the love books a baby never comes of it all, so again I am not prepared. I do not expect the weakness in my legs or the swelling ankles. The tales of burning love never mention how I lie awake, alone in the heat of an August night, and panic. I know the child feels me thinking. It turns over and over, so furiously that I know it must be wound on its cord. I fear that something has gone wrong with it. The mind is not right, just like the father's. Or it will look like the sick sheep I had to club. A million probable, terrible, things will go wrong. And then, as I am lying there worrying into the dark, bottles start going off under the house. Russell's brew is exploding and all night, with the baby turning, I keep dreaming and waking to the sound of glass flying through the earth.

Mary's Night

After Mary hung up the phone on Celestine, she took the crowbar from the top of the refrigerator, where Pete had kept it, too, and went back to her utility room to open the crate that was delivered last month from Florida.

The box had been sitting in one spot so long that drill bits, clothespins, and burned-out light bulbs had collected on top. Mary moved the clutter to a windowsill and began prying nails from the rough pine boards. It was just turning to dusk outside, but she had enough light to see by and didn't stop until she'd pulled off two sides of the wooden box. It contained a cabinet. She switched on the lights in a blaze.

The cabinet was small, elegant, carved of dark-stained wood with ornate cast-iron legs and drawer pulls. Each drawer was decorated with a curving design of amber-colored wood. The top was hinged. Mary opened it, removed the packing, and lifted out the sewing machine. Then she stood back and contemplated. It was like a little black mechanical dragon, with one busy, murderous fang. After a while, she put the machine down and let the hinged top fall over it. Then she switched off the light, went back to the kitchen, and picked up the phone.

It was Sita's number that she dialed, an out-of-town exchange because Sita had just sold the restaurant and moved out to Blue Mound with her scientific husband.

"What do you want?" said Sita, when she heard Mary's voice.

"Nothing from you," said Mary. "I've got something of yours, though."

Sita was silent, trying to think what this thing could be. She finally had to ask.

"A sewing machine," said Mary.

"I've already got one," said Sita.

"I know," Mary answered. "Your aunt sent you another."

Sita had to think for a moment, then she remembered Adelaide and how she had liked to sew. She remembered the fur collars, the turned-out bows, the fashionable adjustments to out-of-date dresses.

"I'll get Louis to pick it up," she said.

"It's in the back room," said Mary.

Then she hung up and put the bar away on the refrigerator. She stood in the brilliance and faint buzzing of the fluorescent ring.

Nothing came back to her from the stillness outside except the faint, restless clinking of the dog's chain, and the acid fragrance of tomato vines he had broken digging bones along the wall. This time of night, Mary usually called her dogs in and fell asleep reading. But tonight was ripe with significance. Tonight was full of hidden signs.

She thought of her tarot pack, kept beneath her mattress to absorb her dream's vibrations as the gypsy instructions advised. She had a Ouija board. A customer had shown her a certain way to crack an egg into a jar of water and read the yolk. But none of these methods came close to duplicating the splendor of the day she had smashed her face in ice and seen her brother as if through a magic mirror. Standing on her clean linoleum, thinking forward, she willed a sign to come.

A steer moaned in the stock pens. A light breeze set up a rustle in the thickets of clenched and ragged roses in the yard. Moths banged the screen door.

Mary turned off the light and went outside. She began to walk. Beyond her fences the backyards were a maze of pens, storage sheds, old boxcars and chicken runs full of rusting equipment. Uncle Pete got his hands on a lot of things in his life. A great iron bathtub, used for scalding the hair off pigs, sat in the weeds

142

collecting ferrous rainwater, breeding midges. Beyond the junk there was Fritzie's shelterbelt of mulberry, evergreen, wild plum and cedar. Around the trees, the grass was cool, layered, densely green. Mary stood breathing the scent of needles and leaves, and thought of Karl.

Again, she saw him gathering the branch, its white blooms and invisible scent to his face so long ago. She saw his eyes close in delicate greed. His lips opened. And then she saw Celestine too, her mouth deep, her arms spread and grasping, her body more solid than the tree Karl had embraced before he vanished.

The yard light cast a faint glow from behind. The evergreens seemed impenetrably dark, even frightening. Mary thought of bums, owls, rabid skunks and mice that the shelterbelt might harbor. Yet, she stepped forward into the overgrown grass. With that first step, she felt gravity collect in her legs. At the next step her eyes itched for sleep. She plunged forward anyway, through the crossed branches.

The earth was damp, cool, and Mary sank into the grass. It seemed, in her trance, that a great deal of time went by. The plums were green and hard when she first lay down, the mulberry pips invisible, the grass green and pliable. Then the moon came up, stars wheeled in sequined patterns, birds took flight. The season waned and Celestine's baby grew large as day.

It was a girl, much larger than Mary's lost baby brother, but just as vigorous, and with a headful of blazing dark red curls.

She peered at Mary, her eyes the gray-blue of newborns, unfocused but willful already, and of a stubborn intensity that Mary recognized as her own. Then the dark deepened and the night grew deliciously soft. From where she lay, Mary heard the wild plums ripen. They grew plump on their thin stems and fell, knocked off by wind. In her sleep she heard them drop through the long brittle grass and collect all around her in a glorious waste.

SITA KOZKA

JUST WEEKS AFTER the food-poisoning fiasco at my restaurant, I quietly married Louis and he resigned as state health inspector to take a county job that would keep us near forever. Louis sold his house in Bismarck and moved all of his scientific equipment to Blue Mound, where we lived in the big split-level house, with colonial details and shutters, that Jimmy had built as a kind of showplace. And there, although we had only been married two months, it was as if Louis and I had been together all our lives. Maybe it was because he had to take care of me. During the excitement of moving and a failing business, my nerves were strained to nothing. Luckily our house has a huge backyard, and while I was recuperating from my troubles, I occupied myself with growing ornamental shrubs, perennials, and climbing vines.

Because of the divorce, I had lapsed from the church. Louis tried to convince me there was nothing to it in the first place, but I was not entirely happy about leaving. For many years Saint Catherine's had been important in my life, and religion itself still had a strict hold. Among other things, the idea of relying only on Louis and myself for answers and assistance was new. I was not sure I liked it. But I tried to be strong, ready for the unexpected, and perhaps for that reason I was not dismayed the morning I found my cousin sleeping, sodden, in my trained clematis. I did not recognize him when I first discovered him. I hadn't seen him in twenty-five years. He had one arm around a suitcase and he held a little book.

He opened his eyes.

"Hello there, Sita," he said from where he lay. He had got into my backyard by rolling beneath the fence. "I suppose you don't recognize me," he said, scrambling to his feet and then carefully untangling himself from the leaves, "I'm your cousin Karl."

A wanderer and a salesman is what I'd heard he'd become. He looked well-trampled by the adventures of life. He was frayed at the neck and cuff. Hatless. His face was handsome in an overly pretty, disturbing way, but his lips were too red, as if he had a hangover. His eyes hung half shut, pouched and weary. His oiled black hair flopped down in strands around his ears.

He looked suspicious, even dangerous in his shabby clothes. Yet I was interested. I knew if he attacked me all I had to do is scream. Louis was in the garage, not ten feet away, feeding his entomological specimens. I gripped my trowel like a weapon while Karl was talking, and decided if he made a fast move I would split his skull. My white canvas gloves would obscure any fingerprints. Louis and I could bury him beneath the dahlias with the murder weapon. In the past weeks I'd consumed boxes of mysteries to soothe my nerves.

"Karl Adare," he repeated. "I'm your cousin, remember? I was on my way to a sales conference. I got here early and didn't want to wake you."

I supposed it was a compliment to have a long-lost cousin visit, even if he crawled in through the flower bed. It certainly would have been news around here, second only to my own divorce and sudden remarriage. With my nerves, and the restaurant, on top of all that, it seemed I had supplied Blue Mound and Argus with gossip all month. The thought gave me a headache. I put down my trowel.

"How nice to see you," I said, remembering my manners, "after all this time. You'll join us for lunch, I hope?"

He nodded yes, and looked around at the yard. "Not bad," he said. The way his voice squeezed shut I knew he was envious of my banks of rich flowers, the tile patio, the house which I'd heard people call a mansion, the largest house in Blue Mound. Louis had inherited good farmland, which he rented out. Even though Louis had closed down the restaurant, we could afford to keep the place up.

"And tell me about yourself," I said, indicating his suitcase and the thick little book in his hands. The book looked familiar, black with reddish diamonds on the cover, and once he cracked the paper glued inside and opened it, I knew why. It was a Bible, a rather typical cheap version of the New Testament.

"There's room to record family events," he said, looking into the cover. "Births, deaths, marriages."

He seemed to be talking to himself, so I made no comment. I didn't want him to try and sell me the book.

"Let's sit down," I said, but he seemed to have read my mind because he didn't snap the book shut or follow me, but continued to look morosely into the cover.

He's preparing a pitch, I thought, and I took his arm.

"You must be tired," I said, "on the road so often."

"I am," he agreed, looking at me steadily and gratefully. "I'm awfully glad to see you, Sita. It's been a long time."

"Too long," I said in a warm voice, although the truth was I'd never missed him, hardly thought about him in all those years, and I was beginning to suspect, just slightly, from nothing I could put my finger on really, that he'd looked me up in the hope of an easy sale.

Just at that moment Louis walked out into the yard. He always looked keenly at people but then never seemed to recall the slightest thing about them once they were gone. Now he stared penetratingly at Karl. Karl smiled back, uncertainly. "I'm Sita's cousin," he called to Louis. "Been a long time!" But Louis ignored him and walked over to the compost pile to gather a few more of his specimens.

"What's he doing?" Karl wondered.

"Digging worms."

"What for?"

"To see how they break down organic matter."

Louis kept me abreast of his every thought. For his new post as extension agent, he was now collecting data about the area pests and local helpers. Earthworms were helpers, and Louis was experimenting with their habitat. What to put in the ground to attract their help.

"They make humus," I informed Karl in a stern voice, for his attention had wandered. He was taking in the details of our home again, my white cast-iron lawn furniture, the clipped and flowering shrubs. He soon included me in his accounts, giving me a slow, bold look. I was not at my slimmest, but according to Louis contentment fit me best, and I knew that my color was good.

"Have I changed?" I said, and then, embarrassed by the coy note in my voice, I answered my own question. "Of course I have. Who wouldn't?"

"Beautiful as ever," said Karl. I turned away. Louis rarely gave me compliments. But then he was often deep in his abstract thoughts. What Karl said meant more to me than it should have, and so I was unable to keep from saying what I said next.

"Gray hairs, a few lines here and there. The years show."

"Oh no," said Karl, "you're prettier now. Maturity becomes you."

"It does?" I was acting foolish as a peacock.

"Yes," he said.

We had a long silent moment between us, almost intimate, and then more words popped out of my mouth.

"All flesh is grass," I said, hardly believing my own voice, and

147

because of the strangeness hearing the phrase as entirely new. We stood uncomfortably, looking at the lawn, and I noticed that the whole yard was covered with the same kind of grass that grew in cemeteries—fine, short-cropped grass of a brilliant green color.

"I'll get lunch," I said, to interrupt myself.

I left my cousin watching Louis pull worms from the mulch, and I went in to make us a plateful of sandwiches for an early lunch. Ham salad. I have a grinder that attaches to my sink. I was mixing the ground ham with capers and mayonnaise when Karl stepped up to the screen door and banged on it lightly.

"Could I use your facilities?"

"Of course," I said.

I let him in. He put the suitcase by the door and laid the book on my kitchen counter as he walked past. He did it so casually that I thought he had done it on purpose, to interest me in it. And so, while he was upstairs, I picked up the book. I examined the dull red diamonds on the cover. Besides being a New Testament, the book still reminded me of something else. It took several moments of concentration for me to place where I had seen it before. Then I knew. Last year at a raffle for the Saint Catherine's Society we had given away a New Testament like this, and Celestine James had won it.

"This may be a coincidence," I said to Karl when he returned from upstairs, "but a book just like this belonged to a former friend of mine."

He picked up the book, weighed it, and pressed it in my hands. "You can have it," he said. "Fill it up."

Then he hoisted his suitcase and went out to sit on the lawn furniture with Louis. I was puzzled by his words until I remembered about the spaces for family events. I opened the book.

Saint Catherine Society, was stamped inside the cover, and then the date. May 4, 1952, and the name Celestine James.

"Aha!" I said, just like a detective in a poorly written crime drama. Then, obscurely ashamed at my discovery, I snapped the book shut and continued mixing ingredients in the milk glass bowl. Having outgrown my acquaintance with Celestine James, I wasn't sure how to handle the Bible anyway. For years I'd had nothing to do with her. I spread the mixture on pieces of bread and cut the sandwiches in triangles and went out. Karl had evidently told my husband that lunch was coming, for Louis had washed with the garden hose, and now the men were balanced on the little wrought-iron chairs. The table came no higher than their knees. The sight was comical. But I had learned not to laugh at everything that looked absurd. Laughter had been one symptom of my thinning nerves.

"Isn't it lovely," I said, "the sun's so mild."

I put the tray down, with everything on it except the pitcher and glasses, and I went back for those. When I came out again I saw that the men had started eating, which annoyed me.

"What bad manners the two of you have!" I exclaimed.

"You're right," said Louis, putting down his sandwich and passing me the plate. My cousin, however, continued to take his food. I watched him pick up a sandwich and bring it to his lips, then bite it with his white teeth. One, two, and the sandwich was snapped down. I stared, wondering if he'd done something to Celestine, perhaps threatened her, in order to get the book. Or perhaps he knocked her out. And then there was the suitcase. Did he have more of her possessions tucked away inside of that?

Louis cleared his throat and spoke in the humoring tone I knew.

"Sita, you're keeping rather a close eye on our visitor, aren't you?"

I looked down at my plate. I couldn't help myself. I whispered.

"The way my cousin eats is very sinister."

"No it's not," said Louis, and cast around for some other topic of conversation. "Hummingbirds are attracted to Sita's trumpet

149

vines," he said. I smiled at Karl, but he was eating faster than ever. I supposed he had not heard my whispered comment.

"Yes," I went on, "they hover with their beaks reaching down into the . . . what is it . . . ?"

"The ovary."

". . . the ovary of the flower."

Karl gulped down a last bite of sandwich and nodded faintly at both of us. I noticed suddenly, although it must have been happening all along, that the sharp iron legs of his chair were digging into the damp lawn. The ground beneath him was evidently very soft, perhaps from all the earthworm activity, and he was settling by slow degrees. The table fit over his knees quite easily now. He seemed not to notice, however, and gave me a tight smile.

I returned the smile, but as we bit into more sandwiches without speaking, I realized why Karl was here.

He had robbed Celestine and we were next. Why else would he have been hiding in the clematis, spying, learning our habits, if not in order to steal from us with ease? And another thing. He had not gone upstairs to use the facilities, but to loot my jewelry box. It seemed as though I had even seen him do this myself. I saw him snap off the tiny lock, pluck up my silver pin, diamond locket, reclaim my necklace of old garnets. I saw him drop my treasures in his pocket. My brooches, my rings, my amethyst.

"I'm going inside, fellows," I announced lightly, and rose.

Louis seemed to sense something. He frowned at the heavy lace of the table. But I was certain of Karl's guilt, now, and went indoors to use the phone.

"The largest hummingbird," I heard Louis say as I walked off, "is a whopping nine inches. Lives down in South America." I knew that Louis was keeping my cousin entertained with some marvel, and sure enough, when I had made the proper phone call and returned, I saw that he had so entranced Karl that my cousin had sunk noticeably farther. He was now at chest level with the table. His arms were crossed in front of him.

"It's sad," I said, fixing him with a look, "how some people just can't keep their hands off of other people's property."

"That's true," said my husband in an earnest voice. "Remember how the little scissors used to vanish from the dissecting kits?"

"Louis taught," I informed my cousin. "He taught in a high school."

"Know where those scissors went?" asked Louis.

Karl's eyes widened and he lifted his shoulders. His mouth was full of sandwich, so he couldn't answer.

"Girls stole them to manicure their nails!" said my husband.

Just then Sheriff Pausch came down the flagstones. He was a little man with a sharp doggish face and a deep, surprising voice that boomed godlike from his bullhorn during tornado alerts. Before becoming a sheriff he'd taught botany, so he and Louis had much in common. They were members of the Blue Mound Mycological Society, which had already had its first meeting in our basement. It seemed odd to have him here on official business, in his tan uniform, with a paper in his hand instead of bread bags full of dried fungus.

Karl's eyes went still wider when he saw the sheriff. His alarm put the last convincing touches on his guilt. He put his hand out and said, "Please, take my seat."

"No thank you," said Sheriff Pausch firmly, motioning Karl to stay seated. "There's been a complaint."

Karl's face turned childish, tipped upward from his low seat, stricken.

"I'll get the evidence," I muttered, rising to go.

"Stay here," said Louis. "What's all of this about?"

"Your wife called me," said Sheriff Pausch, looking surprised and lowering his voice. "She said something about a theft."

I pointed down at Karl, and gave him a cold glare. "He stole

151

Celestine James's New Testament," I said, "then he went through my jewelry box. He took necklaces, pins, whatever he could lay his hands on. Stuffed them in his pocket. Search him!" I urged the two men. "See for yourself!"

"Put your hands in the air," said Sheriff Pausch in his deep voice. He stepped behind Karl and quickly patted him up and down.

"Excuse me," he said, moving back to face Karl, who had gone pale as a sheet. "You can put your hands down now," said the sheriff, flushing down to the opening in his shirt. "There seems to have been a mistake."

There was a long moment of tension. I looked at each of the men carefully. They looked carefully at me.

"It's true," I finally said. "Let me fetch the book."

"I think there has been a mistake," Sheriff Pausch repeated, and just that suddenly, because there was a wary gentleness in his voice, I knew that I had done something very wrong. Worse yet, I knew that something even more wrong was going to happen. I looked down at Karl. The legs of his chair had sunk still farther.

"Stop . . . that," I slowly commanded.

"Sita, sit down now, please," said Louis.

But I was locked in an upright position by Karl's dark strained stare. I could not take my eyes away although I had to bend across the table to see him clearly, he'd sunk so far. The air was very still. The tiny birds, light as moths, hovered in the trumpet flowers. One note sounded. I meant to ask Louis if he heard it as well. But then my cousin leaned over sideways and pulled the heavy-looking case, the one he'd dragged through the clematis, onto his lap. He sat there with the case clasped in his arms, perhaps intending to open it, perhaps intending to go. Instead, something happened.

The case was so heavy, resting on his lap and knees, that his feet began to bury themselves in the earth and very swiftly the

152

lawn rose to his knees. I said nothing. I was paralyzed with fear. I had betrayed him and now I could only watch as the man, the chair, continued to sink. The case submerged. The lawn crept up his oxblood shirt. The grass brushed his chin. And still he continued to go down.

It is too late, I thought, watching him, unless he says the healing words.

"*Mea culpa*," I gasped. "*Mea maxima culpa.*"

But already his mouth was sealed by earth. His ears were stopped. His mild, sad eyes were covered and then there was only the pale strip of his forehead. The earth paused before swallowing him entirely, and then, quite suddenly, the rest of him went under. The last I saw was the careless white cross in his oiled hair. The ground shook slightly to cover him, and there was nothing where he had been.

I stared at the peaceful grass for a long while and then looked up. Louis and the sheriff were watching me. It seemed as though they were waiting for me to tell them what this meant.

"We wake when we die. We are all judged," I said.

Then I went down to the tree where my silver was hung. Bracelets and rings and old coins of it. I put my hands out. The leaves moved over me, gleaming and sharpened, with tarnished edges. They fell off in mounds. The air was a glittering dry rain. While I was down there I said many things. Louis wrote them all on a pad of paper.

I described the tree in detail. It bore the leaves of my betrayal. The roots reached under everything. Everywhere I walked I had to step on the dead, who lay tangled and cradled, waiting for the trumpet, for the voice on the bullhorn, for the little book to open that held a million names.

"You are not in the book," I told Louis. "You are down there with your specimens."

Russell's Night

Over the summer, Russell slowly built himself a fishing shack, and then, in the fall, he dragged it through two fields and left it on the bank where the river slowed and deepened before it bent away from Argus. When the river froze into an angle of black iron, he pushed the shack out onto the ice, drilled a hole with his auger, and began going there often.

Sliding down the steep bank on a raw December afternoon, he caught his scoop net in a nest of old flood debris and plunged into a spider web of thick dead vines that held him. He thrashed for several moments and then quit. The web was oddly comfortable, a hammock in just his shape once he relaxed. He groped for the flask of Four Roses stowed inside the blanket lining of his long denim jacket, then took a pull.

Russell blew into his fingers and put the bottle back in his pocket. No matter how cold it was he never wore gloves anymore, preferring his hands to harden now that he didn't have to count bills or change. He needed callous to tighten bolts, touch hot radiator caps, work lug nuts free and on the weekends clean fish. He looked up into the low clouds and tilted his pint back. Maybe it would snow. The breeze was warm enough. What he liked about not working at a regular job was exactly this. He could lay here all afternoon if he felt like it and just get drunk. But he wasn't much of a drinker, and after a while he freed himself and made his way down to his shack.

He kept a padlock on the door now that Celestine had found his place. Weeks ago, he'd gone in and found everything was tampered with, not drastically, just enough so he knew she had been there. He was positive that it was her, even though she had left no direct evidence. The place had the skewed feeling of something vaguely wrong, but then he realized it was only that everything had been neatened. That was Celestine's habit around the house when she was restless. His coffee cans of fishing tackle had been pushed into a careful row. One of the sandbags he used to weight the house so it wouldn't blow over was patched with cloth tape where sand had trickled out. He always kept the tape in his tackle box. She had put it back. Russell noticed that a can of Sterno had been punched, burned, then replaced on its shelf with the others. His little wire stove was hung back on its hook, and his water can and coffeepot were clean, like he always left them. Still, he didn't like Celestine to visit. He knew she kept coming back because she wanted to talk to him, but he wanted to avoid her for a while longer.

Now, since the padlock was on the door, he knew she hadn't been inside, though her footprints were scattered in the snow.

He took out his key and snapped the lock open, then stepped into the mild green fish-smelling air. Today it seemed warm inside even with no heater. Warmth was trapped in the tarpaper walls. In the middle of the house, black in the center of the ice floor, the hole he'd cut two days ago was still open. He scooped out the slush with a coffee can and dumped it beside the door. Then he baited a hook and a large dangling lure that was beaten and polished like a woman's silver earring. He unfolded the woven-mesh lawn chair he kept propped against one wall, sat down, and started to fish. His eyes had completely adjusted to the dim interior now, and the gray light, spreading down from the small window, one he'd scavenged from a ruined chickenhouse, lit the board walls with a calm and diffuse low radiance.

His leg, the one with the old spiral fracture and shrapnel wounds, the left gimp leg, ached from the fall he'd taken coming down the bank. He rubbed his thigh slowly with one hand and kept the other on the pole he'd stuck through a slat of his chair. He watched the line, the red-white bobber, and thought about nothing. Whenever Celestine came into his mind he put her out of it. He hadn't been home, or spoken to her, except for that one day when he'd noticed the obvious.

Back in July, he'd heard that her boyfriend had left, but Russell had been in no hurry to come down from the reservation. Then one night he'd caught a ride down to Argus, late, and slipped into his room while Celestine was sleeping. He meant to surprise her with breakfast, but she was already awake and up by the time he came out of his door into the narrow hall.

He'd mumbled, looking down, ashamed to be caught in a sagging pair of union long johns. Celestine was wearing nothing but her slip though, and her jutting outline registered.

Before she recognized him, she shouted in alarm, and then she blushed, looked down, and smiled at her news.

"I wasn't going to tell you this way, but you're an uncle."

Russell walked past her without a word and went into the bathroom. He carefully latched the door. Inside, he stared at the brownish speckled linoleum floor until he felt suddenly and strangely dizzy. To clear his thoughts, he shook himself all over like a dog, then washed his face. Celestine banged on the door.

"You don't have to be like that," she said. "I'm married."

"It's your funeral," he answered. Those were the last words they had spoken.

After he was done in the bathroom, he went downstairs and rifled through the refrigerator shelves quickly, hoping Celestine or the salesman would not come into the kitchen before he'd packed himself a lunch and left.

Even when Mary told him that Karl was long gone, he couldn't make himself go back. Something held him.

Now the pole lurched against his hand, pulling down the bobber. He grabbed the line between his fingers, waited seconds, then tugged it gently back, hoping he could secure the hook in the fish's jaw. The line burned off his thumb. He'd done it. The

156

fish must be large, he thought, a half-starved northern maybe, one he'd have to play to land. He reeled in and out, tiring it slowly, until finally he brought it up, not so big as he'd imagined once it broke water, and so exhausted it hardly flopped in the net. It was a long thin many-toothed pike, mottled a dark rich green, beautiful and ferociously cold, and too young. After he'd unfastened his hook and tackle gingerly from its mouth, then wet his hands and slid the fish back beneath the ice, Russell reset his line and settled into his chair again. His body heat and the colorless light had warmed the house. He flexed his hands on his knees to warm the fingers and hoped that he would not catch the same fish twice. As he sat there, waiting, the picture of Celestine in the slip, shadowed in the narrow hall, full and outcurved like the prow of a boat, rose in his mind. This time he let her stay.

She was there when he felt the first tightening in his chest.

Soon it turned into a slow tingling, a nerve throbbing in his arm and a feeling of rich tiredness elsewhere. There was no pain. Only a sharp burst as if the whiskey had expanded, as if it had flooded his brain. He looked around in surprise. As on the day he'd come here weeks ago to find things tampered with, everything looked vaguely distorted. It seemed as though the light itself had now been disturbed. It hung in wavering sheets. Then the pain crashed out. It coiled and uncoiled like a big steel spring, out and in, until it suddenly shrank and collapsed to a black button.

Around five that evening, Celestine came down the banks, falling just where Russell had, but getting out at once and retrieving her flashlight from the snow. When she reached the ice she almost turned back. It was near dusk and he would have needed light. The shack was dark. But then, in the play of her flashlight beam, she saw the unsnapped padlock.

She walked over the hard-packed river snow and opened the door. Her flashlight picked out Russell's slumped form in the lawn chair, and at first she thought, ridiculously, that he'd fallen asleep with the pole wedged in his hands. Then she noticed that the line had snapped. She walked in, touched his back, and spoke his name. When he took a shuddering breath she put her arm around his chest and pulled him out of the chair, dragged him over to the sandbags, and laid him down. After a moment he opened his eyes.

"I'll get help," she whispered. Her voice echoed in the shack, and then everything around her went into slow motion like a nightmare. Things tried to hold her back as she started running. The ice. The snow. The tangled brush. The fields. Even the air. It seemed like hours before she finally reached her car.

WALLACE PFEF

I HAVE NEVER married, but I do have a girl friend referred to by the people of Argus as "Pfef's poor dead sweetheart." She is a long gray face behind glass. Her photograph, in its polished brass frame, keeps discreet watch over my living room. My visitors inquire about the collection of Hummel figures, the souvenir spoons in their rack, the icy bells I collect, crystal bells. But they do not ask about my poor dead sweetheart, although, as they examine my objects, they will pause before her portrait as if to pay their respects.

To tell the truth, I don't know the woman in the picture.

I bought her many years ago at one of those sad Minnesota farm auctions. She was among the empty canning jars, pincushions, butter dishes, and chipped vases in a box I bid out for five dollars. Whoever she is, with her prominent jaw, young worn mouth, and neatly waved hair, she is part of town legend now. I've invented little things about her as they occur to me: her disease was encephalitis. Common at the time, if you lived around horses. She went into a trance from which she never awakened. Her feet were slim and long to match her jaw, and she was tall.

Because of the poor dead sweetheart, I've never had to marry. I've squired women around and made myself available as a sort of one-man dinner-partner service to Argussian widows. Husbands have even hinted jealously of my attentions to their wives. But people have long since stopped believing I would ever desert the picture in my living room.

"She has too strong a hold on him. He can't forget her," they say.

I live in the flat, treeless valley where sugar beets grow. It is intemperate here, a climate of violent extremes. I do like storms, though, and bad weather of all types. For then I have an excuse to stay in bed, reading crime and espionage, dozing occasionally, and listening to the wind, a great hand slapping at my house. *Whap! Whap!* The beams and hidden studs squeak and quiver. I never regret having built so far out of town, on the road out of Argus, heading north, even though it is rarely traveled by any but those who must. It is beautiful here. My view is a stark horizon of grays and browns. I built as an incentive to other home builders, but my only neighbors have been here all along. Celestine and her baby now are my nearest, only the two of them since her brother's unfortunate stroke.

But first, to introduce myself.

I'm Wallace Pfef. Chamber of commerce, Sugar Beet Promoters, Optimists, Knights of Columbus, park board, and other organizations too numerous to mention. In addition to supporting the B# Piano Club and managing the town swimming pool, I am the one who is bringing beets to the valley, beets that have yet to fail as a cash crop anywhere, beets that will make refined white sugar every bit as American as corn on the cob.

There has been resistance to my proposition, and why not? Agronomists value cyclical regularities. They are suspicious of innovation, and my business is courting change. To woo them, I've become the friend to agricultural co-ops and visited each area farmer individually. I've drunk sloe gin and schnapps and nameless basement brews. In town I've joined up with a vengeance, for I know that within the fraternal orders lies power. Eagles, Moose, Kiwanis, Elk. I need to belong. I've gained a hundred ears, pumped hands, exchanged secret passwords with my brothers. I've told them how beets are much more than a simple crop. They are the perfect marriage between nature and technology. Like crude oil, the beet needs refining, and that means Refinery. That spells local industry. Everyone benefits.

I got sold on the beet at the 1952 Home, Crop, and Livestock Convention in Minneapolis. Many of those in the audience around me were salesmen, but none as good as Karl Adare.

I never knew it, had probably hidden it deep away, but I found the attraction as easy as breathing in and breathing out. And so it happened. And there I was, member of the Kiwanis, eating prime rib and accepting choice bits of game hen from the fork of another man. Sheer madness. Yet I felt amazed, as if the clouds had blown away, as if the bare bones were finally visible. I was queer.

I don't know why, either, except that the Pfefs have always been dissatisfied. We came over from the great Ruhr Valley, perhaps even then carrying a race memory of the raw white beet. In America, we moved often, complaining that something was not quite right. Maybe in the end it was us, my father's schemes that failed, and my sisters, who have turned into alcoholic, wasting farmwives. Up until Minneapolis, I was the stability, the surprise in the family.

It was a shock when Karl jumped on the bed and began to bounce. I'd looked for some topic of mutual interest, and hit a nerve when I asked about his sister. I didn't blame him once he told me her name. I knew Mary from grade school. She was ruthless. I'd seen her slow work on Sita Kozka. Mary pulled nerves like string in a blanket until the whole loose-woven fabric of Sita's mind came unraveled. There had been one, two, crack-ups by that time. And, too, Mary was shrewd. She had a reputation for getting and keeping, while I already had a partial sense of what slipped past Karl.

But while Karl went up and down, smacking the ceiling with

161

the palm of his hand, I had no thought of this. I feared some sort of damage, to the bed, not him. I feared he would break the springs in the mattress or the frame would collapse. I can still see it clearly, as in a snapshot: Karl hunched in his tight black pants, tie whirling free, a cutout against the ornate pressed tin of the hotel ceiling.

Then he hit.

I am a good man in someone else's crisis and did not panic. The back was injured. *Immobilize*, I thought. I saw that the right things were done. When he came to in traction, cast in plaster, in what must have been unimaginable pain, he smiled dreamily through grit teeth and rolled his eyes.

"Still here," he observed.

"Of course."

I was not allowed to touch, just look, and I tried to convey everything that way. My mistake. He seemed repelled by my sympathy. Then the drugs sent him back where he'd been, and I was left to sit. I watched for hours. It was midnight before I went back to my room. And even then I racked up a phone bill searching Minneapolis and Saint Paul for a florist who would deliver that time of night.

In the days that followed the accident, Karl hummed tunes or stared at the ceiling all day, living in his own mind, not at all interested in me or the hospital surroundings. He hardly spoke to me; however, I made friends. To this day, I correspond with the morning nurse there. She thought that Karl was mentally unbalanced, he enjoyed his confinement so.

"Good-bye," I said one morning, walking onto the ward. He'd had a private room for one week and not a single visitor except me. I held my hat. My light coat was draped on one arm. "I have to dash," I said. "Everyone in Argus will wonder what's become of me."

He looked well, shaved already, skin freshened, hair combed. It was as though he'd put on the cast for a joke.

162

"Bon voyage," he said, and turned the page of some magazine.

I walked out, angry at myself for being a fool. I thought I'd never see him again.

I had my half-finished house to complete, and I was living in the basement while the top was constructed. I took my time getting it done right. Things went slow, but when the home was finally livable it was perfect. The walls were real plaster. I had an insulated picture window, built-in shelves, and recessed lights to set off my collections. I moved in before the carpets were laid, before the kitchen appliances were hooked up, before the cabinets were sanded. The first thing I brought in was the photograph of my poor dead sweetheart, younger and more earnest than when I'd bought her. I set her on my living-room shelf. She stared out at the raw white room, the primed walls, the plastic-sheeted easy chair and picture window.

"In theory," I said to her, "all this is yours." I drank a toast to her with vegetable juice and got on with my work.

I am good at hiding facts for my own self-protection, at forgetting. So I forgot Karl most days. Yet there were times, walking into his sister's shop for my chop or stew meat, that I found him uncomfortably on the tip of my tongue. I wanted to tell her about him. I wanted to disrupt her smugness. But I was afraid of her grim manner, her cold eye, and couldn't get past the impersonal patience she felt was due to a customer. I only kept going there because The House of Meats had the freshest steak in town, and I preferred to have Celestine wait on me. In spite of her forbidding height and how she stood, knuckles on her hips, confronting each customer, she remembered names, problems, preferences and purchases from week to week. She'd ask how I liked the last of their homemade sauerbraten, or why I'd stopped buying the herring. I enjoyed our chats. I would never have guessed the outcome of things.

I'd just come home from the shop, in fact, one spring dusk, when the call came.

"How's Argus?" said the voice.

I said it was fine, although as usual the farmers were needing rain. I waited for the voice to identify itself, though from the first word I knew it was Karl.

"I'm in the cutlery line now," he told me. "Superior quality. I'm coming through tomorrow morning and thought I'd stop by. Maybe drop in on you, on Mary. Did you tell her about me?"

"Never," I said. I was so shocked that I stuttered and choked over directions to Argus. And that night I stayed up to all hours cleaning the house.

He showed up the night after, very late. In both relief and disappointment, I'd given up and turned off my porch lamp. I had put on pajamas, a quilted silk smoking jacket, tasseled slippers. When he rang the bell I peered from the upstairs window. I knew it would be better if my caller were anyone else.

The dark shape was indistinguishable. But once I'd flooded him with light, there he stood, blinking.

"Well," he said eventually, "you're a sight for sore eyes. Should I just stand here or are you going to let me in?"

"Come in," I said. And in he came.

I don't know how he got to my house. There was no car. Days went by. He seemed to have no firm intentions, besides his knives, and simply looked at me with his light cool eyes when I asked him what company he worked for. I didn't really care. It was enough for him to be there, wearing my clothes and towels, fixing toast for himself, at last making sense of my bed. I never knew what to ask from life, but now I did.

What I wished for and what I expected, however, were two different futures. So it did not surprise me two weeks later when he left one afternoon without a note, without warning.

I thought he might have finally gone to visit Mary, but when I stopped by her shop to pick up the ingredients for my dinner

164

there was no sign of him. I went ahead with the evening's preparations. He'd seemed to like my meat loaf, an unusual mixture
of ground veal, pork, beef, cream, and parsley, crisscrossed with
bacon and baked in a slow oven. I mashed potatoes, strained
squash, melted a little cheese for the potatoes. The careful stirring
and constant checking helped me pass the time. It was a warm
dusk, too. The heat gave me discomfort. That helped divert me,
but yet the night came on.

At last, I put aluminum foil over everything. I had a big glass
door in the kitchen, and beyond that a brick patio with two folding
lounge chairs of blocky redwood. I planned an arbor there, of
climbing grapes, lilacs, roses. I brought a light crocheted blanket
out for comfort, swaddled myself, lay back in the lounge chair,
and let the night come over me. My seeded lawn stretched thirty
feet west, then the field began. It was sugar beets, of course, a
low crop of thick, abrasive leaves. Over it the moon hung, a great
bell in emptiness.

What surprised me, what caused me the worst shock, was
where he went.

A week passed and only one dry, black corner of the meat loaf
remained. I fed it to the dog, a grumpy stray with tattered white
hair and a tail kinked and thin as a rat's. It lived around the edges
of the yard, fading in and out of the tall brush and sugar beets,
hunting cottontails. Sometimes it came directly to the glass door
and I'd feel its dull cold stare. I'd turn just in time to see its
starved haunches whirl. Then it would vanish, having eaten what
I'd set out.

Sometimes I think the dog was a kind of quisling, appearing
like that, leading me eventually to the house. I would never have
gone there myself, but then around dusk, one evening, I was
driving home when my headlights caught her up ahead on the
road toward the James place. She trotted just to the side of the
road, and I was afraid she'd be hit. I stopped ahead, tried to get

her to enter the car, but of course there was no chance of that. So I followed, low gear, straight to Celestine's. The dog went up the dirt drive and disappeared around back. I was anxious. She was so stealthy I thought she'd had a litter. I turned my headlights off, stepped from the car, and followed her into the backyard. I trespassed. Russell had once told me about his gun, filled with bird shot and hung directly over the back door. I felt the hot sting of those imaginary pellets as I crept around the foundation, just under the square of yellow light from the back windows. I heard voices. First there were only mumbles, then rising tones, then Karl.

When I recognized his voice, my brain stopped.

"That's a hell of a good thing," he called from inside. I heard footsteps creak. He came to the back door and tossed a cigarette into the grass. A thin scarf of smoke drifted out, beyond the screen, slow in the humid air. Karl came down the steps and, crouching with his elbows on his knees, lit another cigarette. I could have reached out and touched him. His form was dim, but I could see that he was just in underwear, mine most likely as I'd given him the run of my closet.

The door banged. It was Celestine. She stood on the steps behind him, tall, monumental from my perspective, and clad only in a white bra and half slip. The thin fabric glowed. Her bra was stiff and pointed. She put her hand out. She was holding a small pair of scissors. She sat down by Karl and took his hand. He clenched his cigarette in his teeth when she started snipping his nails.

"Why the manicure?" he asked.

"You scratched me last night," she answered. Karl gave a sudden laugh and nuzzled his face in Celestine's shoulder, beneath her hair.

"Watch out." She drew the scissors from between them and put them down on the steps.

166

I could not take my eyes from the sharp blades.

"Come back in," she said to Karl after a while, "there's mosquitoes."

"They don't like the smoke," he said, lighting another cigarette from the pack on the steps beside him.

It was true. He was driving them all over to my hiding place, adding insult to my injury. At first I thought I could endure the shrill whining. It filled my ears then swelled abominably as more descended, a cloud in fact. Some lit, more of them, and then the blood feast was on. I did not dare brush them off for fear of rustling the long dry weeds.

"I guess you're right," said Celestine, sitting down beside him on the steps.

"Hold this," said Karl, giving her a lighted cigarette. More mosquitoes veered away from their tobacco cloud and then found me.

"What's that?" Celestine said.

"What's what?" said Karl, blowing rings.

"Shut up."

I worked my face, trying to shrug the insects off. They were everywhere, attached to my eyelids, my temples, thick at my neck, sipping at the small of my back.

"Hah . . . don't . . ." said Celestine, shrugging his hand off. "There's something out there. I hear it."

I squinted miserably, hating them, my teeth grinding. Karl's hand was still hidden. Celestine slapped the place beneath her slip where it must have been.

I slapped my own face, involuntarily, when she did this.

"Hear that?" She stood up. "Like an echo."

"Come on," said Karl. "You'll draw them." He lit still another cigarette and put it in her hand. She sat down. I was in agony, almost unconscious of them, involved with my own distress, when the dog slunk along the brush opposite the yard.

"Hey," said Celestine, "that dog's over here again."

She stepped down from the porch steps and crossed the grass, calling softly, intent on luring the dog to her. In perfect time with Celestine, I rose and stepped through the weeds and out, past Karl, whose face went stark with shock when I appeared.

The land was wide, the sky was a comfort. The view from my window was my only haven. In those first weeks, time passed slowly, or not at all. Days repeated themselves, alike in so many ways, but there were small differences that saved me. The dog came back one day, gaunt as before, and I fed her a can of smoked salmon. She moved with less caution around me, and one day as I banked and mulched a Silver Maple I hoped would take hold, she came near and put her head to my leg. She let me pet her. She had a dry silky coat, surprisingly clean, and when I touched her I felt, quite suddenly, all my sadness breaking out. I put my face to her neck. She smelled of grass, dust, rain, and faintly underneath that, skunk. She had borne far worse than I, most certainly, in her dog's life. Still, she stood quietly and did not move away.

Months after what I'd seen in Celestine's yard, I heard that she was pregnant and no one knew who the father was. Of course, there were speculations, a customer most likely, they said, or someone living near, like me. No one but me seemed to know that Karl had been with her.

Sometimes I saw Celestine from a distance. She was hard to avoid since she drove past my house to go to work. I saw the side of her face only, a harsh profile that sharpened thinner in my mind after she went by. Only once did we come face-to-face. This was in town, not long before Christmas. She was tall, swathed in plaid wool, and so enormous that it looked like her baby was due any day.

After Christmas, the winter turned nasty and the pressure dropped

168

until by January a blizzard was taking shape. I was lying up, dozing and reading, jotting in my almanac. I noticed the wind strengthening, heard sleet strike my house, and pulled the covers tighter around me. The dog slept at the foot of my bed now, which was lucky, for had it not been for her whines and her troubled barking there is no telling what would have happened to Celestine, who had taken advantage of a lull in the growing storm to set out for the hospital.

She was in labor, real labor, but the lull was false. The snow swirled and her Buick smacked into a snowbank. My porch lights were just barely visible through the waves of snow, and she started toward me. The fields around my house were blown nearly clean by the fierce wind, a piece of luck. The baby could have been born in that field, if it had not been so easy for her mother to walk the thin frozen crust. Celestine encountered the deepest drifts when she hit the fence around my yard. She says that she split her lungs yelling for help under my window. But think of it! The noise was so loud I did not hear her, or thought her cries were wind. Ever since that time I have gone to my window periodically during blizzards and I have looked out, to every side, and listened closely. Celestine and the baby could have died beneath my window while I read history. In the morning I would have found mother and baby huddled tight against my red snow fence like the foolish pheasants I sometimes find there, drifted out of snow, their feathers lit with such a warm and iridescent glow it seems impossible for them to be frozen, as though the burning colors should keep them warm.

But the dog roused me, pacing and snapping at the air, and after a time, just to check, I went to the door. Even then I did not see Celestine, just snow. I almost closed my door against the wind but then she floundered forward, I caught her, and we stumbled through the door into my living room, ringing my shelf of glass bells. Newly carpeted and finished, with a blue shag rug and walls the color of dark eggshells, the room was my pride and joy. My navy blue brushed-velvet couch had just arrived and was still encased in plastic. Celestine gained her balance and stood up, huge in her plaid coat and farmer pants. She immediately chose the couch. A padded cotton sleeping bag was tied around her waist. Until she lay back and untied it and opened it like a nest, I did not remember she was pregnant. Then I saw her belly, covered in a flowery housecoat material, rising in a mound.

"Take off my snow pants," she ordered.

Then she closed her eyes and began a soft, quick whooping sound, like bitterns in the park make when they fly up from the pond. It was only after the look of concentration left her face and she opened her eyes, so deeply spent of their color, that I saw she was in pain.

"They're coming fast," she said. "Another." Then she made her sounds again. When she began this time, I took my wet slippers off and ran upstairs to fetch some thick dry woolen socks for both of our feet. I came back down and saw that her eyes were shut. Her face was gray, a mask of absorption. She'd taken off her own snow pants and now lay back in nothing but her housecoat.

"Get sheets," she said, before the next contraction.

I ran from the room and collected fresh towels, an ice pack, a first-aid kit. I removed brand new sheets from their wrappings and brought all of this back to her, dumped everything beside the couch. She nodded briefly. So I continued, encouraged, to collect things. I boiled water, sterilized my best pair of shears. I made a bed for the baby in a laundry basket. I warmed up washcloths and wrung out hot towels to wipe Celestine's face. All this time she was working at this, tensing and rocking, sometimes kneeling beside the couch and sometimes on it. The wind was terrible, blowing so hard the timbers rattled. There was electricity, but the phone lines were down.

I was fishing a hot washrag out of a pot when Celestine wailed loudly.

"Gawd! Gawd! Gawd!"

Three times, like someone in the throes of love or giving up their soul. I ran into the living room and steadied myself at Celestine's elbow.

"I felt the head!" she gasped. "Just for a minute. It went back."

There was something in the moment that calmed me then. Perhaps the astonishment in her face, so like the surprise on Karl's in that hotel room when he found himself suddenly on the floor, and yet so much stronger. There was something in her expression that gave me strength too. I knelt at the other end of the couch and held her legs.

She closed her eyes and instead of the whooping sound she made a kind of low whine. It didn't sound to me like pain though, just effort. She roared when the head came. Then she pushed down again and held herself, pushing down, for a long time. The sound she made was a deeper one, of vast relief, and the baby slid into my hands.

Clay blue, dazed, eyes wide open even then, she came out shockingly alive and complete. Fully present. It did not occur to me to slap her because she looked so ready, so formidable. She took breath and turned pink immediately, deepening to red even as I gave her to Celestine, put a clothespin on the cord between them, and cut.

Later that evening, when I'd finally put a call through and we were waiting for the emergency jeep that would not arrive until morning, Celestine held the baby toward me.

"Hold her," she said, "and listen. I've got to name her after you."

Stunned, I drew the baby to me. She'd retreated into a deep hypnotic sleep, but her tiny calm face seemed full of stubborn

171

purpose. I pored over the set of her wide mouth, the pointed and minuscule chin. I was taken with her, completely, and blinded by happiness at the unlikely thought of her having my name.

"What's your second name?" Celestine asked.

I told her, but it was worse than Wallace. Horst.

"Give me her back," said Celestine. "I'll have to think."

When the snowplows came through the next morning, an ambulance was sent out to bring Celestine and the baby back to Saint Adalbert's. I rode along, helped them fill out forms and settle them into their room on the empty maternity ward. Then I drove home, ate a sandwich, and sat down in the living room. The dog curled in the chair across from me, dozing in the complacent way she'd learned. I was unwilling to let the deep significance of all that had happened diminish, and so I didn't turn on the television, pick up a book, or otherwise divert myself.

The phone woke me. I stumbled to the little alcove where I'd had it mounted, and put the receiver to my ear. There was the sound of Celestine's voice on the crackling, ice-laden wire, a dry pause afterward.

"Wallacette," was all she said.

But Wallacette Darlene wasn't destined to be my namesake for long. From the first, Mary had a nickname for her. Dot. By the time we brought the baby into Saint Catherine's for the baptism, Celestine was calling her Dot too. I said nothing. But to me, the child would always be Wallacette. As her male sponsor, I was glad to give her full name for the church records, and her date of birth. But when it came to the names of Wallacette's parents, I paused. I had to gather myself before I said them without a tremble.

Just after Wallacette was born, Celestine had married Karl in Rapid City, South Dakota. I'd pried out the details of her bus schedule and found that she had stayed overnight in some hotel. Honeymoon? I'd never dared to wonder. Nor had I asked if he'd return. Their picture would appear soon in the wedding section of the *Sentinel*, and for the time being that seemed to be the whole extent of their union.

The sacristy was in the rear of the church, next to the doors and uninsulated stained-glass windows, which is to say it was damp and terribly cold.

"We needn't take our coats off," said Father, striding in with his equipment. "Don't unwrap the baby either. We don't want our little girl to catch a chill." He smiled and took the cover off the baptismal font. With a slight tap of his finger he cracked the film of ice that had formed on the surface of the water.

"Say there," said Mary. "You can't pour freezing water on a baby's head!" She stared belligerently into the priest's eyes.

"Of course not." The priest took a small glass jug of water from inside his jacket. "We'll just use a bit of this. It's blessed. Then we'll wipe her head off and cover her back up again."

Mary nodded, satisfied, and the questioning began. The priest held the oblong bundle of our baby and asked what she wanted of the Church of God. Mary and I had memorized the baby's answer.

"Faith," we said.

"What does faith bring to thee?" the priest asked.

"Life everlasting."

Then he prayed and put the stole on the baby. All together we recited the Apostles' Creed and the Our Father. The priest shifted Wallacette slightly in his arms. She woke and stared out at us from under a little green wool beret.

"Wallacette Darlene," the priest asked, "dost thou renounce Satan?"

"I do renounce him," Mary and I replied. Our voices echoed, loud and solemn. Our answers gathered in the cold air and filled

173

the little alcove. I could not help seeing Karl, his thin black moustache, slenderness, his streams of blue smoke.

"And all his works?" the priest asked.

"I do renounce them." My voice was rising. I felt Mary look at me, annoyed.

"And all his pomps?"

"I do renounce them."

Mary outspoke me this time. My voice was barely a whisper, then silence. Celestine reached over and held the wool baby sweater away from the priest's fingers. He dipped them in holy oil and marked crosses on Wallacette's breast and between her shoulder blades. He asked what she believed, and we answered. And then, because Celestine had insisted on this part, the priest gave Wallacette to me to hold. I took her in my arms.

"Wallacette Darlene," he asked, "wilt thou be baptized?"

I answered that she would.

When the priest poured the first small cross of water on her head, Wallacette looked mystified. The next drops came. Outrage screwed her face tight. She opened her mouth as the priest made a pass with the white cloth of purity, and she gathered herself into a long scream as he lighted the candles that Mary held.

He recited another prayer. Mary blew the candles out. Wallacette roared on and on as if she'd never stop.

Celestine's Night

The first summer, Celestine brought her baby to work, and all day the child slept, sucked on her fingers, and woke to watch Celestine from the bottom of an old shopping cart that was padded with blankets. Sometimes Celestine turned around and met the direct gaze of her daughter, a look so penetrating that Celestine's breath caught. She dropped the spice, the string, the knife she was using, and took the girl up in her arms, ready for her to speak as if a spell had suddenly lifted.

When the baby flexed her entire body and struggled to free herself, Celestine put her down. No matter how thorough Celestine's exhaustion, no matter how little sleep she'd had, there was a nerve of excitement running through each hour. Common objects and events seemed slightly strange, as if she were encountering them in the clarity of a strong dream. It was Dot's presence, her heavy sweetness, the milk of Celestine's own body on her breath, the soft odor of her hair, her glorious wealth of pink and lavender skin, that changed the cast of Celestine's daily world.

Sometimes, watching the baby as she slept or reaching for her in the dark, it was passion that Celestine felt, even stronger than with Karl. She stole time to be with Dot as if they were lovers. Days, it was half hours of nursing in the shop's back room, sometimes with the raw smell of blood on her hands. In the evenings, Celestine had the baby all to herself at home. As she read her novels, talked on the telephone, or cooked or sat, Dot slept nearby in a laundry basket, breathing in fits and starts.

In those days and nights, Celestine's mind was flooded, green as jade. Her love for the baby hung around her in clear, blowing sheets.

One night Dot slept past her feeding time and Celestine woke in the half-light of dawn with full breasts. The baby clung like a sloth, heavy with sleep, and latched on in hunger, without waking. She drew milk down silently in one long inhalation. It was then that Celestine noticed, in the fine moonlit floss of her baby's hair, a tiny white spider making its nest.

It was a delicate thing, close to transparent, with long sheer legs. It moved so quickly that it seemed to vibrate, throwing out invisible strings and catching them, weaving its own tensile strand. Celestine watched as it began to happen. A web was forming, a complicated house, that Celestine could not bring herself to destroy.

 **PART THREE**

MARY ADARE

DURING THREE HARD winters after Dot was born, the snow packed so deep that starved deer drifted from the fields to my stock pens, and leapt in. They could not be driven back up the loading ramp. The only other way out was the slaughter chute. But they were useless, full of lung bot, every rib jutting; even their hides were tissue thin. My fruit trees suffered. The snow came so high that rabbits gnawed the trunks and upper limbs, girdling them completely so that even spring, when new buds should have shown, was a time of death. In the shelterbelts, I came across more of the deer's frail hulks and the banks of the river stank of bleached carp. An old man was found, one who for years had lived alone. He was curled in a large drift beneath his clothesline and his arms were full of towels.

As if to repair this sad work, then, the weather turned mild and we had a spate of slow January rains. It was during that time, five years after her winter birth, that I began to wonder how I'd ever kept my distance from Dot.

At first it was the name. If anyone, Celestine should have named her after me. I hated the name Wallacette and I knew it would give the girl trouble for the rest of her life. So I thought up the nickname to Darlene. That was Dot. One round syllable, so much easier to say.

Of course, Celestine never admitted how bad the real name was. When I told her that the name Wallacette was terrible, she only shrugged, looking down at me from all her height, and said that it had distinction. Because having Dot and giving her the name was the first thing Celestine ever did out of the ordinary, she was stingy. She wouldn't really give in to another opinion, not on the name or on other things. Feeding and dressing and burping were her domain. She would be the only one to change the diapers, to give the bath, to cut the soft little nails and even carry the child in and out of the car. I had to sit by watching all of this done. I had to wait and bide my time, and I managed, although it was a struggle because every time I looked at that baby I'd feel a piercing shock. Dot and I had a mental connection, I was sure of it. I understood things about the baby that her mother could not accept.

For instance, she was never meant to be a baby.

Dot was as impatient with babyhood as I. She tried at once to grow out of it. Celestine never saw that, because she, and only she, took pleasure in Dot's helpless softness. Only Celestine was saddened by her daughter's fierce progress. Day by day, Dot grew stronger. In her shopping-cart stroller she exercised to exhaustion, bouncing for hours to develop her leg muscles. She hated lying on her back and when put that way immediately flipped over to assume a wrestler's crouch. Sleep, which she resisted, did not come upon her gently but felled her in odd positions. Draped over the side of the cart or packed in its corner, she seemed to have fallen in battle. But it was only a momentary surrender. She woke, demanding food, and when set free exploded in an astonishing fast creep that took her across a room in seconds.

Celestine moped when her baby stopped nursing, but secretly I was glad. One more independent step. Dot grew teeth. They came in all at once, tiny flat buds with a wide eager gap between the two top front. She grinned, flexed, stood solid, and soon had to be tied up in a neutral corner while we worked, for fear she'd drag down the knives and get into the machinery. She worked her knots free and stumbled desperately toward danger, toward the boiling vats or freezers. The House of Meats, which I'd renamed from Kozka's Meats, was no place for a child. I feared a side of pork would fall and crush her, that she'd crawl into the stock pens or fall beneath the hooves of a dull heifer. But unlike her father, who attracted it, Dot repelled harm. Falling cans bounced past her, and she stepped without looking over open drains.

I think now that maybe she scared off bad luck with the loud volume of her voice. Once she discovered what she had, she became a bully, a demanding child, impossible to satisfy. In our hearts, as time went on, we knew that we were making a selfish girl whose first clear word was MORE. She was greedy, grew fat, because we sympathized too much. We had gone hungry as children and could not deny her a morsel. Celestine tried to discipline her, teach her the word *please*. But she couldn't teach Dot the right way to say it. Dot growled, "PLEEZ MORE," her eyes hard as buttons.

We handed things over. She guzzled milk, screamed, threw her bottle on the floor in a fit, bit Celestine, tore the plastic barrettes from her own head, and the hair too, by the roots. Then she offered us the clump in her hand. It seemed that her hurt was nothing to her, because ours was always worse. We made more fuss than she did over the bald spots, the scraped knees, the purple lumps on her forehead. We were thorough in living through her, in living our childhoods over.

By the time Celestine allowed Dot to enter first grade, she was as big as most children twice her age, strong and spoiled. Her clipped curls were a dark clear red, and her face was square, heavily brooding. I saw my brother in Dot's pout and in the deep-set eyes, and in the eyebrows so straight and fine they seemed traced on with a level and a pale brown crayon. She had my mother's hair. Otherwise, she positively resembled me. Pale, broad, and solid. I don't think I am inventing this, although the one time I pointed this out to Celestine, she puffed large with outrage in her stiff white apron and said, "You're her aunt and that's all. I'm her *mother*," defining for me the sideline role she imagined I would take on. That is, giver of birthday gifts, always a skirt or blouse. Attender of graduations and recitals and school plays. Baby-sitter if a pinch ever came, and, most definitely, not a person to resemble. Not physically, not mentally. Not mentally most of all.

But that was hopeless on Celestine's part. I saw myself in Dot's one-track mind and doubled fists. I indulged the girl royally, I'll be the first to admit.

I went with them on the first day of school. Dot had skipped kindergarten, so the children all knew one another. She walked into the classroom with her mother while I watched, in the aunt's role. I stood outside the classroom of mild-tempered children. I saw the pots of glue, the box of blunt scissors, the stacks of colored paper, the small sturdy chairs. I smelled the dry and sour school smell, the chalk dust and wax, the pink powder that the janitor spread on the bathroom floors. The teacher, Mrs. Shumway, jerked her thin arms, and two boys rose to pass out the red-and-white cartons of milk. Celestine had brought along a box of bakery cookies, a treat she gave to the teacher in order to ensure her daughter's welcome with the other children. But I could see that the cookies didn't matter, not only then, but ever. For Dot was like a wolf ready to descend on the fold. There would be no resisting her. I could tell this from where I stood. Even Mrs. Shumway, a young but wizened, observant woman, would not be able to control her. I knew the teacher was in for a surprise when she put her arm around Dot's shoulders and introduced her as "*our* new girl." Dot swelled at this. Her eyes gleamed. Her chin stuck out. Watching her, the boys went mute and the spines of the little girls stiffened like pulled twine. Children have an extra special sense about each other. They all saw what neither

Celestine and even the tough little Mrs. Shumway could not. They were the sparrows. Dot was the hawk keenly circling. For seven years, until high school, when everything would change, each of these children would be subject to her whims.

And they were, from the very first, for Dot at once set about her business of fiercely pursuing them. She didn't want to hurt them, she just wanted their affection. But this was hard to explain since her means of acquiring their love took such violent turns.

One day, about the time Dot usually clanged through the front door of the shop, Celestine put her knife down and told me this was the day she expected a note from Shumway.

"What for?" I said, intrigued, too much so for Celestine's liking.

"Never mind," she mumbled, "it was just some little tiff Dot had with another girl. The girl's mother called."

Celestine began untying her apron as she walked around the counter. I followed to the door. Looking out, we saw Dot walking slowly up the dust-and-cinder driveway, dragging her thick shoes in a tragic way. She had allowed her hair to droop from its swan-shaped clips and obscure her face. Even through the hair and from a distance, I could tell that her eyes were dull with apprehension. I imagined that her firm mouth trembled.

"I'll go to her," I offered. "Sometimes it's better."

Celestine turned to me. The very flesh of her face seemed to harden when she was annoyed, and her eyes became dark and opaque as if they had been dabbed on.

"What do you mean," she said, " 'sometimes it's better'?"

"For the aunt to go."

" 'For the *aunt* to go,' " she repeated. She put the bundle of her apron in my arms and marched out the front door with an abruptness that was meant to discourage me. But I followed even then, unable to resist, although I stood slightly behind Celestine as she confronted her daughter.

"Give me the note," she firmly ordered. She put her hand out the way a parent must, open and stern. Dot put her hands in her pockets. Her neck reddened and she would not meet her mother's eyes.

"I don't have one yet," she said at last.

"Did you give my note to Mrs. Shumway?" Celestine interrogated.

"Yes."

"No!" Celestine then cried. "You did not! Young lady you have just told me a lie."

Dot looked straight up at her mother in what I saw as miserable appeal. I thought her cheeks blazed in sudden grief, but maybe it was defiance. She was beyond speech, so I stuck up for her. I could not bear it. I reached briskly around Celestine, took her daughter's wrist, and dragged her safely toward me.

"Let's sit down in back," I said. "We'll talk. It can't be that bad."

"Oh yes it *can* be that bad," said Celestine, striding wrathfully beside us up the driveway. "Yesterday your darling knocked a first-grader's tooth out."

"*Pulled* it out," corrected Dot. "It was already loose."

"The little girl's mother called me up last night," Celestine went on. "The tooth wasn't ready to come out."

"Oh yes it was," Dot insisted. "She asked me to get it out. She gets a quarter from the fairy."

"You didn't have to use a rock. A *rock*!" cried Celestine. "And then the note! You were supposed to give the note to Mrs. Shumway to apologize for your behavior."

Celestine suddenly stopped, blocking our paths, having had an arresting thought.

"Did something else happen today, something bad?" she grimly questioned.

"No," Dot replied, with what seemed, even to me, suspicious speed. But Celestine was growing weary and did not pursue the thread.

"It better not have." She took her apron from my arms and retied it around herself. "Now go have your snack, go on; I'll clean up out back and then we're going home and get to the bottom of this."

I went out to the kitchen with Dot, to fix her a sandwich and a cookie and talk in private. That is how I got to hear firsthand about what really did happen that day in the naughty box. That is also how I came to damage Shumway, who probably deserved it, even though Dot was lying through her teeth and even though the naughty box was not exactly the instrument of torture that I pictured. At any rate, I've regretted the episode since and know I should have been more suspicious with Dot when she told me, after I poured her a milk and put some bran cookies down before her, that she'd spent all day in the naughty box where it was dark.

"The naughty box," I said, sitting down with her, upset by the picture of her dim confinement. "Is it a real box?"

But Dot, with her mouth full, let her eyes speak the volumes for her. They glistened with unshed tears of shame. She only cried to get her way, but this afternoon tears coated her hazel eyes in a film that seemed more piteous and noble than sobs. She chewed ravenously, gulped her milk, and went on to describe the box.

"It's a red box in the back of the room, underneath the clock. Mrs. Shumway can fit lots of children inside of it. She pushes you in and slams down the lid. It's big. It's made of wood. It has *splinters*."

Dot stopped in horror, remembering all too well, or so I thought at the time. "And inside the air is very, very black," she whispered. Her gaze was bleak and distant. She put a whole cookie in her mouth for comfort, and while she chewed it she reached for

185

another. But I was never much at correcting Dot's manners. In fact, I employed any ruse to keep from saying no to the girl. That word to her was like an electric shock, inflating her with lightning fury. *No* sent up the voltage until the current flew out of her and jolted us. I let her cram another cookie in her mouth. I thought of Shumway. The teacher's methods gave me a thrill down my neck, as if I was reading a storybook.

"Shumway . . . that Shumway . . . is a witch!" I rose unsteadily to my feet. "She won't get away with this!"

I looked down at Dot, and she looked up at me. In her eyes I thought I saw adoration, innocent trust. I was her godmother of the fairy tales, her protector.

"Just finish your snack," I said, patting her shoulder with adult authority. "I'll take care of Shumway."

Dot's smile turned on full force, was eager and dazzling. I stamped off in its light, got into the truck, and hit the starter. I did not even take the time to put on my hat or drape a scarf around my throat. I drove pell-mell to the school to catch Shumway before she slunk off, to her duplex or wherever Argus first-grade teachers slunk to when they had emptied their naughty boxes and ground their red pencils sharp as needles.

The school was my school, Saint Catherine's, where long ago I had performed a major miracle. Now it had enlarged for our growing population and become more secular, with lay teachers in many grades and no obligatory mass on weekdays. Still, I banged through the new double insulated glass doors with confidence. I strode the deserted hallway until I reached Shumway's classroom. My mind had blackened with rage by then. I couldn't wait to lay my hands on her. And I was in luck. For she was there, just as I'd been hoping, making ready to go home. She was pinning a bright blue beret on her head, eyeing herself in the face mirror of the teacher's closet as she did so. I watched her for one moment and then looked to the back of the room. What I saw doubled my rage past containing.

186

Beneath the clock, in the precise spot Dot had described, there was a glazed box painted a sinister and shining red. It was long as a coffin and twice as broad. I walked past Mrs. Shumway, who jerked her head around in a startled woodpeckerish way, and I threw open the lid. I half expected to find pale children huddled there. But the box was full of toys.

"Do you fill it up each night?" I turned, accusing Shumway.

"What?"

I pointed to the box, then lifted one end and dumped the toys out. Blocks, fire engines, plastic doll furniture and bright rubber rings spilled across the floor. I let it fall with an empty crash.

"Mrs. Shumway, come here," I said.

She walked over to me, not obediently, but with a nervy terrier's menace.

"What is the meaning of this!" she cried. "Who are you?" Her blue hat seemed to lift off her hair in surprise, and her voice shook apprehensively. She stared at me, edged forward. Her face was faceted and sharp, the kind of thin face that wrinkled young. She could not have been more than twenty-six but already her eyes were rimmed in red like a very old woman's. Her hair was cut into a strange elfin shape.

I put my hands on my hips, butcher's hips, used to shifting heavy loads and moving hams down the smoke rails.

"Your little game is up, Mrs. Shumway," I said.

She coughed in surprise. "What are you talking about?" she squeaked. She stepped backward, laughed uncertainly. I suppose, thinking of it now, she merely thought I was harmlessly lunatic, but at the time I took her nervous laugh as an admission of guilt. I reached out and grabbed the shoulders of her camel coat. I dragged her toward the red box.

At first, she was so shocked that her knees buckled and her heels dragged, but when we reached the box, and when I tried to force her in by pushing her and bending her arms and legs up like a doll's, she suddenly regained her poise and stood fast.

She was surprisingly agile, and very strong, so that I had a harder time than you would expect shoving her inside the box and crushing all of her limbs in besides. Also, she was proud. For she made no outcry until she was trapped and all was lost. And then, once I'd sat down on top of the red box, breathing heavily, recovering my composure, Mrs. Shumway began to hammer and howl.

"It's no use," I called down to her, satisfied beyond all measure, "you're in the naughty box! You can't get out until you promise to be good."

There was silence, a period of thought for Mrs. Shumway, who, even in her shock, heeded the sense of my words.

"This is not the naughty box," she said, muffled, below me. "It's on the blackboard."

But the chalkboard at the front of the room was wiped clear and not even black, but a dull and soothing green.

"Mrs. Shumway," I said, "I am not a five-year-old that you can fool."

Again, there was silence.

"Let me out," she said after a long while, "or I'll have you arrested."

"You wouldn't do that, Mrs. Shumway," I answered, having given this some thought. "I'll tell them about the naughty box and they'll revoke your teacher's license."

"There's nothing wrong with the naughty box. It's on the blackboard," she replied.

But I wasn't listening to her excuses. I looked around the room for something heavy enough to weight the lid. There were long wooden tables, chairs, fire extinguishers, and gray tin wastebaskets. There was Shumway's own desk, which I thought I could move and even lift if she would only stay put long enough. But I could see that, since there was no way to keep her inside by force, I would have to intimidate her into keeping still. I picked up a rectangular purple block and beat the cover of the box with it.

"I'll hit you with this if you jump out!" I warned, convincingly I hoped, but nevertheless once I'd left the box and started to push Shumway's desk across the room, she popped out. The red cover of the box crashed backward and out she leapt, still neat in her tan coat and pointed black shoes, her blue beret flattened only slightly. She reached down, grabbed a block like mine, and brandished it as she stepped slowly, backward, toward the door. I moved around her desk and picked up the block I'd dropped. Then both of us edged, at the same pace, into the hall where we then continued our unusual and wary progress through the front doors and out onto the playground, which was where I lost Shumway. She took advantage of the few children who had lingered to play after school, by walking in among them and starting up a desperate conversation. I retreated. But I did so in the secure conviction that I'd revenged Dot, that I'd taught Shumway an unforgettable lesson and, in that way, done something for all of the children of Argus, who would be forced to spend one school year of their lives in her hands.

I didn't think about much besides that, and certainly not about Shumway's threat to have me arrested, but then it turned out she went to the police and told the whole story and presented a list of the badly behaved children, any of whose mothers she suspected of being me.

That's why Officer Ronald Lovchik came to the shop next day. He was a tall, sad, soft-shouldered man with a horror of confronting criminals. The years since the beet had come to town were hard on him. Construction workers from the beet refinery roistered in the bars, and the asphalt haulers set up wild camps on the edge of town where the bypass was going in. All Lovchik needed at the time was a grade-school squabble. Besides, he didn't like to come to the back rooms of the shop at all. He'd always had a hopeless crush on Sita, until he lost her to Jimmy. It pained him even to be in rooms she once inhabited. Back then, he wrote Sita letters and sent small yellow boxes of Whitman's chocolates, which Fritzie and I always ate to save Sita's figure. His very presence reminded me of those chocolates, and made me want one. But he was visiting on serious business. Now he described the incident with Shumway, knitting his brow as if he was unable to look at Celestine for fear she might think he was making an accusation.

"And so . . ." he gulped, bringing his story to a close, "the gist of it is I have to know where you were yesterday afternoon."

"Let me think," Celestine commented, with measured consideration. I could tell that she was impressed with the idea of being a suspect in something she hadn't done, that she relished being asked this dramatic question. I knew she was framing a complex answer in her mind, but before she got the pleasure of voicing her alibi I solved Lovchik's case.

"I did it, Ron," I admitted in a loud voice, unashamed. "I did it with good cause."

"Oh?" He was surprised for a moment only, then resigned. "I'm sorry to hear that." He drooped, dismayed by the conviction in my voice. His eyes took on a wet despondence, and he asked if we could sit down somewhere private to discuss the charge.

"Be my guest." I motioned him down the hall to the kitchen. Celestine, all agape, followed us. We all three sat down at the kitchen table, and Lovchik took a spiral notebook from his shirt pocket and unclipped a ballpoint pen from his tie.

"All right," he said, "what's your side?"

"It was my duty as a citizen," I said. "Mrs. Shumway has been cruel to children."

"In what way?" Lovchik asked, scribbling quickly. I proceeded to tell Officer Lovchik about the naughty box, describing it in detail. As I spoke, his eyebrows lifted, his head shook back and forth, and he hummed disapprovingly beneath his breath.

190

"Just a minute," Celestine said, interrupting my description of the splinters that pricked into the children's clawing hands; "you're talking about the naughty box?"

"You know about it too?" I looked at her, terribly surprised that she had known and never mentioned it.

"Sure I know about it. . . . Mary," she said with a strange look, ". . . its not a real box, it's a corner of the blackboard where children get their names written if they smart off."

I stopped, confused.

"You're sure?"

"I've seen it myself."

Officer Lovchik put his pen down.

"Let me try and get this straight," he said, but then he seemed to despair of that possibility and merely sat, frowning at his knuckles, waiting for one of us to say something.

"All right," he said at last, "it was all some kind of big mistake?"

After putting two and two together in that time, I had to answer that it was.

"Well . . . I'll try and get those charges dropped," he sighed. Then he rose unhappily and walked back down the hallway and out the door.

"Just tell me one thing," said Celestine, after the bell in the front rang behind him. "Did Dot lie to you about this? Did she make the whole thing up?"

I couldn't answer, thinking of the passion in Dot's face, the mute appeal, the unshed tears of her shame—all that had taken me in.

"It sounds like her," Celestine said. "I'm trying to teach her the difference between a lie and the truth."

"That seems simple enough." I busied myself measuring ground coffee into the basket of the percolator. Maybe I didn't know the difference myself, or at least what the episode meant. It's hard to trace these things back, but I do think that the incident over Mrs. Shumway's naughty box was the first time Celestine and I

191

went opposite ways with Dot, and all because I'd been deceived.

"You don't make it any easier," she said, tracing the pattern in Fritzie's crocheted string tablecloth. "In fact you make it worse."

I kept pouring the coffee in, spoonful by spoon, making a strong batch. I didn't want to turn around because I couldn't say anything to defend myself or make much sense, not after stuffing Mrs. Shumway in her toy box. Standing there with the spoon in my hand, I suddenly pictured her telling this story to the police, thin face twitching, her blue beret righteous and flat as a pancake on her elf's hair.

"You should have seen her," I said, then I started laughing, which was the wrong thing to do as far as Celestine was concerned because when I turned around she had gone. All the next day and into the summer she refused to speak to me, and only answered what I said by yes or no, so that it was summer vacation before the whole incident blew over.

That summer, Karl sent Dot a very nice electric wheelchair that he won as a doorprize at some medical-supplies show. The chair was delivered in pieces, which Celestine managed to assemble on the first two days of her week's vacation.

I went over there because she had just started speaking to me on June first, and by then I was as relieved to talk as she was. I knew she'd given herself exactly until that day to maintain strict one-syllable relations. Once June arrived she called me up and babbled all of her pent-up stories of Dot's interesting observations and behaviors. I was the only one in town who'd listen to Celestine and not turn her off. People have long memories in Argus. They still thought Celestine was strange, even disreputable, to have a baby so late in life by a flighty husband who only married her after the baby was born. The postmaster and postmistress, husband and wife, who looked carefully at every piece of mail and were eventually caught steaming open certain bank statements on commission, spread it around about how rarely Karl wrote and what unusual packages he sent to Dot.

Matchbooks. Coaster trays. Hotel towels and washclothes. He sent her samples of whatever he was selling at the time. Fuller brushes. Radio antennas. Cans of hair spray or special wonder-working floor cleaners. These arrived every few months by parcel post. If he wrote, it was on a postcard from the drawer of a cheap hotel. He kept the hotel stationary too, reams of it, and sent it on whenever it piled up.

This wheelchair, though, was something more out of the ordinary. At least the writing paper, brushes, complimentary advertising pens and cans of hair spray could be put to practical use.

"It's got forward and backward controls," said Celestine. "Really, it's very nice."

The three of us were grouped around the wheelchair in the driveway, watching Celestine put in the last few chrome screws. She was hunched, intent, over the complex directions while Dot and I sat together on the steps. During the ban on me, Celestine had stopped all after-school snacks and friendly outings, and the truth is, at Dot's age, it was out of sight, out of mind. I missed her more than she did me. I felt half there without her, absent, forgetful, and blue. Now I was so happy to get back to the way things were before the naughty-box incident that I bore no grudge. While Celestine muttered over the oddly shaped components, Dot and I discussed Shumway's improved behavior and speculated on Sister Seraphica, her teacher-to-be next year, a tall dreamy nun who played the organ and directed choir. Dot expected there to be a rhythm band, and looked forward to hitting sand blocks together.

"I'll teach you the woodwinds too," I said, blowing on a stalk of crabgrass.

But Celestine was finished and Dot was diverted. She jumped

into the seat of the wheelchair and started maneuvering up and down the dirt-and-cinder drive. Celestine came over to the steps to sit by me.

"Somehow . . ." she began, then quit.

"What?"

"I don't think it's the most thoughtful present he ever sent."

I'd taken to defending my brother, not that he would have cared or ever returned the compliment, but out of the sheer bond of blood. Maybe I was grateful that, however accidentally, he'd given me my one tie of kinship, to Dot.

"I think it's inventive," I said. "Different, yes, but look how she enjoys the chair!"

Indeed, Dot had quickly mastered the controls and now zoomed and bumped in mad circles, half tipping, catching herself at the last moment. She was having a good time, but to Celestine the sight of Dot was an unpleasant reminder, or perhaps a kind of bad omen.

"It makes me . . ." She searched for the word through her romantic-book vocabulary: ". . . shudder. Yes, shudder," she decided. "We're not going to keep the thing."

"What!" shouted Dot. Her ears were sharp.

"We're going to give it to someone who really needs it," said Celestine. "It's much too expensive to treat as a toy."

Dot wheeled up and stuttered the machine to a halt. "It's from my father. It's mine!" She lowered her eyebrows and gave us a startling, evil glare.

But Celestine was in one of her determined moods. "Yes," she said again, "we're going to give it to someone."

"Someone who?" I said. I thought she could have let Dot keep it.

Celestine was silent for a while, pondering. Then she turned and gave me a long reproachful stare, as if I had missed out somewhere, as if I should have known.

"Think," she said. "It's obvious who."

Dot jumped out of the chair and wheeled it to the slope in the backyard. She sat down, took off the brake, and gave herself a wild short ride.

"Don't string me out," I said, irritated.

"Russell," she answered.

She was right. I had to see that. After his paralyzing stroke, the attendants took Russell up to the reservation to live with his half brother, Eli Kashpaw, in a little wooden house that Celestine said was full of stretched furs, traps, fox musk, and calendars of bathing beauties, a place where sugar stayed in a twisted sack and all the forks were bent and splayed from opening cans or prying nails from the rough board walls.

Eli had left the reservation only twice, according to Celestine. The first time was three days after Celestine's mother died, when he had shown up at the church, slipping into the back pew quiet as a marten and slipping out again without a word to anyone. To get to know him, Isabel and Pauline and Russell had to track down Eli almost with the same finesse he used on animals. And they often made the effort, because Eli was only shy at first, and after that he was fine company, as the lonely often are. He took a child in, a girl that he raised to trap and hunt, go hungry in the woods, and hide from game wardens, a girl named June, who turned out even wilder than he'd raised her.

Eli kept so much to himself that half of his relations didn't know about his feelings for Russell, who was famous for his decorations. So when Eli showed up at Saint Adalbert's hospital and signed his brother's release forms with the shape of the Kashpaw name—the only shape Eli had ever learned to scrawl—a cousin living off reservation and working at the hospital desk said she was just as surprised as any of them. That was the second time Eli left—to fetch Russell home. And now Russell was living in Eli's two rooms, sleeping upright, letting his brother bathe him, change him, and in good weather wheel him out into the trampled yard, where he was left to doze guarded by ragged and panther-thin dogs.

Celestine went up to see them a couple times a year. In between their visits, it seemed like she couldn't stay off the subject, and that was one reason that I wanted to come along. I wanted to see for myself whether Russell spoke a word yet or ate with a knife and fork or had the use of his hands. I'd always felt bad about the way things had been left between us the last time I'd seen him in the hospital.

I'd come home shaken from that encounter. It had been his silence, or maybe even worse, his speech. Russell had opened his mouth and huge shattered vowels poured out, urgent sounds that wrenched me. Sounds I tried to understand. I'd picked up his pitcher of juice and offered it, then the newspaper. I'd pointed to the bathroom and wheeled him nearer to the window. And eventually, when I'd tried hard enough and offered every possibility I saw in the room, he'd gone dim and silent once more. He'd stared past me and sunk into a quiet I could not crack.

He had thinned as he recovered, and when he sat absolutely still that way he was hard to look at. The contrast between his ravaged cheeks and forehead and his eyes—slanting, deep black, of a delicate shape—was unbearable. I knew that his mind was active. I took his hand.

"Russell," I said, "believe me that I'm sorry."

He stared down at our two hands, mine so tough, with thick split nails and many scars. His long and dry and brown. He was unable to will his hand out of mine, unable to move his hand the slightest distance. I felt such raw anger shooting from his bones that I dropped his hand and jumped up. I left without even saying that I was going, and all the way home in the truck I was embarrassed at my trespass. I tried to pretend I'd done it with no pleasure, or out of sheer attraction like the time summers past when I'd touched the war scars on his chest, but the truth was I'd captured his hand with a thrill. He went to Eli's soon after that, and now it had been years. Six years.

"Your Uncle Russell would appreciate the chair," Celestine called after her daughter. "You can come when we take it up there. It can be from you."

Dot paused in her game, then zoomed off again, determined to extract every moment of enjoyment from her present. Celestine sighed, slapped her knees hard, and stood.

"She's doing her best to wreck it before we go."

"How are you going to haul it?" I asked after a moment. I already knew the answer. My truck. And Celestine knew I knew as well. She looked thoughtfully across the yard at the wheelchair.

"You want to drive?" she asked.

"I'll drive," I told her. "But I never met this Eli."

"Or my aunt," said Celestine. "She's over there a lot now."

"What aunt?"

"Fleur. The one that came down here, you know, when Mama died."

"What a name. Floor."

Celestine looked down at me with strained indulgence. "Fleur," she said. "It's French for flower."

"Ooo-la-la," I said, getting up to go. "Don't be so superior. I took bookkeeping instead of French in high school."

So the next morning, when I came out to the shop, Celestine was wrapping a headcheese in some newspaper, securing it with rubber bands. I gathered we'd take that along, plus a sausage, and if I'd baked we would have taken a sheet cake too. When we visited I always had to shoulder the burden of the food. I took a few bags of gingersnaps from the grocery-section shelves, went back to my room, tied on my head scarf, and then it seemed easy enough to leave. Adrian was there to watch the trade, and nothing special was going on in the way of preparations. It was

197

late morning and Dot was out back with my dogs. She'd ride behind us. The delivery truck was enclosed like a van and padded nicely behind the front seats with foam-rubber pillows. The wheelchair could be laid on its side next to her. So we started out. Before we were halfway through town, Dot sank down in the rubber cushions, dropped her head into her arms, and fell into a sound sleep.

Getting out of Argus was an obstacle course now, with all the orange-and-white drums, oil pots, reflectors, and flaggers ranging down the new highway that was going in. It took us the better part of half an hour to get past them, but then it was a short pretty drive until we hit the boundary line. I stopped the truck next to the sign that announced the reservation and told Celestine it was her turn, she must take over. So she got out and came around the front and slid behind the steering wheel. The roads turned gravel. Dust rose in a tan plume behind us. We left all trace of town buildings and the houses we passed looked strangely abandoned, except for dogs.

Dot crawled into the front and sat between us on the glove case and helped her mother steer. Celestine had cut Dot's thick hair into the shape of a football helmet. In the summer it had gold highlights along with the rust and tarnished brown. One side of her face was creased and reddened where she'd lain. Now that she was conscious there was no end to her questions and exclamations, for Dot was a born traveler, meant to go places, unlike us. My one real trip in life had been the freight train to Argus. I didn't care much for changes of scenery, but Dot was excited by the emptiness and dust, by the solid bands of trees and the half-hidden houses. She was interested in the pitted road that led up to Eli's.

"Watch that," she called sternly, pulling on the wheel. "Go left! Now right!"

Mrs. Shumway had taught her class the concepts of right and

198

left at the end of the school year, and applying them to real life was one of Dot's manias. But there were so many ruts and twists on our way that by the time we came to Eli's clearing she finally grew bored with her game.

Eli's house was tiny, covered with dull gray shingles and surrounded by a narrow yard of dust wallows. Before we were completely stopped, fierce-looking dogs bounded toward us and Dot scrambled across my lap, was out the door and among them before Celestine could open her mouth.

Russell was there, farther on a bit, pushed up beside the screened door in a little wedge of shade. He blended so well into the mottled light and dark of the house, the weathered boards and worn-in paint, that Dot didn't even see him at first. She didn't see Eli either when he appeared, passing soundlessly from a dim tangle of bushes at the edge of the clearing. He watched Dot, the dogs, and Celestine as she got out of the truck. He watched Russell watch his sister.

Celestine carried a headcheese and a long hard stick of summer sausage, and she approached Russell with a smile of eagerness. But in her stride there must have been nerves, because the dogs flew past Dot and landed in a circle of teeth around her mother. She stood, trapped. And then suddenly she swung the summer sausage down, hard, on the nose of the largest dog and yelled, "Beat it!"

Eli walked over to Celestine, holding his hand out to shake hers, and then the door to his house opened and out came the aunt. The only thing that Celestine had told me about Fleur was that she used to work for Uncle Pete, and that she was unbalanced. But Fleur struck me as balanced, and then some. She stood right next to Russell and dropped her hand on his shoulder, maybe to calm him, although he didn't seem to notice us. This Fleur was big-boned but lean, very much the build of Celestine, and had a face like Sitting Bull. Her eyes were black and narrow, watchful. Her mouth was broad. She wore a baggy blue flowered housedress that looked like old slipcovers.

Celestine walked over and kissed Russell on the cheek. He tipped his head away, and gazed off into the woods. Celestine took his arm, but he looked at her hand as if it were a leaf that had fallen on him by accident.

"He's glad to see you," said Fleur.

Dot walked up cautiously and stood before Russell, hands hooked in her pockets. She took him in as if he were frozen in a block of ice or enclosed in a cage of wires.

"Don't stare," Fleur said.

Celestine's breath caught. Direct orders displeased Dot, made her stubborn and resentful. Sure enough, without a word, Dot turned and stamped back toward the truck.

"Help me get *my* wheelchair out," she ordered. So I helped her unload the thing. She wheeled it forward, determined that since she had to give it up she would do so herself. The new chrome gleamed, the leather creaked.

"This is for him," Dot said, pushing the chair up to Russell. No one said a word.

"He's doing all right here," Fleur said at last to Celestine. "You couldn't handle him."

"Hey," Dot called, "I'm *giving* this to Uncle Russell."

"We didn't come to get him," Celestine said to Fleur. "It's just a present."

At that, the aunt seemed friendlier and showed her teeth in something like a smile. "Where did that chair come from?"

I couldn't stop myself from jumping in.

"The wheelchair is from her father."

"Who are you?" said Fleur, with a freezing stare.

"I'm her aunt that owns the sausage plant," I said.

Fleur's eyes caught fire in a flash, then went cold.

"Go on in," she said, gesturing us past her toward the house.

Eli's place was small, mostly the kitchen where we sat. In the next room I could see an old-model radio. On top of two orange crates sat Russell's war mementos, those that weren't in the museum. I recognized the folded cloth flags, small leather cases that held Russell's medals, as well as the shrapnel and bullets that the doctors had carved out of him. A German Luger was pinned up in a web of nails and strings.

Celestine took the headcheese out. "You mind if I put this in your refrigerator?"

Eli had an ancient, fat, yellowing contraption that took up half the wall. On its door an old pencil drawing of a deer was taped and retaped.

"That's well done," I said, touching the picture.

"That's June," he said. "She did that one in high school."

I looked around. There was no evidence of the girl in the room, except what I took to be her photograph, high on a shelf. A little glass jar in front of that picture held a red velvet rose that looked as though it had been snipped off a dress. The girl was dark and pretty, with short black hair and a big serious smile.

"That's her," he said, noticing my glance.

"Your daughter?"

"More or less." Eli shrugged and hefted a coffeepot.

"I just made some fresh," he said, in such a soft voice that I suddenly wanted coffee very much and sat down in the chair near Celestine. He poured three cups.

We heard Dot's voice, subdued but still penetrating.

"I don't have to give my chair away if I don't want to. I could keep it."

"Hush up." It was Fleur's voice, very cold.

We heard a scuffling sound. Some metal clanked.

"I suppose they got Russell set up," Celestine said.

But it was not Russell in the new wheelchair. We heard wheels

201

rip through dirt, a sudden slamming, a wallop as Dot flashed by through a bush.

"Try and get it," she screamed, her voice fading off as she vanished.

"She's showing Russell how to use the thing," I said, making an excuse.

"They hit it off out there," said Eli; "how much you want to bet?"

We listened to the clatter of little rocks in the wheels, to Dot's shout as she reared up and turned in quick short skids, heading back toward the house.

Fleur was just outside the window. "Quit it," she said, when Dot reached her. "That's enough."

Both Celestine and I went tense in our chairs, looked at each other knowingly.

"What?" said Dot as if she hadn't heard Fleur.

"Get off," said Fleur.

During the absence of sound that followed this, I pictured Dot's face burgeoning with rage, her fists becoming rocks. So it surprised me when she tried to wheedle.

"Can't I ride it just a little longer?"

"No," said Fleur in an iron tone.

We pushed our cups aside and stood, ready, silly with apprehension. We were a mystifying sight to Eli.

"Sit down," he urged. "Sit down and have a bun."

Dot's shriek began, low, a growl, gaining in tortured resonances, and we moved toward the door.

"I'd better see what's going on," said Celestine, and then Dot's scream snapped off, suddenly, as if stuffed back into her mouth.

I left my cup on Eli's table and went outside. Fleur was gone. Russell was sitting in his new chair. Dot was sprawled on her rear end in the dirt with an addled look on her face. Celestine stood over them both, her anxiousness changing to satisfaction.

"Let's go," I said abruptly. But she was glad enough. Russell hadn't offered the slightest flicker in her direction. Dot stood, brushed her seat off, and ran to the truck. I bent down and looked at Russell because I had to, at least to say good-bye.

"Remember me?" I asked, then felt ridiculous.

"You look good," I said, although the truth was that Russell's face had sunken to the bone. He was clean. His clothes were ironed. But there was less of him than four years ago, and I turned away as Celestine began talking to him, loud, in a way that struck me as childish.

"It's Celestine. Can you look at me? How you making out?"

Eli came out and, with slow practiced movements, gently pulled Russell to his feet.

"Say good-bye to them," he told his brother. Russell's mouth opened, but no words came out, and his eyes dulled. He leaned against Eli, swaying like a tree half uprooted in a wind. We left them there, braced in the yard, and got back on the road.

We drove twenty miles in silence. I thought that Dot would pester out the details of Russell's case, but she didn't seem interested, put her head down again, and slept. Celestine didn't speak either until around the turnoff to Argus.

"Where did it go?" she said, all of a sudden. She stared out the windshield, her voice rising.

"Where did what go?" I said.

"Everything."

I saw she wasn't really speaking to me, or asking. She didn't look in my direction but to the strips of crops to either side, the neat endless rows that seemed to revolve beside us as we moved.

"Everything that ever happened to him in his life," she said, "all the things we said and did. Where did it go?"

I didn't have an answer, so I just drove. Once I had caused a miracle by smashing my face on ice, but now I was an ordinary person. In the few miles we had left I could not help drawing out Celestine's strange idea in my mind. In my line of work I've seen thousands of brains that belonged to sheep, pork, steers. They were all gray lumps like ours. Where did everything go? What was really inside? The flat fields unfolded, the shallow ditches ran beside the road. I felt the live thoughts hum inside of me, and I pictured tiny bees, insects made of blue electricity, in a colony so fragile that it would scatter at the slightest touch. I imagined a blow, like a mallet to the sheep, or a stroke, and I saw the whole swarm vibrating out.

Who could stop them? Who could catch them in their hands?

Sita's Night

The windows on ward A were regular glass, Louis pointed out, not barred or even locked. They looked out on expansive lawns, just turning from brown to green this early spring. There was even a screened porch. "You can sit out there on warm days," said Louis, "just like home." He put his arm around Sita and watched her face. They stood before a low brick building set off from the rest of the state mental hospital. But Sita wouldn't look at the windows, or at Louis either.

Louis and the psychiatrist had explained to Sita that ward A was a halfway place for patients with a very good chance of returning to society and leading a normal life. She was going there because four months ago she'd pretended to lose her voice, and ever since then Louis and her neighbors had been reading her lips. She grew to like the way they bent close, puzzling out her words, studying her face for clues. She grew to like it so much, in fact, that she lost the ability to speak out loud. Now when she opened her mouth to try and say something in an ordinary tone, nothing happened. But if she came to the state mental hospital, she might be cured. She might speak out loud. The psychiatrist had said as much.

"You've been encouraging her, Mr. Tappe. You've been altogether far too kind."

That's what the psychiatrist said to them both as they sat in his office. They watched him thumb through the dozens of black-bound artist's notebooks that Louis had kept over the years in an attempt to cure her episodes. In those notebooks Sita's dreams were recorded, her conversations with objects and flowers, fantasies she had related to Louis. The notebooks had seemed as private between them as their own embraces. It was a shock to

205

see them stacked on the doctor's desk. And Sita was frightened now. Louis was holding her good brown leather suitcase.

She tried to tell him that she wouldn't stay, that she wanted to go home.

"Wait," said Louis, watching her mouth move slowly, "I didn't get that. Try again."

Sita used her whole face emphatically. She ordered him to take her home.

"I can't," said Louis. He was miserable. "I'm not even supposed to try and understand you unless you verbalize your thoughts."

Sita told him silently that she hated ward A, and him too.

"Come on," Louis sighed, steering her up the sidewalk toward the entrance, "let's go find your room."

Sita let him guide her up the front steps, through a pair of glass doors that looked like they had chicken wire running through them, and down a hallway. The walls of the hallway were a dull leafy color. The floor was green-and-black linoleum tile. They walked up to a very large nurse in a limp white dress and sweater.

"Who have we here?" the nurse said, eyeing Sita, who was obviously the patient since she was being propelled by Louis. "Oh yes," the nurse remembered. "I had a call from Administration. You're Mrs. Tappe."

The nurse walked around the desk and loomed over Sita.

"You'll be getting a private room next week, Mrs. Tappe, but until then we have you in with Mrs. Waldvogel."

Sita pulled away from Louis and moved her lips angrily. The nurse ignored her, striding off.

"Let's bring your bag down the hall, shall we?" she called.

Louis pressed Sita's shoulder gently with his hand and she stumbled after the nurse, down another hallway, also green. All the green made Sita think of an aquarium, of living in a glass tank lined with algae. She wanted to tell this to Louis, to have him write her interesting thought down in his notebook. But then

206

they came to her room and from outside the door Sita saw that the walls were painted mustard yellow.

She tried to make Louis understand that she couldn't sleep in that room. The color made her sick to her stomach. She also hated roommates. Having another woman in her room would remind her of sleeping in the same room as Mary. All night she used to lay awake listening to Mary enjoy her sleep, hating her for each breath of unconsciousness. In the morning Sita would be groggy and tired no matter how much coffee she drank. She tried to say this. But Louis was talking to the nurse, writing down phone numbers and visiting hours on a little pad. Sita's suitcase was already on the bed. Louis kissed her and took her hand off of his arm and led her over to the bed. He sat her down. Once she sat there she couldn't move. The walls paralyzed her with their terrible color.

Sita sat on the bed for a long time, her mouth moving in jammed-up sentences. When she finally was able to tear her eyes from the walls, she realized that Louis was gone and the nurse was putting the last of her things in a steel bureau.

Stop! she tried to call out. Put everything back in my suitcase! I'm leaving!

"You'll have to speak out loud, Mrs. Tappe," said the nurse. "We don't read lips here."

Sita shut her mouth and glared. The nurse smiled into her face.

"Please be ready for supper in one-half hour," she said. "Until then why don't you sit here and get used to your new room?"

As soon as the nurse had left, Sita jumped up to examine the window. It was not locked or barred, but it didn't open very far. Not far enough for her to fit through, anyway. She pushed at the outside screen, to see if it was firmly in place.

"Wanting a little spring breeze, Mrs. Tappe?" It was the nurse again, barging into the room with an elderly lady so docile that she let herself be led in by the wrist. "Mrs. Waldvogel," the nurse said, "here's your new roommate."

Sita looked at the old woman. Mrs. Waldvogel was the perfect grandmother, the type who holds plates of ham in magazine advertisements or sniffs over bouquets of wired flowers on television. Her white hair was held back with a little tortoiseshell comb. She wore an old-fashioned housedress and a ruffled apron.

"I'll leave you two alone to get acquainted," said the nurse.

Mrs. Waldvogel walked up to Sita and took her by the hand.

"What a pretty girl you are," she said. "I hope you'll be happy here."

Sita nodded her thank-you. It was calming to be called a girl. She found herself sitting on the bed across from Mrs. Waldvogel, who took some pictures of her family from her drawer and began to show them to Sita one by one.

"This is Markie," she said, "and here's my son. And this baby in the picture is already four years old."

Sita looked at each picture very carefully. There was nothing strange about the people in the pictures or about the old lady. Perhaps, she thought, Louis was telling the truth. Staying in this place would be a restful vacation. And when the vacation was over she would speak out loud again instead of just moving her lips.

"It's nice to have you here," Mrs. Waldvogel said. "I was beginning to think they wouldn't put anyone in here again."

Sita felt a pang of sympathy for the old woman. Although the walls still glared horribly, and although she was exhausted from the long trip and the anxiety, she smiled. Mrs. Waldvogel blushed as she slowly put away her pictures.

"It's terrible to eat human flesh," she said in her sweet, old, cracked voice.

Mrs. Waldvogel patted her bundle of pictures and shut the drawer. "I devoured the last one," she said.

Sita gasped and turned away. Mrs. Waldvogel didn't notice. She twined a stray bit of white hair back into her hairdo and smoothed down her dress.

"It's time for supper. Shall we go?" she asked.

But Sita sat quite still.

After refusing supper and watching the light lengthen to soft gold in the window, Sita got up from her bed, took a pen and a small dime-store notebook from her purse, and wrote. Then she walked down the hallway to the lounge. The big nurse was working a crossword puzzle at her desk. Sita stood before her and displayed the note she had written.

Please call my husband, the note said. *I will not sleep in a room with a woman who believes she is a cannibal.*

But the nurse didn't even look at the note.

"I'm sorry, Mrs. Tappe," she said, "but I'm not supposed to read your lips or your notes. Doctor's orders."

The nurse waited to see if Sita would speak out loud to her. Sita opened her mouth, moved muscles in her throat, but no sound came out. She hated the absurd picture she must have made, standing before the desk gawking silently. She put her notebook back in her purse and walked over to sit before the television with the other patients.

Rowan and Martin's Laugh-In was on, a show she detested. Sitting before the wide screen, watching the slim bikini girls gyrate, was torture. The jokes weren't funny or the skits either, but the patients howled at the man who rammed trees with his tricycle and fell over, at the spinster in her ugly hair net, at anything.

Sita observed the patients because the show was so bad. Like Mrs. Waldvogel, they seemed normal, except perhaps that they laughed too eagerly and, Sita could not help notice, all of them were badly groomed. The men had a one or two day's growth of

209

beard and were not in the least attractive. Their faces seemed slack and old no matter what age they really were. And the women were even worse. They all had bad permanents. Their clothing fit poorly, or the colors of their pants and sweaters clashed. The air was blue around them because they all smoked. The lounge was full of ashtrays, not breakable cut-glass ones like Sita kept for the charred wet tobacco from Louis's pipe, but scratched coffee cans weighted with sand.

Mrs. Waldvogel came into the room. She sat down on a split plastic chair next to Sita.

"Supper was delicious," she said contentedly. "It's a shame you missed it."

Sita did not acknowledge her. Still the old woman went on.

"I'm having my hair done tomorrow dear. We have a patients' beauty school."

Sita looked around again at the women's ugly uncombed sets and ragged ends. Then she controlled her horror, snapped her lips shut, and walked back to her room. She flipped the switch. She hated stark overhead lighting, but there weren't any lamps.

Patients' beauty school! Even at her worst Sita had always kept her weekly hair appointments. She was proud that she'd never let herself go to seed. But in the patients' beauty school there was no telling what could happen. Frizz. Burned scalp. Savagely applied coloring. Sita's head began to hurt, each hair on it.

The light made the sick yellow of the walls blaze and throb. Sita decided that she would lay down in the dark even if Mrs. Waldvogel came in and bit her. She switched off the light and found her bed. She sank backward into the springs, unfolded a frayed white cotton blanket, and tucked it around her legs. The blanket, the pillow, and the spread smelled like someone else had sweat a sharp medicine into their seams. Sita closed her eyes and breathed into her cupped hands. Before she left, she had remembered to perfume her wrist with Muguet.

The faint odor of that flower, so pure and close to the earth, was comforting. She had planted real lilies of the valley because she liked them so much as a perfume.

Just last fall, before the hard freeze, when she was feeling back to normal, the pips had arrived in a little white box. Her order from a nursery company. The ground was stiff with frost but still workable. She'd put on her deerskin gloves and, on her knees, using a hand trowel, dug a shallow trench along the border of her blue Dwarf iris. Then one by one she'd planted the pips. They looked like shelled acorns, only tinier. "To be planted points upward," said a leaflet of directions. They came up early in the spring. The tiny spears of their leaves would be showing soon.

Lying there, sleepless, she imagined their white venous roots, a mass of them fastening together, forming new shoots below the earth, unfurling their stiff leaves. She saw herself touching their tiny bells, waxen white, fluted, and breathing the ravishing fragrance they gave off because Louis had absently walked through her border again, dragging his shovel, crushing them with his big, careless feet.

It seemed as though hours of imaginary gardening passed before Mrs. Waldvogel tiptoed in without turning on the light. Sita was still awake.

"Sleeping?" the old woman whispered.

Sita watched through slitted eyes as Mrs. Waldvogel took off and folded her dress and slip, then pulled a blue cotton nightgown over her head. She groped her way along the end of Sita's bed to her own. The two were right next to each other. Mrs. Waldvogel fluffed her pillow up and sat down on her covers. Enough light came through the transom for Sita to see her clearly. If the old woman was a cannibal, now was her chance.

Here I am, Sita thought, laid out like a human sacrifice.

The old woman grimaced hugely and bared her teeth. They were strong, white, perfect, and gleamed in the hallway light.

211

Sita's eyes opened in alarm. She sat bolt upright. But then Mrs. Waldvogel calmly and expertly plucked her false teeth out and dropped them into a plastic cup of water.

"You're still awake," she mumbled pleasantly, noticing Sita's stare. But Sita sank down and turned over. For a long time before sleep dragged her under, she stared at the dim wall opposite her bed. Already, she could feel it happening. The knot in her tongue was loosening.

The sun was barely up when she wakened, but even this early she could hear the television's hollow murmur in the lounge. Sita put on her clothing and walked down to the desk. A new nurse and an orderly were there, watching a morning talk show over Styrofoam cups of coffee. Sita had written a note.

I'd like to phone my husband, this note said.

"All right, I guess, although you're supposed to wait till seven," said this nurse. "Take her down there," she told the orderly, a stocky boy with a short black pigtail. He got up laughing at some joke the morning weatherman had made, and, assuming that Sita was mute or deaf, made exaggerated signs that she should follow him down the hall. He unlocked the door to the office that held medications and a phone. He picked up the receiver and held it out to her, then shook his head.

"Wait a sec," he puzzled, "if you can't talk . . ."

Sita snatched the receiver from the boy's hand and held it to her ear. She dialed and waited two rings while Louis groped his way out of sleep. She heard him pick up the phone. Before he even said hello she spoke.

"Get me out!" she cried to him. "I'm cured."

CELESTINE JAMES

ONE NIGHT MARY calls me up to tell me that I shouldn't bother driving in to work tomorrow. Then she waits, holding her breath on the phone, for me to ask her why not. So I ask.

"The shop's burnt," she answers in a satisfied tone.

"What!" I'm horrified.

"Don't worry," she says, "I'm safe. There was mainly smoke damage. The place is crawling with insurance adjusters."

"Should I come over?" I wonder.

"I'm coming over there," she says.

So that is how she ends up living in my house through December.

Mary is not too badly upset about the damage to the shop because, to tell the truth, it isn't doing quite so well as when Pete and Fritzie ran it. This is not Mary's fault. Since the boom with the sugar beet began, supermarkets have been setting up with one-stop-shopping convenience. I can see the attraction, but Mary calls them junk. At any rate, this accident is a chance to renovate. She could not afford to otherwise. She is excited. Workmen start in on the repairs to the butcher shop even before the insurance comes through. A hole burned through the smoke room and spread along the inner electrical connections. Mary is lucky. The only harm to her living quarters is a few gray plumes of smoke blown up the walls. She doesn't want to live with smoke or hammering, with plaster or men tramping through her back rooms, however, and says that she is much more comfortable

213

bedding down in Russell's old room with Dot. If I don't mind, that is.

"I don't mind," I tell her.

But the truth is after three days I'm edgy. I don't know why. Maybe it's that Dot and I have gotten used to our daily ways and Mary disrupts the evenings with her constant reports. She has been to the library for books and has taken her favorite out once more. It is a book by a man named Cheiro and is all about reading the lines in your hands. Mary has been doing this for years, and I'm tired of it. I know what the lines in my hands mean.

"No love, no money, no travel to Hawaii," I tell her when she asks for a look. "No thanks."

"I just want to see if that island in your Head Line has shrunk," she says, consulting her book. "It could mean a tumor of the brain or a nasty blow."

We are sitting in the front room around the gas furnace. I watch its blue ripple in the little crosshatched window. I tell Mary that there's more mystery right there in the jumping flames than in all of Cheiro's books.

"Well then answer me this," she says, leaning off her chair for emphasis, "a child is born with certain lines in its hand. Those lines and no others. How do you explain it?"

The flames reflect across her face, so ordinary yet so fierce. She has taken to wearing a different colored turban each day, covering her hair. She is wearing a white one now. Her slanting eyes are sharp yellow, and the little purple spider veins in her cheeks have darkened like stitches. If you didn't know she was a woman you would never know it. She could be the famous Cheiro himself.

"There's nothing to explain," I tell her stubbornly. "They're just lines."

But Mary isn't listening. She is looking into Dot's palm, which she has already read at least a thousand times before. It's the one thing Dot never tires of, however. Now she wonders if Mary can figure out the initials of the boy she will marry. Dot is almost eleven, but already, more than once, she has been deeply in love. I can hardly stand to see her lose out when it happens and she gets a crush. To attract attention she has developed a loud, booming voice, and like me, she is big and imposing, with a large-jawed grin full of teeth. She frightens off the other children with her hot pursuit. To get boyfriends she knocks them down and grinds their faces in the snowy grit. To get girls, she ties the string waistbands of their dresses to her own dress strings. She drags them around the playground until they promise to write her a note.

The nuns don't know what to do with Dot, and I don't either. So I do the wrong thing and give her everything until there is nothing left. I try to be the mother that I never had, to the daughter I never was. I see too much of myself in Dot. I know how it is. I was too big for all the boys. But I never went so far as to beat them senseless, which Dot has done.

I discourage violence and love-crushes, but Mary eggs her on.

"I see an S," she muses, "then a little j. S.j., S.j."

"It's not him," says Dot, disappointed. She broods into her hand as if her stare could rearrange the lines.

"Take your homework in the kitchen," I say, "and get it done."

I can feel Dot make a face behind my back. A sense develops in a parent.

"I'll help," says Mary, too quickly. So they go in, leaving me alone. For a while then I hear them snicker as they flip through the pages of Dot's books. I have no doubt that they are laughing at me, and I know I will feel this way later on as well. Mary will sleep in Dot's bed and Dot will flop out on a cot. As I am trying to sleep I will hear the two of them whispering, but I won't tell them to be quiet, because I know that Mary will not obey.

That's it, I realize now, looking at the gas glow. That is why I'm so depressed since Mary has been around. It is like having two unruly daughters who won't listen or mind me. I am out-numbered, the only grown-up.

When Mary and Dot come back into the room, I am all set to ask how the work on Mary's house is coming and maybe suggest she could live back there quite soon. But before I can open my mouth Dot announces that she has a secret that she has been keeping for one week. By the way Mary smiles knowingly and by the way she sharply gestures for me to listen, it is obvious that Dot has already told her. This upsets me, but with effort I form my face into an eager mask.

We are quiet. Then Dot speaks in a loud voice.

"I am going to play Joseph, father of the Christ child," she states. "We've been practicing for the Christmas play next week."

I think it's terrible that they picked my little girl to play the father of Christ in their pageant. Then I look at Dot, imagining her in a long grizzled beard and coarse robe. I see the carpenter's maul wielded in her fist. I sigh. I try to smile. It's true that she will be convincing.

Dot hands me a folded-up mimeograph from her teacher, and I read that there will be a Christmas play the second week in December. Parents are invited to attend, and also to bring a pan of hotdish or dessert for a potluck afterward. There is a dotted line on which I'm supposed to write the dish I'll bring. But the dish is already filled in with the word *Jell-O*.

"Jell-O salad," Mary says, noticing my stare. I look at Dot and try to be reasonable.

"I'm proud of you," I tell Dot. "Of course I'll be there."

Then I ask Dot to put her pajamas on and wash her face. She says no. I say yes. Mary acts the coward and stays out of it. One hour later, excited and satisfied at having caused a delay, Dot tramps upstairs, loudly singing her favorite carol, which has a

216

chorus of "Pa-rup-pa-pa-pum." Listening to her footsteps in the upstairs hall my heart fills up. Even though she's difficult, I'm her mother. I'm the one who should sign her Christmas mimeograph. But I can't say this to Mary because it seems small and foolish, so instead I blurt out something more idiotic yet.

"I suppose you're going to put your damn radishes in the Jell-O!"

I say this suddenly, in a grating voice that seems to echo.

Mary's answer is an attempt to act innocent. She says that she thought she'd save me trouble by bringing along the dish. She thought because I was so busy she would make one of her special Jell-O salads. I do not say I am glad she has done this, because it isn't her place. And there is another thing as well: she knows I don't like her Jell-O salads. I've said so before. She puts in walnuts or chopped celery, macaroni, onions, miniature marshmallows, or, worst of all, sliced radishes.

Even thinking about her strange Jell-O makes me furious. Nothing she cooks is normal, not her bran cookies, not her sheet cakes, not her liver casseroles. I don't want her awful cooking to reflect on Dot.

"All right," I say coldly, however, "do as you like."

Dot comes down the stairs in a woolly nightgown, fresh and washed. She is so happy about having stayed up an hour late, about her starring role and our acceptance of the invitation, that I don't have the heart to put a damper on any of her joy. But she puts the damper on herself, for a moment, in a startling way.

"I forgot to tell you what the play is called," she says. "It's *The Donkey of Destiny*."

And then her expression changes suddenly.

"I hate the donkey," she says, almost as if to herself.

"Dot?" I ask.

But already she has turned, surprisingly with no more argument, and run upstairs to climb in bed.

217

That night, I keep Mary downstairs talking for a long time. I am still annoyed with her, and really, the reason I talk so late is merely to keep her from keeping Dot awake. I don't let Mary go to bed until her eyes droop. She yawns, exhausted, and can hardly drag herself from the chair.

I'm tired too. And I know that by diverting Mary I've left Dot to face her problem with the donkey alone. Whatever that problem is, I should have helped her. I should have gone upstairs after her and got her to admit what was wrong. But I know if I had, Mary would have climbed right after me and tried to take over the situation.

This must stop! I think, getting into bed when the house is quiet. I decide that no matter what, even if it causes a misunderstanding, Mary must go back to her own house after the Christmas play is finished. Until then I will endure her acting girlish with Dot. I will try to stand them whispering late across the hall and telling secrets to each other. But just until the play is over. After that, I decide I will keep my daughter to myself.

But the next day I have to remember all that I intend and bite my lip. For Mary tells me something I do not know about my own daughter, although I would have known if it hadn't been for keeping Mary up the night before.

We are at the shop. It is late morning and after having been closed for a few weeks we're opening for business in a few hours. We've started back into preparing orders for our regular customers, which seems to me a hopeful sign. Repair work is going on around us. I want to urge the men with their aprons full of tools to work quickly. But they are going as fast as they can already. To me, their frenzied hammering and the whine of their drills is a cheerful industrious sound. To Mary, it is irritating.

"It gets on my nerves," she says, wrapping pound after pound of bratwurst.

"The harder they work, the sooner you can move back home,"

218

I answer. I am unable to keep a note of anticipation from my voice.

"Well," says Mary, with a close glance, "I could always check into the Fox."

"Oh no," I answer in a voice I cannot keep sincere. "Don't go to a hotel. I'm sure that your presence is very beneficial to Dot."

"I'm sure it is too," Mary says, giving me the same narrow-eyed stare she uses often on hard cases who want credit. But I do not want credit. She is the one in that position. She wants to stay with me and weasel her way into Dot's affection, not that I don't understand: Mary is alone, I know. It's her way of doing it that I object to. Wallace Pfef, for instance, likes my daughter very much, but he never butts into our business the way Mary does.

So I return Mary's stare with blank windows she cannot read, and hit the cash button on the register. I am adding up an order. By the time I find the total she has recovered and swung around.

"Do you know what it was about the donkey last night?" She asks this as soon as I slam the drawer shut. I do not want to have to ask her.

But Mary doesn't wait for me to ask.

"Dot *loves* the donkey. One half of it, that is." She fairly crows. "The little boy who plays the front end is her beau."

"That's no surprise to me," I say calmly, but inside I am thinking that I really could be driven past my limit. I really could be forced to do something I'd regret.

I turn from Mary and start thinking. If she has been able to worm her way into my daughter's heart to this extent, where will it leave off? If Dot ever runs away I think she'll hitch into town and live with her aunt. What a victory for Mary! I'll be fired and barred from The House of Meats. I'll have to hire a lawyer to get my daughter back. It isn't fair. I'm the one who has to be strict and tell Dot to do her homework. Mary is the one who keeps her up late, having fun, so that the next day she dozes off in school. I'm the one who tries to make Dot eat lima beans and wash her neck. Mary tells lies looking into the palm of her hand. I ached for a mother because I never had one. I would have been glad for a mother to tell me what to do. But Dot has always had me there no matter what. I've been steady but unexciting. For dinner I make hamburger casserole, while Mary would serve anything that fell into her hands.

A week goes by, and then it is the morning of the Christmas play, bleak and cold and with the usual traveler's warning. Dot is spinning with excitement, nearly out of control. She bolts down her breakfast and in a surge of affection hugs me, then Mary. I can see that Mary is so touched and surprised that she has no words, can't even say good-bye or wish Dot luck. Dot forgets to brush her hair and jumps out the door, looking wild and unruly. Hug or no hug, I run after her with a hairbrush, slipping and sliding. I catch her at the bus stop.

"Dot," I say, "stand still. Calm down or you'll be tired by the time you get on stage."

Her cheeks glow and her eyes are dagger bright. She is carrying an old bathrobe of Wallace's and a pair of my leather sandals in a paper sack. The rest of her costume will be supplied by the nuns. The wind is harsh. My legs are bare. The road is slick and welted with frozen grime. Dot struggles while I brush her hair and pluck lint from her blue plush coat. The bus rescues her. She leaps in the very second its thin door swishes open.

"Next time you see me I'll be *disguised*," she screams.

The gears of the bus groan impatiently, and she runs down the aisle to sit in back with, as I have heard, the other trouble-makers. She waves, though. Her face is a pure blob of light through the caked dust of the window. The bus pulls carefully down the road, and she is gone. I walk back to the house with my plan firm in mind.

The first thing I'm going to do is call Wallace Pfef, because my car has one rotten snow tire and tonight, in this ice, I'm going to need a ride. I can't ask Mary, because I'm bringing along a special secret dish that I don't want her to know about. Not until the play is finished, that is, not until the parents are wandering hungrily toward the back of the auditorium where the long hot-lunch tables are set, full of uncovered dishes. Then she'll find out about it. Soon enough. For I've decided to go more hog-wild than Mary would have the nerve to. I've decided a jealous mother has the right to be unpredictable. And I've also fixed it so all the strange looks will go in Mary's direction and not toward Dot or her mother. We'll be eating off our paper plates, talking to Wallace Pfef, ignoring the scratched heads and titters at the table. Mary, for her part, will be someplace else. I don't care. I don't even plan to sit with her during the play.

When I get back to the house she is already prepared to drive into town. I'm glad she's going early. I'm taking the day off. That way I'll have time to perfect my special dish for this evening.

"Don't bother to wait for me," I say as she is going out; "just find a place in the auditorium tonight, and sit. It will be crowded."

She nods at me and drives off, squinting forward to see through the little antifrost square of plastic fixed onto her windshield. I call Wallace and agree on a time and think that everything will go like clockwork. But of course, as with most things in life, it doesn't.

The gymnasium that night is packed full and noisy. I walk into the confusion with Wallace and my foil-covered pan, but before I can safely deposit it on the table, along with the offerings of the other parents, we are caught by Mary. She is dressed to the hilt, in a black turban with a rhinestone buckle, and a new rayon dress. The material is so unusual I can hardly stop looking at it. The background is blue, covered everywhere with markings that could have been drawn by prehistorics with charcoal sticks. It is writing of a sort, legible yet meaningless. It almost makes you want to lean forward and decipher it.

"I saved us seats," she says, "right up front. Come on, before someone grabs them."

"I'll find you," I say, pushing Pfef to go with her. Luckily, she is so anxious to get back to the seats that she doesn't notice I've brought a dish. So I am able to slip it in among the others. I say hello to the teachers who are standing at the back marshaling the paper cups. Even Mrs. Shumway gives a pleasant smile tonight, although her eyes, darting over the crowd, light a moment on Mary's flashing buckle, and take on a glazed wariness.

At length, I make my way to where Mary has kept the seat open between herself and Wallace. She has nothing to say to Wallace since he has become Dot's friend. She also blames him for sugar beets, which have brought the new franchise supermarkets that have cost her so much business. We look around, caught up in the excitement of it all. The lights blaze in steel-mesh buckets. Dads with rolled sleeves are lifting additional folding chairs from side carts and settling mink-collared grandmothers. In front, by the entries to the stage wings, nuns are huddled together in their black veils. The gym is run-down, a parish all-purpose room used for wedding and funeral dinners, budget meetings, bingo. The purple velveteen curtain is a shabby cast-off from the public school. The wood floor creaks and wavers. But the walls shine, decked in strands of tinsel. The feverish noise mounts and mounts, then, suddenly, it hushes and there is only the sound of programs rustling. In whispers, we find and admire Dot's name. The lights go down. There is complete silence. Then the curtains squeak open. The spotlight shows a boy wearing a knit poncho and a huge sombrero of the kind people who have been to Mexico hang on their walls. This boy makes a long sad speech about his friend the donkey, who he must sell to the glue factory in order to buy food. On a darkened set of bleachers behind him, a chorus of first-graders laments the donkey's fate.

The boy pulls the rope he has been twisting in his hands, and the donkey bumbles out of the wings. It is wearing gray pants and tennis shoes. The body is barrel shaped, lopsided, and the paper mache head lolls like it was drunk. The mouth, painted open in a grin, and the slanted black-rimmed eyes give it a strange expression of cruelty.

Parents *ooh* and *ahh*, but some look startled. The donkey is an unpleasant creature. Its dyed burlap-and-rug hide looks moth-eaten. One ear is long and one is short. Mary must be the only person in the crowd who thinks the donkey is cute. "Oh look at it prance," she whispers into my ear.

Her tartar eyes gleam softly; she bites her lip. Her gloves are in a tight ball like socks. She smiles as the boy and his donkey start out on the long road to the glue factory. Tragedy, her favorite element, is in the air. Her eyes sparkle when the chorus wails.

"Amigos! We are amigos!" the boy shouts from beneath the sombrero. Then they slowly begin to walk across the stage. They are weeping. But before they reach the glue factory, Saint Joseph appears.

My heart jumps. I am so afraid that she will trip or say the wrong thing. But she is just right.

She wears a long beard of spray-painted cotton, an old piece of upholstery fabric tied to her head, and the brown towel-cloth bathrobe that Wallace loaned to her. My summer sandals look biblical on her. As in my vision of her, she is carrying a wooden maul. Mary nods proudly, and I guess that the maul is her old sheep knocker. I don't like that. Saint Joseph should carry a construction tool, I think, not an instrument of death. Perhaps because of the maul, Dot looks grimmer than the mild church statues, and more powerful. I believe in her as Saint Joseph, even though she is my daughter. The donkey sidles up to her with its evil, silly grin. She stands before it with her legs spread wide, balancing on the balls of her feet. All I can see of the boy who, according to Mary, she loves are the gray corduroy knees and frayed black shoes. Dot grabs the donkey around the neck, and the gray legs twitch for a moment in the air. Then she sets the donkey down and says her lines to the donkey's amigo.

"Señor, where are you going with this donkey?"

"I must sell it to the glue factory, for my family is hungry," says the boy sadly.

"Perhaps I can help you out," says Dot. "My wife Mary, myself, and our little boy Baby Jesus want to flee King Herod. My wife could ride this donkey if you would sell it."

"I will sell my donkey to help you," shouts the boy. "He will not be killed!"

"Of course not," says Dot. "We will only ride him across the desert to Egypt."

She takes some large coins made of crushed aluminum foil from her bathrobe pocket and gives them to the boy.

And so it is, the transaction is accomplished. The donkey of destiny now belongs to Dot, who then tries to pat its snarling paper mache muzzle. But here is where the episode occurs which, I later hope, will not scar the mind of my daughter for life. The donkey balks. Is this in the script? I glance at Wallace, then Mary, wondering. But Wallace shrugs and Mary's look narrows to a flashlight focus of premonitions.

"Come along little donkey," says Saint Joseph through grit teeth. She pulls, perhaps a bit roughly, at the rope on its neck. Suddenly, a hand snakes from the front of the donkey's neck flap and rips the rope out of Saint Joseph's surprised knuckles.

My hands fly up, helplessly, as if they could stop everything. But too late.

The audience twitters, a few loud men guffaw, and Saint Joseph hears the audience, laughing at her! She jerks the rope back from the donkey. The hand slips out again, and this time pulls the cotton fluff right off Saint Joseph's chin.

Dot's arm tightens. I can feel it. Her face goes red with fury, purple, white, and she raises the maul, high! I know what will happen. The audience gapes. Then she brings it down clean, like swift judgment, on the cardboard skull of the beast.

The front of the donkey drops. The head flies off, smashed. The last of that scene that we see is Saint Joseph standing in criminal triumph, maul gripped tight, over the motionless body of a tow-haired boy.

The curtain has closed and the audience is in a rumble of consternation. A fat blond hysterical woman flies down the aisle, no doubt the mother of the donkey's felled front end. I sit rooted.

"Come!" Mary hisses, hoisting her handbag on her elbow. "Or the nuns will take it out on her hide!"

We leave the chairs to Wallace and find the side door. We slip behind the curtains into the backstage area. Angels and shepherds are standing in dismayed clumps. The Virgin Mary has torn off her veil and sobs in a corner. The painted wood silhouettes of sheep and cattle look stupidly baffled.

"Where's Dot?" Mary's voice booms. Everybody swivels.

"She escaped out the back door of the gym," says one of the sisters, tight lipped.

"Get out a search party then!" says Mary. "She's barefoot in the snow!"

But no search party forms at her words.

I take Mary's elbow and steer her out the back entrance.

"We'll look for her in your truck," I say, "and don't worry. I'm sure she put on boots."

We drive slowly up and down the streets of Argus. There are so many new streets that sometimes we hardly know where we are. We drive back, stop in at Mary's, and finally make it all the way home where we find Dot bundled in a blanket, sitting on the living-room coffee table with her bare feet by the heat ducts. The pair of red boots she took are drying out on a plastic mat.

"Young lady!" I shout in relief, marching toward her, but Mary gets there first.

"Wait," says Mary, holding me back. "She *is* hurt."

Sure enough, Dot is hiding something. She sits, clutching her play beard, shaking with the cold or maybe holding herself together. Defeated, wrapped in a blanket, she looks, oddly, like an ordinary middle-aged man. Her face is pale, streaked with misery, and her blue eyes are distant, unfamiliar with not even a hint of anger.

"Dot," I say, opening my arms.

She hesitates, wants to come, won't let herself, won't look at my face, but she starts to move toward me. Mary, however, is in the way between us. Mary kneels with a stiff creak and then suddenly, fiercely, lunges and catches my daughter full across the chest and neck with a stranglehold. Right then, I don't even care it is Mary who holds her, because I can only feel Dot's sadness. But Dot charges suddenly into my arms, runs right over Mary like a bull, sends Mary tumbling in a heap of black signs. Then Dot bolts up the stairs. The door to her room slams.

Mary thumped so loudly, falling over, that I pause just a moment to help her. But she is not hurt and even tries to look perversely delighted over what Dot has done. She pushes away my helping hands and lifts herself up.

"That's my girl," she says, adjusting her turban.

I go upstairs.

"Dot," I say, tapping on her door.

After a while I hear her muffled voice and so I enter. I sit down with her in the dark, on the cot where she has thrown herself, and slowly let my arms fall around her, as if by accident. She doesn't move, but she is tense as an animal in fear, ready to snap or go limp beneath its keeper's grasp. I adjust my hands, flattening my palms so that I touch her by inches. When I move them, pressing my fingers in her hair, stroking down the side of her neck, she almost shrugs me off. But she cannot, the fight has left her and she needs me too much to resist when I gather her close. Her heavy head falls against me, salty, smelling of sour wool. Her shoulders rock, but I can't tell she's crying until my skirt sticks to my thighs damp, and she breathes out, harsh and deep.

It is so long before she draws another breath that I almost shake her in alarm. But she is just asleep, and nothing will disturb her now. I don't leave, even though my arms go numb and Mary waits downstairs. I don't leave when she tosses in her first dream, throwing more weight against me. I sit perfectly still.

Then her fingers uncurl, as if sand is trickling out, and she seems lighter. The radiator shudders in the corner. Dot's room smells like the nests of shoes and socks she has made this week. It smells of the mildewed stuffing of her battered and abandoned dolls and of the sawdust where her hamsters hide. It smells of oil that she puts on her softball glove, lilac water that she dumps on her hair. It smells of cold grit between the window and the sill. It smells of Dot, a clean and bitter smell, like new bark, that I'd know anywhere.

I fall asleep sitting in the peace like that, and when I wake up I can't tell how late it is. I go downstairs and see that Mary is sitting by the gas heater. She has a piece of bread and butter in one hand and a mug of weak coffee in the other. The clock says midnight.

"I made a pot." She gestures toward the kitchen. "Get some for yourself."

So I do, and for a while we sit munching and sipping without a word.

227

"Wallace must have stayed back to talk with the parents," I say at last. "I suppose somehow the nuns salvaged the event."

"That kid deserved it," Mary says. "He was really the donkey's ass."

I agree with her. Mary speculates that he is a new child in the area, one of those who live in the big six-plexes known as cardboard acres. I tell her that children have had their moments of violence since time began, and this will pass. She begins to talk about the supper, about how they'll all mill back and fill their plates and talk about her specially concocted Jell-O. She has found a recipe she never tried before. I am dreamy and half-asleep after sitting with Dot and so, when I tell her about the dish I brought, I don't think.

"Did you notice that I brought in a special pan?" I ask.

"No," she says. She doesn't even ask what it was. I touch her chair and laugh.

"Well listen a minute," I say. "It had your name on it."

"My name?" She is interested.

"I taped it on the bottom of the pan," I tell her, "although I made the dish myself."

She is silent now and curious.

"What was in it?" she asks.

"I made a Jell-O salad."

"Oh," she says, "what kind?"

"The kind full of nuts and bolts," I say, "plus washers of all types. I raided Russell's toolbox for the special ingredients."

Her pupils harden to pinpoints. She trains a long look on my face. Then she turns away and huffs on her coffee, as if to cool it. I expect she will laugh at any moment and see the joke. I expect from her anything but what actually happens. For she never speaks. Her shoulders slump down and her back relents. And then, in the odd print of her dress, I finally read that she is hurt. She won't admit it, I know, but Mary wanted this evening

228

to be successful even more than I did. She wanted to taste here and there among the hotdishes and discuss them. She wanted to boast about her niece's starring role. It was the first time that she was ever included to this extent in the life of Dot, and unless a wind hits and the shop is completely leveled, this will probably be the last. She has no excuse to stay here, even now.

"I'm going," she says. "I left the shop unlocked and the dogs are out."

She puts on her coat and walks out of the door. I am left standing in the entry as her lights swing away into the dark. I hardly ever think about Mary's feelings, but now I do. I think of her alone in the small throbbing cave of her vehicle. She has worn thin, fancy gloves for the play, and now the night is so cold that she can only keep one hand at a time on the wheel. As she drives, she blows on the other hand to warm it. Then she changes hands. It is three miles between my house and Argus, and the road is bad. I watch Mary's car move cautiously down the dangerously frozen gravel ruts. Her red taillights tremble at the far intersection, then wink out.

The Birdorama

For days, Adelaide's silence and the brooding look she turned on the rain-wet leaves outside the tiny window of their bedroom warned Omar that she was building up a fit of anger. Her rage had nothing to do with him. It damned up regularly as water and there was no use in his trying to stop it. When she let loose, Omar stayed out of her way and let her pound on tables and chairs, let her kick and curse and bang screens and break whatever brought her peace.

In blue darkness, awakening to find her gone from their bed, he sneaked downstairs to spy on her mood. She was sitting at her kitchen table with a cup of cocoa. Adelaide's skin had gone paper white with age, and her hair too, a halo that stood out, electric. Her throat and slim waist had stayed supple. Her touch was quick and hard. She snapped when she spoke, and her eyes gave off a cool harsh light that subdued the customers who came to see their birds. Now, her housecoat heaped around her in a white billow, Adelaide poked at a little jade plant in a pot with a sharpened pencil. Omar watched her for a moment then retreated upstairs, dressed himself, and climbed down the flimsy back stairway.

Outside, the steam was rising from the grass and the palms were gray blue, alive and shuddering with breezes that stirred at dawn. The first few waking birds were starting to complain, to throw themselves back and forth across the inside of the wire dome. They hung for a wingbeat and then fell, flapping two or three times depending on their span, to the other side. Every morning they had to test the limits of their quarters and find the shape of it all over before they could calm down to sing and feed. Their brains were tiny, the size of watch mechanisms, accurate

230

but stupid. They couldn't hold one idea in their heads overnight.

When Omar stepped into the great silver gazebo that glittered through the palms and attracted visitors from the local resorts, all the birds wheeled up, threw their claws out, and beat the air in circles, then settled to hone their beaks on the dead tree limbs planted in concrete. The arched ribs of the cage soared, black against the pearl-gray sky. From across the yard, Adelaide began. He did not look back, but her wordless scream caught him in the stomach. Out in the boat sometimes his trawling buddies tied two trash fish together, threw them out for seagulls, and watched the birds snap the fish up and kill themselves, bewildered, bound through the guts. At times like this, he and Adelaide were tied together just as viciously. He felt her pain like it was inside of him, but could do nothing.

He walked through the dome, back to the feed room. The birds knew the routine and collected, their eyes bright as snakes'. They had to eat more than their weight, and their morning frenzy was unpleasant to watch, even though it was the only time they seemed intelligent. Their heads bobbed in greed like pistons and their beaks stabbed up bits of fruit and animal fat. Turning away, Omar heard glass begin to break in long silvery muffled waves inside the house. Adelaide was sweeping ornaments off shelves, or perhaps she had pulled down the kitchen rack of wineglasses. She never hurt herself, and there was really no reason to stop her. Glassware was cheap and the closest neighbor was a quarter mile off. It was the waiting that oppressed Omar.

To pass the time he imagined what they would do once Adelaide came back to herself. He saw them holding hands in the front yard, behind the jacaranda, laughing at some foolish thing a customer had said. He saw her beating him at cards, tossing down the whole deck in a sprawl. She found a flat glittering stone from their driveway and held it against his cheek. She looked into his eyes. Gave him a piece of soap. A section of a ripe

231

orange. A newspaper. He saw them sleeping, curled tight in their sagging bed.

The house went huge with quiet and he got up to go. The birds were talking to each other now, oblivious of him. The sky was low and dense, the heat already close, and the rain an invisible warm spray. He heard the sound of Adelaide's broom and waited outside the door until the dustpan spilled musically, twice. Then he went in. She stood in the middle of the kitchen floor, her feet smeared with blood. Her hair was combed tight into a bent steel clip, and the cumulus puffs of her white gown hung flat. Her lips were pinched pale, and her spent eyes held his, frightened. She picked up a coffee cup, poured it shakily full, and he reached forward to take it from her hands before it spilled.

WALLACE PFEF

THEY LOVED DOT too much, and for that sin she made them miserable. Sometimes it was as if all of her family's worst qualities were crowded into her—Mary's stubborn, abrupt ways, Sita's vanity, Celestine's occasional cruelties, Karl's lack of responsibility. I went through fits, avoiding Celestine and Dot for months, then giving in. Dot had one trait that always drew me back.

She feared nothing. Not darkness, heights, nor any type of reptile. She jumped off high dives, climbed my ladders, walked through night as if she owned it. She showed me jars of loathsome creatures, which she watched tenderly for hours—slugs and caterpillars, even a yellow spider, and black snakes with orange stripes running their full length. She kept other small animals too. In the summer, she gave off the hay smell of the pressed alfalfa pellets she fed her rabbits, and the sewery odor of turtle food. But she was kinder to her dumb animals than to her mother and aunt.

Them, she starved.

I think that Dot's behavior was partly the result of Celestine and Mary's squabbling. Sometimes I thought the friction between the two women would grind Dot to dust, but instead she hardened between them, grew tough. She stood solid in the yard when she was five years old, put her fists on her hips and yelled at cats. When she was ten, she could do a full day's work, if she ever wanted.

Sometimes in the afternoons Dot came over, supposedly to

233

prune the spirea and flowering crab trees, or rake up the fresh-mowed grass clippings. I had prospered along with the sugar beet. Those acres I had bought up hit the ceiling once beets came in, and I had part share in the new sugar refinery. I could afford time off to putter. She watched me do it, all the while taking chances with my tools. She loved to hammer, and anything was vulnerable to her steel. Floors, pots, tables, walls. I convinced her to build a birdhouse, which turned out enormous, skewed, big enough for a pack of dogs. We put up a drainpipe, and nailed together a dead drunk trellis.

The nicest thing she ever did for me, the one present I re-member, was a cardboard egg carton filled with neatly broken eggshells. Each shell held a teaspoon of earth and, she assured me, a surprise seed that would grow if sprinkled diligently. I kept my carton on the windowsill, sprinkled, and a few seeds did germinate. They sent up split fragile shoots that paled and with-ered before I could tell what they were.

I was proud that when Dot ran away, she ran through me. I came upon her suddenly, once, curled up, spent and drowsing at the top of my cellar steps, and sat down beside her. She was barefoot, in summer shorts. She had wrapped herself in an old gray gardening sweater that I kept on a downstairs hook.

"I'm running away," she said. "I even left a note."

"Why?"

"I'm going to live with my dad."

"Now, now," I said in a soothing voice, "just tell Uncle Wal-lace and he'll make it all right."

Dot's eyes widened, shooting rays of burning disdain.

"It is all right. He sends me things," she said, "neat things like soap. He sends me bus schedules and doll watches. He wants me and he's not what Aunt Mary says."

"What does Aunt Mary say he is?"

"A bum."

234

I hesitated. Once I would have defended Karl. It took seconds to realize that my loyalties had shifted through the years, that it had happened without a word to myself, without acknowledgment.

"I wouldn't exactly call him that," I got out.

She took that for approval.

"I know," she agreed. "If he's nothing but a bum where'd he get that big wheelchair? A bum couldn't get a wheelchair like that."

"That's right," I said, thinking of the ridiculous gift.

Dot considered this, suspicious.

"You know," she said at last, pointing her chin at me, "all the matchbooks in my collection? They're almost all from far-off places. Sometimes he sends an Iowa or Minnesota, but hardly ever. He's been around the world!"

Her claim didn't stand up, even in her own ears. I knew by the way she turned aside, unable to stare me down.

"Dot," I said, "come on upstairs and let me make a sandwich for you. Toasted cheese and tuna?"

She followed but was not to be distracted from her purpose by any one of her favorite foods, not even the cookie she loved called Mystic Mint. I kept a box of them on ice for her. We both liked them better frozen. She made me tie half a dozen in a plastic bag for her to take on her trip. Not until I asked her where she thought she would find Karl did she stop chattering about the bright future, the things they'd see together. It took a good while longer before she let me phone Celestine.

"Look here," I said to Dot after I hung up. "You should forget him."

She put down her sandwich and looked hostile.

"How come?"

I took a deep breath. My heart was pounding, foolish I suppose, but thinking of Karl just then made it hard to breathe normally.

Something had happened in the long period of time when I had not let myself remember him. Unexamined, unaired, feelings can change, rot to shreds or brew poison. I found myself saying surprising things.

"He's worse than a bum," I told Dot. "He got your mother pregnant and ran away. He stole some money from me and then went to Aunt Sita, took a handout, drove her into an asylum, then disappeared. He tries to sell things, but they don't work. He drinks and lies, can't make a living, cons and fools people. He's a nothing . . . he kicked my dog."

I stopped, out of breath, astonished and sick. But I needn't have worried so, for Dot's whole face gleamed. She was transported by my words, ready to fly off, find him.

"And," I said, mustering a desperate lie, the only one, "he hates children."

"Not me," Dot cried, jumping from the chair, stamping up and down in a dance that became a frenzy. "Not me, not me, not me!"

I had the awful urge to twist her arm, hiss, kill her fantasy. Yes you, I wanted so much to say, especially you.

But of course I didn't go that far. Celestine was at the door. She barged in and went straight through the house like a freight train, almost wailing. I would have been touched if I hadn't been so distressed with myself. But then, as time passed I learned the lesson parents do early on. You fail sometimes. No matter how much you love your children, there are times you slip. There are moments you stutter, can't give, lose your temper, or simply lose face with the world, and you can't explain this to a child.

It was a year so many other things began, things of greater and more terrible import. There was a war building up overseas, and death seemed to stalk our public heroes. The government could not be trusted, either, not even close to home. Here in North Dakota the missiles went in, a series of underground silos that

236

didn't store grain. Right in town, there was an uproar of construction and new plans. Our developers were running out of the usual street names and had started naming cul-de-sacs for their wives and children.

But for all that was going on out there, that year stands out as the one I failed Dot.

Christmas is hard on a man alone. I was always included in someone's family dinner, but then I had to go home. It was the time of year I felt the emptiest, and sorry for myself. Books diverted me only for a short time, television made it worse with all those Christmas specials, movie stars dressed in velvet, singing carols, taking sleigh rides, wrapped in big white furs. The one event I truly looked forward to that year was seeing Dot play Saint Joseph in the Christmas pageant. She'd invited me herself and even borrowed an old bathrobe I kept around. Her starring role of Saint Joseph could have been that of Christ himself, she was so proud. It wasn't only for her size that they gave it to her, but also her voice. She had developed her vocal cords keeping up the outfield chatter for her baseball team all summer, droning like a maddened locust, "Humm baby," and "Hey battah, hey battah, hey battah." I don't remember Saint Joseph ever saying much in Christmas plays, but Dot claimed that she had twenty lines. And so I looked forward to the pageant night, was happy when that night came, and hummed Burl Ives Christmas tunes driving out to fetch Celestine. I wasn't prepared at all for the disaster.

I'm speaking of the private disaster, my secret one, not about the boy who enraged Dot or the punishment she delivered with Mary's old sheep mallet. That was not so surprising, for the fact is Dot was often in trouble for her temper. I don't know why the nuns even let her play such a vital role. The disaster that shocked

237

me, that pierced me through, happened right before the public one, when I saw Karl.

It was the old brown bathrobe that I'd lent Dot for a costume. I'd been a fool to forget its significance. That bathrobe was the kind of thing you lend to a man who comes to visit, but I'd not thought of that for years, or how he looked standing in the doorway.

And then he appeared.

It happened when the boy's hand snaked out of the donkey's coat and pulled Saint Joseph's beard off. I did not think that Dot resembled Karl, but I was wrong. For there he lounged, suddenly, half in shadow, with the light behind him on the white woodwork. His eyes lowered so his lashes brushed down, then lifted to look me full and square so that there was no distance in the room and none between us.

I started up, stood. The gym was a hive of golden insects buzzing, floating, gathering the honey that filled me. I was in tears. My glasses fogged. Nobody noticed, for which thank God. Through a gap in the crowd I saw the front of the donkey fall in a heap. Then its back end pitched forward, and a boy scrambled from the husk of gray carpet samples, shouting.

I turned my head, slapped my hands to my temples, but it was no use. Karl was still there, across from me in the morning, at the table, pouring coffee and stirring in three spoonfuls of sugar, combing his black hair from his eyes with his fingers, licking the drops of milk from his moustache.

The curtains swept shut. One of the sisters emerged to announce that the play would have to end. Applause spattered through the audience, and people began to fill the aisles. "Shouldn't we at least eat?" someone asked. I was forced to answer, forced to mop my brow and clean my glasses off with studious care. Then I walked through the clumps of people who were already finding comfort at the back table.

The Pyrex covers of the dishes had been removed. Cups of

urn coffee were poured and handed out. I went through the line mechanically, collected mysterious dollops, ate in frantic haste. Between mouthfuls I made excuses for Saint Joseph's temper, and soon the topics switched as always to sugar-beet forecasts and mortgage rates, bond levies and pavement costs. Then I almost cracked my tooth on a metal bolt.

"Someone's idea of a joke," said the principal, to whom I'd been talking. "No one knows who did it. Some teenage prank perhaps. Whoever it was filled a whole pan with hardware, but if there was a name attached to that dish it fell off."

"It's very strange," I said, nudging the piece of hardware aside.

The bolt brought me to my senses. It was time I went home, out of harm's path, where I could soak my delusions away in the bathtub. A hot bath was what I wanted desperately. I looked around, but Celestine and Mary were nowhere in sight. I thought after the fiasco they had probably taken Dot home in Mary's truck. I should have thought of Dot then. I should have wondered what drove her to fell the donkey. But I was too far gone, dragged under by memory, by the strain of keeping Karl under too. I left the school gymnasium, got into my car, and drove home. And in that whole drive I did not let Karl come up once, although he struggled beneath my hands, although his body was pale and lean and his cries were soft. I held him down with all my might.

At home, I stumbled over to my couch, too exhausted to weep or thrash about, too bitterly sad to answer the door the first time the bell rang.

Then she rang again. I don't think I would have answered even then if I hadn't schooled myself since the night of Dot's birth to believe I should always be available to a person in distress. Anyway, the dog was barking. It was cold and I'd left her tied in the backyard. I went to answer the door and stood behind it, patting my hair back into place, gathering myself before I'd see what she wanted.

"Uncle Wallace?"

There was no need to wonder. I heard her voice and it was dangerous with need, like his. I opened the door a tiny crack.

"Let me in, it's freezing cold."

"No," I said. "I mean, please go home."

Dot was silent, unbelieving. "I've got something to tell you," she insisted. She put her foot in the space and then barged through, just like her mother, or more like her father perhaps, the salesman.

"No," I said again, catching her by surprise and spinning her back toward the door. "I mean it. Go!" I fairly threw her out, and then tried to salvage something.

"Dear, I'm sorry."

But her face had clenched like a pale wax-paper mask, into a ball of hate. It was strange. She looked transparent with the cold, like a child of glass. The snow's blue light shone through her when she tore off my old robe and stood a moment, facing me. I saw that she was anyone but Karl, and half frozen in nothing but a little girl's sprigged undershirt and cotton panties, which glowed whiter as she jumped down off my steps, across the crumpled brown robe.

"Come back!" I cried, but even then, and most unforgivably of all, I did not mean it enough to rush after her. She headed home. But it was almost one-half mile. I folded the bathrobe into my arms, told myself that I would stand outside on my step the length of time I thought it would take her to get there. That way I'd convince myself she was all right. Within minutes I was shivering from deep inside and my face had numbed.

I ran inside, grabbed my keys, and tore hell for leather out of my garage, following her. I thought of the first time I'd headed for that house through the night, following the stray dog. Even then, Dot had existed, a small collision. She could have curled into the crook of a typed question mark.

I looked hard but couldn't see her, drove slowly, alert to any movement in the ditches to either side. She might be hiding from my headlights, and it was cold out, so cold. I reached the house without having found her, but then a light went on, and suddenly I saw her through the window, a shadow bolting up the stairs.

All my Christmas presents to Dot that year netted nothing but a thank-you note written by Celestine, in a hand that was supposed to resemble her daughter's. I phoned. Celestine forced Dot to speak to me, but all my fond questionings and jokes left her cold. I racked my mind for something that would win her back. I thought of giving her a dog, but I knew that Celestine had refused dogs from Mary. Celestine would hate me if I gave her daughter a pony. An automobile perhaps? Had she been old enough I would have dipped into my savings account to purchase a little runabout. Or I would have bought her a ring of pearls and diamonds. Dot hated jewelry. She liked parties, though. I called Celestine and asked her what she was doing for Dot's eleventh birthday next week.

"Nothing, I mean I don't have plans."

"Then let me plan," I said. "Let me give her the party."

Celestine was easily convinced. Parties were to Celestine an unpleasant task. I knew full well that she only gave them to try and help Dot make school friends, and that so far they'd done the opposite. That was mainly because of Mary, who had to be invited. Children were afraid of Mary's yellow glare, her gravel-bed voice. She organized games with casual but gruesome threats, and the children complied like hostages with a gun trained on them. They played mechanically, with an anxious eye to her approval. Their laughs were false. But Mary didn't notice this and took no hint from Celestine to stop her intimidation tactics. As for Dot, she became Mary's sidekick, second in command, and carried out her aunt's orders with grim and businesslike dispatch. It didn't seem to bother Dot that when the party finished, the other children dashed from her yard in relief.

"Maybe you can get Mary to lay off the children," Celestine said now. "She will be on unfamiliar turf."

If it were up to me I wouldn't have invited Mary at all. But that was the wages of being allowed to give this party. Naturally, I had to have Dot's aunt. But if I had to have Mary, I decided, I would also have Louis and Sita. They'd not been much in circulation lately, although Louis had said it was important for Sita to socialize. I knew Louis from the Lions, from local town government, and of course through his job diagnosing the few pests that threatened sugar beets. He was an important man in our area, always called on in times of crisis. He'd been the perfect man for Sita when she needed care—strong and skillful. But it was obvious how caring for Sita had worn on him. Every time I saw Louis now, he looked thinner and grayer. He had developed angina and had to carry nitroglycerin capsules. Still, I thought that his reasonableness and authority might temper Mary.

"This will be a mixed gathering," I told Louis on the phone. "Family, a few of Dot's school friends, perhaps a fellow Lion or two."

"It's been years since I've been to a birthday party," Louis said. "We've missed out on them with no children of our own. We'd love to come."

"Where?" It was Sita's voice; she had picked up the other phone and was now on the line.

"I've asked you not to do that, dear," said Louis.

"I know," said Sita, "dear."

"I called to ask you both to come to Dot's eleventh birthday." Sita's line clicked.

"We'll be there. She's truly fond of the girl. We'll see you then," said Louis.

When they were all invited, Dot's school friends and Mary too, I sat back and for the first time considered the fact that I

242

was asking Mary and Sita to coexist for several hours when they hadn't sat beneath the same roof at the same time for years. I considered that I was asking Louis to attend also, counting on his stable influence, but that if he couldn't make it at the last minute I'd be lost. Without him, I thought that I would never keep the caldron of elements I had mixed from boiling over. As it turned out, his influence was not enough.

In spite of the potential problems, I took joy in my preparations. I decided that Hawaii would be our birthday theme. We'd have an indoor luau, "South Pacific" playing in the background, Pin the Tail on the Wild Pig. Dot would have a basket of crepe-paper leis to deck each guest with at the door. We'd have a pineapple upside-down cake for the birthday cake. I bought a windup cake stand at the gift shop downtown. I imagined how the cake would revolve as the music box within the stand tinkled out "Happy Birthday to You." We'd sing. There would be lots of exotic drinks made with canned juices, crushed ice and paper umbrellas on top. I'd give Dot a ukulele that I ordered down in Fargo. Most important of all, she would forgive me.

January 18 dawned. Eleven years since I had answered my front door in a blizzard. The day was calm and not terribly cold. In town, the sun gleamed off the street pavement, melting the snow in patches, and the children I picked up seemed eager, if a little nervous. Perhaps they'd been to Dot's other parties. But this one would be different.

There were four children, Dot's only friends, three hefty boys and one small fresh-faced girl with a sweet expression. When we got to my house, however, and Mary's truck nosed up behind us like some big dark red predatory fish, this little girl's face sharpened.

"Don't worry," I began as we scrambled out, but whatever I might have said to reassure her was drowned out by Dot's yodel of delight and Mary's rasp.

"Let's get cracking. We've got a birthday to celebrate!"

243

Mary's face was ruddy with excitement and she hardly even noticed me, so deeply was she concentrating on the children. She rounded them up behind her and marched them to the door before I could get organized enough to intervene.

"Company halt!" she yelled.

Then she opened the door to my house and they entered. Dot had trooped in behind her but the other children dragged their feet and looked back with imploring eyes.

"Don't worry!" I called again, but the door shut and I had to gather up the last-minute purchases—paper cups, extra clothespins for Drop the Clothespin in the Bottle, and special party straws—before I could rush to protect them.

Inside the door, however, there was little to be done. The children stood in a resigned clump, bending their heads to let Dot or Mary slip the leis on. The exposed backs of their necks were delicate and vulnerable. I tried to liven up the party, dressed in a loud orange Hawaiian shirt, beach-bum trousers, a big straw hat. First thing off, I handed out the favors, little bird whistles that soon had the place chirping like an aviary. Celestine walked in and stood at the living-room entrance, looking expectant, but no one noticed her except for me. Her face darkened as she took in the situation.

"See what I mean about Mary?" she said.

The children stood in a straight line as Mary numbered them off for some team that she was organizing. Each one had the look of being singled out for the firing squad.

I lifted my hands in a gesture of defeat.

"I couldn't stop her," I said.

"I never can either." Celestine shrugged.

As we stood there, Sita and Louis drove up in their big silver car. They walked in. As always, Louis was calm and controlled; he also looked more frail. His eyes were tired and shadowed. Perhaps Sita had had a difficult night. Still, he smiled at the earsplitting bird whistles that had begun again. Mary had organized whistling teams. Louis gave Dot his coat and he kissed her when she put the lei around his neck. She kissed him back, enthusiastically, and hugged Sita too. I'd been the only one except her mother that Dot had not showered with affection.

I trusted that, minutes from now, her attitude would change. The ukulele rested in its case. The graceful blond-wood instrument came with clear instructions, and a beginners book called *Island Favorites*, from which Dot would be able to learn "Tahitian Lovesong," "Beyond the Reef," and "A Papeete Lullaby."

Sita tapped me on the shoulder. She'd gotten too thin and lost her bloom in the mental hospital, I knew that. But she seemed to have gone downhill even since then. Her face was cavernous and delicately wrinkled like a fine thin notepaper. She looked ill, yet she was still striking with her fine bone structure and her fashionable clothing.

"It's very nice," she said, indicating the green crepe paper strung from the light fixture, the plastic hibiscus, travel poster, the centerpiece of coconuts. "Where is your powder room?"

I directed her up the stairs and she gracefully ascended. That was the last we would see of her until the refreshments were served.

Meanwhile, it was time for the wild pig. And now it was clear that the plan to inhibit Mary had been a failure. There was no advantage in holding the party at my house. She was in charge. I had painted a large brown pig on a piece of cardboard and hung it on the wall. I had cut out a curly paper tail and stuck that on a hatpin. Mary held the tail and the hatpin now. Blindfolded, brandishing the long wicked-looking pin before her, she had every child in the room, save Dot, backed against the wall. Dot fearlessly dodged the pin and gave her aunt a great push forward. The pig was impaled with such force that Mary's arm buckled. She ripped off her blindfold.

245

"Who's next!" she cried, wiggling the pin and the tail loose.

"I am," said Louis in his low, calm voice. He took the pin and the tail from her hand, let himself be blindfolded and spun. The children hung closer, as if he was safe, King's X. He held the pin within the shelter of his body and suddenly the whole game was comical and fun, the way it should have been. Only Mary, no longer the center of attention, seemed less interested.

She followed me into the kitchen, where I went to baste the luau ham, a fifteen pounder covered with pineapple wedges, scored, and dotted with red maraschino cherries.

"That's a decent-sized ham," she commented. I knew what she was trying to get at, but I held my own.

"On special at Dotzenrud's Super Valu," I said.

She leaned close to the ham, inspecting it, then grabbed a knife from the top of the stove and, before I could move to stop her, cut a wedge right out of the center, ruining my pineapple and cherry design. I stared in shock as she popped the bit of ham into her mouth and chewed, narrowing her eyes critically.

"It's cured with cheap chemicals," she said at last, "not wood. And the water content. I bet you could squeeze two gallons out."

I slammed the oven shut and clenched my teeth. If it hadn't been for Dot I would have asked the aunt to leave right then.

"Why Mary," I crooned instead, acting the good host, "you haven't had the special drink yet, reserved for VIP guests in this house."

"No, I haven't."

So I went to make it. I was merely going to mix her a stiff one. But when I opened my cabinet the first bottle that my eyes lighted on was the one an Elk had left, Everclear, just about pure grain alcohol. If she hadn't cut through my decorated ham I wouldn't have done it. But she had, so a percentage of Everclear went into the drink, disguised by Hawaiian Punch and a can of purple passion Shasta, that would have knocked a prizefighter

246

sideways. I thought of setting the little Chinese umbrella on fire as I served this drink, just to signal its potency. But I did not. It would be better to let Mary discover its effects on her own.

She took a healthy gulp.

"Bottoms up!" I smiled, upending my own glass of punch. To my horror and delight, Mary drained the entire concoction.

Once she'd set her empty glass down on the counter, I asked if I could refill it.

"I wouldn't mind," she said, and then she actually smiled. The effects of the drink were stronger than I'd imagined. Still, I threw an extra shot into the next one. She walked out of the kitchen with the drink in her hand. I followed. She was steady on her feet, but when she reached the entrance to the living room she paused. Her head tipped to the side, and then tipped farther to rest against the woodwork as she surveyed the scene. I edged around to get a side view, and even in profile I could see that her smile was uncharacteristically dreamy. She sipped lightly now, and made no move to join the game of Drop the Clothespin. She merely stood, watching the children take aim from atop a chair, and even nodded approvingly when Celestine handed out the prizes—more leis, plastic watches, rings with glass stones.

When everything was finished, laid out on the carefully set table, when the cake in all of its upside-down splendor was placed on the Happy Birthday cake stand and the tropical punch was poured, I walked out to call the guests. At the last moment I had set three little bears riding motorcycles on top of the cake with the candles. I would light the candles soon. The party had turned warm and joyful with Louis and Celestine in charge. Mary watched from the floor. As I came out of the dining room I saw that she had collapsed where I'd left her, in the doorway. I bent down and touched her arm. The material of her dress was the color of orchids, splattered with dark little marks that looked like accidental stains. As I assisted her into the dining room I saw that they were stains.

"Don't bother," she said, when I offered to fetch a damp sponge. "They'll blend in." She laughed, throwing her head from side to side, and offered the empty glass. I took the glass and mixed her another drink, just strong enough to keep her mood from evaporating. She took a sip as soon as I put the drink in her hand, and then, looking me full in the face, spoke in a voice that was almost tender.

"From now on, you get your ham from me, you get it wholesale."

"I'll hold you to that," I joked, guiding her forward. Before she fumbled into her chair she turned and gave me an even more benign gaze. Her eyes changed color, softened from the harsh yellow of two gold coins to a radiant amber.

"I mean it, you old coot," she whispered affectionately. Her turban had gone awry. It had slipped back off her forehead and barely stuck to her head, so that her hair, which I'd rarely seen, fell out in gray wisps. She leaned across the table and spoke to Louis.

"Where's my crazy cousin?"

Louis gave her a surprised look then glanced involuntarily at the staircase where Sita sat, peering at us through the cast-iron leaves of the banister rail. I'd noticed her from the corner of my eye for some time now, drawn to us warily but helplessly, like a starved deer. She resembled one. Her cheeks were hollow, her eyes were stark, and her ribs were caved in. She melted back from our attention into the shadows of the upper landing.

"Join the party!" hollered Mary, straining in her chair.

"Let her alone," said Celestine, reaching over the heads of two children and tapping Mary's back. "It's about time we toasted the birthday girl."

But Mary shrugged Celestine's hand off and pulled herself

laboriously to her feet. Her eyes had now deepened to the color of caramel, like sugar coming to a boil. She staggered to the bottom of the staircase.

"Ready or not here I come!" she cried. But Louis brushed past her before she could move, and she slammed herself back against the wall just beneath the electrical connection to my doorbell chimes, setting them off in a merry *tink-tonk*. She whirled, her face uncreased in delight. The bell kept playing. She continued to whirl and hop in a strange dance. Evidently the chimes had shorted somewhere in the wires. The children watched Mary with rapt attention. Even to them it was obvious that something was abnormal. I climbed a chair quickly and disconnected the bell, but the damage was already done.

"She's completely plowed," Celestine noticed.

She rushed to Mary's side and dragged her back to the table.

"What was in that drink?" she said, frowning.

Sita saved me.

"Here I am!" she called in a voice so loud and bright it temporarily froze her. She recovered though, gripped Louis tightly, and accompanied him over to the table. They both looked ashen, almost skeletal, and I noticed Louis pat his pocket to make sure of the presence of his nitro capsules. They sat down and then we were all, finally, assembled.

But what an example to the children we had set. They'd go home traumatized as every year before.

The thought spurred my determination. I would rescue this event from what had begun to happen by at least allowing Mary to sober up. As soon as everyone was served and eating happily I went out back to put the coffee in the percolator.

While I was gone, the whole thing blew.

Much later, I was to piece together what happened from conversations with Celestine, and with Mary, who was chagrined at the results. For it was Mary who took a House of Meats matchbook from her pocket while everyone else was eating, and lit the birthday-cake candles. That didn't seem so terribly bad, though a little off the traditional timing. No one stopped her. And what she did next would not have been out of line either, except for the fact that in her mind's disarray she wound the cake stand so tightly that it sprung.

I came back into the room as the cake began to move. The music box tinkled the birthday song, but quickly, so quickly that Mary's mouth could not keep up with it. Speed built. The brown glaze blurred. The candles fused into a single flame, and the toy bears began a mad chase that led nowhere.

"Stop!" I cried, lunging for the controls.

"HappyBirthdayToYou!" Mary cried.

Then the cake stand's spring snapped. It whipped around once, jerked, and flung the entire cake at Sita. She went backward with it, clutching thin air, fending off the bulk as if it were alive and attacking her. She flung bits of it from side to side and slapped her arms, thereby effectively demolishing what survived, mashing the rings of pineapple, beating the cake itself to crumbs.

The little wheels of the bears' motorcycles spun themselves out against the wall. Sita's high laugh rose above the sounds of surprise. Louis leaped up, grabbed Sita, and held her pinned against his chest. The children combusted in a frenzy of pent nerves, and Celestine had her hands full, calming them. As for Mary, she sat quite still. A statue couldn't have been more motionless. A gaunt and Halloweenish grin was plastered to her face. Her eyes had gone a full black, and her hands were pressed together on her heart. Although Louis was the one I should have worried about, for even then he was reaching around Sita and into his pocket for a capsule, my one thought was that Mary's heart had given out. She'd had a stroke. I rushed around the table and checked her pulse. The beat was slow, even. It then seemed very clear that the tall purple drinks had turned her to stone.

Sita began to scream with laughter and point her finger in Mary's direction. Whatever Mary really felt about the cake accident, her face was a mask of devilish glee. And she sat there like that, smiling without moving, as the party broke up. Louis spoke calmly to Sita and convinced her to leave. The children were ushered into Celestine's car with all of Dot's presents to be opened en route. From my front porch, my party in ruins, I saw them out. But as they backed from the drive, the last minute before they were obscured by my decorative hedges, Dot rolled down the window.

"Uncle Wallace!" she cried. "That was the best birthday ever!"

I stood there until the last of the engine's noise had disappeared, and back inside, even as I swept up the crumbs of my lovely cake, even as I plastic wrapped all the remains of my luau, I was pleased.

I looked at Mary, but with guilt now, for thanks to me she had made a complete horse's ass of herself. As far as I knew, she rarely touched spirits. She sat in the same chair. Her grin had not faded. From time to time she rolled her eyes. I sat down beside her.

"If you can hear me," I said, "blink twice."

Blink. Blink. So she was conscious.

"Are you all right? One blink means yes and two means no."

One blink.

"Shall I call the ambulance?"

Two blinks.

"Shall I do anything?"

Two more.

So I just left her sitting at the table as I continued to clean up the litter of paper plates and party favors. After perhaps a half an hour passed she began to speak in a slow drawl.

"Wallace," she called out. A long minute passed. "I had a good time."

I came into the dining room wiping my hands, put the dish towel down, and sat across from her at the table. Mary's face was coming back to life.

"That's nice," I said.

She nodded. Her first sentence had taken an effort. By the way she cocked her head I knew that she was still drunk, but sobering up. It crossed my mind that she'd be hell with a hangover, and I should really try to get her home before the Everclear wore off. I made the suggestion.

"No," she said. "Let's talk."

I wrapped my hands in the dish towel. I wasn't sure that I wanted to talk to her. We had never been friends. She had wounded me when possible, beginning with the first day she gave my namesake, Wallacette, the unremarkable nickname Dot. She had resented me, taken jealous potshots at my friendship with Celestine, been perpetually cunning where she could have been kind, and tried her best to spoil this party. There was no warmth in her, no generous heart. She was a tough case.

"What's there to talk about?" I said. "I'll bring you home."

She leaned across the table and waggled her finger.

"There's lots to talk about," she said. "I don't want to go. I've got your number in the book of numbers. I know what card you played."

"You're making *no* sense," I said, trying to be firm. I was not going to let her get underneath my skin.

"Coward."

"What?"

"You're two yolks in the same damn egg," she said.

"You've lost me."

"You're lonely."

I looked at her. I shook off the dish towel, smoothed back my hair. I touched my eyeglasses, chin, cheekbones, as if I were putting myself together.

"I'm not lonely," I said to her. "I am a member of three fraternal orders and have a social life that's, well, I'm in *demand* Mary."

She blew air through her teeth, then suddenly, so quick I couldn't react, snatched across the table and drew my hands into hers.

"Liar," she said. "When I pass sometimes, late, you're up burning the midnight oil. A couple times I've stopped and looked right in your window."

I was indignant but also fascinated.

"Why?" I said. I tried to pull my hand back but she gripped it tight.

"I've thought about things."

While I was trying to decide whether or not I wanted to know what she thought about, she turned my palm upward in her hand and gazed down into it. Her mouth moved as if an article was written there. She finally said "It's no good," dropped my hand, and looked straight into my eyes. I was too curious to keep quiet.

"What?" I said.

"Say, do you have a cigarette?"

"A few stale ones," I muttered, looking down into my palm now that I had drawn my hand back. I got up and took an old pack from a drawer in the highboy. I gave it to her with some matches, and she lit one, blew the heavy smoke out with great authority.

"You have a big cross on your mount of Venus," she finally revealed, "and no marriage line."

I sat down and kept looking into my hand. There were lines there I'd never noticed. Tiny crisscrossing hatch marks, long swooping lines, braids and ropes.

"I'm not surprised," I said.

"Too bad," she said, rising unsteadily. "But you two could still chance it."

I must have looked confused.

"You and Celestine."

I couldn't believe my ears.

"Oh," I said, "well . . . that's something. Yes."

"What are you trying to say, Wallace?"

"I'm trying . . ." I couldn't go on.

"I read you like a book."

"Yes, well. I'm flattered. But she's already married."

"Karl hasn't been back since Dot was born," she said, and then, after a moment of frowning she lifted her eyebrows. "She deserves better out of life."

She was waiting but I wouldn't say what she wanted me to say. Her figure made a dense patch of jungle-dark shade, and her eyes glared out like the points of two tacks. She was holding herself up by pushing down on the back of the chair. Neither of us moved until the cigarette burned completely down to the filter. Then I reached over the table and drew the end from her fingers. I put it in the blue club-shaped ashtray.

"Time to go," I said, walking around the table. I took her elbow when she swayed.

"My coat's on the front couch," she said. We walked into the living room and I helped fit her into the woolen armholes. She buttoned the thing around her like a shield.

Outside we opened the car doors without speaking and got in. We drove in silence. The early dusk fell and the shadows on the road spread in insubstantial pools. I thought at least the strange afternoon, the conversation, might bring us closer. But by the time we reached the shop, so many stubborn seconds of silence had accumulated between us that we were back where we'd started.

The ox Motel

Karl liked motels with strange or inviting names, so he pulled in when he saw the blinking sign, even though the town was Argus. As he stepped out of his car into the sweet, fresh night, he saw that it was merely the Fox. The *F* had burned out. He checked in anyway.

He found his room, turned on the television, showered, and stretched out naked on the bed. He paged through the telephone book, found their names. He planned to stop with that, but then he dialed Wallace Pfef's number. The phone rang once and Wallace answered.

"Hello? Hello? Hello?" By the third hello, Wallace's voice sounded strained, bewildered. Karl held the phone away from his ear, then lowered it toward the cradle. Wallace's voice turned tinny, comical, and was finally cut off. Karl thought of dialing Mary's number next, but felt embarrassed at talking to her with his clothes off. He could have slipped on a pair of pants, but instead he called Celestine.

"Guess who?" he said when she answered.

He listened to the thin empty hum of the open line. It did not occur to him that she might not recognize his voice, and when she finally said, "Who is this?" in a sharp suspicious tone, he had a sudden blue pang that he covered over with talk.

"You know who it is. I was passing through and stopped for the night, unexpectedly you know, and since I was here I thought maybe I'd just drop by."

When she still did not answer he went on.

"Or you'd come meet me for a drink, maybe. Or I'd take you and Wallacette out for dinner."

"Karl," Celestine said at last. "You promised you'd stay away."

He waited. "It's been fourteen years."

"I'm not going to dredge up old times."

"Fine, just fine."

"All right," said Celestine after a moment. "I guess you have a right to see her. Just give me a minute to think."

She thought.

"I suppose you'll be pushing on tomorrow," Celestine said. "Why not breakfast then, seven-thirty, over at the Flickertail?"

"I'll be waiting there," said Karl. There was an undertone of longing in his voice that surprised him. He pulled himself up against the pillows. "Don't be late!" he said harshly.

But the line was already buzzing.

He woke too early, got ready too soon, and found himself sitting in a booth drinking cup after cup of coffee before they finally arrived. By the time they walked through the door he was jittery and faintly ill from the caffeine on an empty stomach, and all the cigarettes he'd smoked. He stood up but he hardly knew what to say, the sight of Wallacette was so unexpected. She stood in the café entrance with her mother, a short solid girl with light olive skin, brown-red hair, the dangling hoop earrings and tight short skirt of a juvenile delinquent. It surprised him to see the clothes her mother let her wear, so cheap looking, and the eye makeup. She scanned the people in the booths through narrow black slits. Under blue hoods, her look was eager. She passed him over, came back when he raised his hand and smiled at them. He stepped forward and her face fell.

Later on, thinking back, he would brush away her disappointment. He had aged, become shrewd and hard and gray, with frown lines down the side of his mouth and many small marks of strain around his eyes. He was so used to driving, so used to distance and movement, that he sometimes found it hard to focus properly on anything within the reach of his arms.

So he saw his wife and daughter most clearly when they stood in the doorway. When they slid into the booth across from him, their faces smoothed and blurred.

"Sorry to be late," said Celestine. She didn't look sorry. She looked like she wanted to be somewhere else. Her coat was thick and rough, furlike, sewn of light and dark gray patches. She kept it draped over her shoulders and squeezed Dot into the corner of the booth. Their faces stared at him, from fur and hair, fuzzy, almost like animals from a den. Karl could make out Celestine's big, raw features best. Her face was bare of makeup. Her lips were pointed in the middle, brown, and her dark eyes like drops of molasses. Her cheekbones and her nose stood out, and her hair, in lake-brown waves, sprung stiffly around her skull. He wanted to press it down, to get close enough to breathe the pepper that clung to her skin from sausage making.

But her eyes stopped him. He looked at Dot.

Her face was bolder, vivid in its rouge and orange cake. Her hair was cut in a long shag that looked like a flattened mane. Her neck was powerful.

The two watched him closely. He adjusted his tie, straightened his collar, smiled, tried to dazzle. He nudged the menu at Dot's place.

"This is on me," he said. "Order anything you want." He tried not to stare at Wallacette Darlene, but she was staring at him, frowning in unblinking concentration, her lips slightly parted, her breath shallow. Karl's eyes kept darting back to meet hers, his lips kept forming a nervous smile.

He said in a hearty voice, "How old are you now Wallacette?"

"Fourteen," she said, and her expression changed, as if she had decided something. She sat back and lowered her powdered lids. "Didn't you tell him, Mama," she said through one side of her mouth, "that I'm Dot?"

"Dot," she said to Karl, "Dot."

257

"She goes by Mary's nickname," said Celestine. Then she gave Karl a look of resigned complicity that warmed him a little. It was the kind of look that nuns had exchanged in the halls at Saint Jerome's. It was the kind of look that passes between adults over the heads of their children.

Dot caught the look between them and blew the stiff bangs off her forehead. "I'm out of the ordinary enough," she said. "I don't need a weird name." Her voice was hard and final. Karl found nothing to say to her.

"You're not what I expected," she said coolly, to his face.

Karl looked to Celestine for help, but she was studying the menu.

"You're not," he raised his eyes to Dot's, "what I expected, either."

This stirred her a little, took her by surprise. She held the menu up and mumbled, "I'll have the number two with coffee and tomato juice. Where's that waitress?"

They were all three silent, reading the typewritten sheets behind the plastic, the combinations of eggs and hashbrowns and toast. The waitress seemed to have forgotten them, however, and they sat, suspended among the other customers, farmers and construction workers already on their coffee breaks. Across the street a new building of tan aluminum was rising. Hammering and the muffled whine of electric saws filled the street. The sun shone on the stacks of candy under the counter, on the coffee urns and the spigots of the milk machine. The waitresses had just come on their shifts. The cook, a large blond woman in an orange bib apron, said things that made the men at the counter laugh into their cups. The radio blared livestock futures and farm reports into the bacon-smelling air. But none of this suggested anything that the three in the booth might say to one another.

"Does Dot have some sort of, well, male influence in her life?" Karl surprised himself by asking this, and then realized during Celestine's pause that he wanted very much to know.

"Wallace Pfef is like a father to her," Celestine said.

Dot pretended not to hear at first, but in the silence Karl kept after Celestine's hard answer she spoke. "I go up to Uncle Russell's a lot now. Eli's teaching me to fish."

Karl nodded, remembering Russell as a ravaged-looking Indian with a box of clanking tools, a man who didn't like him.

When the waitress made her way at last, they all ordered. Celestine tried her best to make talk about the shop and Mary, but carefully did not ask whether or not Karl planned on visiting there. Karl tried too. He told Celestine all about his new job, high pay, even though he hadn't known much about stereo components at first. He was working for a budding chain of hi-fi and record stores, in the supply end.

Celestine smiled at him for the first time.

"That explains the record player you sent."

"The latest," he said, pleased even though she hadn't called it a portable stereo system, which it was, and of the best quality.

"Did you like it?" he asked Dot, who looked down at her hands and regarded her chipped pink nails as if they had something to tell her.

"Of course I liked it," she said to her fingers.

Karl decided to take a chance and tried to get her attention. "D.O. Double T.I.E./Dottie is the girl for me," Karl sang. "Do you know that one?"

Dot's face sprang into an ugly mask.

"No," she said. "I listen to hard rock."

"Do you know," said Celestine, embarrassed and a bit flustered, "that Dot tried to run away and find you once?"

The waitress put their steaming plates down, and Dot lowered her head to the food. She ate fast, without looking up. The long dangly loops in her ears hit her chin every time she took a bite. Karl watched her and had the sad thought that he could have influenced her taste in music if he'd been around more. Maybe not living with them, but at least settling down in the area, maybe not seeing her that often, but at least once in a while. He felt reckless and desperate, suddenly, with the loss of this unattractive girl.

"I'll tell you what," he said, "would you listen to some records if I sent them?"

"It depends," said Dot.

Her voice had an edge of knowing. She was conscious of where she stood. She put her fork down and frowned into her plate for such a long time that Celestine finally turned on the bench and put her hand over Dot's.

"Honey," she said, "would it kill you to say yes?"

"Yes," said Dot.

 PART FOUR

CELESTINE JAMES

"WE ARE VERY much like the dead," Mary argues, "except that we have the use of our senses."

We are talking about the afterlife, her pet subject, and she is kneading Polish sausage meat with bare hands that have thickened and calloused through the years so they look like tough paws. We're getting old. Mary's hair has grayed to the color of a mouse, and she wears it pinned just over her ears in two pugs. Her back is curved like a shell, and her face is set in deep folds of conviction. She is being mental again, going off to flights of fantasy. She slaps down a ball of meat and sends up a cloud of white pepper. It is always my job to bring her back.

"Sounds like Tol Bayer," I joke. "He had all the symptoms of an alcoholic except that he never drank."

Mary still brings out my worst, and I can't help myself from pulling her leg. This time I've gotten to her. She walks over to the salt barrel and stands there, looking quizzical, before she picks up a handful. She walks back, throws it in the meat, starts kneading while she thinks. And for a while that is enough of her boolah about the dead.

Mary tries to get her imagination to mend the holes in her understanding. I come to see her in the grape arbor the next day. It is Sunday, so the shop is closed down and quiet. We're barely keeping even with our layout of expenses now, but we don't care. We won't open Sundays like the chain store and discount parlors.

Mary is sitting in a lawn chair picking stems off the sour blue grapes that she claims make fine jelly. When she sees me she puts her basket down, reaches underneath her chair, and then hands me a common red brick.

"This flew in my window," she says. "Smashed it too."

I know she won't hire a glazer to fix the window. It will be a taped-up eyesore to go with the peeling exterior. Along with us, it seems that everything about the shop, the business, is going to seed. But I don't care. When Mary sells the place, which has become valuable real estate, we both plan to live off the money. I have insisted that Mary give me retirement benefits.

"I hope you caught the kid," I say to her.

"There was no kid."

I tell myself not to argue with Mary, but I can't help arguing like I can't help the man in the moon.

"Someone chucked it and ran off," I say.

"Nobody chucked it."

"So what do you suggest did happen?"

"This brick is a sign," she says.

"Of what?"

"Trouble."

That does not surprise me. Mary has never had a sign announcing something good. She goes in to wash casings, and I finish cleaning grapes in the arbor. I don't give her red brick a second thought. I don't want to hear any more of her mysterious claims.

But then, that night, something happens that is unlike me. I have a dream.

I dream that Sita is standing in her front yard underneath the Mountain Ash. I see the orange berries glowing behind her, the ferny leaves tossing in the air. She is twisting her hands in a fancy hostess apron and looking out on the road. She is watching for someone.

"I call and you don't come," she mutters.

"What?" I say.

Her eyes have retreated in bruised pits and her cheeks are sunken, pale as dough.

"I call and you don't come," she says again.

Maybe it is the brilliance of the berries in the tree, the blue and white lace of the apron, or Sita's long look of sickness. Whatever it is, the dream is more real than life to me. I awaken and the sky is the dim gray of predawn. I cannot sleep again but lay in bed watching the windows gradually lighten.

In full morning I walk into the shop and right away I ask Mary to come sit down before we get to work. I put her percolator on the table between us and then I tell her about my dream.

"She's got an illness," says Mary.

"She looked half dead to me."

"She's asking for you."

I lift my shoulders and say, offhand, "I haven't talked to her in years. I don't know what she'd want to see me for."

Yet I think back to the days when Sita and I were best friends. That was before Mary appeared off the Argus freight. Sita and I grew up together, thick as thieves, fighting and making up. I never got the best of her. She was not as tall as me, but she was stronger than she looked, and she got so hysterical in a fight that I always gave in. Then she would sit on my chest and bat me with her long heavy braid. Her hair is short now, fixed by a beauty operator and curly as a poodle. In the dream, it stuck out in spikes, flattened on one side and gray at the roots. So I know she has not been to the hairdresser in some time.

"I'll go along with you," says Mary. "After all, she's my cousin. I should go."

So we sit there and discuss what we're going to do.

Dot is no problem since she can take care of herself, but I still hate to leave her because she has been so anxious. Since she was nominated as a princess in the contest that Wallace has invented for the Beet Festival, Dot spends half her time trying to lose weight and the other half writing in a secret diary that she keeps locked in a drawer. Sometimes I find her on the back steps, glaring in a morose way at the pages of a book. Other times she mows the grass furiously short. Each night she goes to work at the concessions counter of the Argus theater. She watches the movies from the back of the aisle, smoking cigarettes. I cannot stop her from doing that. Her clothes are stale with the smell, along with the popcorn oil and licorice. It seems to me that the films she watches depress her, give her strange ideas, put bad language in her mouth. I think that perhaps I should not leave her for Sita, but Dot says that's crazy.

We decide to motor thirteen miles to Blue Mound and answer Sita's call. She's close, but very far. In the years since she's been there, she has never called or asked us over for a meal. We don't even know what her house looks like inside, except from hearsay. Yet it seems very natural that in her hour of need we come, and just in case we have to stay there long, we pack our nightgowns, one of Mary's sheet cakes, and two summer sausages in the delivery truck. We leave my cousin Adrian in charge of the shop, but he will not care for Mary's dog, Dickie, so we must visit Wallace Pfef on the way out of town.

Wallace has painted his raised ranch a dull-looking tan color I don't like, but he says it blends in with the fields. Earth colors are his theme. When he shows up at the door, we see that he's even dressing in them. His pants are gray. His shirt is the same color as his skin. Flesh color.

"That shirt is unbecoming," Mary tells him.

He looks down and pinches some of the cloth between his fingers. Meanwhile, I see that we can't leave the dog here. Pfef's nasty female dog glares unblinkingly at us, then snaps. Little Dickie strains and yaps back from the safety of Mary's arms.

266

"Let's go," says Mary. "I don't care for Little Dickie to get pounded."

"I'm sorry," I tell Wallace. "I didn't mean to disturb you."

He tells us to give his best wishes to Sita and waves us off. We have no choice now but to take the dog along. Dickie yaps at strangers when they come into the shop, but there is no harm in him beyond that. I do remember Sita hates dogs, and I ask Mary if she thinks Sita will mind.

"She'll have to take the bad along with us," says Mary. "After all, it was her that asked you."

"Yes," I say. "But of course she asked in my dream."

"There's no difference," says Mary, and I know there is none to her. She wants to do some knitting, so she tells me to take the wheel. As soon as we are on the road, she pulls out her yarn and needles. She casts on, and begins the sleeve to a sweater she is making for Dot. Her clicking needles start me thinking about Mary's sewing machine and how Sita accepted it even though it was the only thing given to Mary by her mother. Sita was the one who told me about it, proudly, when we met in town by accident. I told her she should not have taken it. If my own mother had lived, I know I would have forgiven her anything and in my middle years accepted that machine. But Mary gave it up. And that machine was a nice cabinet style, antique by now. I think that we could haul it back in our truck, providing that Sita still has it sitting in her garage.

"Maybe we could get the sewing machine, Mary," I say.

"What sewing machine?" She will not admit it was ever hers. She holds the first knitted rows up to admire them, a cream background with dark red lines. She is making the sweater pattern up as she goes along. It is a maze like the kind that scientists train rats to run through. We drive in silence and then, after a few miles, she turns to me and says, "Sita hasn't got long now."

"What makes you think that?"

Mary takes the brick from her pocket and spits on it. The spit will dry in the shape of a calendar date, she says. She stares at the brick like it was suddenly going to talk, and my patience wears through. "Put that thing away," I tell her.

Although her eyes have gotten ever harsher and brighter, she has aged like an ordinary enough person. It's the way she dresses that makes her look like such a fringe element. For the trip she's wound her head in a black silk scarf with tassels. She's hunched over like an old turtle, and her purple dress is all straining seams. I can't help wondering, as usual, what's going through her mind. She's got the dog in her lap and she's eating raisins from a little bag.

Sita lives in the only new house in Blue Mound, a big white ten-room house, landscaped on two levels, that she calls a colonial because it has shutters that do not shut and a tall, heavy, carved oak front door with a brass knocker on it. She is standing on her front lawn when we turn into the drive. Just like in the dream, her hands are twisted in a stiff lace apron. Just like in the dream, the orange berries glow behind her head. She looks sick. We get out of the car. Unlike in the dream, she puts her hands on her hips and yells.

"Get your damn dog out of my roses!"

Then she reaches into her tree, pulls down a hard clod of those berries, and throws them at Little Dickie. The dog scampers away.

"He was just watering them for you," says Mary. "Don't get all set back."

I try to smooth the situation over by complimenting Sita. Admiration usually calms her, but this time it doesn't work.

"You look good," I tell her.

Her eyes pick me apart.

"So do the leaves before they fall," she states.

At that, Mary starts to laugh, which turns Sita's face white.

"I'm sick," says Sita, glaring nowhere, "sick as a sick cat."

Then she turns on her heel, stamps up the columned entry into her house, and slams the door shut behind her. Mary catches Little Dickie and then we tie him to the ash tree with a piece of clothesline. We get our bags and our sheet cake from the delivery truck, and Mary follows me up the walk with the summer sausages.

Looking at her, all in mournful purple and black with those sausages wrapped in white paper, I think she reminds me of something. What is it? I pause at Sita's door and look back at Mary. Then I know. She's like the picture of the grim reaper on the month of January. The hem of her black skirt drags. She looks like she's seen it all. And she carries those sausages like they were symbols of her calling.

Inside of Sita's house everything is neutral. What I mean is, Sita doesn't let things pile up, so you don't get any feeling about anyone who lives there. Sita's tables have nothing on them but an ashtray. They are not like Mary's, for instance. You walk into her back rooms and right away there is a deck of cards on the table, balls of wool, or a *Fate* magazine to tell you who she is.

We hear Sita upstairs in the bathroom, the water flushing. So we walk through the house to the kitchen, hang the sausages in her pantry, and put the sheet cake on her big Formica kitchen table. It is here that we particularly expect to see a few signs of Sita's sickness and neglect. But the kitchen is clean and lighted, the plants watered. Every pot is washed and put away. The steel sink is shined, and even the tile floor is freshly waxed.

"I don't know how she does it," I say in a loud voice, thinking she will hear me. But Sita isn't on the stairs, coming down to greet us. The water is still gushing.

"The answer is she has a cleaning woman," Mary says.

We set our traveling bags on the kitchen floor. Not knowing

what to do with ourselves, we shift aimlessly from foot to foot until at last we grow tired and sit at the modern dinette arrangement in her breakfast nook.

"I suppose she's trying to get fixed up a little," says Mary after several minutes go by. We listen. The water stops flowing through the pipes, but then it slaps and gurgles, as if she is bathing.

"At least she can manage that by herself," I say.

Mary is looking at the pot with a longing expression. "I'll brew some coffee. It'll be nice and hot for her when she gets down here," she says.

"We'll all have a snack," I agree, hungry for the uncut cake.

Mary rifles through the cupboards for the coffee, but of course it's on the counter in the green cannister labeled COFFEE.

"Naturally she'd keep it here," says Mary.

I agree. "Sita does things by the book."

She is taking her bath by the book now, washing every inch of herself. From the early years we spent close, when I slept over some nights, I know she is using exactly one capful of bath powder. Afterward she'll dust herself with talcum. Then she'll sit down on the edge of her bed, wrapped in a towel, and file her nails into perfect ovals.

"As for me," says Mary, reading my thoughts, "I like to rub a lemon on my face."

"That's why your skin's all puckered up," I blurt. I hate for her to read my mind, but now I've hurt her feelings.

"I'll knit," she says after a moment, subdued. She rummages in her strained valise for the sweater sleeve and can't seem to find it. I have gotten touchy. I begin to question whether we should have come. The Sita in my dreams was more desperate and hospitable. Outside, Little Dickie begins to bawl and whine. He's probably wound so tight to that tree trunk he cannot move.

"I use my coffee cannister for trading stamps," I tell Mary. "It fills up exactly the size of two booklets."

270

Mary brightens and draws her hand out of her bag.

"The flour bins," she says, "they're too small in those sets. That's where I like to keep my screwdriver and my canning tongs. . . ."

She looks over at Sita's cannisters, sharpens her eyes at me, and listens up the stairs to see if Sita is still occupied.

"Go ahead, look," I say. "See if she keeps flour in her cannister."

So Mary opens the green container.

"Wouldn't you know it," she whispers. "Of course she would keep her flour where it belongs." Then, suddenly, she snaps her head down and peers closer. "What's this?" She cups the bin in the crook of her arm and plucks out an orange capsule. "It's crawling with pills." She puts her hand into the flour, digs around, and comes up with more. We don't know what to think.

At last, there is a sign that Sita isn't managing for herself. I feel reckless. I can still hear Sita moving around upstairs.

"Throw it out," I say. "There's no telling how old those are. She must be losing her marbles."

"She could poison herself," says Mary, fascinated. If it were her choice, I think she'd run upstairs and show them to Sita. "All right," she says at last. She opens the cabinet beneath Sita's sink, finds the garbage can, and dumps out the pills and the flour.

She puts the empty cannister back in place. We are just pouring the coffee out in three of Sita's matching cups and cutting the cake, when she walks down the stairs.

"We just brewed up some coffee," I say in a pleasant voice.

"There wasn't any made," says Mary in an accusing tone. Then she remembers some sort of manners. "This cake's fresh," she says.

Her black scarf has slipped down over her forehead in a little visor, and when she stares at Sita she looks like she is placing a bet.

I turn to Sita quickly, meaning to comment on how she's fixed herself up. But Sita looks exactly the same, no fresher than when we first met her in the yard. She hasn't changed her clothes, and her hairdo is still lopsided. I wonder if she still sleeps in a roll of pinned toilet paper all week to save her hairdo, like she did as a model. And she does. Now I find another sign of the strain.

As she turns to the refrigerator to get out the cream, I see a neat pink square of toilet paper has been left pinned to the back of her head. When she turns back I don't say anything. But Mary is smiling at me.

"I hope you enjoy this," she says in a sweet syrupy voice, setting the brown and yellow square of cake before Sita.

Sita opens a drawer and takes out three white paper napkins with scalloped borders. She sets those carefully beside our plates. Then she sits down and takes a bite, and a sip, and another bite. She's about to take a third bite when she looks at her fork.

Mary and I have nearly finished our slices, and I am thinking how empty this kitchen looks, with no sign of cooking. Does Sita eat from a can or box?

Sita is gazing with shocked attention at something on the end of her fork. She puts the cake down, and then, prinking her finger, delicately draws a transparent scrap out of the cake bite and puts it on the edge of her dessert plate.

We see that the scrap on the edge of Sita's plate is a finely baked amber wing, brittle and threaded with fragile veins.

"That's a wing," Mary observes, putting down her fork.

"It is the wing of an Indian meal moth, to be exact," says Sita. Her voice is acid, her mouth pinched and dry. "They usually don't get to be this size."

Mary gazes at the wing for a moment, politely, but not as though it had anything to do with her. She picks up her fork and begins to eat her cake again, relishing it even.

Sita's head slowly turns. The toilet paper on the back of her

272

head flutters like a feather. Her eyes watch the cake moving from plate to fork to mouth of Mary. Sita looks like an outraged hen sitting there, so boney beaked and peckish.

"How do you know the name of it?" I ask, to divert her attention. Then I remember her late husband had something to do with infestations. "Did you learn that from Louis?"

"After he resigned his post as health inspector," she says between her teeth, still intent on the moving bites of cake, "Louis was the county extension entomologist." I try to signal Mary not to take another piece, but already she is lifting the square out of the pan.

"Bugs can't hurt a person when they're cooked," she tells us.

I don't want to look at Sita. I sip my coffee as long as possible. Then I do look at her and see that all the color has left her face, she is fearfully pale. She is so mad that her lips have turned blue. I put the cup down and brace myself, knowing from those early years that her rage must fall.

"You won't bring those filthy insects in my house!" Sita shrieks, jumping up so suddenly that the piece of toilet paper floats off the back of her head.

Mary looks uncertainly at her fork, but it is too late.

Sita picks up the sheet cake, and without a word or glance, takes it out the back door. I hear her walking down the steps, the trash can clanging, and then she slams back in with the empty pan and puts it in the sink. She walks behind Mary, snakes a thin arm around, and plucks the saucer away and the fork from her hand.

Now Sita has gone too far. When she walks toward the door again, meaning to shake the cake off the fork and throw the crumbs in the garbage, Mary leaps up. Her head scarf drops over her eyes, so she has to jut her chin in Sita's face to see beneath it.

"You should talk!" she shouts. Yellow sparks are spinning from her eyes. "Talk about the pills in your flour, Miss High Nose!"

Sita looks stunned, then she rushes to the cannister, rips the cover off, and sure enough it's empty. She stands there so long, peering into the bottom of the metal cannister, that I wonder if the shock has been too much.

"What have you done with them?" she says. "Where are they? Tell me this instant."

When Mary points, Sita falls to her knees before the sink and opens the cabinet. She drags the garbage pail out and starts to paw through the flour. It falls through the air, covers the floor, flies up into her face. Her arms are white with its dust. In her hand she collects a few brilliant capsules, orange and blue, and holds them tight to her chest, guarding them from our sight.

Poor Little Dickie. We have forgotten his food, so in the days that follow we give him scraps or go down to the corner market for expensive emergency cans. A dog living in a butcher shop gets spoiled. Often Little Dickie has to fend for himself. He digs holes in Sita's iris borders, looking for a bone. That first night, he sneaks into the garbage can and gobbles up the sheet cake, bugs and all. We can't keep him on the cord, because he bites through it with his strong little teeth whenever he feels like roaming. He's a house dog. But of course we can't keep him inside.

Sita hates him. You can tell it in her eyes when he begs at the door. I fill the holes up behind him and replant the irises, hoping she will not be too hard on Little Dickie. If she notices the patched ground, she never says so. We can see now that Sita is as sick as my dream said, and yet she won't let us take her to the doctor. Every time I suggest a visit, she says she's already been there and got a five-year dosage of medicine. Sometimes I catch her smashing pills together in a cup, or rolling them about in her hands before she pops them down. They are pain medicine, she tells me. She's been taking pills for many years, so I don't ask questions.

I worry that Mary will make some mean remark about Sita's behavior that first day, but she cleans up the flour without a word and settles in to this visit. It seems to me that she blooms in the presence of illness the way some women perk up around a good-looking man. She removes her black fringed scarf and pins her hair up in a skinny coil. She wears a dress with yellow flowers and hums as she cooks custards and broths to tempt Sita's picky appetite. She shakes her can of brewer's yeast in everything she makes, while Sita grinds and swallows the bitter pills that do nothing but set her on edge and then exhaust her with sleep. Everything we eat is flavored with the stale yeast powder. But Sita hardly notices what she eats anymore.

Indeed, she moves less, says less, as the days go by. In the evenings, when we sit on the porch, she wraps up in her best afghans, the ones that Fritzie crocheted so long ago. It is a bad sign. No woman uses the best afghans on herself. But who else is there to save them for?

The visit lengthens from days into weeks. I go back and forth between Blue Mound and Dot, but Mary stays because Sita is in such a weakened state.

One night Sita is talkative.

"Why did you come here," she asks, "you and my cousin and that damn little dog?"

"Because I dreamed you were sick," I say.

"You dreamed I was sick." She rocks in the falling blue light. Her face is like a carved bone. "Oh yes, you dreamed you might inherit something that I own."

This gets my goat. "We're good to you because your mother was good to us," I tell her. "We're not here because we want anything of yours."

She sits there, creaking in her chair. There is a long silence

275

between us, but then I think how superior she has always been, and I know I won't be able to help myself from asking what I thought of in the truck.

"But you could will Mary the sewing machine her mother sent her," I say.

The rocker stops. Sita's mouth is open, black and wide as an attic. A bat could swoop in there and perch. Her mouth opens even wider when she starts to laugh. I realize I haven't heard her laugh yet, not since we got here, then all of a sudden she chokes to a halt.

"That hoary old thing broke down ten years ago and I gave it to the Grinnes."

I know the Grinne family. They are the disreputed prodigals of Blue Mound who live mainly off their sales of balled aluminum foil. I know that Grinne girl couldn't sew with that machine, wouldn't sew with it, never intended to sew with it in the future, and probably chopped the cabinet up to kindle fires one cold winter.

I have nothing more to say to Sita. I leave her creaking, her wasted bosom shielded in her arms, and I walk upstairs to see what Mary is doing.

We share the upstairs guest room, which is decorated with dull, perfectly blended pinkish colors and pictures of the same tree through different seasons. Some nights in that room I lay awake for hours as Mary rambles in her sleep. She has long threatening conversations with unknown people. "Hand it over," she says. "I've heard that one before."

One night, as I am listening, I realize what she is doing in her sleep. She is collecting outstanding bills. She has her foot in the front door of the dream. She shouts when it closes on her foot. "You signed the note," she hollers. "I'll see you in court!"

Mary has spread out in the room. Her valise unpacked a surprising number of things. The red brick is on the stand beside her bed, wrapped carefully in a washcloth so none of its cosmic powers leak into the air. She is not one to hide her clothes, even underclothes, from view. They are stacked or draped on bureaus or the backs of chairs. Only her great white cotton bloomers are neatly hung, clothespinned to hangers and swung off the closet doorknobs because Sita will not allow her to dry them out on the line. A chipped green statue of the Virgin Mary is set up behind the brick. She has stacked her astrology books and knitting yarns in handy corners. I see now that she has finished Dot's sweater.

She holds it up for me to admire.

The red lines run in zigzags and squares within squares, forming paths that lead to dead ends.

"Where's Start?" I ask.

Mary doesn't understand until I trace the pattern with my finger, trying to find an exit. She begins to search along with me, through the tangle of pathways across the chest, down the undersides of arms, across the shoulders. But we can discover no way out.

I pick up a book that is on her bed, and flip through it.

"The night sky is full of baffling holes," I read.

This is a subject that has been on Mary's mind, and she is happy to explain. She tells me about holes in space that suck everything into them. They even suck space into space. I cannot picture that. In my mind I see other things, though, drawn away at high speed into the blackness. Just this morning I discovered a pocket of junk in Sita's house. In an old cabinet in the basement, behind the recreation room, I found a disorganized clutter, spider nests, real dirt. The shelves of the cabinet held old bottles and cans. Venetian shoe cream. Moroline. Coconut hair oil. KILL-ALL Rat Tablets. And a book called *The Black Rose*, by Thomas B. Costain. There were papers too, a whole scrap pile of Sita's newspaper clippings and rent receipts from the years she spent in Fargo as a single girl. There was a letter. It was stamped, sealed, and ready to mail. I read the envelope carefully, wondering and wondering what to do with it. The address was written out to a Mrs. Catherine Miller, Minneapolis. There was no telling exactly how old this letter was, or when Sita had forgotten to mail it.

I closed the cabinet and walked upstairs. I put the letter in my purse. In the end I decided to retrieve it, and sent it off to this Mrs. Miller with a few cents more postage. But all day today, any time I have thought of the cabinet of junk, a sadness has taken hold of me. Sita is the reason all those things are there, and when she goes they will still be there. They will outlast her as they have already outlasted her husband. They will outlast me. Common things, but with a power we cannot match. It makes me sad to think of them, so humble yet indestructible, while Sita, for all her desperation of a lifetime, must die.

And now, as Mary is talking, I have a strange thought that everything a person ever touched should be buried along with them, because things surviving people does not make sense. As she goes on and on about invisible gravities, I see all of us sucked headlong through space. I see us flying in a great wind of our own rubber mats and hairbrushes until we are swallowed up, with fearful swiftness, and disappear.

Everything is getting confused. Nothing seems to matter. I'm not even angry when Mary reads my thoughts again and says how the Indian burial mounds this town is named for contain the things that each Indian used in their lives. People have found stone grinders, hunting arrows, and jewelry of colored bones.

So I think it's no use. Even buried, our things survive.

The dog is barking under the window. The evening is growing chill, and I realize that Little Dickie has bitten his rope and gone digging in the iris beds again. I hear Sita, yelling from the porch. Her voice is rising and rising until it cracks off. Her chair tips,

278

or something else goes crash. I hear Little Dickie barking and grunting. Or is it Sita? One of them is groaning. We open the window and Mary leans out to see, but it is too dark. Lilac branches shield Little Dickie from our view. We hear panting and pounding.

"He found something," says Mary. "Sita's going to kill him if he digs up her border."

"Get out of there! Scat!" Mary yells.

But the panting and pounding still goes on.

So Mary reaches behind her. Two things are within her grasp. The chipped statue of the Virgin and the special brick. She flings the brick out the window. There is a thud, silence, then Little Dickie whines.

We run downstairs. The moon isn't up yet. I fumble for the porch light but can't find it, and follow Mary down the front steps. I have to grope my way, holding on to lawn chairs and rose stakes. I cross the grass, and then I see their huddled shapes. Mary's flowered dress patches into the bush, but the white shape on the ground—that is Sita. I know her afghan by touch. It is the cream-colored pancake-posy stitch that Fritzie made before she left.

I am kneeling, bending close to her. She does not move for many long seconds, and then her body gives a rippling shudder. It flashes into my mind that it's time. Things are being snatched from our grips. The scattered dirt is dry and cold. She whispers in my face.

"You'll eat shit with the chickens someday too."

That's Pete's phrase. It means that no matter how high and mighty, we all get to ground level someday. Sita's hair is wet where the brick slammed down on her head. I think that she's right. She's right. I'll eat shit with the chickens. We carry her indoors. She is light as toast. We lay her on the long beige couch in the living room. I'm almost afraid to switch on the lamp, but finally Mary does, and then I see how bad Sita looks. Black shadows arc in her cheeks.

I sit with her the rest of the night, bathing her forehead and listening to her breath fall and sink. I pack the best afghans around her. The rippling stripes and whirling clouds. The mouse-and-trap stitch. Mary is dozing in the chair with her head on her hand, not moving, so that sometime in the night I forget she's there.

I forget Little Dickie too. That dog got pounded anyway. I forget what we have come here for. At some point Mary begins to mumble, so I know she is asleep.

"Don't argue with me," she says. "I have checked your account."

Sita smiles at those words and opens her eyes. She looks peacefully around, then focuses at me and frowns. I don't know if she's frowning at me or someone else, but I look down into her face.

She takes a deep troubled breath. I don't hear when she lets it out, because I am suddenly remembering how she used to look when we were girls and she got the better of me. She sat above me like I am sitting above her. Her pink lips curved. Her teeth were white and square. She swung her long thick braid over her head. It whipped down, plopped against my cheek, brushed my nose and mouth. I remember, now, that Sita's braid did not hurt. It was only soft and heavy, smelling of Castile soap, but still I yelled as though something terrible was happening. Stop! Get Off! Let Go! Because I could not stand how strong she was, her knees against my chest. I could not stand her holding me down helpless in the dirt.

SITA TAPPE

Ever since they came with their cake full of bugs and their spicy sausages, I've taken to sleeping downstairs on the pool table. It's not just that Mary talks in her sleep so loud that she can be heard from the end of the upstairs hallway, or even that Celestine is up and down all night fetching glasses of water, eating cereal or frying eggs. It isn't just that I never asked for their companionship, don't want it, even wish they would fall sick themselves and leave. I sleep downstairs for many reasons of my own. The pool table itself, for one. I like the feel of green French baize. I like the smooth surface. I like the pockets, useful places for rolled-up magazines, tumblers, my hairbrush. Sleeping, I breathe a grade-school scent of blue chalk dustings, along with the grown-up odors of spilled cocktails and ash. I've explained to Celestine and Mary that the hard flat surface of the pool table is good for my back, but the truth is I like sleeping in the basement.

My first husband used to call this large, windowless area his recreation center. Jimmy had it soundproofed and paneled in expensive oak, but the wall decorations are gifts of junk from his friends in beverage distribution and local taverns. Along one side of the room there are shelves full of stereo equipment, drawers of records, a color television console. When I got married again, Louis added classical to Jimmy's country-western and easy-listening records. Sometimes Louis did experiments in the unfinished areas of the basement or held meetings of his fungus group. He put in a shortwave radio set and called places behind the Iron Curtain. There is so much here of both Louis and Jimmy that the room is a kind of monument to both of them and to neither one.

It is mine now. I've moved all of my favorite things down here.

There is a nest of jewelry in the tape case, photographs of my father on the Mexican end tables, and folded in a pile three of my best cashmere sweaters and a pair of Italian leather sling-back shoes. I even cleaned out the bathroom just behind one wall. I scrubbed it three times with Dutch Cleanser, then with Lysol. I threw away Louis's darkroom chemicals and the pint bottles left underneath the sink by Jimmy's brothers. Now the bathroom cabinet holds my makeup, but not what's left of the pills, the little stockpiled prescriptions that were Louis's legacy. I have a safer, surer, place for them.

At one time I used to have the pills stashed everywhere. But I kept forgetting where I hid them. They'd turn up unexpectedly, and that was undependable. I couldn't stand to lose a one after Louis died because there is no doctor in town anymore who will write out a ticket. "You'll become addicted," they tell me. They want to cut me off. They think I am cut off. They don't know what Louis left.

The room is dark at any time of the day. I do not like being wakened by the sun anymore. This morning, even knowing that I have to get up soon and meet Celestine and Mary, I lay flat on my back, swathed in covers that have absorbed an earthen smell from the basement air.

Lying here, I imagine all that I could do by remote control.

Louis was the one who ran wires beneath the shag carpeting. He liked to sit in his wing-back armchair and push buttons. Jimmy, I know, would have lounged on the fat Mediterranean-style couch and cursed with awe at what Louis had done. From here, I can turn on the television if I want. The face of the Morning Hostess might be flipping in a blur, but I can stabilize her with one twist. Headphones are at my elbow. I can push on the stereo power, the radio. I can listen to 8-track tapes, or, in silence, watch the brightly lit dials and barometers slide and flicker. I can operate the light control to dim or illuminate the imitation Tiffany overhead. I can turn on all of the beer lamps and watch them. One is a long silhouette of a stagecoach pulled by horses that flee silently around and around a lit screen of mountains and desert cacti. Another is of a canoe endlessly revolving in a blue lake. Some are Hamm's, some are Schmidt's, some are simple diamond-shaped Grain Belt. On the far side of the room, Jimmy installed a wet bar shaped like the letter U and padded with thick black vinyl.

Since the night Mary tried to brain me with a thrown brick, there is less pain. It was as if the blow shorted out a series of nerve connections. That was one reason I did not call the police when I finally could—that and the fact of the pills. I had a fear they would make an examination, search the house, find what's left of them floating in the toilet tank, in the waterproof container Louis used to keep his matches in whenever he went out to the field to gather botanical specimens. I almost hate to take the pills anymore, there are so few left. A month, month and a half from now, what will happen? I'm just lucky that the brick jogged the nerve ends out of kilter. That makes the whole prospect easier to bear. I am more comfortable. However, I have lost the use of my left arm and must hold it crimped up at my ribs like the wing of a chicken.

I should rise, before they make their deliveries and come back to get me in that truck that smells of blood and scorched leather. Later on sometime, today or tomorrow, I can't remember, they want to take me to watch the Beet Parade in Argus, and then the coronation, which will be held in a grandstand of hard backless seats. I refused at first, but they insisted.

"You'll get real enjoyment from seeing Dot crowned," coaxed Celestine.

"You'd be surprised," I answered, "at how much enjoyment I can get from laying down."

Mary, still sullen at having almost killed me prematurely, tries to downplay what she did. She will take no responsibility. She says we're wound up and we don't stop until we wind down.

"So you might as well have a day out," she said, without enthusiasm. Her lack of it was probably what made me agree.

Getting up is no light task, however. It involves the use of too many muscles, and of my legs, which I prefer to pack in warm knits and pillows. The recreation room is chill, not something I mind much in this summer heat, except during that first long walk across the carpet, or the moment I have to step onto the frigid bathroom tiles.

I roll onto my stomach and lower my legs from the table. From the left side pocket I lift a tumbler of water, and drink deeply. I have not removed the colored pool balls from within the table, and now they roll and click in their hidden channels. I find it a friendly sound, soothing and distracting. The table is built so solid that they only move when I get on or off. I begin to walk across the carpet. But this morning I do not even get as far as the heavy couch. There is something changed, a weakness deeper than I've felt since the brick smashed down. I wish that I'd asked for some food before the two went out or that there were even a few stale pretzels left behind Jimmy's bar. But then, I remember, the pretzels would be fifteen or maybe twenty years old by now. I do not mean to do this, but I find that I am laying very suddenly upon the floor. I do not think I've fallen, but I am unmistakably stretched out, flat on my stomach, my face pressed into the shag strands that are like a thick wool grass. I have to lay there. I can't call out for help. I don't know how long it takes before I gather back my strength, crouch up on all fours, and crawl. I have my pride, but I must save it for even harder moments and for times when Mary and Celestine are around to watch.

Death is a weekly chore to them, I think, no more than that, no more than the sound that causes it. The rifle report. The dull blow. The fork in the chicken's neck. I'm sure that they never hear the sounds the animals make. But as a girl, before I left the butcher shop, I always heard the cries and bellows. The pigs screamed like it was our neighbors being murdered in their beds. And when the chickens got their heads knocked off, their wings flapped and flapped, beating the lime sand into a brilliant cloud.

I still hear their wings. They sweep the ground in a hopeful frenzy. Even brainless the body continues its puppet dance. When it happens to me, I do not want Celestine or Mary to hear the sound. That's another reason I sleep in the recreation room. I remember Jimmy's truckload of acoustic tiles, his special insulation. I remember Jimmy testing the stereo full blast downstairs while I stood up in the kitchen, sensing the bass drum's vibration, hearing no music but a faint insectlike whining.

Now the bathroom. The door. The switch.

Jimmy had steel handles installed. He said he put them in for the handicapped, but of course he meant his brothers, who could not aim straight even with the handrail, being soused, and left the evidence of their drunken relief on the pale blue tiles. I am glad for the handrails and the no-slip strips now. I bring myself to the toilet. Lifting the glazed ceramic top off the tank is the most demanding event of my day. I always fear that it will crash to the floor as I slide it over. This operation takes every ounce of my control. I pluck the waterproof box out. I put the cover back, not over all the way, just enough so it won't slide. And then I breathe easier. I fill my toothbrush cup with water. I open the little bottle and shake three into my palm. Not three. No. No. I have limited myself to one. I put two back. Then for some reason I empty the whole container. I'm just curious to see how many days I've got left before they're gone. That's when I see how few there are.

I stare down at the bright orange capsules for I don't know how long. It is as though we are held in a beam of comprehension.

Only half a bottle left to go. I want to swallow one now, but the capsules won't let me. I have to listen. I have to know what this means. So we look at each other, up and down, and up and down. It isn't really very long before I understand.

Without us, they say, without Louis, it's the state hospital again. It's the cannibal ward. The needle. It is sights that you won't like seeing in your garden.

There is no question. I know quite suddenly that I've come to this moment over time. I have walked over empty spaces to get here. I have arrived.

And then it's easy. I swallow them all.

Sometime after that, I lower myself onto the toilet with my good arm. I do not think ahead. I get up in a crouch that takes me over to the sink. I would like to bathe. I don't think past the thought of water. That makes it easier to let myself down into the tub. And then, when I am sitting and I have turned on the taps, the pills take hold with the rush of hot white water, and at once I begin to float.

I love plants. For the longest time I thought that they died without pain. But of course after I had argued with Mary she showed me clippings on how plants went into shock when pulled up by their roots, and even uttered something indescribable, like panic, a drawn-out vowel that only registered on special instruments. Still, I love their habit of constant return. I don't like cut flowers. Only the ones that grow in the ground. And these water lilies. Printed in a toxic paint upon my bath curtain, they melt me with their purity. Each white petal is a great tear of milk. Each slender stalk is a green life rope.

Such a sound. Such a cascade of water is coming down. I've never seen a waterfall or even heard a moving stream. It is too flat for the water to make a rushing sound where I have lived. I know the river though, its punishments and torn banks. I know it as a tongue of destruction that dwindles by summer to a foul mud rope. No, the river is not the marvel of clean water from a spout, hot and wild, buoying me up with this strange illusion that I'm well.

Out, dry, the pills blocking nerve pathways, I stand.

There is a mist on the mirror. I wipe it off with a hand towel. I have to wait for my hand to stop trembling before I take off the rose-plastic puff of the bath cap and brush my hair. My color's sea gray now, and really I'm too thin. But I take the garnet necklace from its embroidered case and fasten the old filigree clasp very carefully around my throat. Naked but for the blood-red stones, I think of my aunt. I listened beside the door once as Fritzie told some friend the tale of Aunt Adelaide's coldhearted flight. They thought she was cracked by misery, but how I understood her! I saw her sucked up into a cloud. Her bones hollowed like a bird's. Her wings never made that terrible chicken sound, thrashing earth, but no sound at all. She didn't have to flap, but effortlessly swerved into the streams and the currents that flow, invisible, above us. So she flew off. That's what I should have done instead of transplanting phlox. Their roots were tough, and I could never find the proper place to put them, the proper fence to set them off. White phlox up against a white fence. It never worked. I should have painted the fence blue. I should have brought down a more attractive dress.

This one, with its white pleats gone dull in the shower steam, with its belt of lavender and prickling lace at each pulse point, I don't like. I don't even think it does justice to the necklace, but I'll wear the garnets anyway, for Mary's benefit. She's never seen them on me before, but then, she probably doesn't care. She is hard, not a woman of sentiment. I never got to her, or Celestine, except through the daughter.

On one of those few times I had to go to their shop on business, I encountered the girl. Dot sat at the counter eating a lunch, took large gobbling bites of the spiced-meat sandwich, licked her fingers. She had her father's same bad manners. I told her that. She stopped, seemed interested. I told her that she wasn't like her mother at all and resembled, around the nose and eyes, her grandmother Adelaide. I said this just to spite Mary, who never talked about the woman. I went a step farther, told Dot what Adelaide had done. I made it romantic, almost like a legend. Dot was riveted to me, demanded more. I hushed her when Mary came.

For an instant I had taken Dot away from them both the same way Mary stole Celestine. All these years and I still remember that terrible small moment when I stood in the graveyard with my shirt off.

So many things run together. One odd memory I have from the notes Louis kept, was my vision of those underground children on the Day of Judgment.

The horn sounds, I said. All the sirens go off. The municipal water tower spouts blood. And then, I told him, the tough-rooted sod parts over each small resting place. Out the children walk. They are pure bone skeletons. They are surprisingly tiny, made of ivory, carved with precision tools under a jeweler's glass eye. Magnification would show the symmetry of each small joint. But there is no time to marvel, for as they walk down the streets of Argus, their bones are swathed and enveloped in flesh and wrapped in skin and then, finally, in clothing.

What kind of clothing, though, and of what era?

And what will they do, I asked Louis, about their parents? What if their parents had sinned themselves into hell? Would there be schools, bus lines, orphanages, stepmothers and stepfathers, some kind of organization to care for them all? If not, what terror! Imagine the poor children left to wander, searching through the ranks of the dead for someone or something familiar.

It is too heartbreaking, Louis, I'd said.

Now I'm ready. The necklace gleams, sharp as malice, against the ruin of my throat. It's too late to change the way I am. I do not take the necklace off. My arms creak as I shrug into the dress. There is the makeup, the hair, and all the concentration this requires. The effort of moving each separate finger, of grasping the tiny brushes and tubes, is immense. Who would believe the strict will this demands? I amaze myself with each light stroke. The results are a vast improvement. And necessary. I must do a good job up here to draw attention from my legs, for I cannot bend to pull on my stockings anymore. I cannot wear stockings. So I will not look down except to admire the tips of my white glove-leather pumps.

And now the lights. Out. The bathroom door. They will drive that truck into the yard and lean hard on the horn. I will be up-stairs for it, whenever they come, out on the front porch. I'll rise to meet them. But before I climb the fourteen deceptively simple, deep-carpeted stairs, I rest. I rest right here. I sink back in the dim, cool room, on the couch of maroon leather that Jimmy loved and where once, long ago, the only time in my life, in fact, I surprised myself by taking no precautions and lay afterward, in Jimmy's arms, awed at the blank window into the future.

Such were the possibilities.

Papa would have loved a grandchild, and Fritzie too. They never dared say anything right to my face about it, but I knew from their small broad hints. When they came up north to visit they always looked into my face for some sign, some softening, a change in my body's weather. Fritzie lingered over children we happened into, and once, in a fit of her old fierceness, asked if I was going against the church with some method.

Papa loved Jimmy's beer lamps. When Jimmy and I first married, Papa would come over and the two would sit and watch them while drinking beer and listening to records. Later on they'd come upstairs glazed over, hoping for sandwiches and pickles. I'd provide, but I never went downstairs with them. I thought the lamps were vulgar. That was then. Not until I moved down here for good did I understand what a comfort they can be, almost hypnotizing, more soothing than any real scenery you might find, and with the added advantage that I can watch in a darkened room.

I wonder how long it will take if the pills do work. I touch a switch by my right hand and a beer lamp comes on. It is the one of sky blue waters, my favorite. Again and again, waiting, I watch the small canoe leave the Minnesota lakeshore and venture through the sleek waves. The pines along the shore stand green black and crisp. The water shimmers, lit within. The boat travels. I can almost see the fish rise, curious, beneath its shadow.

MARY ADARE

As WE DROVE up to the house we saw Sita, all in white, standing upright in the yew bushes and inspecting us through the curling dry needles. She looked impatient. Her purse was by her feet and her legs were oddly set, propped to support her as if they were made of wood. I steered the truck halfway around the circle of her driveway.

"First she didn't want to go, and now I suppose we're late," I said to Celestine, who was annoyed that Sita had decided to go. She wanted to enjoy the parade and the crowning of Dot with no interference and no judgment from Sita, no worry about the state of her nerves. Turning off the engine, stopping to get out, I could tell Sita was going to be unpleasant.

There was no greeting from her. Not one grudging sound. Celestine sighed loudly and pushed her hair up off her neck. She slammed out of the truck with an angry air of having to make the best of it. Then she stalked across the lawn, calling. I followed, distracted by Little Dickie's barking. He was tied up out back of the house, and I thought that I should give him some water from the hose even though I'd no sooner suggest this than Sita would frown at the delay.

So we stood right up next to Sita and touched her arms, thinking to help her from the tangle of branches.

Celestine and I both noticed her coldness at the same time. Sita's expression never gave her away. Her eyes were open, staring right at the place our truck had stopped. Her lips were set in exasperation, as if she had just been about to say something and found out her voice was snatched in death. Celestine picked Sita's purse up to give it back, but then she held it, dangling from her fingers by the strap. She didn't know what else to do with it. I was no help. I suppose that we were in a state of shock. I don't know how long we stood there, half listening to Little Dickie bark, smelling the dry, hot air and, strange thing, Sita's French perfume, a penetrating scent from the stoppered flasks that she kept in the basement bathroom.

"What should we do?" Celestine finally asked.

I looked at her, but Celestine did not seem to be asking me. Rather, she was asking Sita. I looked at Sita too, then, as if to consider her opinion. That was when I noticed details, like the necklace of red stones, familiar looking and antique, which had snagged on a broken branch and held her head up, and her arms, which she had managed to wedge at even heights in the scrawny, divided trunks. She had dressed very carefully, as usual. Maybe she had gotten tired of waiting and leaned back in the bush. Maybe she had been about to say, To hell with them. They're late. She had taken to using words like *hell* and *damn* around us constantly, something she hadn't done even when she'd quit the church. Sita was never easy to live with. We had to bring her trays down the basement stairs and serve them to her while she lounged on the pool table. Even then, she turned her nose up or picked her casserole suspiciously apart as if she thought I had hidden more insects between the noodles.

"I suppose we should take her down," I said.

"But then what?" wondered Celestine.

Celestine's cheekbones were colored with rouge. Her hair twisted back in waves, gray brown, newly set. But she looked rattled.

"We have to think clearly," I said.

"Have you got an idea?" Celestine asked. She was annoyed that Sita died in a yew bush on the morning of her daughter's glory. I don't think it had entirely struck Celestine yet that Sita's condition was permanent.

"Is there a funeral parlor in Blue Mound?" Celestine asked.

"This town's too small," I said.

What Sita's death meant was sinking into our minds. Langenwalter's. That was the funeral home in Argus, a long place made of pink and orange stucco, with a Spanish tile roof and black-grilled windows. To think of Sita in one of its familiar rooms was impossible. Besides that, there was the Beet Parade. Everyone would be there, even the Langenwalters. "They probably won't be available," she said, "either to fetch Sita or take her in."

"We'll bring her with us in the truck," I said.

Celestine shook her head. "I thought we'd just put her inside the house, lay her out on the couch."

"Celestine," I said, "do you want strangers to haul her off?"

"No," said Celestine.

"We'll take her with us," I said again.

But then we just stood still, drawn back into the circle of Sita's silence. I heard the hum of crickets in the flax field across the road, the drone of some machinery far off.

"Take her other arm," I finally said. I reached out, lifting Sita by the elbow. We unhooked Sita's necklace from the twig and her head fell a fraction to one side so that she seemed, now,

292

more alert and observant than she had been in weeks. She seemed to have fixed on some fascinating scene that she disapproved of and yet could not be diverted from watching.

We supported her between us and walked toward the truck. She was higher on Celestine's side and dragged on mine, and she was heavy. That struck me. She'd been so light and thin before. It was as if death had entered and filled the marrows of her bones with sand. The truck seemed immeasurably far across the lawn. Sita's feet scraped.

"Hold her up more," said Celestine. "You're getting her shoes dirty."

I tried to hoist her higher but her weight was immense. I was panting and my breath came like fire by the time we reached the truck. It had been my intention to lay her full length in the back. Celestine held her propped up and I opened the double doors. Once I looked inside, though, I couldn't see loading Sita in like any common delivery.

"On second thought," I said, "let's put her up in front."

"Are you nuts?" said Celestine.

"No I am not." I felt sharp toward Celestine because I thought she just didn't want to ride behind and run her stockings. I didn't say another word to her, just opened the passenger's side door and helped move Sita toward it. But once we got there we found that Sita was so stiff she didn't want to bend. It was a problem. Celestine put Sita's legs in and I tried to fit the rest of her. But no matter how we did it, legs first or head first, Sita ended up leaning onto the driver's side, looking like she was thrown there. And she was getting more bedraggled as we pushed and shoved. Then, suddenly, in the middle of our exertions, Celestine hit Sita's back in a certain place and it was magical, as if she'd touched a hidden spring. Sita folded into a perfect sitting position right in the seat. There she waited, with her hands in her lap, her head slightly cocked, gazing out the front windshield.

293

"All right," I said, gaining back my breath, standing away from the truck, feeling a little dizzy. "Let's go."

Celestine didn't answer, and I saw the reason when I looked at her. She was staring at Sita, wordless, running over with tears. Her face was completely drenched with them, and the bosom of her dress too. I shoved my handkerchief at her, but she didn't even take it, or understand. Then she put her hand up and found that her cheeks were wet.

"Oh," she said, in a surprised way, as if she'd hurt herself.

I put the handkerchief into her hands and walked around to the driver's side. Celestine bent over, fastened Sita in with a belt, and put the white leatherette purse in her lap. Then Celestine climbed through the back and sat down just behind me. I started the motor and drove out of Sita's yard.

With the air cooling on and the vents and windows shut, we were enclosed. The fields spread, dry and failed, between Blue Mound and Argus. Dust rode on the horizon in buffeting shapes. The drought had turned the landscape a uniform white-brown. But all of that was outside our vehicle. We almost seemed to float. Ditches skimmed by in a blur. We had the road to ourselves for a long while and drove in silence, our minds distracted. I didn't notice the speedometer.

The siren and the flashing lights gave me such a start that I wrenched the wheel hard, pulling over, still thinking to let the police pass and surprised when the car stopped behind me.

"He's walking over to the truck," said Celestine in an amazed voice, looking out the back window. I could see him from my side mirror now. Officer Lovchik.

"Hello Ronald," I said, rolling down my window when he bent to speak to me. "I thought you'd be directing the parade."

"Or in it yourself," said Celestine.

"I'm on my way there," said Lovchik, "but I clocked you at eighty."

I had no answer.

"Morning, Sita," he said, smiling across me into the passenger's seat. Since Louis had died Ronald Lovchik had renewed his old pursuit of Sita, even sent her boxes of those chocolates. I knew because I'd found a stack of Whitman's in her cupboard, still sealed in cellophane. I'd eaten some and they were fresh. But now he had no chance. Sita looked forward, sternly, into the distance. Lovchik looked down, hurt but unsurprised, and flipped open his pad of tickets. Then he sighed and closed it.

"What the hell," he said bitterly, straightening so I looked at the tight tan buttons in his shirt. "It's your first offense, right?"

I leaned out and said yes.

"I won't ticket you," he decided. "First warning. That's all."

Celestine tapped me. "Thank him," she hissed.

"Thanks," I said.

"I hope I didn't disturb you, Mrs. Tappe." His voice floated over the roof of the car, and then his footsteps retreated. His car door thudded; he veered around us and flashed down the highway.

"Why didn't we let him take over," I asked, restarting the truck.

Celestine did not answer.

My voice rang too loud in my ears. I drove carefully, well under the speed limit, into Argus and followed Eighth Street down as it led into Main. We planned on getting to the fairgrounds by the most direct route. So I cut through an alley and entered a line of cars that was pushing slowly onto the congested corner of Main. It was somewhere in the crowd of cars, misdirected and confused, that we made our mistake. Perhaps the windows shouldn't have been rolled up so tightly or the air on so high. I didn't hear the high school band, is what I'm saying, or the squeak horns of clowns until they were upon us. Until then, I didn't realize that we were in the parade.

By then there was no turning back. I swung in behind a float made of spray-painted sheets and Kleenex, and wire that was shaped into a gigantic sugar beet. It loomed before us, fat and white. Long crepe paper leaves floated off the top. The beet bobbled in the hot wind, drawn lurching behind a high schooler's car. From time to time tissues sheered off, blew into the crowds on either curbside, or settled on our windshield. The pace was slow. Behind us a club of precision marchers displayed themselves in uniforms of gold and blue. Every so often the parade stopped to let them form a scene or letter with their bodies.

"Wave and smile," said Celestine. "Those people are looking at you."

It was true. Although the huge beet and the drill team took up most of the crowd's attention as we passed, there were some curious enough to peer in at us and wave. Perhaps they glimpsed Sita, imperial and stern in her gleaming necklace, and assumed that she was someone important, an alderwoman or the governor's wife. Others in the crowd were customers and waved simply because they were pleased to recognize us.

"There's Langenwalter standing next to Adrian," Celestine whispered.

"You wave," I told Celestine. "I'm keeping both hands on the wheel."

So as we moved along, close to overheating in first gear, Celestine occasionally flapped a hand at the window.

It seemed as though hours passed before we made the turnoff, coasted slowly down the incline into the county fairgrounds, and cut the engine under a tall horseshoe of elms. We parked directly behind the grandstand where it was cool, in the dim shade where we hoped no one would linger or notice Sita.

I left the motor running with the air cooling on and climbed out. We stood under a big tree, looking through the windshield at Sita.

"I guess we have no choice," said Celestine. "We have to leave her."

We waited there a moment longer, hesitating as if to make sure. Under the dappled light that turned through the leaves, Sita's expression had shifted now to a deeper watchfulness. She stared right through us, past us, and then beyond us to the other side, where booths and games were set up in the clearing of trampled grass.

Most-Decorated Hero

The orderly hoisted Russell out of his wheelchair, rolled him onto the bed, and stripped him of his thin cotton pajamas. Eli Kashpaw sat at his kitchen table with a coffee, watching. Fleur was stationed in the shadows of the next room, supervising the orderly with stern attention. She unpacked Russell's uniform from an old cracked valise. The green wool exuded naphthalene. The orderly dressed Russell in it, moving carefully under Fleur's eye. He strained to lift Russell back into his chair. Fleur took Russell's medals from a leather case and pinned the whole bright pattern over his heart. Then she put his rifle, in a long bag of olive drab, across his lap. Russell waited for his hat to be set on at an angle, the way it was in his portrait-studio pictures.

When everything was done, he locked his hands on the armrests. He could use his arms to push. The orderly wheeled Russell into the morning heat, across the yard of tough grass, and up a ramp into the nursing-home van. He slammed the door. The van pulled out and then it was driving the back roads. There were no windows on the sides, but there was a plastic bubble in the ceiling. Tipping his head Russell saw sky, clouds, and after a while some crisscrossing wires. After an hour of driving, they stopped. Outside the van he heard horses blowing and stamping. An amplified voice called out numbers and directions.

Suddenly his chair was yanked from behind and, in one swoop, went down the ramp out of the van backward. Across the street, in a parking lot of armory trucks, he saw lines of antique cars, drivers in goggles, women under old-time parasols. A majorette was stretching her golden legs out on the ground. Legionnaires passed him, not feet away. Nobody looked at him. Finally the son of his old boss at Argus National clapped him lightly on the arm and bent over his chair.

"What a day for it," he said, and that was all.

The air was dry and the sun far away, veiled by clouds of dust. A jeep rumbled up, hauling his float. It was the same one the American Legion always used. The orderly strained to lift Russell onto the float, then strapped him upright between raised wooden bunkers. A field of graves stretched down before him, each covered with plastic grass and red poppies. A plain white cross was planted at his feet.

Very soon, the parade would start to move. The skirted, flimsy high school floats and go-cart clowns were falling into place. The announcer's high-pitched voice had gone ragged. The bands tuned up, hoisted their drums and tubas.

The float moved.

Russell felt the small jolts in his face as they bounced over potholes. With each lurch, the cross above the grave at his feet shook. He sat high, hands clutching his knees, and stared above the crowd as he passed. There were men with children on their shoulders, girls in bright dresses. His float continued past the glass storefronts and banks, past the bars that featured dancing girls and Happy Nites, past the post office. The drums rattled and the plastic horns squawked in the clown's go-cart. The noise was tiring. Russell tried to hold his head high, to keep the fierce gaze smoking, but his chin dropped. His eyes closed, and suddenly the noise and people seemed far off.

He thought of a distant storm. Low thunderheads collided and the air was charged with a vibrant, calm menace. Before him he saw a large hunched woman walking slowly down a dirt road. He started after her, and then he recognized his sister Isabel, dead these many years. Now she was walking this road, wearing a traditional butterfly-sleeved calico dress and quilled moccasins. Her black hair hung loose. She turned and signaled him to follow. Russell hesitated, although he felt it happening. He felt his mind spread out like a lake. His heart slowed and numbed and seemed to grow until it pressed against his ribs.

"He looks stuffed," cried a shrill woman from the curb. Russell heard her clearly. At one time her comment would have shamed him, but now he simply opened his eyes to the blurred scene, then shut them down. His sister was still there, not far in front of him. Isabel looked over her shoulder with her old grin. He saw that she'd had a tooth knocked out.

"Wait for me," he called.

She turned and kept walking. The road was narrow. The grass on either side flowed off forever, and the clouds pressed low. He followed her, thinking that he might see Celestine. She might join them. But then it occurred to him this wouldn't happen, because this was the road that the old-time Chippewas talked about, the four-day road, the road of death. He'd just started out.

I'm dead now, he thought with calm wonder.

At first he was sorry that it had happened in public, instead of some private place. Then he was glad, and he was also glad to see he hadn't lost his sense of humor even now. It struck him as so funny that the town he'd lived in and the members of the American Legion were solemnly saluting a dead Indian, that he started to shake with laughter.

The damn thing was that he laughed too hard, fell off the road, opened up his eyes before he'd gone past the point of no return, and found himself only at the end of the parade. He quickly shut his eyes again. But the road had gone too narrow. He stumbled. No matter how hard he called, his sister continued forward and wouldn't double back to help.

WALLACE PFEF

DOT GREW ANGRIER each year, frightening us, making havoc, causing danger to herself. Some nights she stayed out till two or three and, once, she didn't come back until dawn. She smoked in her room, filling the windowsills with stubs, and kept secret diaries that she locked with small gold keys.

It wasn't hard to guess the sort of things she wrote in the books.

She was persecuted, miserable, plotting her revenge. Instead of her grade-school lack of friends, she now had active enemies. And there was Celestine, me, and Mary. We were the banes of her existence, until she needed us. Then we gave her all we had, which she resented. She filled boxes with papers. Her diaries collected. And she told us these things to our faces too, not sparing us a single word.

More than anything we had in common, Dot's spite drove Celestine, Mary, and me together. Dot had not been an easy child, but before this we'd been able to out-talk her. Now she out-talked us, listed each fault, left us stricken. She ate our hearts to the bone, devoured us, grew robust on our grief and our bewilderment. More than anything, we were shocked by what we had created. Dot wore fishnet stockings and a vinyl skirt to classes, teased her hair into a nest, came home with merchandise she couldn't have purchased on her minimum wage at the Argus Theater. Her friends were hoods, drinkers, smokers, motorcycle riders, and assorted deadbeats who haunted the street of bars that did not donate to the Christmas Lighting Fund.

We tried to interest Dot in hobbies, in school sports, in scholastics. But she only seemed happy when she was riding in a souped-up car, or parked in one. That was not my observation, but Celestine's. Mary observed that if Dot were not all she had in the world, she would have disowned her niece. My reason for sticking by Dot, though, was different. I had faith, fundamental and abiding, in Dot's courage.

True, her lack of fear had become quite tedious and rude. Her utter honesty turned teachers and classmates to stone. But she was what I was not. She was not afraid to be different, and this awed me. Besides, I loved her and wanted to make her happy.

But I couldn't entirely do that alone.

I had a theory, that if those who really loved Dot could hardly stand her, what could she think of herself? One spring, in order to help her, to give her pride in an accomplishment, to allow her self-image to soar, I gave her a twenty-pound shot for the shot put. It was the best investment of my life, or so I thought, because at first Dot took to it and would not be parted from the iron ball.

That was the first spring of the drought. The days were unremittingly fair, the rainfall at a record low. All that month Dot walked past my house, carrying the shot to and from the corner where her bad influences dropped her off. She was trimming down, she said, for the track-and-field tryouts. She was serious about all of this and it seemed like a new start. In the late afternoon, she stopped by if she saw my car parked in the drive. This was also new, and she would be so pale with hunger, having eaten nothing all day long, that she wouldn't have the strength to point out my failings. Besides I would disarm her. I'd sit her down at the table with a quart of milk and a pan of walnut brownies. She'd plow right through them while telling me her plans.

She would live by the ocean like a movie star, or disappear

like her Aunt Mary, who told Dot she'd hitched a boxcar. Dot would own a fried-chicken chain. She would drive trucks, bull-dozers, fly off forever like her grandmother Adelaide. She would travel the world and seek knowledge, or live up north on the reservation with her uncles Russell and Eli. She'd put the shot in the state track, from there to the Olympics. Argus would display her gold medals in the county museum right next to Russell's war mementos and her now-famous diaries.

Dot was either lit up by her imaginary future, or depressed, a dark lump, by what she saw as her life's realities, harsh and awful. She told of parties to which she was not invited, good-looking hoods who ignored her, girls who filled her locker with balled-up paper towels, teachers who asked her questions in class they knew she couldn't answer, even janitors who waxed the halls so she would slip and embarrass herself.

In her worst moods, the world was out to destroy Dot.

"You think I have a bad attitude," she'd say. "You think I'm just feeling sorry for myself, but listen to this!"

And then she'd relate another grievance.

Dot had started to collect things that worked against her, and she took a morose satisfaction in telling them to me.

"Show your bright side," I'd say to her.

"You're out of your head," she'd answer.

I was raking the winter leaves off my lawn the afternoon Dot came around to the back entryway. She was carrying the shot. It made a deep *thump* when she dropped it into the grass.

"I made the team," she announced, but she did not sound very pleased. "They said I'd be a good shot-putter because I'm dense for my height."

"Dense?" I was indignant. "You're perfect. I'll get out my insurance chart and prove it to you."

"Those things lie." She hefted the shot, held the iron ball dreamily within the curve of her neck. "Sometimes I fantasize—

like, you'll think this is completely absurd, Wallace, but—I'm picked out by a magazine to pose on their cover. They discover me living like a nobody here in Argus, and they take me and dress me up, do my hair, and suddenly I'm gorgeous." She spun into a sudden crouch, turned, straightened her arm and lunged forward. The shot arced and fell, directly into my rose bed.

"I didn't think I could throw it that far," she said, satisfied. She retrieved the ball. I didn't have the heart to tell her she had broken my favorite bush, Intrigue. Besides that, her words were percolating deep below the surface of my thoughts. I fed Dot and sent her on. But all that evening I was distracted. I could feel it slowly surfacing. And then it took shape when I was tucked between my sheets.

Wallacette Darlene must think well of herself, have a fantasy come true for once, be perfect, on top. This would change her whole view of the world as against her. Give her confidence. Inspire her. But which fantasy? Which wild plan? Which hope? It was not in my power to do much, and her list was so farfetched. But I was determined. I would be like the godmother in a children's story, grant one wish. But which would it be?

I thought through them all and came up with the last.

There will be four queens in Argus, I imagined, just like in a deck of cards. There was already a Snow Queen, a Pork Queen, and a Homecoming Queen. There would be one more queen, and she would be queen of the beets! Yes! And the Beet Queen would be queen of them all, because in Argus the sugar beet is king!

I could see it so clearly, from the moment it first occurred to me. Dot ascending foil-covered steps, her face bright, the tiara catching spotlights and sunlight. I saw the Beefeater roses, plump and breathing, dark red. I saw Dot's eyes, that light amber color so strangely like Mary's, running over with tears of shock, of pride. And I also saw myself, for we do things for our children so many times for our own benefit. I was among the audience, but I was behind it, the cause and prime mover. Dot's eyes were trained upon me, full of amazed respect. People stopped me, shook my hand, said "Wallace, she's gorgeous," "You've done it again," or "I don't know when I've had such fun." For of course I had already begun to see the crowning as part of something larger. My mind just works like that. It would be one long extravaganza, drawing people from out of state. A five-day festival, a fair, a big show in honor of the sugar beet, and topping it all off—the queen.

I was too excited to sleep that night. Such possibilities ran through my head. I saw the carnival, floats, a long parade that would celebrate the changes that ten years of the beet had brought to Argus. I planned an elegant float from the Farmer's Cooperative, and another from the new Sears outlet. Our franchises could be persuaded to donate refreshments. Fried chicken. Hamburgers. The sugar beet had been bigger than I had ever dreamed, and Argus had become its capital. A celebration was overdue, the more I worked it out.

I sat at my desk and typed up my inspirations while the dog snored on my feet. The night passed and the April dawn came early, a gray suffusing light. I collapsed to sleep the morning out. But I was up in only hours, talking my idea around with the other chamber of commerce members, club presidents, the doers and the shakers of the town. There was uniform acceptance, enthusiasm, excitement. We began to see the festival as something annual, a must-see in travel guides as well as a local attraction. We took donations, started raising money from the local beet cooperatives, town businesses. We'd have a sidewalk sale, a big craft show. Things blossomed beyond my farthest hopes.

Between the night of my vision and the day it dawned, however, the months of preparation were long. For one year, I hardly thought about anything else but the festival, even though I had

305

a committee made up of concerned young Jaycees and Jaycee-ettes. "Wallace," they told me, "leave some of this to us!" But I just couldn't. I was obsessed by every detail, down to the order of the floats in the parade and the young person we must hire to clean up after the horses of the Western Riding Club. There was a city ordinance on horse manure that I had drafted myself.

Most important of all, the thing I never lost sight of, was the crowning of the queen. It had to be more than perfect: it had to be regal. All of Dot's fantasies rolled up in one and come to life. I wanted posters. I wanted flyers with the royal candidates prominently displayed. I hired Tommy B.'s Aviation, just west of town, a fellow Moose Lodger who dusted crops and seeded clouds. He would be sworn to secrecy and then skywrite the queen's name just above the grandstand at the moment she was crowned. Driving into town some days with all the sky stretching out blue and aqua before me, I saw the loop-de-loop of her name:

Queen Wallacette That's how I saw it. Never Dot.

I don't care how much she pouted or insisted, or grew up, I don't care how brief her skirt or thick her makeup and blue her language, she would always be Wallacette in my heart. Sometimes I sat on her couch, the one she was born on, and time collapsed. I saw reels of home movies in my head. Dot taking two steps at a time, always running off the edges of steps or landings because in her eager frenzy she never looked down. Dot older, full of swagger in the outfield, practicing her swing on the dried heads of dandelions, filling the air with downy seeds. And lately, Dot a hard-faced girl, despised by classmates, and feared. But I knew once the crown dazzled and drew attention to her sense of command, her unusual bearing, and, yes, her beauty, the town would see it too. Girls would envy her, boys would flock. I wished her enemies would go further, eat dirt to please her, bow and scrape, but I would settle for seeing her crowned.

I'd rig the vote.

306

To that end, I worked like a Trojan and broke my health. The exhaustion, the strain, the loss of weight, these were nothing new. I started running myself into the ground long before I'd even thought up the festival. It was my nature to attend to the details of any event, down to designing posters and composing slogans. I typed long into the night, making up my own press releases, preparing committee reports. Besides that I had enlarged my weekly column "About 'n' Around" to include a community-events calendar spiced with interesting commentary, many pertinent asides, and reportage of gatherings I'd attended.

"Don't think twice," began one of my columns, "before putting aside these dates on your calendar: July 8–12, 1972. These five days will be the acme of entertainment. Games, floats, prizes galore, and of course the crowning of a local reigning lovely."

Who would be Dot.

The only thing that wasn't cooperating was the weather, and that was beyond my control.

We needed rain, a soaking rain that began very slow and steady to open up the earth's pores. We needed it to stop, collect, and to start again next day or day after, sinking deeper, longer, never driving down harsh enough to flay off the topsoil or fast enough to gully the fields. We needed a kind rain, a blessing rain, one that lasted a whole week. We needed water. We tried things, cloud seeding, but the chemistry wasn't right once, and another time the clouds blew off. Whole congregations prayed for the drought to cease. But the days were rainless, hot, and everywhere the earth dried and cracked. For the first time in years there were crop failures, land for sale. And as July neared I couldn't ignore the fact that I was drained, pulled tense, my face sagged with the rapid weight loss.

"It's simple nervous exhaustion," my doctor said, and wrote out a prescription for a muscle relaxant, which I never had filled. I never took his advice on a vacation either. Instead of quitting,

I went at it harder. Perhaps I made my condition worse with the guilt as well. I had nomination ballots printed up so that everyone in town could vote in their bank lobbies. Then I collected the votes myself. I spent one whole night filling out a new set of ballots in different colored pens and pencils, changing my style of X. The same thing when they cast their final votes for the queen. I had to rehearse myself in the bathroom before I presented the results to my friends on the festival committee, and still, when I said Dot's name, my smile shook. I had never been dishonest in my life.

Things went from bad to worse. The drought did not relent. There were those who wanted to cancel the festival, but I told them there was no turning back. The governor and his wife had been invited, along with nine high school marching bands and a precision motorcycle-riding team. The contract for the carnival had been signed, and we had also signed with the rock bands, polka bands, a stunt and stock-car show. We had a demolition derby featuring The Battle of the Mammoths, a fight to the scrap heap between two tractor combines. There was a tractor-pulling contest and a guard alert in which we would see the readiness of our local reserve forces. Once you start the ball rolling like this, there's no stopping it. I said so. But there were those who just looked up at the drained white sky and shook their heads and walked off.

I didn't blame them, for desperate times had hit the beet. But desperate times had hit the area before, and we'd survived. I worked harder. I saw all the more reason for the town to have a big bash, take their minds off the daily weather, which had become the one topic on everyone's lips. People quoted Dewey Berquist, the weatherman out of Fargo, and dragged out scraps of folklore, examined tree rings and the depth of sloughs. But when the river dried to a thick narrow trickle, the banks revealed, all lined with dead fish and twisted hulks of cars, I wished I could call it quits, too. The heat shriveled my enthusiasm. And then, almost the last day, something happened even worse, something so improbable I finally cracked.

One morning, I bumped into Celestine at the post office. She had just reached into the box for her mail.

"What do you know," she mused. In her hand she had a flyer. Dot glowered off the front, her eyes dark as two pools of steam. The other sugar-beet princesses were pictured, too. Their smiles were sweet but their faces were forgettable. Celestine also held a long white card.

"What's this," she said, turning over a postcard.

The card was printed with a logo: ELMO'S LANDSCAPE SYSTEMS. Beneath the logo the words *I'm on my way* were printed, and the name *Karl*.

The high cool ceiling of the post office suddenly seemed to stretch upward forever, collecting the echoes of our voices. The brass fronts of the numbered postal boxes held a thousand small glass mirrors that gave me back the face of an old man, lined and ancient. My hair had thinned on the crown and changed from light blond to gray. Even my new square wire-rimmed glasses seemed, now, a sad attempt to grasp at youth. I was in no shape to see him, or be seen.

There was no turning back, no stopping, and the day finally came in a swirl of grit and dead heat. I woke up more exhausted than I'd gone to bed. Nothing helped. I was worn to the bone and knew I'd have to stumble through the day on sheer willpower. I made it through that morning, and then through the parade, by drinking gallons of weak iced tea. The waxed cups thinned and softened in my hands; the paper shredded. After twelve noon no ice was to be had anywhere, and even the stuff in the soft-drink cannisters was expanding, seeping out of the pressured lids. I was on the edge of collapse, and so what could have been fun or easy became an awful challenge, almost life and death. I staggered on, until I reached the first task of my afternoon.

The Lion's Club had constructed a dunk tank as a community fund-raising device. It was simple. A padded stool was placed several feet above a deep wide stock tank full of water. Under a bigwig's dangling feet a small round lever, supporting the chair, would spring away if it was hit by a three-for-a-dollar softball. The seat would slam backward and the VIP would get doused. The mayor, police chief, sheriff, and the members of the town council had a stint at the tank. To be included was a status symbol and the tank was a popular stop on the midway. For my turn, I wore a costume of course, just as all the dunkees did. To acquire the courage I needed to don my outfit—the orange Hawaiian shirt, straw hat, the beachcomber's pants, the same getup I'd worn at Dot's long-ago luau—I'd convinced myself that Karl wouldn't show. I looked all around the booth before I dared to appear. The mere climb winded me. Once I got there the water glittered in my eyes.

I hadn't known it would be so hard to keep my balance on the dunking stool. I gritted my teeth and held on, sick. I tried to joke with my friends, each of whom took three or six or nine tries and left me sitting.

"He's here! He's the one you've been waiting for!" cried the ticket taker, Arnie Dotzenrud, a slow and uncomprehending fellow Lion. I swooned, gripped the edge of the stool. Yellow stars turned.

"Let me down, please," I whispered, and that's when I saw Dot walking toward me from a distance, dressed in a green cloud. She was electric, tense with life. Just the sight of her was a transfusion. I doted on her sturdy form, the way she swung her arms, and her walk, bold with purpose. I didn't understand the menace that was there as well.

She stood in front of me, and everything else faded out and

blurred. It was like looking at a stopped tornado. Her face was ready to explode and her stormy green dress stood out like an invert funnel. She walked up to the ticket taker, slammed down a dollar bill, and said, "I'll take three." She locked her teeth and cocked her arm back. The green mesh sleeves strained across her muscles. I had watched her pitch a thousand softballs, and so I knew that when she concentrated she never missed the strike zone.

"Please don't," I said, holding my hands up. "Wallacette?"

The first ball slammed. The seat crashed out from under me and I went down. Even through the water I heard the next two hit home.

The Passenger

After they planted the beets in Argus, and put the new bypass in that connected the town with the interstate, most everything that the town needed came by truck. It was the same way with what the town produced. People came to Argus by way of the interstate too, but not Father Miller, who didn't much like traveling by car, and only drove long-distance as a last resort. He took the train across the border from Minneapolis, into North Dakota, and upward in a long curve that brought him to Argus. The coach was nearly empty, and he was the only passenger to disembark, even though there seemed to be a celebration going on. He stepped off the portable footstool, waved off the conductor's helping hand, and answered the perfunctory "watch your step, Father," with a burst of worried enthusiasm. How, he wondered, would the Empire Builder continue the level of excellent service with no passengers? The conductor made his chin long in rue and said he didn't know. Both men paused a moment beneath the blistering Dakota sky, and then the train made a starting lurch. The conductor threw the footstool aboard, swung himself behind, and soon the priest stood alone on the apron of new cement that skirted the Argus depot.

He rocked on his heels, looked side to side, flapped a large white handkerchief out of his pocket, and touched his forehead. The hot dry air fueled him, set him at a boil.

He was here to find out the truth behind the letter that his mother had put into his hand two days before. At first he had not even been curious. He was reliable, a man of good sense, a satisfied priest admired for his tactful sermons and his warmth with the elderly. His first reaction to the letter had been annoyance, worry for his mother. But she was very weak now and not overly concerned about anything besides her illness. Later on, sitting in his office over some accounts, he began to wonder. He tried to imagine what the town was like, the people, the butcher shop. But he now saw that there had been no need. Nothing about Argus was unusual.

He lifted his black case and stepped purposefully beneath the wide cool eaves of the old depot. His foam-soled shoes were soundless on the octagonal tiles, and when he stopped before the brass-barred ticket booth, he made an important-sounding cough to attract the attention of the young man behind the counter.

"Is there a butcher shop close by?" he asked.

The ticket agent thought so, or maybe it was a grocery.

"How about a family named Kozka?"

The man had no idea, so Father Miller walked over to the telephone booth and began to page through its slim directory. He found no uncle and aunt in its pages, but when he drew Sita Kozka's letter from his suitcoat again, and read it, he decided that he might try to find the butcher shop. From her description, the enterprise that her parents owned was located on the eastern side of town.

Father Miller slipped off his jacket, slung it over one shoulder, and started down the main street of Argus. He was a medium-sized man, trim but not muscular. His main exercise was walking, and his stride was energetic and swift. It took him only a few blocks to find The House of Meats. The town had grown large around the shop, and the property was something of an eyesore among the neat modern buildings on Main Avenue. A cracked blue electric sign on stilts announced it from the street, and an unpaved drive led, between tall grown pines, to a low slate-green shingled building with several chimneys of pointed tin. The place looked run-down but not deserted. Johnny-jump-ups flourished against the front wall and leggy white geraniums bloomed in the dirt. The grass was unevenly mowed. The windows were dim

313

and dirty, but patched with tape. From the end of the drive, he could see the black cardboard in the front and read the bright pink word CLOSED.

There was no telling whether the Mary Adare named on the broken sign was a relation or not. More than twenty years had passed since the letter in his breast pocket had been written, and who knew what had taken place during that time? The name *Sita Kozka* was all he had to go on, and this derelict building.

In the heat his wiry curls were beginning to spring to life. He combed his fingers through his dark red hair and looked down at his hands. He privately thought they revealed a side of his personality. They were oddly unlike the rest of him—sinewy and long, nimble as a monkey's, with delicate oval nails. They were the hands of a safecracker, devious and finely tuned, and so sensitive to cold that he invested in fat goose-down mitts to keep them from getting frostbitten when he made his winter rounds. Now, regarding them on a street in this town, the gnarled knuckles and sharp tips dizzied him. They belonged to someone else.

Down street, the muffled flourishing of drums, waves of clapping, beeping horns and cheers began. Jude Miller put his hands in his pocket and the crowd collected around him, pressing him fast where he stood, mingling their sweat and hair spray and food smells with hot asphalt and the faint alkaline dust he scuffed up beneath the blue glass sign. He closed his eyes and tried to think of his mother. Catherine Miller's long broad serious face was turned away from him. He strained up on his toes like everyone else, or bent toward the street, hoping that the first glimpse of the gold and pink majorettes, the banners, the antique cars and cartwheeling clowns would put everything back into perspective. But his heart quickened as the crowd surged together in a pack. His hands popped free. His face streamed in the heat. His body was shoved and molded, arranged into a new form by the crowd's hips and elbows. He squeezed tight, held his breath,

314

barely fit. All around him the noise of the parade rushed and rolled and the colors spun in a blur so bright he could not contain the picture. He tried to keep his mind in check, but still the thought came. All that held him together now was the crowd, and when the parade was finally over and they drew apart he would disperse, too, in so many pieces that not even the work of his own clever hands could shape him back the way he was.

KARL ADARE

ALL MY LIFE, I traveled light. I made a habit of throwing out worn clothes, books I finished, even Celestine's notes. I only had one piece of furniture, an expensive portable stereo, and once I got tired of a record I simply left it behind in a motel room. But then, in the past few months, I started to miss recordings that I'd ditched ten, twelve, fifteen years before. Even tunes I left behind in the last week would run through my head, only missing a line or a word. I started hearing them at work. I had gone from treating Dutch elm disease, thrips, and leafy spurge, to selling and installing preplanned landscape designs down in booming Texas. It was a living, I scraped by, but there was nothing to the job I liked. So I got careless. Dreamed things. Heard things. Laying out the seepage fields and septic tanks on graph paper for a contractor, suddenly I'd think of a song. Irving Berlin's classics, "All By Myself" and "Happy Talk." Eddie Fisher's smooth deadpan backed up by Hugo Winterhalter and his Orchestra. Patti Page's "Throw Mama from the Train." "Softly, Softly." Jaye P. Morgan's voice would fill my head. I'd hum along. I'd get a strange look from the contractor.

"Never mind," I'd say, "just listen. What comes after this?" I'd sing, " 'Throw Mama from the train a kiss, a kiss. Throw Mama a kiss good-bye. Throw Mama from the train a kiss, a kiss.' Then what? It's something about her old country ways."

The guy would either laugh and shake his head or I would get a stranger look and lose the job. But I'd stopped caring. Where was Joe "Fingers" Carr? Where was "Tequila"? Where were the old hits they never played on the radio anymore?

The Great Ones are gone, I would think, sitting at the edge of the dry motel pool with a margarita sweating in my hand. But it was more than that. I had outlived something careless in myself. Most men get to my age and suddenly they're dissatisfied with all that they've accumulated around them. Not me. I wanted everything I'd left behind.

I wanted the cars repossessed after fifteen payments, the customer's houses into which I never got past the doormat, the ones I did get past, their rooms and rich smells of wax and burned food. I wanted the food itself, burned or not, and the women who had left it in the oven too long. I wanted their husbands. I wanted the men in blind alleys, truck beds, the men who had someone else or, like Wallace Pfef, never anyone before. I wanted the whole world of people who belonged to each other and owned things and cooked food and remembered old songs.

But it didn't hit me until I had lived month after month in dissatisfaction, that what I really wanted was their future. I wanted their children. So when Celestine's note caught up with me in the Plano branch office, I shouted out loud, showed the clipping around. It was a newspaper photograph of the Beet Queen candidates, and Dottie's name was circled. Behind them, with a big square grin on his face and new wire-rimmed glasses, stood Wallace Pfef. I crowed over Dot and altogether made a fool of myself, until one of the managers couldn't take it anymore, sneered, asked me the last time I'd seen her.

I quit the place.

It had been a comedown anyway, and I had no feel for the merchandise.

I went back to my hotel and packed everything I owned in the trunk of my old Plymouth. Then I sat down beside the pool, just a moment, to think what I would do next. There had been plenty of times like this in my life, lulls of indecision. They lasted longer and longer though, and this one lasted longest of all. I sat there drinkless and coatless, my hat on, my keys dangling off a ring, until the sky turned orange and one by one the neon signs around the place flashed in bows and zippers. They made no sense. They were just moving figures. Nothing around me spoke. And as I sat there and the shadows gathered and the lizards scraped along the tiles, I made less and less sense, too, until I made none at all. I was part of the senseless landscape. A pulse, a strip, of light.

I give nothing, take nothing, mean nothing, hold nothing.

This is what I said to myself in that strange false dusk. I shut my eyes against it. I shut my mind against the thought. I held my breath. And in that darkened, bleak, smothering moment, something came back to me. One thing. Not an object, not a plan, not even the nagging words to a song, but a sweetness. That's the most I can describe of it. Just a breath, but so pure.

I opened my eyes, walked down the steps, and got into my car. I started driving north and didn't stop but to gas up, because of the date on the newspaper clipping, because of Dot. I linked her with that moment of sweetness even though I'd wondered, since I last saw her, whether she was still at large or locked in jail. As I drove I began to link other people with that moment too, even people I thought I had left behind forever, like my sister.

The last time I saw her I got a slight concussion for my trouble. This was during dinner, when she hit me with a can of oysters. I picked the can up and rubbed my temple. I said, "You've got no family feelings." And she answered that she had no family. She was a hard one, with no reprieve. Then there was Wallace. As his only experience, I was some sort of God he worshipped by acting like he was my personal maid. He ironed everything I wore, washed my shirts fresh, brought coffee, squeezed oranges because I said I liked real juice, and cooked up big dinners every night. An ash wouldn't drop from my cigarette but that he'd catch it in his bare palm and brush it into a wastebasket. Sleeping with him was no different from that. He'd do anything to please me, but didn't have the nerve to please himself. I like a person to be selfish so I can stop thinking that they're thinking something that I can't understand. He drove me out of my mind with attention, and even though I did feel sorry for him there was no question, ever, of staying.

And yet I was coming back.

I drove into Argus on the day of the parade, just at dawn, with all I owned packed in the trunk and flowing over the backseat. I sailed right through. It was as if my hands had stuck to the wheel. Or maybe I'd been driving in a straight line so long I had forgotten how to turn. Sunup, with the air so full of dust and reflected light, looked ferocious. All the merchandise was burning in the big plate-glass windows on Main Avenue. Even the street signs gave back a red glow. The streets looked glazed and hot. They turned back into highway and far in the distance, on the other side of town, the air folded in glossy continual waves of rising heat. Two silver grain elevators floated above the ground and I started toward them, thinking maybe I could park in some shade, catnap, wake refreshed and then drive back in once the festivities began.

I stopped on the shady western side and parked in tall wild mustard. I got out and stood in the weedy gravel. With day, a wind had come up, so loud it filled my ears and made them ache. I had forgotten the force of a Dakota wind. It was so long ago that I had the territory that included the Badlands, where Celestine and I went for our justice-of-the-peace wedding. We said our vows, and then I took her and the baby out to dinner at the Alex Johnson Hotel, the fanciest place in Rapid City. I tried to bring up the subject of my living with them again because I hoped that Celestine might be having second thoughts. But she only showed her harsh white teeth, forked up her salad, and jiggled the baby curled in her lap.

"Let's not get carried away." She nodded at the table between us, as if it was representative. "This is only a formality."

I could tell that she hated having marriage thrown on her, and that even though she bought our Black Hills Gold wedding bands herself, in the Alex Johnson lobby, she wasn't fond of hers. During dinner, she worked it on and off her finger like it hurt. Once she removed it entirely and set it on her coffee saucer. The busboy nearly ran it through the dishwasher.

That's where we parted company, and where I got back on the road. And that's also where I really became a father for the first time. One thing they never say, one thing I've never heard about, is a man's side of having a baby. Nothing happened in me while Celestine was actually pregnant, because of course I never knew her symptoms, pleasures, and complaints firsthand. It was after seeing baby Dot that I got hit.

I left Rapid City by route of that endless stretch of highway that runs beneath the border between the two Dakotas. During long drives my trick was usually to hit on a catchy tune or talk back to the radio, but after a while I switched it off. I found it pleasant to have the peace of the afternoon around me, to be at the center of unchanging fields of snow and brown branches. The landscape stayed so much the same, in fact, that at one point I seemed suspended, my wheels spinning in thin air. I hung motionless in speed above the earth like a fixed star.

A wind had drawn me along, the same wind blowing now, only sugar beets had taken over, mile after mile, and no one grew grain around Argus anymore. The elevator was a hollow shaft of two-by-four studs and flapping tarpaper. The accountant's office was nailed shut with boards. The tracks of the rail spur looked overgrown, the banks undercut, some of the ties were missing. I was probably trespassing, and from the way I looked I would not have blamed the state police for picking me up.

I was disreputable, unshaven, unwashed, covered with road dust, and I was hungry. I waited until my watch said nine o'clock, then I went to the Flickertail and sat in a booth with coffee and a bismarck roll. I sat there long enough to watch the whole parade, or at least the backs of people in the crowd and the tops of floats, and then I washed up in the restaurant bathroom, combed my hair, and shook out my jacket. I slapped cold water on my eyes. But I still looked like a bleary old bum with my three-day beard and cheap blue suit.

I felt worse than that when I finally got to the fairgrounds. The parade was breaking up, and in the confusion I drove through the wrong entrance and parked on the other side of everything. I started wandering, stumbling in a haze of exhaustion, in a whirl of canned organ music from the merry-go-round, in a big stew of noise and confusion. It was such an awful mess that I was almost glad when I got to the edge of a long row of booths and saw The House of Meats truck. It was parked in unmowed grass, in the slanting shade of elms, and Sita was sitting in the front seat, alone.

Although her face was shadowed and distorted by the dusty windows of the truck, she didn't look as though the years had told her tale. If anything, age had made her more attractive by refining her features to the bare minimum. Her head was tilted in a modest way, but her gaze was sharp and queenly. She was wearing a rich red garnet necklace.

The necklace made me look away.

Sometimes a small thing, a trinket, brings back a whole world of memories. I hadn't thought of my mother since I don't know when, but the necklace was similar to the one she called her treasure. Maybe it was the necklace that made me take the chance and cross the parking space, or maybe it was the wishful thought that if Sita still looked so well and hadn't changed after all these years, maybe I hadn't either.

"Do you mind?" I slipped into the driver's seat, shut the door,

321

and was suddenly overpowered by tiredness. The air conditioner was on high, and the cab was so wonderfully comfortable that I let all the strain of the road, all the anxiousness, the heat and noise, fall away from me. I sank into the seat and simply let go. I thought I heard myself apologize to Sita as I slowly leaned forward. I folded my arms on the steering wheel and rested my head there.

"Just let me close my eyes for a minute," I heard myself saying. "I'm so damn tired." And then I think I even dozed off a second, or hallucinated, because I jerked suddenly back, gripping the wheel, thinking I was driving.

I glanced at Sita but she was still staring straight ahead, ignoring me so intently that I looked too. Across the dry grass, a crowd surrounded a plank booth. I could hear the tiny faraway hoots and jeers they exchanged with a shrunken-looking figure, absurd in clashing colors, who sat high on a wooden board above a pool of dark water. It was Wallace Pfef.

"Well there he is," I said, "making a perfect ass of himself." But the truth is I didn't feel that way. He wasn't acting the fool. Even from where I sat, above the sound of the air conditioner, I could hear Wallace yell down some remark from his perch. I couldn't make out the words, but the customer laughed and pitched his softballs wide, without taking aim. That was Pfef. People liked him so well that they wouldn't even dunk him on a hot day for a joke.

I was just about to remember my manners, to explain myself to Sita and get on with finding my daughter, when I looked down the row of booths past Wallace and saw Dottie round a corner. It was odd. After driving all this way to see her, I hung back, didn't go to her. She trudged along, her head lowered like a bull's, so I got a good view of her hairdo, anyway, swirled in front, flipped in back, with ringlets hanging down and the whole thing sprayed. It looked indestructible.

"How could Celestine have let her do it?" I said aloud. And the dress too. Dot was squeezed into the heart-shaped top and kept tripping on the bell skirt. As she walked, she swung her muscular short arms and flexed her gloves. A long swatch of white material trailed behind her. I could swear she was looking for trouble. Even from that distance I could see the glitter of her eyes. She reminded me of sailors on shore leave, the dangerous numbers, all pent up from months at sea and looking for a place to use their fists.

She lunged toward the booth where Wallace sat, moving with mechanical purpose. She never even hesitated at the counter, but stripped off her long white gloves and bought three softballs. She hefted one. Testing the weight of it, she took her aim. I watched in a kind of wonder as she threw the balls. One, two, three—each went true, but the first was enough. Wallace disappeared in a flash of orange. His hat seemed to float down after him.

I shot from the truck, caught myself, stumbled, went on. I had let myself smoke too much and I was no longer young. My back pinched, but I put every ounce of speed into my legs and sprinted. He was out cold. I had to get there. I was running for my life.

I pushed past the crowd and fell into the tank with Wallace. I went down on my knees, waded forward to where he rested on the shallow plastic bottom, heavy as a sleeping child. It looked like he was taking a nap there. It looked like he was already drowned. When I pulled him up, streaming water, bewildered and thrashing, sick to the bone with amazement, he threw his arms out, struggled. I dragged him close, and the right words came back.

"Screw the management," I said.

The Grandstand

Celestine and Mary were torn as to whether they should sit in the upper seats of the grandstand, beneath the wood-and-shingle awning, or down front in the burning glare close to the royal platform. They chose to suffer. They sat together in the first row middle, silent, each enclosed in her thoughts. The sun was terrible, and their rayon dresses held the heat of it close to their bodies.

"This is the same way you cook a turkey," said Mary after half an hour passed. Notice of the coronation had come over the loudspeaker system, and people were now beginning to straggle to the seats. A red-haired priest sat down in the first row near the end. Celestine and Mary could see him clearly because the grandstand curved around home plate.

Both of them thought of Sita.

"Maybe we should get him," said Celestine.

"I don't know about that," said Mary, pressing her lips together. "She left the church."

"That's true," said Celestine. But she wished she had performed some sort of last rites on Sita herself. It seemed as though she should have done something. She continued to watch the priest, as if he offered hope. He looked solid, and she was sure that if they approached him when this was over he would know what to do.

"They're wheeling Russell up," said Mary. "Look over there."

The orderly had driven the long way around town to get to the end of the parade before Russell's float. Now he pushed Russell over the bumpy diamond.

"Russell's probably burning up in that old uniform," Celestine worried. It seemed to her that everyone must be miserable. The

324

priest, sitting opposite, had folded a program of the ceremony and was now fanning himself with it. Celestine and Mary had programs too, but they wanted to keep them perfect to remember the day.

At last the princesses filed up the platform steps, each holding her skirt in a bunch as she walked. Celestine compared them closely. In their frothy confections, they were like magazine models or mannequins in store windows. Sita had always looked perfect in the same way that they did, lips gleaming, hair held in place by spray. Dot was not among the girls at first, but then she came tramping down the left baseline.

Her dress had gone limp in the heat, like a wilted plant. She didn't even bother to hold it away from her ankles as she ascended the steps.

"There's my girl," breathed Mary.

To her, Dot looked ravishing. The sun reflected off Dot's hairdo. Her dress glowed where an uneven iridescence had been woven into the fabric. Mary thought that her niece resembled an ancient pagan goddess. She had been reading about Atlantis in her *Book of the Unfamiliar*, and she could picture Dot touching the waves with an iron scepter.

Celestine thought that Dot looked uncomfortable and maybe desperate. Her shoulders were hunched and her face sweat in gleaming streaks. She sat in the last folding chair, fists in her lap, and squinted off into the hot white sky.

The whole crowd, uncomfortable, sighed and fanned and frowned beneath the sun, waiting for the mayor to begin. Celestine and Mary stared at Dot, willing her to look at them, exchange some form of recognition from her royal spot. But Dot was completely self-absorbed as if she were alone in her room, and they couldn't catch her eye. Then Wallace sprang with nervous vigor up the first-tier walkway, distracting them. Karl followed in his wake. Both men were steaming, sodden.

"She knows," Wallace gasped, falling into a seat directly behind Celestine. Karl sat down more slowly and deliberately, in back of Mary. He nodded, his eyes haggard, but did not say a word. He surveyed the platform, the banners, the folding chair disguised with streamers and higher than the others, on a dais, empty until the queen was announced.

"Who knows what?" Mary twisted around and took Karl in with shrewd eyes, hiding everything. "You're sopping wet."

"I know," said Karl.

"You made it," said Celestine.

Wallace leaned forward and put his face between the two women. Water from his hair and ears dripped on their shoulders. "Dot knows," he said desperately, "I concocted this all, changed votes, rigged everything, got her elected."

Celestine's eyes snapped open, her mouth went down. "You couldn't have," she said.

Mary was impassive, as if she'd always expected the worst. "There will be hell to pay," she pronounced, not taking her eyes from Dot, who sat among the preening beet princesses and did not smile or wave or dimple, but continued to stare into the wide sky like she'd been struck a blow.

"She'll collapse from the heat," Celestine muttered. "They should hurry up."

The sudden roar of the airplane, starting up in the outfield, drowned her words. The platform dignitaries swiveled as one to watch it take off. The flimsy home-run fence had been taken down and a long flat burnt field stretched beyond that—a perfect runway. The mayor shouted across the engine's noise.

"Welcome . . . first annual . . . be writing . . . up there for all to see . . . doing double duty since . . . puny little clouds . . . wish luck . . . cloud seeding is a . . . success rate . . . Tommy B.'s Aviation . . . technical expertise . . . and now . . ."

Dot moved then. Throwing up her dress in a bunch, baring

326

her strong short legs, she stamped across the board platform and jumped, landed on her toes, then ran, leaving tiny black spike marks in the beaten earth of the diamond. She ran toward outfield, toward the small white plane that was perched there alert and graceful as a bird. And when she got to its doors she vaulted in without a hand up, or permission. There was a pause, as perhaps she argued with the pilot. And then the mayor gained his voice and shouted, "Oh, hey . . ." Celestine and Mary, Karl and Wallace were on their feet, poised to do something, but the pilot leaned out the door, tipped his black mesh tractor hat, and taxied forward. The plane moved with startling, swift, lurching hops and gathered speed until the roar was overpowering, and up it rose, over the booths and canopies, over the tall old elms, over the flat river of mud, over the grandstand and over the town.

The mayor was the mayor of Argus because he never completely lost his footing in any crisis, but could always be counted on to respond with dull remarks. Now he droned with the plane's engine, sticking to his written speech, explaining the story of the beet in Argus up to the present. The crowd grew restless. The people trapped upon the platform fixed expressions of interest on their faces, but what they really followed was the progress of the plane, which went so high it vanished once, then sparkled like a sequin and bored straight into a solid-looking cloud and out the other side again. Then through another and another. It wheeled and banked in turns and loops and then began to write.

Down on the ground, Mary had thrown her hands out, clasped them, put them to her face, and finally kept them there as if her expression would crack if she took them down. Celestine was at a loss, numb with fright, unable to be furious with Wallace, who was so appalled and anxious that he trembled. Only Karl's face was thrown back in wonder.

They watched. Their faces were characters that caught the light. The plane tipped, glided, formed Queen Wallacette out of smoke and vapor, and when it was done veered away, disappearing over the treeline.

There were a few seconds of silence on the platform, and then the mayor, halting, pronounced Dot queen and handed fresh red roses around the wire backstop to her mother. Then he stepped down with the princesses and Legion post commander. Russell sat still. There was a murmuring, a rumbling of footsteps on wood, as the crowd left the grandstand. Only the four stood rooted, heads tipped back, ears straining for the engine's return. They made a little group, flung out of nowhere, but together. They did not lower their eyes, but kept watching as above them Dot's name slowly spread, broke apart in air currents, and was sucked into the stratosphere, letter by letter.

DOT

"THIS IS SO fucking hideous," I said, staring down at the wet-looking green material of the dress I was supposed to wear. "I think a dinosaur shed this or something."

Aunt Mary sighed with pain, as if a knife had twisted deep inside, then set her mouth firm to endure me. My mother put her fingers to her lips.

"I don't care," I told them. "I'm not going to wear this even if Aunt Mary paid two hundred dollars."

But you can see how far that got me, because of course that's exactly what I've got on.

I'm standing in the armory parking lot with all these floats made of spray-painted Kleenex and chicken wire. Uncle Wallace is handing the drivers red numbers so they know their order in the parade. It's a mess. All the guys driving the cars that pull the floats are dopers from the Autobody Club. They're half buzzed and slumping against the fenders or laughing their heads off once they get behind the wheel. I don't care about that because those guys are friends of mine, not boyfriends or anything. They let me hang around. What I do care about is wearing this dress, which is like Thumbelina's nightmare. But at least I've got this white lace shawl that looks like a curtain I pulled out of someone's front window. I have it wrapped around me because I'm afraid if P.J. or Eddie or Boomer or any of the guys get a good look they'll split a gut and ram each other. Life is funny enough through their eyes.

And then there's the other members of the royal court. When I see them floating toward me all in simple white eyelet or pastel blue, all slim and tanned orange from laying on their garage roofs smeared with iodined baby oil, I'm irritated. I know from the way that Wallace acts that this is my day. He knows the outcome. I don't have any doubt who will get the crown and think that, really, I should have this float to myself alone.

Some National Guardsmen have taken Uncle Wallace's place organizing everyone, and now a slender man in crisply starched olive drab directs us to get in line. The sight of a uniform brings our driver down to earth, and the five of us girls climb onto our float. It's a tractor-trailer bed. Old sheets are stapled onto the splintered wood, and tinsel garlands left over from Christmas hang off it here and there. Five sheet-wrapped hay bales are arranged for us to sit on. Behind us a big white scalloped fan of cardboard spreads, labeled THE QUEEN AND HER COURT. One hay bale is placed a little higher than the others, and I take it. The princesses spread below me in a swirl.

The streets are still damp, because the fire department sprinkled them down with what was left of the river. The dust only settled for a little while. I can feel the drought. It draws on me, tightening my face. As I drove into town this morning with Uncle Wallace I saw the fields lifting. Low in the sky, flaring like smoke, the dirt moved, and I said, "What's the forecast?"

"Dry," he answered. "More sunshine." His face looked tiny and shriveled when he said this, as if the drought was withering him too.

The parade lurches into motion, and about a half block away, I see this beefy orderly from the rest home unload my uncle from a special dome-top van. Russell's strapped into the wheelchair with harnesses that look like they are part of his uniform. All his medals are pinned on, a bright patch that spills down his chest.

The guy is bumping him, dragging him up the side of the float, tipping him so that he sags over once.

I stand up, scream off the edge of the moving float.

"He needs a drink! Can't you see he's thirsty? Give him a drink!"

People turn. I point at Russell and stand up and yell it again until a Legionnaire comes running with a full canteen. It seems like I'm in command, already queen, because the Legionnaire and orderly put Russell gently in place now, in the middle of his fake battlefield, which is planted with those wire-and-plastic poppies veterans sell every year. Russell drinks from the canteen, tilting his head up to swallow. I see the water go down in gulps and then the whole parade is moving off down the street, and Russell is wedged between the bunkers and crossed rifles, staring into the open back of the National Guard jeep that's going to pull him.

P.J. hits the horn and I sit down on my hay bale. I've dropped the lace shawl, and in some part of my mind I'm aware that my fellow candidates are feasting their eyes on my plantlike dress. But I don't give a crap. I begin my windshield-wiper wave, as instructed by our gym teacher, who has been a contestant for Miss North Dakota. Back and forth very slowly. Smile, smile, smile.

Although the street is wide, people have parked it full of cars and are now standing three deep right up to the sides of the floats. As we pass, they wave, hands fluttering inches from our faces, and we wave back without speaking, our palms only inches from theirs. The illusion of our grandeur encloses us like a bubble. It is as if we're isolated, deaf and dumb to our admirers. That is how I hear the conversation about me so clearly that there can be no mistake.

"Which one'll get it, do you think?"

"Oh, that one. The stocky-looking redhead."

"You're kidding."

"No, she's it for sure. I heard. My brother knows that Pfef."

"Yeah?"

"He rigged it. Got her nominated and then counted the votes himself."

"He related to her?"

"She's supposed to be his niece or something."

"Oh."

"Her mother's that big Indian woman. That six-footer."

"She don't take after her."

At first, I think I go a little numb. Everything outside of me is a whirling blur. I keep wiping at the air, but the crowd just smudges. I smile until my cheeks ache. And then little by little things start coming clear. I am facing up to reality, like for instance the fact that all the other girls heard that conversation, too. I turn to sneak a casual glance down, and all four of the princesses swivel greedily to meet my look. I can tell that they're very pissed off, but also glad at the same time. They're crazed with eagerness to get this story out into the open.

I sink far into myself. In some part of my mind I knew that Uncle Wallace set this up. But that's not something a person really likes to admit, so I never did. I thought at least he would keep it a careful secret. But now it's the latest gossip. One of the princesses starts quacking.

"I don't think it's fair, I don't think it's fair." All the while she is saying this she's waving and smiling. Her head bobs on her long neck, and I decide, as queen, that I will chop it off. "Someone should say something. Someone should tell." She won't stop.

"Be my guest," I shout in her ear. "You think I want to be queen?"

She holds her head and looks at me with a pained expression, but the others take over.

"Why not? Why wouldn't you? You get a gift certificate from

every store. You get to keep the crown. You get a big write-up in the *Sentinel*. I'm sure you'll take a cute picture, like, in curtains, and I hope you wear your dress. It looks like, *I mean really, it's mashed lettuce.*"

They are making me dangerous.

"It's a goddamn designer original!" I scream. This shuts them up, or at least makes them hiss among themselves, just loud enough for me to hear.

"I bet you got it with trading stamps."

"I know *just* where she got it—on sale in the window of the Big Gals shop in Grand Forks. I even saw it when I was over there. There was this dummy with the dress on and a little sign around the neck that said 'ninety percent off.' "

I realize that what they are saying about the dress is probably true. The Big Gals is where Aunt Mary likes to shop. She's hard to fit, being built like a cement root cellar, and this place always has fantastic sales.

"I'll kill you," I threaten, wishing I could choke them right there. But I cannot shut them up, of course, and even they can hear that there is a lack of conviction in my voice. There is also stark gloom and depression. I have never felt so desperate.

Far ahead I can see each float or band turn off at the fairground entrance. They move so slow and turn so awkwardly that this last part seems to go on forever. We're trapped in the blare of trumpets, the clatter of high school drums, and an endless medley of the theme from *Doctor Zhivago*. Wherever the high school bands pause, the Old Folks Band takes up. The senior citizens are riding in a hay wagon and all, strangely, dressed in vests and hats made from flattened beer cans crocheted together around the edges. They lift their instruments. They nod three times and all begin. Their music is off-key, tuneless as the wind.

Perhaps the unbearable music affects my mind, because as I am sitting there I start to think revenge.

I've only been mad at Uncle Wallace once before, and when that happened I was madder at him than anybody, ever. But the anger I felt long ago was a pinprick, mere spite. This is real. *How could he do this to me?* I wonder, climbing down from the float. We're at the end of the parade. A red haze drops across my eyes.

There are booths set up everywhere full of 4-H calves and very clean pigs. Catholic Daughters has a bingo shed in full swing and a pie concession. There are carnies too, hucking those enormous pink dogs nobody ever wins, and everywhere the salty warmth of fresh-popped corn, the sugary heat of cotton candy, bright blue syrup, the sizzle of foot-long hot dogs. I feel like I'll faint if I don't stop and eat, but I plunge ahead. Already the crowd is drifting toward the grandstand where the emcee is gabbing on the bullhorn. I run along the edge of the booths, past the shaded stand of elms. I know Uncle Wallace will be somewhere among the charity projects, organizing them or working behind a counter. And sure enough. It's too easy. I find him posed as a complete sitting duck, the world's easiest target. I buy three balls for the dunking tank.

I pick up the first. I can hear the emcee inviting people to the grandstand for the crowning of the Beet Queen.

"Wallacette, please don't!" calls Uncle Wallace.

When he says that name the red curtain drops.

"You told!" I scream. "Cheater!"

For a few seconds, just as the last ball is in the air, I feel good. But then at the splash I turn, almost blinded by what I've done, and I walk toward the grandstand, shamed. Uncle Wallace's face looked so old and thin that I can't stand to think of it. I want to run. I want to jump into P.J.'s Classic and get him to drive me to Canada. First Russell, now Wallace, and next the low point of my life. I don't have to go through with this, I think, I really don't. I could duck through a canning booth, hide out in the cattle barn. There is a plane at the edge of the field, warming up its engine. Even as I step onto the platform where the mayor, Uncle Russell, and the princesses are already sitting, I think that I could fake some sort of massive convulsion. The ambulance would arrive in a wail, lights flashing, and the guys in white would dash for me. They'd hoist me like a feedsack and throw me on a stretcher. They'd fumble me at the ambulance door like they did to Russell. But I do none of these things. I am getting a much better idea.

The sun is a fierce white ball, and under it the boards of the platform have scorched. The seats of the aluminum folding chairs are hot as stove tops. I sit down. This dress comes in handy, useful for something. I adjust the leaves of my skirt to make a cushioning layer, and right there, beneath the eyes of my family and the town, the plan in my head commences to take shape, take form as a kind of logical outcome. There is a thread beginning with my grandmother Adelaide and traveling through my father and arriving at me. That thread is flight.

Before me, in the grandstand, I know that my family sits with eyes like set traps. I do not look at them but turn, instead, to Russell. He sits down the row of burning chairs. His lip has curled, a swatch of hair fallen across his forehead. The lines in his face, deep and brown, jagged, running sideways, are like the dry earth.

"It is with great pleasure," the mayor says, adjusting the microphone, "that I welcome you all to the first Sugar Beet Festival."

There is just barely time.

"The Queen is supposed to fly!" I holler at Tom B. Peske, the pilot. "It's a publicity stunt. Come on. Take off!"

He lets me jump in and as we taxi across the field I tell him that I'm old hand, working on my pilot's license. So he is surprised when, about a hundred feet up, I shut my eyes and drop my head in my lap. The plane wiggles, shudders, spins over like a carnival rocket. I feel too light, unconnected. I sit up and open my mouth, shriek at him to take me back down. He refuses. He's got to write my name. My whole long awful name. Ten letters.

I breathe deep and slow until the world comes clear through the windshield of the plane, and I dare to move. I move by inches, adjusting myself, amazed to find that I am too deathly sick, because of motion or shock, to be afraid. The hugeness up here, the flat world tipping, no end to sky and earth, shakes me. Tunnels of hot air flow straight upward from the plowed fields. Every time we bump over one, every time I think of how we look from down below, I make noise. It's the only thing that distracts me from throwing up. I yell so hard, going over the tops of the letters, that the pilot, Tom B. Peske, shouts that I deafen him. The only thing I do right is help seed clouds. We veer due west, where a group of cumulus are massed. I load the silveriodide cartridges into the flare gun just the way Tom B. says to, and then I hold it out the window while he flies blind. My fingers rust to the gun's smooth side. My throat tastes like iron. I concentrate on Tom B.'s hands, steady on the panel of instruments. I concentrate on shooting the gun. An hour passes before we come back and circle above the grandstand.

I decide, when we finally descend, to die with my eyes wide open. So I see everything, the sudden magnification as we swoop, the rushing earth, the carnival and fairgrounds like a painting that smears and then suddenly focuses as we slow. The semicircle grandstand is where we stop, just in left field.

Tom B. takes down a clipboard and begins to log in this flight. He hardly notices when I let myself out, or maybe he's disgusted and glad to see me go. I'm so happy to touch the ground that I don't care, and I don't care either that the air is dense, humid, and I'm smothered in my own dress again. The cloth is damp with sweat, scratchy, clinging like a burr-filled sheet. But I could run down third baseline. Home. I start walking, wobbling a little, righting myself. The platform is empty, the chairs disordered, the streamers fallen, and the grandstand is dotted with people catching a stray breeze, eating drumsticks, pie. No one points at me or notices, no one rises in their seat to hail the queen. No one screams and points, either, which is something. The mayor is gone. The princesses. Russell is gone, and Wallace. Aunt Mary is gone too and I stop, struck by a wild pitch.

All the time that I was in the plane, I imagined that they gasped, cried out, covered their eyes and prayed. I was sure that they would wait forever, or until the plane came back down, but they have not.

It is a lonely thought, and not entirely true. For as I am standing there I look closer into the grandstand and see that there is someone waiting. It is my mother, and all at once I cannot stop seeing her. Her skin is rough. Her whole face seems magnetized, like ore. Her deep brown eyes are circled with dark skin, but full of eagerness. In her eyes I see the force of her love. It is bulky and hard to carry, like a package that keeps untying. It is like this dress that no excuse accounts for. It is embarrassing. I walk to her, drawn by her, unable to help myself. She comes down the steps, stands beside the dugout, and gives me the tumbled batch of roses. Heavy, half-opened, the heads have wilted on the stalks.

"Let's get going," she says. "I wonder, can you walk in those shoes?"

I take them off. The soles of my feet are tough as canvas, and we start out. My mother tells me I have to brace myself about Aunt Sita, but I don't falter for a step, just keep walking through the crowd that mills sheeplike, dazed by heat, onto the griddles of asphalt streets and sidewalks. The tar sticks, burns through my callus. On the road to our house past Uncle Wallace's she tells me Aunt Mary is at the funeral parlor, half crazy with worry about me. Then she stops. This is not what she finds so hard to tell.

"He's back, isn't he," I say to her. "He's waiting at the house."

But he's not. As we pass Uncle Wallace's closed, cool place my mother points with her chin and says, "That's his car."

It's an old, lean model, with sprung shocks. It is bruised with unpainted weld marks, coated with thick dry dust. The car is backed into its parking place, ready for a smooth exit.

I put my heels on. The stickers beside the road are mowed short and cut like glass. I touch my mother's arm for balance as we walk. The clouds spread over us. We breathe a powder of hot blowing earth. My dress is unbearable, a prickling mess that I strip off once we walk into the house.

I put on an old soft T-shirt and cutoffs and then come into the kitchen. She has rolled her stockings down to the ankles. She has taken off her tight belt. She has lifted a carton of cold juice from the refrigerator and we sit down at the table to drink it, talking about everything that has happened, then trailing off. Night comes, black and moonless, still and very hot. I sit motionless while my mother cooks, eat the toast and eggs that she prepares, drink the milk poured from under her hand.

I want to lean into her the way wheat leans into wind, but instead I walk upstairs and lie down in my bed alone. I watch the ceiling for a long while, letting the night deepen around me, letting all the distant sounds of cars and people cease, letting myself go forward on a piece of whirling bark until I'm almost asleep. And then it begins.

Low at first, ticking faintly against the leaves, then steadier, stronger on the roof, rattling in the gutters, the wind comes. It flows through the screens, slams doors, fills the curtains like sails, floods the dark house with the smell of dirt and water, the smell of rain.

I breathe it in, and I think of her lying in the next room, her covers thrown back too, eyes wide open, waiting.

P.S.

Insights,
Interviews
& More . . .

About the author

About the book

Read on

A Conversation with Louise Erdrich

Where were you born, Louise?

I was born in Little Falls, Minnesota, and grew up in Wahpeton, North Dakota.

You have a rich ethnic heritage—Ojibwe and French on your mother's side, German on your father's side. How would you describe this mix?

The result has been a peculiar sense of humor, or at least some see it that way.

In an earlier P.S. you owned up to throwing "terrible tantrums" as a small child. How would you characterize your childhood between tantrums?

Between tantrums I was a model child and made my parents very happy.

What is your earliest memory of reading and being influenced by a book?

I was astounded at a young age by Orwell's *Animal Farm*—the greatest pig story ever written!

Is it true that you wore cowboy boots at Dartmouth?

Red ones, with very pointy toes.

Do you have any unusual or otherwise compelling anecdotes about your collegiate experience?

Working in the stacks at one of the last open-stack libraries was a source of great joy, as was Orozco's devastating mural in the basement. One panel shows a great skeleton in a black

> 66 *Is it true that you wore cowboy boots at Dartmouth?*
>
> Red ones. 99

academic cap and gown giving birth to baby academics contained in bell jars.

Is it true that you once worked as a flag-waver for a road crew? If so, what are your memories of the job?

Tears of boredom and hot feet.

Speaking of jobs, you opened a bookstore in Minneapolis (BirchBark Books and Native Arts) in June of 2000. Do you spend a fair amount of time there?

Mr. Brian Baxter, my friend and bookselling mentor, manages the store. I get to work the floor a little and suggest books, but I am not allowed near the computer cash register. My daughter works there too. I check in every day. Otherwise I am busy writing.

What's been your biggest surprise in operating a bookstore?

Ha! That it is impossible! A quixotic, enjoyable effort by obsessive book lovers. Yet we make it work.

You have said that both sides of your family were given to oral storytelling. Do you find yourself prior to writing each novel sharing its basic story aloud with, say, your daughters?

Often, yes. My daughters are great at letting me know if my ideas suck, or don't.

Do you have any writerly quirks? When and where do you write? PC or pen?

I write by hand in large notebooks, then transfer the draft to computer.

What do you rely upon for stimulation when you are writing? Do you observe any particular beverage ritual? ▶

Meet Louise Erdrich

Bettina Strauss

LOUISE ERDRICH is the author of eleven novels, as well as volumes of poetry, children's books, and a memoir of early motherhood. Her novel *Love Medicine* won the National Book Critics Circle Award. *The Last Report on the Miracles at Little No Horse* was a finalist for the National Book Award. She lives in Minnesota with her daughters and is the owner of Birchbark Books, a small independent bookstore.

❝ I write by hand in large notebooks, then transfer the draft to computer. ❞

3

A Conversation with Louise Erdrich
(continued)

I drink a huge cup of coffee as I bring my five-year-old to school in the morning. Sometimes I walk the dog and think about what to do. Then more coffee and work.

Do you have any pet hates?

Loud, persistent buzzing noises of mechanical origin. For instance, leaf blowers. Besides that, unkindness small and vast.

What single thing would improve your quality of life?

Not having to do publicity. But I would do any amount if I could just turn back time and make Al Gore our president. God himself has told me that the whole world would be better off now.

What is the most important lesson life has taught you?

Never rationalize anything that feels wrong.

What engages your time outside of family, the bookstore, and writing?

That seems to take up most of it, but I do study the Ojibwe language.

What are your goals and dreams?

To raise happy children; to write the best books I can; to be accidentally "raptured" — although, come to think of it, the most interesting people will surely be left down here on earth. ◡

The Beet Generation
Louise Erdrich on Farming, Dating Bad Boys, and Creating Her Alter Ego

LOUISE ERDRICH GREW UP in the Red River Valley of North Dakota, formerly known as the "breadbasket of the world." *The Beet Queen* is set at a turning point in agricultural history—the small towns of the Western frontier have gradually disappeared and are being replaced by a huge commercialized farm belt where great tracts of land are given over to agribusiness. "Farming evolved slowly here," explains Louise. "It started off with small homestead farms, then more and more of the land got merged together into 'bonanza farms,' and then it changed to monoculture . . . mile after mile were planted with wheat and corn and rye; huge fields were covered in one crop." And then the sugar beet moved into the valley. "It's an industrialized method of farming," says Louise. "The beets are put in the ground, then have to be hoed, sprayed with herbicide, dug up, and processed mechanically in huge sugar beet plants. But they're kept in immense piles first; they ferment and stink like hell. And when they're being processed the smell is even worse. But," she adds philosophically, "people need to make money to live, and in North Dakota the sugar beet was the crop of choice."

Louise has had personal experience of the crop she describes as "an unattractive plant, with leaves that are big and floppy." When she was twelve, she spent the summer working on a sugar beet farm. "That's how kids earned money; it was good money and it wasexciting but, oh God, it was grueling." ▶

> " 'Farming evolved slowly here,' explains Louise. 'It started off with small homestead farms, then more and more of the land got merged together into "bonanza farms," and then it changed to monoculture . . . huge fields were covered in one crop.' "

The Beet Generation *(continued)*

Up at five thirty in the morning, she washed, dressed, and headed out to wait for the farm truck (cushioned with hay bales) to appear. "My mother would pack me a great lunch in a big cooler. She'd make soup, and I'd have all kinds of good stuff—nice sandwiches made from homemade bread, cookies, and muffins. My mom is a great mom, the quintessential mom. Even my old crew boss still remembers her soup." Louise would head off to the truck—the same truck that would later be used to haul the beets—and join the other kids and grown-ups who'd be working that day. "We'd go out to this beet field, and the girls would all strip down to their bikinis and tennies to get a good tan." Work would start at six thirty and continue until about one or two in the afternoon. "You'd take out the weeds with a really sharp hoe and get a rhythm going; you definitely didn't want to hit your leg with it." They'd go down the rows, chopping weeds and thinning out the plants a careful ten inches apart. "That was it," Erdrich recalls. "We did that all day."

She describes *The Beet Queen* as her most autobiographical novel. The landscape of Argus, the book's fictional setting, is obviously based on Louise's childhood surroundings. But it's not just geography that makes her second book so personal. "Dot is definitely me, for sure," Erdrich says. "I rarely let her out. Inside, I was always furious and stomping around, but outside, I was a nice girl. Sometimes I tried to be bad, but really I was good. I loved my parents; I didn't want to upset them."

The furiously grumpy, continually angry Dot is Louise's alter ego. "Blessedly, I could live through Dot, let out my dark side, and allow my true nature to show," observes an Erdrich still glorying in Dot's rebellion. "That's how I would have loved to behave. But the thing was,

‘We'd go out to this beet field, and the girls would all strip down to their bikinis and tennies to get a good tan.’

6

when I was growing up you were supposed to be very, very nice; you got no points at all for being angry." She says that all her "repressed rage and fantasies of revenge" bubbled over in Dot. "I was the good girl who hung out with the bad kids. I liked the idea of the bad guys. I'd date them for a while and think: Oh he's soooo cool. But after a couple of dates I'd realize they were bad kissers. Sloe gin or Boone's Farm wine was the drink of choice and did not do much for me either." She ended up with a "very sweet boyfriend" who pumped gas at the service station and was on the high school wrestling team.

Her opinion of the sugar beet industry is less complimentary: "I know that land can't be ruined beyond recovery; it can always be brought back. But I don't know how long it would take sugar beet fields to recover. The crop depletes the soil. It absorbs all the nutrients and turns them into nonnutrients." Erdrich laughs. "It's the most ridiculous thing: they're taking this incredible soil and turning it into this nonnutrient . . . which I am at present dumping into my tea. It's been that way for some time. I grew up surrounded by sugar beets. But another crop has come in to save the landscape: sunflowers. There are fields and fields of sunflowers. They are more gorgeous than you can imagine . . . the hot blue skies of North Dakota and, against them, golden sunflowers." ∾

> 66 'I liked the idea of the bad guys. I'd date them for a while and think: Oh he's soooo cool. But after a couple of dates I'd realize they were such bad kissers.' 99

The interview above was conducted by Eithne Farry

A Critical Eye on
The Beet Queen

NOVELISTS ANGELA CARTER and Anne Tyler, both fervent admirers of Louise Erdrich's debut, *Love Medicine,* were further enthralled by *The Beet Queen.* Tyler called it "a perfect—and perfectly wonderful—novel." Angela Carter, meanwhile, marveled at the newness and breadth of Erdrich's insight into America. "[V]iolent, passionate, surprising . . . small towns, the prairies, sexual obsession—all the matter of the classic American novel," she wrote. "Louise Erdrich is so thoroughly in tune with the surreal poetry of America that when you read her you can hear America singing, the discordant chorus of its multitudes of voices, its rough music. *The Beet Queen* imparts its freshness of vision like an electric shock."

Critics admired her ability to create heartfelt drama from the details of domestic life. Paul Bailey, writing in *The Observer* (London), said the "range of her sympathy is astonishing. . . . Erdrich shares with Faulkner the gift of transcending the mundane." The *Chicago Sun-Times* reviewer lauded *The Beet Queen* for its dialogue ("brilliant from start to finish") and its "original and powerful characters who, like their relatives in *Love Medicine,* left me exhilarated and very grateful to this immensely gifted novelist." Erdrich touched upon the book's characters and dialogue in an interview with the *New York Times.* "These are works of artifice, invention, and fiction," she said. "But there's a reality to the people. The people whose lives were similar to the lives of characters in the books have read the books. One of the most wonderful things anyone has said was, 'You finally got it down the way people talk around here.'"

Among Erdrich's many talents, reports *Newsday,* are her "extraordinary power, compassion, and insight into the human heart"—talents that have "vaulted Erdrich into the front ranks of American lit." Reviewers consistently noted the poetic qualities of her prose. Writing in the *Sunday Times* (London), Bernard Levin called Erdrich a novelist of "formidable strength and imagination" and said "she presents the fruits of both in a prose of flexible, haunting beauty." The *Los Angeles Times* concurred: "She is a luminous writer and has produced a novel rich in movement, beauty, event. Her prose spins and sparkles, and dances right on the heart when it needs to." Poet Robert Bly, reviewing *The Beet Queen* in the *New York Times Book Review,* dubbed it a work of "power and precision"—a book that "provoke[d] in me amazement at this splendid feisty talent."

The ultimate accolade, however, was accorded by Philip Roth. "Louise Erdrich," he said, "is the most interesting American novelist to have appeared in years." ❧

An Excerpt from Louise Erdrich's Latest Novel, *The Painted Drum*

"One of her best novels. . . . Erdrich's writing has become richer, her voice wiser and gentler even as she tells the harshest of stories. She shies away from nothing."
—Minneapolis Star Tribune

"With fearlessness and humility, in a narrative that flows more artfully than ever between destruction and rebirth, Erdrich has opened herself to possibilities beyond what we merely see—to the dead alive and busy, to the breath of trees and the souls of wolves—and inspires readers to open their hearts to these mysteries as well." —Washington Post Book World

One
"Revival Road"

FAYE TRAVERS

LEAVING THE CHILD CEMETERY with its plain hand-lettered sign and stones carved into the weathered shapes of lambs and angels, I am lost in my thoughts and pause too long where the cemetery road meets the two-lane highway. This distraction seems partly age, but there is more too, I think. These days I consider and reconsider the slightest of choices, as if one might bring me happiness and the other despair. There is no right way. No true path. The more familiar the road, the easier I'm lost. Left and the highway snakes north, to our famous college town; but I turn right and am bound toward the poor and historical New England village of Stiles and Stokes with its great tender maples, its old radiating roads, a stern white belfry and utilitarian gas pump/grocery. Soon after the highway divides off. Uphill and left, a broad and well-kept piece of paving leads, as the trunk of a tree splits and diminishes, to ever narrower outgrowths of Revival Road. This is where we live, my mother and I, just where the road begins to tangle.

From the air, our road must look like a ball of rope flung down haphazardly, a thing of inscrutable loops and half-finished question marks. But there is order in it to reward the patient watcher. In the beginning, the road is paved, although the material is of a grade inferior to the main highway's asphalt. When the town votes swing toward committing more money to road upkeep, it is coated with light gravel. Over the course of a summer's heat, the bits of stone are pressed into the softened tar, making a smooth surface for the cars to pick up speed. By midwinter, the frost creeps beneath the road and flexes, creating heaves that force the cars to slow again. I'm glad when that happens, for children walk this road to the bus stop below. They walk past with their dogs, wearing puffy jackets of saturated brilliance—hot pink, hot yellow, hot blue. They change shape and grow before my eyes, becoming the young drivers of fast cars who barely miss the smaller children, who, in their turn, grow up and drive away from here.

As I say, there is order, but the pattern is continually complicated by the wilds of occurrence. The story surfaces here, snarls there, as people live their disorder to its completion. My mother, Elsie, and I try to tack life down with observation. But if it takes a lifetime to see things clearly, and a lifetime beyond, even, perhaps only the religious dead have a true picture of our road. It is, after all, named for the flat field at its southern end that once hosted a yearly revival meeting. Those sweeping conversions resulted in the establishment of at least one or two churches that now seem before their time in charismatic zeal. Over the years they merged with newer denominations, but left their dead sharing earth with Universalists and Quakers and even utter nonbelievers. As for the living, we're trapped in scene after scene. We haven't the overview that the dead have attained. Still, I try to at least record connections. I try to find my way through our daily quarrels, surprises, and small events here on this road.

We were home doing pleasant domestic chores on a frozen Sunday in the dead of winter when there was a frantic beating at our door. In alarm, Elsie called me. I came rushing from the basement laundry to see a young man standing behind the glass of the back storm door, jacketless and shivering. I saw that he'd lost a finger from the hand he raised, and knew him as the Eyke boy, now grown, years past fooling with his father's chain saw. But not his father's new credit-bought car. Davan Eyke had sneaked his father's new automobile out for an illicit spin and lost control coming down off the hill beside our house. The car slid toward a steep gully lined with birch. By lucky chance, it came to rest pinned precisely between ▶

trunks. The white birch trees now held the expensive and unpaid-for white car in a perfect vise. Not one dent. Not one silvery scratch. Not yet. It was Davan's hope that if I hooked a chain to my Subaru and backed up the hill I would be able to pull his car gently free.

My chain snapped, and the efforts of others only made things worse over the course of the afternoon. At the bottom of the road a collection of cars, trucks, equipment, and people gathered. As the car was unwedged, as it was rocked, yanked, pushed, and let go, as different ideas were tried and discarded, as the newness of the machine wore off, Davan saw his plan was lost and he began to despair. With empty eyes, he watched a dump truck winch his father's vehicle half free, then slam it flat on its side and drag it shrieking up a lick of gravel that the town road agent had laid down for traction.

Over the years our town, famous for the softness and drama of its natural light, has drawn to itself artists from the large cities of the eastern seaboard. They have usually had some success in the marketplace, and can now afford the luxury of becoming reclusive. Since New Hampshire does not tax income, preferring a thousand other less effective ways to raise revenue, wealthy artists find themselves wealthier, albeit slightly bored. Depending on their surroundings for at least some company, they are forced to rely on those such as myself—a former user of street drugs cured by hepatitis, a clothing store manager fired for lack of interest in clothes, a semi-educated art lover, writer of endless journals and tentative poetry, and, lastly, a partner in the estates business my mother started more than fifty years ago. ❧

Have You Read?
More by Louise Erdrich

LOVE MEDICINE

The first of Louise Edrich's Argus novels (and winner of a 1984 National Book Critics Circle Award), *Love Medicine* is set on and around a North Dakota reservation; the book tells of the intertwined fates of two families, the Lamartines and the Kashpaws. Their world is harsh and hazardous, full of old grievances and bad decisions, but is illuminated by the kind of love that can leave a person crazily empty or full to overflowing with its spellbinding magic.

"A powerful piece of work. . . . Louise Erdrich is the rarest kind of writer; as compassionate as she is sharp-sighted."　　　—Anne Tyler

"A dazzling series of family portraits. . . . This novel is simply about the power of love."
　　　—*Chicago Tribune*

THE BINGO PALACE

Seeking direction and enlightenment, charismatic young drifter Lipsha Morrissey answers his grandmother's summons to return to his birthplace. As he tries to settle into a challenging new job on the reservation, Lipsha falls passionately in love for the first time. But the object of his affection, the beautiful Shawnee Ray, is in the midst of deciding whether to marry his boss, Lyman Lamartine. Matters are further complicated when Lipsha discovers that Lyman, in league with an influential group of aggressive businessmen, has chosen to open a gambling complex on reservation land—a development that threatens to destroy the community's fundamental links with the past.

"Beautiful. . . . *The Bingo Palace* shows us a place where love, fate, and chance are woven together like a braid, a world where daily life is enriched by a powerful spiritual presence."
　　　—*New York Times*

TRACKS

"We started dying before the snow, and like the snow, we continued to fall." So begins Nanapush as he recalls the winter of 1912, when consumption wiped out whole families of Ojibwe. But the magnificent Fleur Pillager refuses to be done away with; she drowns twice in Lake Matchimanito but returns to life to bedevil her enemies using the strength of the black underwaters. This is a book about memory, love, and loss, and the way desperate emotions can cause a person to take desperate measures.

"Erdrich is the most interesting American novelist to have appeared in years."

—Philip Roth

THE ANTELOPE WIFE

Rozin and Richard, living in Minneapolis with their two young daughters, seem a long way from the traditions of their Native American ancestors. But when one of their acquaintances kidnaps a strange and silent young woman from a Native American camp and brings her back to live with him as his wife, the connections they all hold to the past rear up to confront them. Soon the patterns of their ancestors begin to repeat themselves with truly tragic consequences.

"Spiritual yet pragmatic, Erdrich's deft lyricism affirms while it defies the usual lines separating the mythical from the daily. Erdrich leads every event in her book to its outer limits, so no detail is mundane. And each scene contains bits of hilarity, extravagance, and horror."

—*Boston Globe Sunday Magazine*

TALES OF BURNING LOVE

Jack Mauser has women problems; he's been married five times and none of his wives really know him. This becomes strikingly apparent when all his disgruntled wives, marooned in the same snowbound car, start to tell stories about their onetime husband. He's a man with a talent for reinvention and a less than circumspect regard for the truth. But as the women talk, their stories begin to revive them; they start thinking about Jack in a whole new light.

"Erdrich's finest novel in years. . . . Shockingly beautiful prose."   —*San Francisco Chronicle*

THE CROWN OF COLUMBUS
(cowritten with Michael Dorris)

A gripping novel of history, suspense, recovery, and new beginnings, *The Crown of Columbus* chronicles the adventures of a pair of mismatched lovers—Vivian Twostar, a divorced, pregnant anthropologist, and Roger Williams, a consummate academic, epic poet, and bewildered father of Vivian's baby—on their quest for the truth about Christopher Columbus and themselves. When Vivian uncovers what is presumed to be the lost diary of Christopher Columbus, she and Roger are drawn into a journey from icy New Hampshire to the idyllic Caribbean in search of "the greatest treasure of Europe." Lured by the wild promise of redeeming the past, they are plunged into a harrowing race against time and death that threatens—and finally changes—their lives. A rollicking tale of adventure, *The Crown of Columbus* is also a contemporary love story and a tender examination of parenthood and passion.

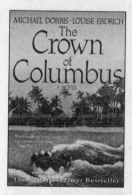

"The rare novel that is both literature and good fun."   —Barbara Kingsolver

Have You Read? *(continued)*

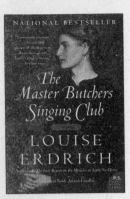

THE MASTER BUTCHERS SINGING CLUB

Fidelis Waldvogel leaves behind his small German village in the quiet aftermath of World War I; he sets out for America with his new wife Eva—the widow of his best friend, killed in action. Finally settling in North Dakota, Fidelis works hard to build a business, a home for his family, and a singing club consisting of the best voices in town. But his adventures in the New World truly begin when he encounters Delphine Watzka, a local woman whose origins are a mystery, even to herself. Delphine meets Eva and is enchanted; she meets Fidelis and the ground trembles. . . .

"An enrapturing plunge into the depths of the human heart." —*Washington Post Book World*

"[A] masterpiece. . . . Erdrich never hits a false note." —*Pittsburgh Post-Gazette*

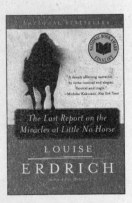

THE LAST REPORT ON THE MIRACLES AT LITTLE NO HORSE

Cecilia lives for those hours at the piano when she can play her beloved Chopin. The very air of the convent thickens with the passion of her music, and the young girl is soon asked to leave. Cecilia makes a decision that will change her life forever when she comes across the corpse of a drowned priest. Hiding her figure beneath the heavy clothes of the dead man, she begins a journey north to the tiny community of Little No Horse—and into the fierce hardships of her new identity as a missionary.

"A deeply affecting narrative . . . by turns comical and elegiac, farcical and tragic."
—Michiko Kakutani, *New York Times*

FOUR SOULS

The strange, compelling Fleur Pillager
takes her mother's name, Four Souls,
for strength and walks from her Ojibwe
reservation to the cities of Minneapolis and
Saint Paul. There she seeks restitution from
and revenge on the lumber baron who has
stripped her reservation. But revenge is never
simple; her intentions are complicated by her
dangerous compassion for the man who
wronged her.

"Full of satisfying yet unexpected twists. . . .
Four Souls begins with clean, spare prose but
finishes in gorgeous incantations and poetry."
—*New York Times Book Review*

THE BLUE JAY'S DANCE: A BIRTH YEAR
(**nonfiction**)

The Blue Jay's Dance is a poetic meditation on
what it means to be a mother. Describing her
pregnancy and the birth of her child, Erdrich
charts the weather outside her window and
the moods inside her heart. It is, she says, "a
book of conflict, a book of babyhood, a book
about luck, cats, a writing life, wild places in
the world, and my husband's cooking. It is a
book about the vitality between mothers and
infants, that passionate and artful bond into
which we pour the direct expression of our
being."

"The language in this book is stunning, elastic,
often full of silence. . . . Erdrich is forthright
and tough-minded in her intentions, generous
in her speculations, and courageous in her
vulnerability before her readers. *The Blue
Jay's Dance* is a book that breaks ground."
—*Boston Globe*

ORIGINAL FIRE: SELECTED AND NEW POEMS

In this important new collection, her first in fourteen years, Louise Erdrich has selected poems from her two previous books of poetry (*Jacklight* and *Baptism of Desire*) and added new poems to create *Original Fire*.

This profound and accessible collection anticipates and enlarges upon many of the themes, and even the characters, of Erdrich's prose. A sequence of story poems called "The Potchikoo Stories" recounts the life and afterlife of the questing trickster Potchikoo; here Erdrich echoes the wit and humanity of the inimitable Nanapush, who appears in several of her novels. Similarly, the group of poems called "The Butcher's Wife" contains the germ of Erdrich's novel *The Master Butchers Singing Club*.

THE GAME OF SILENCE (for children)

Her name is *Omakayas,* or Little Frog, because her first step was a hop and she lives on an island in Lake Superior. It is 1850 and the lives of the Ojibwe have returned to a familiar rhythm: they build their birchbark houses in the summer, go to the ricing camps in the fall to harvest and feast, and move to their cozy cedar log cabins near the town of LaPointe before the first snows.

The satisfying routines of Omakayas's days are interrupted by a surprise visit from a group of desperate and mysterious people. She learns from them that all their lives may drastically change. The *chimookomanag,* or white people, want Omakayas and her people to leave their island in Lake Superior and move farther west. Omakayas realizes that things so valuable, so important that she never knew she had them in the first place, are in danger: her home and her way of life.

"Sure to be a children's classic." —*Seattle Times*

Don't miss the next book by your favorite author. Sign up now for AuthorTracker by visiting www.AuthorTracker.com.